SPiN

SPiN

ROBERT RAVE

St. Martin's Press ♒ New York

This is a work of fiction. All of the characters, organizations, and events portrayed in this novel are either products of the author's imagination or are used fictitiously.

www.stmartins.com

Library of Congress Cataloging-in-Publication Data

Rave, Robert.
  Spin / Robert Rave. — 1st ed.
      p. cm.
  ISBN-13: 978-0-312-54436-2
  ISBN-10: 0-312-54436-7
  1. Young men—Fiction.   2. Public relations—Fiction.   3. Self-
realization—Fiction.   4. Celebrities—Fiction.   5. New York (N. Y.)—Fiction.
I. Title.
  PS3618.A935S65 2009
  813'.6—dc22

                                                              2008044064

First Edition: August 2009

10 9 8 7 6 5 4 3 2 1

*Dedicated to the two people who, to this day,
still don't understand what it is a publicist does:*

my father, Ron, who can tell a story like no other;

*my mother, Jane, an expert at editing
the stories my father tells*

Gratitude is the heart's memory.
—French proverb

Acknowledgments

My sincerest gratitude and love to my parents, family, and friends, without whom this would be meaningless.

Heartfelt appreciation to Paul Aaron, who believed in me and the characters in the novel from the very beginning. To my friend and literary agent, Jason Allen Ashlock at the Marianne Strong Literary Agency: you're a rock star. Thank you doesn't seem to suffice for all the guidance you both have given me.

A GIANT thanks to my editor, the *incredible* Sarah Lumnah at St. Martin's Press, who has made this journey such a joy. I'd also like to thank Sally Richardson, Matthew Shear, John Murphy, Dori Weintraub, Steve Troha, Elizabeth Catalano, and the wonderfully talented people at St. Martin's Press. I feel truly honored and grateful to be part of such a magnificent publishing house.

Thanks to three very extraordinary women who inspired me more than they'll ever know: my high school English teachers Mrs. Jacqueline Garibay and Mrs. Gloria Schweinberg. And my English professor at Illinois Wesleyan University, Dr. Kathleen O'Gorman.

ACKNOWLEDGMENTS

To Michelle Jubelirer for her business acumen and friendship.

To Matt Groeber for his indispensable help with the novel when it was only a draft.

To James Jayo for his encouragement and belief in the novel.

Thanks to those who have listened to me talk about this book until they finally changed their phone number: Jennifer Gill, Scott Seviour, Marc Malkin, SuChin Pak, Greg Baldwin, Eunice Jordan, Blaire Bercy, Richard Chung, Peter Jacobson, Halle Sherwin, Billie Myers, Elizabeth Daro, Bryan Jacobson, Laurie Jacobs, Reyna Morenoff, Francesco Friscioni and Vinnie, Richard Mensing, Heidi Krupp Lisiten, James Waugh, Matt Altman, Amy Shiftman, Gary Loder, and Rob Bragin.

And finally, my thanks and love to Andre, Stanley, and Freddy.

SPiN

Prologue

You Ain't That Good

T*AP, tap, tap.*

What the hell? It's way too early for housekeeping.

Tap, tap, tap.

My head is too heavy to lift off the pillow, my tongue too tired to speak. I try to *will* the tapping to go away. Perhaps, I think, if I just concentrate hard enough . . .

Tap, tap, tap.

What the fuck? I open my eyes, and they burn like hell. I see an outline of two figures against the TV screen. An anchorwoman's muffled voice talks about the morning commute. I hear the time: 6:17.

Tap, tap, tap.

Jennie's crouched over the Ligne Roset coffee table, impeccably dressed. She's wearing her usual uniform: a tiny black dress with a cardigan sweater. And I can smell her from where I lie. I haven't even taken my morning piss, and I can smell her: day-old smoke nesting in hair burned by a blow-dryer and Thierry Mugler "Angel" seeping from her pores. I want to bury my face in the pillow to escape the stench, but any movement would show signs of consciousness, and, frankly, I don't want to deal. Not after last night. So instead, I'm forced to lie here, caught up in all that is Jennie.

Tap, tap, tap.

My eyes now able to focus, I see my prepaid phone card lying on the table: a gift from my mother, a less-than-subtle reminder to call home. When my mother stood in the checkout line of her local Sam's Club with this plastic card in hand, I doubt she imagined it would be used to cut lines by her darling son's boss.

Jennie straightens up and stares in the mirror. She's tan. I guess you would call it that. She resembles a carrot from her daily dose of Mystic Tan. She pats down her harshly dyed hair to smooth out any strays. She looks just like she does when she's walking one of her clients down the red carpet, and the sun is only now beginning to rise.

"Fuck," she says in a tone that is equal parts Long Island hell-raiser and Upper East Side Empress. "These fucking morons can never get it right."

Yesterday she had her L.A. hair guy, Jacob, come to the hotel and give her another blow-out. Ninety dollars for every time she blows out her hair; which is every day. I don't get it, but then again, I don't get Jennie.

"That fucking Jacob," she says, petting her head feverishly, pulling her blond hair, exposing the jet-black roots. "You would've thought he'd be good since he's black, you know, since he has to deal with kinky hair every day. Not this one. He has no business working in Randolph's salon; Weave-City or some other ghetto place, maybe."

I can feel her watching me in the mirror. I shut my eyes tight, her image emblazoned in my mind. She's only a few years older than me, but she looks a full decade older. Jennie is twenty-eight, nearly five-foot-eleven, but that varies depending on her shoes, and slender—and by slender I mean bloblike with no visible muscle tone. Her frame, especially her unusually wide shoulders, is akin to a rugby player's. People don't know what she does, who she works with, or even who she is; but they have seen her in pictures with Madonna and Britney, so that must mean she's somebody.

Tap, tap, tap.

She's going to be wired for days.

Through squinted eyes I glance at her hands. Considering her large stature, they're shockingly stubby, and fat. She has the hands of an ogre; an ogre with French tips. I first noticed them when she was flipping through the guest list at a Gucci fragrance launch. "Jesus," I gasped when I saw them, quickly covering by complimenting her rings. She looked at me suspiciously like she always did; but I quickly changed the subject, and she went back to uninviting guests after they'd already RSVP'd; the social future of half of New York rested on those stumpy little fingers.

I want out. I've had enough of this shit. But I simply hate confrontation. So instead I just lie here, hoping for a house to land on this wicked witch of the red carpet. Or at least for her to go back to her own room.

Though she knows there is no way I could possibly still be asleep with the noise that she's making, I still pretend, knowing she'll be barking orders at my first noticeable twitch. She thinks of me as one of the maids she had while growing up, and I'm just as expendable. It doesn't matter that I work on her biggest accounts or that without me she wouldn't have a clue as to what's going on with any of them. To her, I am as useful as the person who pours her coffee.

Someone knocks at the door. Jennie quickly disposes of her morning treat before answering. Jacob, the human hair dryer, comes in.

"Okay, let's try this again, shall we?" Jennie says condescendingly. She turns to Adam, and smiles. "Get out of the way so he can do me." Instead of sitting on his empty twin bed, Adam sits at the foot of mine. He is unnaturally attractive to anything with a pulse, and is well aware of this. His shaved head and chiseled face are only outmatched by his lean, sinewy body.

"Is it cool to turn this on?" Jacob asks quietly, hair dryer in hand.

"Yeah, why?" she says with a sneer.

Jacob nods in my direction.

"Fuck him," she says. The hair dryer goes on, and my respite is over. I sit up in bed, pretending to be waking up at that very moment. Her long, painted, strawlike hair is being pulled like Silly Putty, so hard her eyes well with tears. For a moment, I wish I were him.

"Damn it, Jacob! That fucking hurts!" she finally says. He stops momentarily as she studies her hair in the mirror. "It's still kinky!"

"If you'd let me—"

"Go!" she shouts.

"What?" he says, wounded.

"Go. I'll do it myself," she insists.

"B-b-but . . ." he says.

"OUT!" she shouts.

"I still need to be paid," he says, rebounding.

"Send a bill to my office in New York. I don't have cash on me," she lies, and ushers him out the door. I'd heard this before.

He might as well forget getting paid for three months, if at all. She grabs a blow-dryer from the bathroom and sits back down in the chair in front of the mirror. "Taylor, I need you to do my hair."

I kick the sheets off, and like a robot I get out of bed and walk toward her.

"Good morning, Sunshine!" Adam gleams. *Yeah, I'm sure it is for you, Adam. You're not about to be emasculated as you blow-dry your boss's hair.* I walk past her.

"Where are you going?" she barks.

"I have to pee," I grumble as I slam the door.

"Lose the attitude," she says through the door.

I stare at myself in the mirror while I stand at the toilet. I need a new job. I look down at the sink and see the selection of complimentary Kiehl's products the Mondrian gives to their guests. Maybe the Mondrian is hiring. No, Jennie will kill any job prospects. I'd witnessed it before. Lacy, another faceless twentysomething, quit almost immediately after I started. When Merrill Lynch called about her previous work experience, Jennie told them she was incompetent and had a drug problem; neither, of course, was true. The job wasn't even in a competing field, still she sabotaged Lacy. When I was in school, I was told that it was against the law to talk disparagingly about past employees. But of course the law is only a minor detail to Jennie, something easily sidestepped.

I stick my hand out midflow and get it nice and wet. I glance at the mirror again, as I watch piss splash on my palms and roll down my fingers. I know I should be repulsed; the old me would have been sickened.

"Taylor!" Jennie yells.

After zipping up, I avoid the sink, but move the faucet with my elbows to pretend I'm washing away with the expensive soaps. Then I open the door, and walk out like normal.

I stand behind her, my hands still wet, and pat her hair down with my urine-soaked hands. That's the closest I will ever come to pissing on Jennie Weinstein. I continue to smooth out her curly hair.

"Did you use the patchouli soap?" she asks.

"Yes, why?" I say innocently.

"You smell like a lesbian," she says, disgusted, yet strangely delighted with her taunt.

I turn on the blower as she's about to say something. Adam is scanning the *New York Post* online.

"Our item is in," he shouts over the blow-dryer.

"Read it to me," she shouts back. Between the blow-dryer, the shouting, the TV turned up to the max, and the fact that it's not even seven o'clock, my head is going to explode.

"Daily Dolce is closing down their Wooster Street restaurant, leading to speculation the ubertrendy boite fell because of owner Jonathan Edendale's costly drug habit and his penchant for 'anything in a skirt.'"

I see her mouth moving in what is most likely a laugh. It looks more like a pig at a trough.

"You are so fucking good!" Adam shouts.

"He should've done my brother's party for free," she snickers back. I turn off the blow-dryer.

"What are you doing?" she asks.

"I think I'm done here," I reply. Oh yeah, I'm *done*. I was *done* months ago. Jonathan Edendale's wife had a baby three months ago, and everything in that Page Six piece is bullshit, manufactured by my illustrious boss to get even. Oh yeah, I'm definitely done.

"I guess you are," she says, checking out her pee-ridden head in the mirror. I sit back down on the bed next to Adam.

"You should be a hairdresser," she says, patronizing.

"No, I don't have the patience to deal with assholes," I say. She ignores it, and Adam nudges me.

"Chill," he says under his breath. Jennie gets up from the table and grabs her purse.

"You ready, Adam?" she asks. She takes a cigarette from her Prada purse. She loves cigarettes. I think she would eat them if she could. I wish she would. Truth be told, she'd be as big as a house if she didn't smoke. Ashes fall all over the carpet and desktop. She treats the room as she does her employees: like one big, giant, ashtray. I know: I'm bitter, but soon you'll see why.

Adam grabs a leather-bound black folder. "Where you guys headed?" I ask.

"We have to do a walk-thru with Jackie's label and breakfast after," she snips.

"Jackie? She's my client," I say, a bit panicked.

"*Your* client?" she says angrily.

"You know what I mean," I say.

"You better lose the attitude, Taylor, real quick," she says.

"I'm sorry. It's just that I brought Jackie in, and I thought I was going to be a part of her entire launch."

"You are part of it. You're just not needed right now," she explains.

And Adam is going with you because? I want to scream. But I don't, instead offering, in my typical kiss-ass fashion, "Okay, no problem. I'll start creating the tip sheet here while you guys are doing the walk-thru."

She walks for the door and the smell returns. It's sweet yet dirty; perfumed garbage. Adam smiles. "See you later, bro."

"See ya," I say with a smirk. Something isn't right.

She opens the door, turns back, and says, "I forgot the combination to your safe, and I need to get my Cartier watch out of there before the event tonight. Call hotel security and have them open it for you."

"Do I get to keep what's inside?"

She looks at Adam, then back at me, and says, "You ain't that good."

"Okay," I say, already reading the *New York Post* online. The door slams shut. Temporary freedom. I pick up the phone while reading in Page Six about the alleged rape at Crobar. Was this story real or planted? Who the hell knows anymore? Gossip writers don't know because the publicists give them the stories. The publicists don't refute the story because it gives their client publicity or at least allows them to barter for a story on another client. One big game. No wonder I don't know my head from my ass anymore.

"Hi, this is Taylor Green in 622." God, I hate the sound of my own name. It's too theatrical, too gay-sounding. No doubt a result of my grandmother Ethel's persuasive powers over my mother. "Yeah, could you send someone up to open the safe? I've forgotten the combination, and now it's shut down altogether . . . Thanks." Even at this hour, I'm still able to muster up the required pleasantries.

I sit back down on the bed and look around the room. The heavy curtains are pulled to block the looming sunlight. Normally, I would rush to open the drapes to start my day. But not today. I'm exhausted. It's been one helluva trip. The TV glows against the stark white wall. Adam's clothes are scattered throughout the room, while mine are neatly folded in my suitcase. God, I'm so uptight. You'd never know that I was staying in a four-hundred-dollar-a-night room in an Ian Schrager hotel. At present, it looks more crack den than like Phillipe Starck.

I open the closet door to make life easier for the guy coming to open the safe. Wooden hangers line the rods. A striped button-down shirt and a pair of black pants from Banana Republic hang next to my Tommy Hilfiger jacket, the remnants of a Midwestern boy's regimented dress code.

"It looks like the Gap threw up in here," Adam said when he first saw my closet in New York. He's right, but a trendy job affords me nicer things now. I wear Varvatos, and have a leather YSL jacket that was meant as a freebie for Ryan Phillipe, but never quite made its way to him. Wearing clothes not meant for me, working in a job that isn't me, in a poser society that doesn't accept me; and until now I couldn't see any of the signs telling me to leave, or at least that's the way I learned to spin it. So good at my job I learned to spin myself.

I hear a gentle tap on the door. I answer it and a burly man in beige enters the room.

"Can I see your ID, please?" he asks.

"Sure," I say. I catch a glimpse of myself in the mirror. I look like hell: my hair looks like a bird's nest, my skin is breaking out from stress, and I look like I haven't slept in days, which I haven't, thanks to *her*. I grab my New York driver's license from the desk.

"Here you go," I say, handing it to him. He nods and goes into the closet. I sit down on the bed and wait for him. Once again, I'm waiting on Jennie, fixing her mistakes.

The safe opens and he pauses, staring quietly into the metal box.

"I know, it's pretty amazing, right? I've never seen something so beautiful either," I say.

"Sir, we have a problem here," he says as he turns to face me.

"Problem?"

"Please remain seated. I need to make a phone call," he says, his eyes following my every move.

"Um, okay, sure. What's the prob—"

"Sir. Could you please be quiet?" he says, his tone changing. I stop talking and begin to sweat, though I don't know why.

He picks up the phone and dials. "Hi. Becky? This is Larry from security, and I'm in 622. I'm going to need some assistance up here. Could you please phone the police and let them know I have a situation?"

"Police? Situation?" I say shakily, standing up.

"Sir, sit the fuck back down," he says, throwing me onto the chair.

"Okay, okay. I'm sorry, but could you please tell me what the problem is?"

He walks back to the safe and pulls out three eightballs of cocaine.

For a moment I'm outside myself, watching a burly man holding cocaine and a half-dressed skinny boy sitting frightened in a chair. I start to tell him that the drugs aren't mine; that if he knew me, he'd know that I'm not someone who does drugs. In fact, I've only tried drugs twice, and that was very recently and thanks to my addict of a boss. If he also knew that my mother was very religious, and would crucify me herself if she thought I did drugs, he'd know that they couldn't possibly be mine. But I don't say any of these things because I know any explanation will be futile. I've seen these drugs before. I know where they came from, and I was there when they were purchased. It doesn't matter that the drugs aren't for me. I don't know the specifics of *how* the coke wound up in my safe, but I sure as hell knew *why*. This wasn't going to end well . . . for any of us.

You fucking bitch, you ain't that good.

**Jennie Weinstein
Public Relations**

Cordially invites you
to the grand opening of

domino

**Friday, March 3rd 10P.M.
11 Gansevoort Street
New York City**

Please RSVP to Mia Cadelo
(212) 555-0100
Mia_Cadelo@JWPR.com

This invitation is *nontransferable*

1.

The Birth of the Yes Man

MY weakness for the world of celebrity can be traced back to the days of "Calling Doctor Love" and "Beth" by the band KISS. Their music was a commercially intoxicating mix of head-banging rock anthems driven by infectious hooks, pop ballads powered by loud guitars, and overly sentimental melodies that wailed through my speakers. More importantly, they were total badasses. As a scrawny eight-year-old, I would dance in my room for hours, screaming at the top of my lungs that I wanted to "rock and roll all night," or at least until my eight o'clock bedtime. I would fall asleep dreaming that I had suddenly and inexplicably become best friends with the band, a friendship that usually involved the lot of us going to Shakey's and gorging ourselves on breadsticks and pizza. In my mind, this was the life of a rock star.

But at the same tender age of eight, I learned the harsh reality of stardom. Inside one of the album jackets was an order form for official merchandise, a flyer that had all things KISS: hats, embroidered jackets, T-shirts, jean-jacket buttons, shoestrings, and to my delight, KISS makeup. I imagined my friends driven insane with jealously when I strutted my way to the monkey bars in full Peter Criss makeup. I was going to be the shit at the Montessori school. I sat at my mother's kitchen table and asked my grandmother Ethel to help me fill out the order form while my mother was working at Roland's department store. Ethel floated me the eighty-nine bucks without reluctance, since, after all, it was going to the "arts" as she called it (had I asked for the same dollar amount for some Chicago Cubs memorabilia, I would've been out of luck). And so I ordered every available item: the tour jacket, the baseball cap, the Dr. Love T-shirt, and yes, the makeup. Excited to the point of nearly pissing on myself, I had no idea how I would survive the grueling four to six weeks for delivery.

Four weeks came and went, and then six. Then eight. Finally, three months later, and still no official KISS merchandise. The devastation set in. My heroes, such as they were, had let me down, and there was no consoling me. My mother, Elizabeth, didn't even try.

"The sooner you get your head out of the clouds and realize that people are a disappointment, you'll lead a much happier existence," she told me. Not exactly the "let's go eat a peanut-buster parfait at Dairy Queen" kind of speech you'd expect a mother to give to her dispirited eight-year-old. I had stopped expecting those pep talks long ago.

My father left my mother two weeks before my fourth birthday. I don't think he said good-bye. He told me he was going to the store, and I never saw him again. His timing was as perfect as his irresponsibility. He disappeared two months after my mom's dad had passed. We moved in with my grandmother Ethel temporarily until my mom found work at the only department store in town. She had given up college when she married my dad, and so was forced to work retail for minimum wage alongside the sixteen-year-old high-school dropouts.

After my father left, my mother found herself a new man: Jesus. Jesus did not approve of KISS, or any men who wore makeup, or most of the people with a Beverly Hills zip code. To my mother, nothing could take me further away from the Lord then the sinners of Hollywood.

Ethel, on the other hand, felt otherwise, and tried her best to cheer me up after the KISS fan-club debacle. One morning when my mother had to do inventory at the department store, Ethel led me into her bathroom, a place I'd only walked past, a place I was never EVER allowed inside. I paused before entering, not sure if it was safe to proceed. The room looked like someone had filled a hose with Pepto-Bismol and sprayed every last corner. She lowered the toilet lid with the crocheted pink cover, and sat me down. She opened a large Le Sportsac makeup bag and grabbed a giant sponge that looked like it had already been used to scrub a pickup truck before I arrived. She pulled a large, mysterious tube of translucent glop from her bag and began to slather it on my forehead.

"Where did you get this?" I asked.

"You're lucky to have a grandmother with such a colorful past in the theater, my boy," she said. I hated when she slipped into that dramatic stage voice. She sounded like Kathleen Turner. In her youth, my grandma Ethel (as in Merman, she always reminded anyone who might remember) lived in New York, working as a dancer and actress. Growing up, I was fascinated by Ethel's stories of New York City. She had lived in Greenwich Village, and was a working dancer and actress for several shows "that were so Off Broadway you could consider it New Jersey," she said. She knew firsthand the allure of show business. In fact, she relished her time as a dancer and would have continued it had she not met my grandfather, who swept her off her feet. After "falling in love," which she now refers to as a "stumble," she was forced to move back to the Midwest, where she remains in "the hellhole" that she currently calls home. She often points out that the other Ethel also made mistakes. Remember Ernest Borgnine? Don't worry, I didn't either until I looked him up.

By this time, I was sweating so profusely that the white goo dripped down my face, and I looked like some sort of creepy clown.

"Okay, not to worry, not to worry; we had a fella like you in the chorus of *West Side Story*, a real sweaty pig," she said. She grabbed one of my mother's favorite red guest towels and wiped away the dripping white mess. Then, clutching a bottle of Ban Roll-On deodorant (lavender-scented), she began to roll it all over my face. She blew on it for a few minutes. Her breath permeated a mixture of Baileys Irish Cream and wintergreen Certs. I politely asked her to stop blowing on my face, and she began reapplying the white face makeup. Within minutes my face was stark white. She covered my lips with candy-apple-colored lipstick, my eyes with her black eyeliner, and the pièce de résistance: tiger stripes on my cheeks. I looked at my reflection in the mirror. I looked less like KISS drummer Peter Criss and more like a character on *Geishas Gone Wild*. But I appreciated the effort, and I prayed the kids at school would as well.

A half hour later, I got out of Ethel's car, and stepped onto the playground in full makeup. In retrospect, the look would have been much more convincing had I forgone the chinos and polo. Less than five seconds passed before I felt an apple hit the back of my head. A few moments later, a punch in the face from Tommy Salinger, causing the eyeliner to get in my eyes. Before classes started I was sent home, bleeding, embarrassed, and with a nasty eye infection. I hated KISS.

Fifteen years later, my thirst for celebrity returned with a vengeance.

I was standing on the wrong side of the velvet ropes desperately trying to get into the opening of Manhattan's hottest new restaurant, Domino. I'd been invited to the opening by my upstairs neighbors, a lesbian couple named Lauren and Allison.

When I had arrived in New York, it had quickly become apparent that Midwestern charm meant jack to New Yorkers. The prevailing attitude seemed to be: "Just do what you have to do and save your pleases and thank-yous for the county fair." I got to New York at the end of June, with a humidity level that rivaled Rio (a comparison that would be more powerful had I actually ever traveled there), and little knowledge of city navigation. Imagine sitting in a steam room fully clothed with a hat and scarf on, and that's what it's like in New York at the end of June. That I had arrived wearing a pair of jeans, a long-sleeve T-shirt, and a sport jacket from the Salvation Army did not help. I wanted to look New York cool but succeeded in looking Midwest stupid; I lacked only the fanny pack. When I arrived at the apartment I had subletted from one of my grandmother Ethel's old theater friends—a place on West Eighty-sixth Street between Columbus and Amsterdam, right across the street from a housing project—I was looking more like a junkie than one of the project's newest residents. Lauren was the first one to help point me in the right direction. For a moment I considered the remarkable possibility that she might be hitting on me. Lauren had a pinup-girl look about her. With her jet-black hair, she definitely had a Betty Page thing going on. Her body was tight, and slightly muscular. *Yeah, I can see myself with that.* Then Allison stuck her tongue down Lauren's throat. Allison was taller than Lauren and had a pixie haircut that made her look like a teenage boy. She was striking, yet didn't have Lauren's smoldering sexiness. They were the first real-life lesbian couple I'd ever encountered, and they quickly took me under their wing as their adopted child. I gladly accepted.

Allison had just turned thirty and was the senior vice president of original movies for Showtime, hence the invitation to the restaurant opening. Allison's seen her fair share of partying, but she's been nesting ever since she landed Lauren. I shamelessly begged them to take me when I saw them reading the invitation in the elevator. They had looked at each other, then at me, and with pity agreed.

As we waited in the cold March air, the rumblings in line were that Leonardo DiCaprio, Tobey Maguire, and Lukas Haas were in the ultraexclusive third-floor lounge. Flashbacks of Peter Criss drumming a KISS anthem swirled in my head, and I wanted very badly to be part of Leo's "pussy posse," as the tabloids called it. This was my first real party with actual celebrities! It was taking every last bit of strength to keep from turning into a screaming eleven-year-old girl.

We inched closer to the front of the line, and were held momentarily so Sandra Bernhard and Patricia Velasquez could be ushered inside. While we waited, Allison explained to Lauren and me that for a New York City restaurant to survive, it must create the right kind of buzz. A publicist would have been hired to cultivate the crème de la crème for a series of tastings that had been orchestrated to boost business. "For these types of things to work, there has to be some type of celebrity connection attached," Allison continued. "Why else would a food critic want to visit another so-so restaurant? But if they believe they'll get a chance to mingle with some entertainment-industry elite, they'll line up for hours. It's rather pathetic," she finished.

"Um, that's Mr. Pathetic to you, thank you," I replied, smiling. Anybody who was somebody was there, and I needed to cross over finally from the anybody sideline. Even though I had a powerful lesbian duo with me, I still was very nervous that we wouldn't be allowed past the velvet ropes.

With invitation in hand, we inched closer and closer to the velvet ropes.

"You're going to get a stiff neck," Lauren teased.

"I'm so nervous," I said, bouncing slightly on my toes.

"I'm not good at these things either. It's more Allie's thing than mine," she said.

"Whatever! When we went to that screening the other night, you practically begged me to go. I didn't even know what that so-called art-house movie was supposed to be . . ." Allison jumped in.

While they argued over who loved their status more, I stood in front of them adjusting and readjusting the wristwatch my mother had given me for Christmas a few years before. I knew she'd saved up for quite a while and had used her employee discount at Roland's to get me that watch. It was Gucci, with a leather band and gold trim. Unfortunately, its fashion shelf life had worn out roughly four years ago.

"Name?" a woman screamed. She stood in a black trench

coat with what appeared to be nothing on underneath. She was so sexy even her cigarette seemed like an invitation to get naked. I imagined that she could have been very pretty, probably gorgeous, but hard partying and heavy smoking were masking the beauty. She was, as it turned out, a city-hardened twenty-six.

"Christina Miller," the girl in front of me said in a Long Island accent.

The doorwoman looked her over and didn't even bother to check the list. "Nope, you're not on my list." She brought her cigarette to her lips and took a long drag and blew the smoke in the girl's direction. "Next."

"But I'm sure I was put on the list," the not-quite-Versace-clad girl whined.

"Try T.G.I. Friday's," the door diva proclaimed. The young woman slinked away, fighting back tears.

As I waited on the sidewalk, I was in awe of the brazenness of the guardian of the velvet rope; had she never read about public stonings? Drive-by shootings? A bitch slap?

"Did you see that? We're never getting in," I said.

"Don't worry, we'll be fine," Allison said leisurely. "If there's any problem, I'll just show them my business card, and that will be the end of that."

"I don't think it matters to these people," I replied.

"I'm with Taylor; I say we bail," Lauren chimed in. "I'm not prepared to be assessed and rejected by some Boston College dropout."

"I didn't say we should bail!" I said loudly. "We can't leave! Julia Roberts and P. Diddy are supposed to be here!"

"And what does that mean to you?" Lauren snapped. "As if you're going to be sipping Cosmos with them!" I ignored her and turned away, but she had given me the visual of sitting comfortably with Julia, discussing her reasons for doing *Mary Reilly*. To this day it weighs heavily on my mind.

"Are we done here? I've got half of the Upper East Side waiting to get in, and you're polluting the air with your noise," the door bitch said. She came at us like a bat out of hell, spiked heels smoking. Her Gucci perfume caused my eyes to water. "Name?"

"Allison Jacobs, VP of Movies and Minis at Showtime. I'm sure I'm on the list if you could be so kind to check for me." Allison held out her business card, but I knew she had made a fatal mistake; she had been polite.

"Nope, not on here," the doorwoman said, without removing her eyes from Allison's.

"You better check again, or this could get ugly," Allison said as she took a step closer. This was better, I thought, but much too late.

"Oh honey, look in the mirror," the vixen said. "You're a few days past ugly." In one swift motion, Allison lunged at the ropes taking a swing, nearly landing a left hook. The door girl did not flinch. Clearly, she had seen worse.

"Security, get these people out of here; they're not on my list." Two huge, burly security guards came toward us.

"Wait!" I shouted. I had prepared for a situation like this, having caught a glimpse of a name on her clipboard while she berated the previous woman. "Could you check the list again? I'm certain my name is on it."

She gawked at my bloodshot eyes. I had her attention. Her face appeared calm, but in a bipolar kind of way: serene but ready to snap at any minute and make an example of the three of us. I proceeded with caution, "Kyle Milton."

She looked at me and paused before looking down at her clipboard. I nervously began to spell the name, "M-I-L-T . . ."

"I know how to spell!" she snapped, then looked back up, stunned. It was as if I had just puked all over her new Louboutins. She regained her composure and looked long and hard at the three of us.

"Well, are you going to unhook the rope or do you want me to try my uppercut? And this time, I promise I won't miss," Allison said, looking directly into the woman's eyes.

"I'll open the ropes, but not for you," she said to Allison.

"But I'm on the guest list!" I said, hearing the ice crack below my feet.

"As unfortunate as that may be for everyone inside, that is true. But Ellen and kd Lang here are not. And you, Mr. Milton, don't have any pluses," she said, pleased.

I turned to Lauren and Allison. Lauren whispered, "Go."

I did not protest: They knew me far too well.

"I'd rather snort broken glass than give this bitch the satisfaction of going inside," Allison said, loudly enough for the entire line to hear, evoking a few laughs.

"Are you coming in or what?" the door chick barked at me.

I looked back at them one last time. Lauren smiled, and said, "Just give us a full report in the morning." She winked.

The doorwoman reluctantly unhooked the rope and glared at me as I walked to the other side. I will never forget what it felt like crossing the threshold of the velvet ropes for the first time. A burning started in my stomach and worked itself up my spine and into the back of my neck. My face was flushed, and a smile crept across my face. I had beaten the Tonya Harding of velvet ropes. I was in.

The restaurant was hardly crowded, however. Apparently, having a huge crowd outside your party for everyone to see was much better than having everybody inside for no one to see. I grabbed a Bacardi lemonade—the only drink you could order since Bacardi sponsored the party. It's difficult to look cool walking around with a Day-Glo drink in a martini glass.

My first move while in the throngs of hipness was to plaster myself up against the wall so as not to be noticed. I was too afraid someone would come up to say to me, "Excuse me, aren't you the boy from Indiana? Sorry, there's been some sort of mistake; you're not supposed to be here. And please, how old is that watch? I see you go to Supercuts. Are you here by yourself? Are you kidding me with that girly drink? Why are you here? Who invited you? GET OUT!"

I sucked on the mint leaves and imagined I was being followed for one of those celebrity profiles on *Showbiz Tonight*. It beat acknowledging the fact that I was standing by myself, and more importantly, allowed me not to break into a full panic attack. I'd suffered a severe panic attack when I was eleven at my neighbor's thirteenth birthday party. I didn't know any of her older friends, and when her mom pushed me into the group to make friends, I stood speechless. Speechless was better than what followed; in a panic I threw up all over Bonnie Griffin.

I pretended the crew was instructing me to look like I was "playing it cool," and waited for people to come to me. The waiters were my assistants, and the busboys my closest friends, who walked back and forth from "the confessional," where they said really flattering things about me.

I could have stayed there all night, watching the crowd.

Suddenly it was an hour and a half later and I was sitting at a table alone, grinning stupidly and talking to myself after a few too many lemonades. I had to leave immediately.

As I inched toward the edge of my empty booth, I heard two women arguing by the booth next to me.

"I can't believe you're pulling this shit on me tonight, at *my* event," the dark-haired woman said.

"*Your* event? The last time I checked it was my name on the door, not yours," said the peroxide blonde.

"I'm the one that sent out the invitations and called the press to come to this party. It was me who begged these C-list celebrities to show up. You didn't even know the event was tonight until I told you!"

The dark-haired woman stepped to the side, and I could see the blond woman's face: I knew exactly who she was. I had seen her picture on the cover of magazines alongside her celebrity clients. Her name was Jennie Weinstein.

Jennie's tall frame was imposing, and she was nothing special in terms of physical beauty. She didn't quite fit the physical mold of the rest of the pack of waiflike Manhattan publicists. She wore a tight black Prada dress and a pair of black heels. No jewelry except for a Bvlgari watch. To the unobservant, she seemed a simple girl from the Upper East Side. But I knew different.

Since moving to New York, I had read all about Ms. Weinstein, the reigning queen of everything "hip" in Manhattan. Her upbringing had become urban folklore. The youngest of five kids, Jennie was born to a megamillionaire hedge-fund manager father and a shipping heiress mother. She attended the prestigious Nightingale prep school on the city's Upper East Side, and was the most popular kid in school, a girl who liked to party. She regularly skipped school and sunbathed with the downtown set by the Piers. She usually managed to make a quick pit stop at home for an outfit change, and to keep up the schoolgirl appearance to her distracted parents. Her industriousness was best evidenced early on by cutting deals with the building's doorman—giving him roughly three hundred dollars a week in return for his silence—so she could go out dancing at places like Area, Robots, and the Palladium. She was a Madison Avenue girl with Tenth Avenue aspirations. She attended Brown University, but rarely studied, graduating by the skin of her teeth. After college, at age twenty-three, having been brought up with other very well-heeled kids (figuratively and literally), all of whom loved to party too, she chose the one job that allowed her to talk on the phone all day to her friends, decide which places would be the next cool spot to hang out, and party more than ever: She became a publicist. Her competition both feared and hated her, and with good reason. She was ambitious, fearless, and irreverent, with nothing to lose and nothing to gain. While staring at her, I felt both excitement and shame that I knew so much about her. It was like a twisted teenage crush.

"Do you honestly think these people came because of *you*? They saw my name on the invitation and knew it'd be a good party. Most of these people here don't know who Heather Richardson is, or give a fuck for that matter," Jennie trounced.

"Then maybe you ought to tell them," Heather said.

I inched closer as the argument got nearer to my table. I didn't want to miss a word.

"I could hire anyone to do your job and get the same results. Everyone's replaceable," Jennie snapped.

"I'd like to see you try to find someone who'd put up with your bullshit," Heather fumed.

"I will. You're fired, Heather."

I could barely believe what I was witnessing: the notorious Jennie Weinstein in action! Jennie turned to me.

"Hey, you. Wanna job?" A stunned Heather was motionless.

I felt my stomach churning. I calculated that I was approximately thirty seconds from another Bonnie Griffin incident. I blurted, "Actually I work in PR too, for MPK Publicity."

Jennie stared at me blankly.

"It's a huge firm in Midtown," I explained. "We mainly have corporate clients."

That, of course, was a lie. The truth? MPK Publicity was simply Mitchell P. Kern, a friend of Ethel's, and there were no partners. Mitchell and I did not do corporate PR; we pitched Off-Broadway shows to small theater publications. His office was the size of a walk-in closet.

"Hello?" Jennie repeated. "You want a job?"

"I do, but, I have a job, and—" I tried to respond.

"Well you just quit. Now you work for me."

Heather rolled her eyes. "Well . . . what would I have to do?" I said, regretting the seven previous cocktails.

"Go to the most fabulous parties in Manhattan and hang around a bunch of famous people," she said, and smiled.

"Well, I'd have to give notice and . . ."

Jennie interrupted, "Yes or no?"

"Yes!" I said.

Heather glared at me in disgust and turned to Jennie. "You're too much. I've been with you since you started, and now you replace me with some clueless kid? You'll regret this in the morning when the tequila and nose candy wear off."

She then turned back to me. "Be careful. Not only does she bite, but she leaves quite a mark."

Heather stormed off, and I immediately stood up, grabbed Jennie's hand, and shook it feverishly. "Thank you so much for this opportunity. You won't regret this, I promise."

Jennie gave me a confused look. She started to walk away, when I grabbed her.

"So when do I start? Where do I go?"

"All my information is on the Web site. Come by a week from Monday." And she melted into the crowd.

The party was still hopping, but I had accomplished plenty for one night. I had just landed a job at one of the hottest PR firms in New York City.

Fuck you, Peter Criss.

The following morning, I got up early and ran to the newsstand to buy the *New York Post* and read Page Six. Even though I hadn't spoken to a single celebrity who attended the opening, seeing the party in print made the experience seem real. I hurried to tell Ethel that I was in the same room as all of these famous people. My mom and Ethel may not understand exactly what I do for a living, but they do understand famous people and the newspapers that write about them. Last night, *I* was at a Page-Six-worthy party.

"When it's your name in the paper, then I'll be excited," Ethel said. She clearly didn't understand the utmost importance of Page Six to a New York insider these days.

"It's basically the diary of the who's who in New York and beyond. The section is scattered with bits and pieces of gossip about anyone and everyone. There are even some private citizens like us who try outlandish stunts just to get their names in the column," I explained. "Like the guy who peed off his seventh-floor balcony . . ."

Even as the words escaped my mouth, I found myself bemused at the entire concept of Page Six, bewildered by people's fascination with gossip columns. What should one make of educated and intellectual human beings consuming information such as where Gwyneth Paltrow gets her hair done while on holiday in St. Barts? (Salon Cristophe, in case you were wondering.) What is it about other people's business that is such a turn-on?

From a Page-Six party one night to mac and cheese in my apartment with my dog Algebra the next: That was the reality of my life. My Midwestern roots, like the roots on the head of my future boss, refused to go away. So, I was happy to say "YES!" to Jennie, though even then I had a feeling that sooner or later that Yes would bite me in the ass.

The Monday after the party at Domino I showed up to work at ten and waited for Mitchell to arrive. I'd never actually quit a job before, and I'd had excruciating stomach cramps the entire morning. But I couldn't let my guilty conscience interfere with a shot like this. By eleven o'clock, I had given Mitchell my notice. Needless to say, he wasn't very happy since I pretty much was the glue that held the office together. However, he did leave me with some interesting and poignant words, "Anyone thinks they can be a publicist these days. These young socialite bitches plug in their laptops and forward their calls to their cell phones and boom! Call themselves publicists. It's more than just throwing a party or placing an item in Rush & Molloy, Taylor. Not all of us have unending trust funds, especially you. My advice to you is, be careful!"

I think in the back of my mind I knew he was right, but the

starstruck side of me didn't care. After only knowing Jennie Weinstein for a total of five minutes, I had quit a job that paid decent money, had health insurance, and was stable. Five minutes. I was about to learn just how much I would ultimately sacrifice for Jennie.

Jennie Weinstein Public Relations JWPR

FOR IMMEDIATE RELEASE

Contact: Jennie Weinstein
Jennie_Weinstein@JWPR.com

JENNIE WEINSTEIN IS PLEASED TO ANNOUNCE TAYLOR GREEN'S ARRIVAL TO THE JWPR FAMILY

After an extensive and exhaustive candidate search, I am delighted to announce that Taylor Green has been named Junior Account Executive to Jennie Weinstein Public Relations. With his hiring, Taylor will implement and manage press campaigns for a number of high-profile JWPR clients in addition to adding new clients to the company's ever-expanding roster. He will report directly to me and will remain based in the company's New York headquarters.

I congratulate Taylor on garnering this well-deserved position after beating out an extremely competitive field of applicants. His client-first approach and press savvy were two of the principal reasons for his hire.

Of his appointment Taylor states: "Getting this job has been nothing less than exhilarating, and I am excited by the challenges that lie ahead as my role expands under Jennie's guidance. It's truly an honor to be working with one of New York's biggest tastemakers, and her work ethic is awe-inspiring to me."

Taylor came to JWPR from the esteemed MPK Public Relations, a theater publicity team, where he served as a coordinator with a primary focus on house seats for various Broadway shows. A recent graduate of the highly touted Indiana State University, Taylor holds a Bachelor of Arts degree in Communications.

Please join me in congratulating Taylor and wishing him continued success.

2.

Shock and Awe

I woke up in a full-on panic. My Sony alarm clock, the same one I've had since high school, literally scared me out of bed. I grabbed Algebra's leash and raced down the steps. I couldn't be late. It was my first day at work, and I couldn't fuck it up. I had nearly reached the front door and felt like I'd forgotten something. I searched my pockets for the keys. Check. I looked at the ground. I had forgotten something . . . *Algebra*. I raced back up the stairs, nearly knocking Lauren's coffee out of her hand.

"Late already?" she shouted up the stairs.

"Not yet," I said, painfully optimistic. I fidgeted with my keys and finally opened the front door, to find Algebra patiently waiting.

"Sorry," I said, expecting him to understand. We raced down the steps together and out into the city streets.

"All right, no sniffing around today. Just do your business, and let's go. I can't be late today." He ignored me and smelled the fresh pee off the light pole. After a few minutes of that, I shouted, "Algebra let's go!" Defiantly, he sat down and stared at me. "I don't have time for this, you either go or you don't." I pulled his leash, dragged him up the steps, and I made a mad dash for the shower.

I showered so quickly that I barely rinsed off all the soap. I decided not to shave. I hate shaving, and on those special occasions that I do, I look like I'm thirteen. I reached for an old black suit that practically drowned me in fabric. It had belonged to my grandfather, and I didn't have the courage to tell Ethel that it felt too creepy wearing a dead man's clothes. Nor did I have the money to buy a new one. It had worked when I interviewed with Mitchell, and it would have to do for Jennie Weinstein. I threw on a pair of mismatched dress socks and dusted off an old pair of black dress shoes.

I glanced at the clock—9:15. Fuck. I was going to be late. I dumped some food in Algebra's bowl, darted outside, and hailed a cab. No time for the subway, and besides, I was sure Jennie would let me expense it. I couldn't imagine that *her* people took the subway.

Thirty-five minutes later, I was cursing myself for not taking the F train (that's F for "fucking faster than sitting in traffic"). I felt guilty for quitting Mitchell. After all, I'd sort of fallen into publicity like 99 percent of publicists. I don't think anyone ever actually sets out to be a publicist, not anyone with any real ambition anyway. I could hear Lauren and Allison's advice: Stay Jennie's protégé long enough to network your way into a top Manhattan job of your choice. "Use her, like she's sure as hell going to use you," Allison had said.

I burst out of the taxi eight blocks early and began to sprint. I'd never been late for anything my entire life, and I was about to be late for the most important job of my life. I slowed my run down to a power walk as I triple-checked the address on the card Jennie'd given me. I saw a large, pristine New York brownstone ahead. Just as I looked for the numbers on the door, I saw two of the hottest girls on the planet walking inside.

"Hold the door!" I shouted, racing up the steps. Just as I was about to reach the door, I tripped on the last step. *God, I'm an asshole.* The girls politely smiled and saved their laughter for the ladies' room. Perhaps I should have taken that as some sort of sign, but instead I continued on, anxious to get my keys to the kingdom—especially if everyone in Jennie's kingdom looked like those two.

I followed them into a modern, minimalist office with a single table at the entrance. The place was refined without being sterile, expensive without being showy. The receptionist was blond, probably around nineteen, and drop-dead gorgeous. Like Claudia Schiffer, but with more curve. So *that* was my new home. Busy dreaming of how plush my private office was going to be, I didn't hear the receptionist.

"Sir, can I help you?" she repeated.

"Oh, I'm Taylor," I said.

"Do you have your comp card?"

"Comp card? I need one of those?" I said, as the sweat beads began to form below my nose. The hot girls I followed in looked at me like I'd ridden the short bus all my life.

"If you want to get in here you do," the receptionist answered.

"Oh. I didn't know. Jennie just told me to show up. I didn't know I needed a photo or anything." The sweat seeped between my lips, and I was not sure if I should acknowledge it. As I smiled to diffuse my obvious embarrassment, the sweat dripped into my open mouth.

She stared at me with a dull expression until finally she said,

"Jennie? Ahhhh, you want the office up the steps and to the right."

"Yeah?" I asked.

"Yeah. That's Jennie Weinstein PR, and this is Fox Models," she explained.

"Fox Models, eh?" I said with a smirk.

"Don't."

I scampered out of Fox Models as quickly as I could and headed up the steps.

As my fingers got ready to push the bell, and I prepared myself for the entry buzzer to the glamorous world of public relations, I heard Jennie shouting through the door at her staff. I took a step back and immediately considered begging Mitchell to forgive me, but my mind flashed to Ethel, then to my high-school football coach (split screen of course) and re-membered I was never supposed to back down from a chal-lenge! Sufficiently motivated, I took a deep breath and pressed the bell.

The door opened, and a thick layer of cigarette smoke es-caped into the hallway, causing my eyes to burn. Smoke was nothing new to me—I lived in New York City—but it was un-like anything I had ever known. I couldn't even see the face of the middle-aged woman who sat at a desk less than two feet in front of me. I coughed like I had taken my first drag. I saw the outline of big hair with a headset poking out.

"Hello?" she said with a deep, raspy voice.

"Hi. I'm Tay—"

"Jennie Weinstein Publicity," she said loudly. I studied her closely; she had fire-engine red hair that looked like it had once belonged to a clown, and humongous fake breasts that looked like they'd once belonged to Pam Anderson. She wore a psychedelic catsuit, pumps, and makeup that was caked on. For a moment I thought it might be Wynona Judd, and I almost told her that my mother was a big fan.

"Yes, thanks, I realize that now," I explained. "Where were you five minutes ago when I was making an ass out of myself downstairs in front of a half dozen beautiful women?" I laughed. "Anyway, Ms. Weinstein told me to come—"

"Jennie Weinstein Publicity. Hold," she said again.

"Right. Anyway—" I interrupted.

"Jennie Weinstein PR. Hold." There was a layer of smoke thicker than L.A. smog, but could she really not see me standing in front of her?

"I'm cool. Go ahead and get it. I'll just wait," I offered. The receptionist continued to stare straight ahead, zombielike.

Finally, her eyes shifted in my direction. "Hi. Anyway, I'm Taylor and today is my fir—"

"Jennie Weinstein PR. Hold." *You've got to be kidding me!* I grunted louder than I intended, and through a layer of smoke I saw a somewhat familiar face. There, dressed in dingy sweatpants, a long-sleeve T-shirt and no makeup, her hair curly and big, was the door bitch, looking very different when not working the velvet ropes.

"WHAT?" she screamed. She held a cigarette in one hand and pressed a cell phone to her ear with the other. These people and their phones. The receptionist a few floors below was more along the lines of Audrey Hepburn's style and Princess Diana's disposition. Mia was a cross between Courtney Love and Roseanne. Strangely, however, I was digging it.

"Hi, I'm Taylor Green," I said politely.

"And?"

"And I need to see Ms. Weinstein."

"Sorry, no solicitors," she said, and turned to walk away.

"Wait! I recognize you. You're the girl who worked the door at Domino last week. Mia, right?" She needed to know that *I* was there, that *I* was among New York's hippest. I prayed she didn't remember she'd denied me. She had the same intensity as before, and I was once again attracted to it.

"No, it wasn't me," she said, obviously lying.

"Yes, it was. You were just all done up then."

"You think I come to work 'all done up'?" she snipped.

"Are you going to let me in?" *Am I back at the ropes again?*

She gave me the once-over. I felt fairly comfortable with my attire. In fact, I felt damn fashionable for wearing a corpse's clothes.

"I'm your new coworker," I offered.

After surveying every inch, she relented. "I guess. I don't know what gets into Jennie sometimes."

"Try a fifth of vodka and a gram of coke," I said.

"Come in." She rolled her eyes but had a hint of a smile. She nodded toward the receptionist, and said, "You can flirt with Bob later, but I'm not sure you'll get very far because I think she's pretty much deaf, dumb, and blind from what I can tell," Mia said. "Come on, I'll give you the grand tour." Her New York accent was so thick that I imitated it in my brain as preparation for later impressions for Lauren and Allison.

"Something funny?" she asked.

"Nothing," I said, and grinned.

"Learn to be a better liar if you want to work here," she said.

"Your New York accent," I said. "It's just . . . adorable."

She rolled her eyes again, then we walked into a large open space.

"Welcome to the dungeon. This is where the magic happens."

Instead of the meticulously decorated space, something straight out of an issue from *Architectural Digest*, the office was "shabby chic." But without the chic. If you could get past the avocado green carpeting and stained lounge chairs, you would still have to deal with the walls—which had once been white but were yellow because of the smoke. Had I not read the sign on the door, I would not believe that this was the same Jennie Weinstein PR that handled J-Lo's album release, the Beverly Hills Polo team, Lexus, and the Oscar after-party.

Judging from appearances, this was the place where hangovers were born. Ashtrays overflowed, trash cans were filled with empty vodka and aspirin bottles, memos were strewn all over the desks. The dungeon people, like my tour guide, had phones in their ears and cigarettes in their hands. And not one of them was wearing a suit or anything that resembled one. The room was filled with the deafening sound of phones ringing—a stark contrast to the quiet mornings on Mitchell's Upper West Side. Every conversation—no matter how trivial the topic—maintained a frantic intensity. Suddenly, I felt strangely excited. I had more energy than someone who just downed a six-pack of Red Bull, and I was a bit dizzy. Within a few months, I would be sitting at one of those desks, shouting into the phone about my night out on the town. Within a matter of weeks, I would be speaking flippantly about the celebrities I encountered ("Yeah, it was a cute party. Ashton, Demi, Cameron, and Jack were there," I'd say with a lackluster tone, as if ordering a burger.) I would learn all the tricks of the trade and invent some of my own.

And I did.

We reached the reception area outside of Jennie's office.

"So, the receptionist," I said.

"What about Bob?" Mia said.

"You know. Is that a . . ." I whispered.

"Secretary? No, she prefers office assistant," Mia cracked.

"Bob, could you be a dear and buzz us in please?"

"Sure, no problem, sweetie," Bob said in a high-pitched voice. She called Jennie on the phone and mumbled something. Within a few seconds, she told us to go in. So many checkpoints, like trying to get into one of her high-profile parties.

We reached Jennie's office and stopped abruptly. Mia informed me that one always knocks before entering, then counts to ten to give Jennie ample warning. I was puzzled, but nodded in agreement.

Mia knocked on the door. "You're not counting," she complained.

"I'm counting quietly in my head," I said. She did not care.

"Okay, that's more like twenty. It should be safe now," she said, and turned the knob. I stepped inside Jennie Weinstein's office.

It was a sharp contrast to the shit hole I had just come from. Plush. White-leather couches, a huge Romero Britto painting on the wall, hanging next to a plasma television.

I've never been a huge man of faith, but looking back that was God throwing a small pebble at my head, trying to get me to wake up to avoid potential disaster. Yet much like most major catastrophes in my life, I walked straight into it . . . eyes wide open.

Jennie's back was to us, and she talked excitedly into her headset as we entered.

"No. Uh-uh. I told you I'm not about to do that. Marcello, you need to try harder," she said.

"Jennie?" Mia asked. She motioned Mia to enter while her back continued to face us. Mia directed me to the couch.

I whispered to Mia, without taking my eyes off the back of Jennie's head, "She seems busy. How about we come back when she's free?" I turned, but Mia had bolted, closing the door behind her. She'd left me with one of the most powerful women in New York.

"Listen, if I do that, what are you going to do for me?" Jennie said, her tone changing. I began to shift on the couch, attempting to make my presence known.

"Now, what about your other hand," she said, smiling. She paused, then gasped. "You kinky son of a bitch. I knew you were into ass play."

Ass play? I thought. *Did she just say the words "ass play?"*

"Can you fit two in?" Jennie continued in her businesslike demeanor. Is she . . . no way . . . oh my God . . . she is . . . She's having phone sex! *I shouldn't be here right now.*

"Bring that Latin heat, Marcello," she said, and I decided it was time to go. I stood up from the couch and walked toward the door, when suddenly Jennie snapped her fingers and pointed at the couch. I felt like a dog she'd just scolded for peeing on her shag rug. Reluctantly, I sat.

"You, you, you. It's all about you. I'm getting nothing out of this, Marcello. It's no good for me," Jennie scolded him. I shifted uncomfortably and pretended to look up at the Britto.

"I gotta run, Papo. Let's finish this later. *Ciao,*" she said, and hung up.

"Sorry about that," she said, looking up at me from her large desk.

"No problem," I said cheerily. "I just wanted to say how excited I am to be working here, with you. Yeah, so my boss was pretty pissed when I quit. And like I said the other night, he is an old friend of the family, so I did feel kinda guilty, especially without giving him any notice. But honestly, I know an amazing opportunity when I see one, and I just wanted to say thank you so much for it. I guarantee you won't regret offering it to me."

"Yeah . . ." she said trailing off, then finally, "Who are you? Todd, did you say?"

"Actually, my name is Taylor Green," I said meekly. God, I hate my name.

"Uh-huh. I'm sorry, but have we met?"

I laughed, hoping this was some sort of office hazing every new recruit must endure.

"I'm sorry—something funny?" she asked.

"No, not at all. We met last week at the Domino opening. You offered me a job, remember?"

She stared at me blankly. "I don't remember interviewing anyone for a job."

"Well, it wasn't exactly an interview," I explained. "You flat-out offered it to me when you fired someone named Heather. You were a little buzzed, so you might not remember."

Jennie gave me the once-over. "It's Taylor, right?"

"Yes."

"I don't know who the hell you are," she said.

I stared at her blankly.

She continued, "At our client launches, I'm so busy working and making sure things are going according to plan that I can't remember every single tiny conversation that happens."

"Tiny?" I became angry. "I quit my job."

"Now, I'm sure I didn't ask you to quit your job. Besides, you look like a bright kid; I bet you'll find other work. Real easy." A bright kid? She was only a few years older than me. Jennie's phone rang. "Yes?" she said into the intercom.

I heard Bob's high-pitched, throaty squeal. "Phil Reynolds from *The Scoop* on line two for you."

"Great, I need to place Tropical Tans in there this week. Don't lose him!" She clicked off and looked up at me. "I really need to take this call, but leave your contact info with Bob, and we'll put you on our event mailing list," she said.

Under other circumstances, this would be thrilling. Jennie does every major party on the East Coast. "That's not good enough," I balked.

"Again, I'm sorry, but I don't have any open positions at this time. Send us your résumé and we'll put it on file and contact you if something opens up." I stared at her for what seemed like an eternity until she picked up the phone and started talking.

"Phil! Hey, baby! I haven't got you anything on Britney yet, but you've got to give me more time." I walked toward the door. "You never told me you were on deadline, honey, hold on one second, let me see what I can do."

I reached the reception desk and saw Mia standing over the fax machine. "Thanks so much for your time," I said, with cheerful sarcasm. "I've never been treated so rudely in my life."

"I tried telling you," Mia said.

As I walked out I heard Jennie's voice over the intercom, "If someone doesn't give me some dirt on Britney Spears right now, you're all fired!"

"Here we go again." Mia sighed.

"That's really too bad," I said to Mia. "I saw Britney last

night in front of my building." I was not about to go back to the other side of "Nobody Land" just yet.

"What?" she quizzed.

"Yeah, her hairstylist lives upstairs."

"Are you serious?"

"Why would I make something like that up?"

"Come with me, quick!" Mia said, pulling me toward Jennie's office.

Just as Mia was about to knock on Jennie's door, I stopped her. "Don't," I said.

"What?" Mia asked.

"Maybe I'm not meant to be here. Perhaps it's a sign. Something's telling me that I could potentially be avoiding a major minefield."

"You're right; maybe you're not meant to be here. Maybe you're supposed to go back to work for some garmento. Or better yet, maybe you're supposed to be back in the Midwest, which, based on your attire, is where I'm assuming you're from," she said. Then her tone changed. "Are you kidding me? This is potentially the biggest opportunity in your life, and you're suddenly having second thoughts about it?"

"I don't know. She didn't even remember who the hell I was, for God's sake."

"If you stay, I can promise you she'll forget who you are almost weekly. Thanks to a cornucopia of various drugs, prescription and not, you can never be sure what you're going to get. There will be yelling and screaming. There will be times where you will have your self-esteem trampled on in front of anyone you've ever respected. But consider this, Taylor, when was the last time you were able to give your mother earrings from Chopard?"

"What?" I asked. "There's no way I could afford those."

"My point exactly."

"I need some answers, or you're all fired!" Jennie yelled over the intercom again.

"Yeah, I don't know; a pair of earrings isn't worth all of this," I said, defeated.

"When was the last time you invited your grandmother to a movie premiere that they'd normally watch on E!? Or when did you last get into Manhattan's busiest restaurant without any notice? Or go away for the weekend and not spend a dime? Or send your family and friends gifts on a regular basis without ever opening your wallet?"

Before I was able to answer, Mia tersely explained, "This is the currency that publicists have. Not a bad life for a kid from the middle of nowhere."

It was a good speech. So good that I suddenly began rethinking my feelings on working for Jennie Weinstein. And perhaps my feelings toward Mia.

She knocked on Jennie's door and counted to ten faster than anybody I knew. It was a knock that would forever change my life.

She barged in, and shouted, "He saw Britney last night!"

"Where? Who was she with?" Jennie barked at me like I was her man slave.

"I'd really love to help you, but I can't remember everything when I have so many other things going on," I said.

"Don't get cute with me. You want a job? Fine. Tell me where the fuck she was." She picked up the receiver, "Phil, I'll be with you in one more second."

"Are you hiring me?" I questioned.

"I said yes. Now where was she?"

"She was dropping off her hairstylist in front of my building. It's kind of a weak item, but . . ."

Jennie picked up the receiver. "Phil, I got it, and it's good!"

I looked at Mia in disbelief. "Britney was seen getting it on with her hairstylist in the back of her limo, and my spy tells me she was pretty fucked-up." My mouth dropped.

"I told you it'd be good. Of course it's real!" she shouted into the phone. She continued, "So I can tell Tropical Tans they will be in next week's issue?" She paused, then said, "Perfect. I'll speak to you later, baby! *Ciao.*"

"I never said Britney was making out with her hairstylist. Actually, I'm pretty sure he's gay. And I highly doubt either one of them was drunk, since the man's a recovering alcoholic and, actually, so is she," I protested.

"It doesn't matter. Let Britney's publicist worry about it; I got my client in next week's *The Scoop,*" she said, and laughed. Mia burst out laughing along with her, but Mia's laughter seemed manufactured.

"Anyway, I like your instincts. Ballsy move, but it worked."

"Thanks," I said, confused.

"Mia, could you show Taylor to his new office?" Jennie said sweetly.

"New office? We have no space for an office. That's why we have the dungeon, remember?"

Jennie glared at Mia. "Oh. That office," Mia said. "Sure, follow me, Cornbread."

We walked down a long and winding corridor until we finally reached a door at the end.

I asked the obvious. "Is this a supply closet?"

"No! More like a junk room. And from this moment on, it will become your new office," she said.

I supposed it was better than nothing. And who was I to complain. I was standing at the front gates of Oz.

"This is . . . great," I bluffed.

Mia wasn't convinced. "Again, work on the lying. Anyway, Jennie would like you to reorganize this space. Put the bottles of alcohol from our liquor sponsors on a shelf, the sample-size clothes for the celebrities need to be logged, CDs organized, party flyers and old press kits filed." She surveyed the room, then continued, "That should about do it, I guess. Oh, and anything else that looks messy, you know, just straighten it up."

Was she kidding? I'd seen segments on HGTV where they did that sort of thing, and it took them days to finish. And they were professionals!

"Any questions?" she asked.

"No, I think I'm good." I was so screwed.

"Welcome to Jennie Weinstein PR," she said.

I looked back into the room. It was worse than I thought: a Martha Stewart's worst-nightmare candidate. I needed my mother.

I took off my suit jacket and hung it on the back of the door, loosened my tie, rolled up my sleeves, and grabbed a stack of empty vodka bottles. Every trip to the trash bin demanded I pass the rest of the staff, all of whom cheered me on with obvious glee.

"Hey, Todd, I have some stuff that needs to go out too!" Louise Phillips, senior publicist, mocked.

When finally I returned to my "cloffice" the organization began. That was my specialty. My mother and Ethel were so neurotic that my T-shirts were organized from light to dark, and primary colors were separated from pastels. I could handle a storage room. I picked up bottles of vodka and tequila, dusted them off, then meticulously organized them on the shelves. I feverishly read old press kits. The celebrity tidbits were riveting. Did you know that the décor at the chic restaurant Gotham is made from recycled Glad trash bags? Or that while studying for her high-school midterm exams, Neve Campbell drank gurana berry shakes to stay awake? She was a 4.0 student! This was the stuff that Ethel found riveting—that's where I'd learned to eat it up. There were bios of some of the biggest names in music, fashion, and nightlife. The harshness of Jennie aside, the press kits were why I had come. Hers were the hippest clients in both New York and Los Angeles. And there I was, a kid from a small town in the Midwest, holding those people's professional and very public lives in my hands.

An old invitation fell out of one of the folders, to a party I had read about. The invitation alone must have cost at least fifty bucks. It was for the launch of some new skin-care line by Heidi Klum. The whole invitation was completely biodegradable. In fact, if you lit it, it became incense that gave off smells of the Brazilian rain forest. You could find what's left of the company at your local Dollar Store.

I placed the invitation on the shelf and smiled. I found an old CD boom box and plugged it in. Ironically, it played Missy Elliot's song "We Run This." The only "running" that I was doing was to the trash. There were so many promotional CDs in that closet that I could have sent them out to all my friends and family for Christmas, and there would have still been leftovers.

I went through Missy, Run DMC, and the Best of the Bee Gees before I finally finished resurrecting the space. Still unsure of how it was going to be my new office, I looked at my watch—almost nine o'clock, and I was bushed. I shut off the light, passed the dungeon where a few remaining people were still working the phones, and made my way toward the door. I breathed it all in for a minute. Maybe I did have a chance in the PR business . . .

On my way home, I dialed Ethel.

"How's my star?" she asked.

"I'm great," I said.

"And your first day?" she asked anxiously.

"It couldn't have been better."

"And your boss? I bet she just adores you already," Ethel gushed.

"Yes, she even gave me my own office," I said.

"I knew it!" she said excitedly. "What does she have you doing?"

"Well, um, right now the office is undergoing a sort of reorganization of sorts, and Jennie put me in charge of that."

"Wonderful," Ethel said.

"Listen, tell Mom I said hi, and I'll call you tomorrow," I said, avoiding any more questions.

"Love you," she said sweetly.

"Love you too."

And so, exhausted, I headed home, where I found a surprise from Algebra waiting for me, just as I had predicted.

The Daily

Just Asking

Which sex-bomb actress recently dumped her magnificently hunky boyfriend because she caught him in bed with another man? The goddess immediately rushed to the doctor for a complete series of tests.

3.

Blind Item Betty

EVERY day before I walked through the front door of JWPR, I had already read Page Six, Rush & Molloy, Liz Smith, and Cindy Adams. Initially I had no idea what I was looking for in their columns. It was difficult to see what the significance of Jonathan Adler's choice of fabric for the Parker hotel in Palm Springs actually had to do with our clients or pitching to the press. The details all sounded a lot like insignificant lunchroom gossip to me. But what seemed to be useless bits of information would prove to be invaluable in the future, when I had to carry on conversations with reporters. It seemed like whatever was on Perez Hilton or D-listed was all anyone ever talked about at parties. Imagine watching the E! Channel on a twenty-four-hour loop—that was my day. But with less Seacrest, thank God.

Each morning before Jennie arrived and each afternoon after she left, the staff placed bets on the blind items. Blind items are the really nasty bits of gossip that newspapers can't print using any real names—not without a lawsuit anyway. The reading public—me included, sadly—spends many unremorseful hours attempting to name these anonymous subjects.

It was near the end of one of these workdays, and the phones had finally stopped ringing. Jennie's strict rule demanded the staff remain in the office until seven o'clock, no questions asked. At a quarter after six, no one felt like doing anything useful, but we all were forced to wait until Jennie departed before letting loose.

Finally, her office door opened. I saw her grab her oversized Louis Vuitton bag.

"Good night, Jennie," Mia said, and smiled. Jennie simply glared at her, tossed a glance at the rest of the dungeon, and walked out without saying a word. All of us listened in silence as Jennie's shoes echoed down the stairs.

When we were certain that she was gone, Mia asked, "Anyone up for a little friendly gambling?" The room erupted.

Not until after my fourth full day did Adam Hanes finally notice my existence at the company, and boy did he *notice*—to the point it made me a little uncomfortable. He was the resident office stud, whose initials seemed to give Jennie the right to call him Ass Hole. From what I'd "observed and overheard" (otherwise known as the "Big O's" in PR), he was a very handsome, obnoxiously straight young man who moved to New York from Middle America with aspirations of becoming a model after meeting a talent scout at his local mall. The scout, not surprisingly, was full of bogus promises and a handful of roofies, but Adam managed to land modeling jobs here and there, and a few were even with Abercrombie & Fitch. I think it's safe to say that he slept his way to the middle. He had been working as a waiter for a catering company when he first ran into Ms. Weinstein at a private party at Donatella's town house. As Adam tells it—and he tells it well, and often—he went home with her and "banged the shit out of her," and he was so good she offered him a job just as she was about to cum. Perhaps Jennie has a much different scenario of the story, but who would dare to ask? Jennie'd kept him on staff as a junior publicist almost exclusively to serve as an eye candy escort for clients. He was more of a . . . male socialite, for lack of a better term. Some called him a "walker" since he's quite a dedicated escort to some of Manhattan's richest women—and apparently even a few men—to all of Manhattan's A-list parties. He reveled in finding his photo in society publications like *Avenue*, *Quest*, and *Gotham*, and on the Web sites of celebrity photographers like Patrick McMullan and David Patrick Columbia.

"So . . . have you fucked her yet?" were Adam's first words after welcoming me to the office, and I think my silence came as a surprise to him. "Jennie," he said. "Have you? Well? Fine. Whatever, dude. Don't tell me. It's all good."

At the moment he was trying to swindle what was left of everyone's paycheck in a game we called "Blind Item Betty."

"You in?" Mia asked him.

"I've got my twenty bucks right here," he shouted.

"How about you, Louise?" Mia looked at Louise Phillips, the bookish one. She filed press clips in the drawer. She once was a freelance writer for *Allure*, until one night Jennie promised her a much higher salary working for JWPR if she'd write a piece on Tyler Thomas, a fledgling chef and JWPR client. Louise complied with an eight-hundred-word love letter complete with a photo of Tyler, which had appeared at the front of the magazine. With dreams of working on some of the fashion industry's biggest darlings, Louise had quit the magazine world and set her sights on publicity. Unfortunately, after a month or so of working with JWPR, Jennie'd lost interest in her and relegated Louise to the world of filing and handling the corporate clients, who never really sought press as much as they did a write-off.

"Are you in?" Mia asked her.

"Okay, but this is the last time. I lost too much on the Ricky Martin Men's Room thing," she said.

"Okay, that's twenty for Adam and twenty for Louise, and I, of course, am the house, which means I get 10 percent. What about you, Bob?" Mia asked. As Bob pranced into the dungeon, I was baffled as to why no one ever discussed his/her true gender. But I was not about to bring it up.

"No, I think I'll just watch," Bob said. "I'm getting a facial later and need the tip money." Why the facial, who knows, as his/her face was already glowing.

"Wait!" yelled Carol Wallace, the account rep for Luca, Yosi Sneakers, and all the hot nightclubs. "Put me in for double!"

Much to my surprise, Mia walked to the edge of the dungeon and poked her head around the corner. "Hey, Taylor, you want to get in on a little Blind Item Betty?"

I pretended not to know what she was talking about. "Maybe. What is it?"

"Simple, we take an item from Page Six and place bets on who we think they're talking about," she explained.

"Sure, why not? I'm usually pretty good at those, put me in for five bucks."

"Oh, big spender," she taunted. "There's actually a twenty-dollar minimum to enter."

"No problem," I said just before Mia hurried back to the

dungeon. The truth was I didn't have an extra twenty to gamble.

I quickly made my way to the dungeon, where Mia rustled through the newspaper. "Okay here goes . . . Which sex-bomb actress recently dumped her magnificently hunky boyfriend because she caught him in bed with another man? The goddess immediately rushed to the doctor for a complete series of tests."

Carol paced, thinking, while Louise nervously broke pencils. Adam sat motionless and stared into space. I was stumped as well.

Finally, Carol broke the silence. "Is it Madonna?"

"No, it can't be. I don't think people consider her an actress," Adam quipped.

"I got it! It's Keira Knightley, right?" Adam guessed.

"Who is she even dating these days? There's been so many. I lost track after Ashton," Louise said.

"Nope, she's single, or at least she was when we did our Lazaro's Jewelry launch," Mia proclaimed.

"Oh yeah, that's right," Louise said.

"You got a guess, Cornbread?" Adam asked. He busted up laughing. The ladies quickly joined him.

"I think 'Cornbread' is wearing thin," I said. "And actually I don't really pay attention to the blind items because I think they're pretty childish. But since there's money on the line, I'll say Donna Harris," I said.

"Who the hell is Donna Harris?" Louise asked.

"She's the young blonde who has three, no, four movies coming out this year and just recently broke up with the guy who has that show on the CW who everybody thinks is gay," I explained.

"Okay, any other guesses before I call Richard to get the answer?" Mia asked.

"Wait a second, I thought these items were supposed to be blind," I said coyly.

"Yes, but if you're a close friend of the guru at Page Six, he'll leak. Just ask Mia," Adam said.

"Not to mention he gets 5 percent from the house," Mia added. She would later tell me that she waited until the dollar amount accrued to at least a hundred dollars before sending payment that usually was in the form of a Starbucks gift card. She picked up the receiver and dialed Richard Johnson. She spoke into the phone, "Hi, it's Mia. Yeah. Good, thanks. So anyway, we're doing Blind Item Betty. Yeah, today's item. Uh-huh. Yeah, with the bisexual guy." Mia paused, then screamed, "NO! Wow, who knew? Thanks, honey. See you soon. *Ciao.*" She hung up the phone and strutted to the front of the dungeon. "It looks as though we have a winner," she said.

Adam stood up, grinning cockily, and walked toward her to collect the money. "Sit your ass down. Congratulations, Taylor. You were right." She handed me the stash of cash and walked back to her desk. I got no applause, no congratulatory pats on the back. Instead, the staff simply walked back to their desks and packed up for the night.

Depending on whom you ask, my job was either sociology or anthropology: I had to know all the eating and mating habits of Hollywood's finest. Since I was new to the firm, I worked extra hard to make sure I knew everything about everyone. I spent hours reading, all out of sheer terror of being fired. Fear is a tremendous motivator. And this was like some sort of fucked-up fraternity initiation. Knowing every celebrity's dirty laundry became my biggest concern. Many times I witnessed Jennie leaking her own clients' dirty laundry to the press in order to secure coverage for one of her lesser-known accounts. It reminded me of a grown-up version of Monopoly, wherein a notable person getting caught in a compromising position at a venue a publicist represented was akin to landing on Park Place with three houses on it. There was a heavy fine to pay in both cases. "You landed on my nightclub (doing coke in the bathroom stalls, no less). Give me two mentions on Motorola and Diamonds.com or go directly to jail without passing Go." The dirty trick was that the collateral was an entertainer's personal life. I never realized that the countless hours spent playing that game with Ethel and my mom would pay off later in life.

All this left me with a bigger issue to grapple with: Who was I supposed to protect my clients from, the tabloids or us?

I was about to walk back to my office when Bob tapped me on the shoulder. "So what are you going to do with the money, babe? Get a massage? Facial? Or spend it all on cheap liquor and expensive hookers like I would? Or is it the other way around?"

"Maybe on the weekend. Tonight, I'm going straight to bed. I haven't been sleeping a lot lately. Jennie's been having me work late."

"The cigarette-and-Diet-Coke run at 1:00 A.M., right?" Bob grinned as I nodded. "She used to do that to me when I just started."

"Why?" I asked.

"She has to come down off the pot."

"I thought she was more of a coke kinda girl. You know, Speedy Gonzales," I argued, while mock grinding my teeth.

"During the day, sure. But she does pot at night to chill out, then cigarettes and caffeine-free Diet Coke to put her to sleep. This is real-life *Valley of the Dolls* shit here."

"I guess a hot bath and some chamomile tea is out of the question," I offered.

"When you're as stressed and pressured as she is, you'll do anything to keep up your momentum. You'll see. I give you three months until you're hooked."

"Nah, that's not my style," I argued.

"Funny. Jennie said the same thing when she started," Bob said as he picked up his purse and walked for the door. "See you tomorrow."

"Hey, Cornbread!" Adam shouted. "Do you want to take your winnings, and hang out for a while?"

"Basically, you're broke and want me to buy us beers and pizza," I said, smirking.

"Beer and pizza? God, you really are so Midwestern," he replied.

"Uh, yeah. I'm from Indiana."

"So you agree that you are Midwestern," he said, almost surprised.

"I might be missing something here, *dude*, but aren't you from the Midwest too?"

"Yeah, but I'm not *Midwestern*; not like you," he said defensively.

"Whatever. Where we headed?"

"Pravda," he said. "It's right around the corner from my place." Then he pulled an American Spirit out of his pocket and lit up. Too cool for Marlboro Lights, apparently. We walked into the crowded elevator as he continued to smoke.

"So anyway, it will be fun; lots of pussy there. Russian chicks

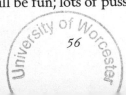

all over the place. Most of them are hookers, but I just tell 'em I don't pay. Look at me for chrissakes," he said. The other passengers did.

The idea of hanging out with Adam was fascinating to me. He was everything I wasn't: confident, gorgeous, funny, and sexual. At the same time, I hated the whole idea of getting to know him. I hated breaking out of my comfort zone, and I usually avoided talking to anyone for fear of having nothing to say. I might end up being too quiet, then be mistaken for the creepy, loner guy at the bar. On the few occasions I had mustered enough courage to carry on conversations with women, I had tripped all over my words and stared at the ground most of the time. Rainman was more approachable than me; at least he danced with a girl in a penthouse suite. Ironically, in a work situation, I would shine. I could bullshit with the best of them and turn on the Midwestern charm at the drop of a dime. So I made a conscious choice in the elevator to think of Adam as a client. He might have had all those amazing surface qualities that I didn't, but I had something he didn't: a brain. And if I was eventually going to be Jennie's right hand, I had to learn how to play Mr. Abercrombie to my advantage.

Forty-five minutes later, we walked into Pravda, and I immediately grew tense. The bar had an appropriately clandestine vibe to it—it was underground, and the entire interior cast a glow, perhaps because of the golden ceiling. And it was Russian tacky: Moscow tchotchkes adorned the walls, while models and the old banker types who loved them sipped giant martinis in distressed leather chairs at miniscule tables. They served food there, if you can call caviar food. My "Blind Item Betty" money might get us two drinks with a small tip.

"I could live here," Adam declared while inching his way to the bar. Somehow I got the feeling he already did.

"Vlad, what's up, bro?" he said, shaking the tall dark-haired Russian's hand across the bar. "Two Leninades," he said.

I laughed.

"What?"

"Lenin-ade? As in the infamous Russian dictator?" I said.

"Oh yeah, it's funny, right?" He had no idea what I was talking about.

I noticed him checking out a girl who was sitting at a banquette with a group of girlfriends. She was blond, sophisticated, and had legs for days. By the rest of the country's standards, she was beautiful. But in New York, she would have been considered "cute." She wore a tight, black miniskirt, so short she was almost giving a Sharon Stone.

"She's hot," I said.

He gave me this *maybe-for-you* glare. "I guess," he said. "Retail."

"What?"

"She works in retail. High-end retail, but retail nonetheless," he said.

"Shut up," I said. "How could you possibly know that by just looking at her?"

"Look at her calves. See how big and toned they are? You don't get that from the gym; you get that from standing all day in designer knockoff shoes. And check out her makeup. It's too much, like she had it done at a makeup counter," he said, as if he was a med student performing an autopsy.

"No fucking way," I said, taking a sip from a "Leninade" the size of a fishbowl. "And for a straight guy, you know a lot about women's shoes and makeup," I added.

"You'll learn," he said, putting another cigarette in his mouth but not lighting it.

I rolled my eyes. "Anyway, I better hit it soon. I gotta be in the office early tomorrow to make sure Jennie has her shit for her eight o'clock."

"Jesus Christ, you have no balls, man!" he said loud enough for the lady on my right to give *me* a dirty look. "Vlad, give us two more . . ."

"Adam, I really gotta break out of here," I pleaded.

"To go," he said to the bartender, glaring. Vlad handed us two large Styrofoam coffee cups with sippy lids, and handed me the bill. *There goes my cable for the month.* I looked at it closer. *And my electric.*

It was almost eleven. I knew I should start walking toward the B train and head back to the Upper West Side. I returned to work mode and calculated the exact amount of time that I needed to sleep and still be functional in the morning. I needed to be home in an hour—an hour and a half at the most.

"Where you going?" I asked.

"I live two blocks from here," he said. "Let's get some food."

We walked for what seemed like thirty blocks, and finally turned down Rivington. On the left side of the street was a nondescript walk-up, exactly like all the others on the block. For a city so full of energy and personality, such buildings are Ritalin. For someone who lived a life that revolved around attending parties in the public eye, for someone who was in fact the very definition of a socialite, Adam's accommodations were underwhelming.

"How do you tell them apart?" I asked.

"The block is a bit bland, but you can't beat the location.

I'm three blocks from SoHo and a six-dollar cab ride from the meatpacking district," he justified.

"I get it, I was just saying that—"

"Just shut the fuck up," he snapped, unexpectedly. He walked to the glass door, and pressed the key panel to the left. I imagined that the sound and the wires pulsating inside the walls would send every rat in the building scampering. In a matter of minutes they'd all have been outside, and they would have been pissed.

"You have to ring the buzzer at your own apartment?" I said anxiously. "Are you sure this is your place?"

Nobody answered the buzzer, and I began walking to the subway to avoid the imminent rat exodus.

"My roommate should be here," he said, confused. I was surprised to learn that Adam lived with someone—it didn't fit with his playboy lifestyle. Unless his roommate was as much of a pig as Adam. I imagined some crack den where they stayed up all night doing lines off a hooker.

He pressed the buzzer again, and that time its sound was syncopated with Adam's "fuck-you-answer-the-door."

Within a few seconds, a barely audible cracked voice came through, and we were in. I trailed behind Adam as he walked up the steps. The old prewar floors had lost their luster, and the hallways smelled like Lysol; but at least it was clean. We stopped on the second floor, and he knocked.

The door opened, and a short, slightly chubby girl appeared, wearing a pair of navy sweatpants and a gray T-shirt that was so tight you could see the creases in her fat. That was the last person I'd ever expected to answer Adam's door. Her face was flushed, and she had a few beads of sweat on her forehead.

"Hi, babe," she said, leaning in and kissing Adam on the

lips. The kiss looked familiar, like a ritual. "Sorry about the door. I had my Carmen Electra workout DVD on full blast to get me motivated," she said, and laughed. Her optimism was sad, but infectious.

She turned to me, and said, "Check out this ass, it's just like Carmen's, right?"

"Absolutely," I said, without hesitating.

She turned back to Adam, "Are all your friends publicists?" She burst into laughter. "No really, honey, you can lie with the best of them."

"I'm Taylor," I said as I shook her hand.

"Ellie," she said. She resembled a stuffed animal that you wanted to squeeze and love but would never have any sort of sexual fantasies about. Adam stepped inside and walked down the hallway and into the kitchen. I tried to follow, but I was stopped.

"Now tell me what this one has told you about me: that we slept together? We were each other's first love? He's still madly in love with me? It's all true," she said with a smile so warm that it could melt ice.

"Actually, I didn't even know you existed until just now," I said, grinning back.

"You could've lied," she said, as her smile faded. She walked into the living room and turned Carmen Electra down. Adam returned with a bottle of chilled vodka. I opened the lid to my sippy cup, and he poured.

"Sorry," I said to Adam. "I think I accidentally pissed her off."

"No problem. She's just a little sensitive," he explained. "Hey, El, we're going to order some pizza from Angelo's, you want something?"

"Pizza? How do you expect to go to all those fancy events

getting superfat from eating pizza? Those ladies don't like fat guys on their arms," she said. Until then, I hadn't realized that a walker had such strict guidelines. The man had to be in incredible shape, well dressed, somewhat cultured, and most importantly, know when to step aside when the press went to snap a photo of his socialite date. A walker was a nicer way of calling a guy a "himbo."

Adam walked into the kitchen, opened the refrigerator, and grabbed two plastic containers. He put them both in the microwave.

"Those are my Zone meals," Ellie said, without even looking toward the kitchen. I gathered Adam stealing her diet meals was a regular occurrence. I could tell it unnerved her, but she politely smiled and pretended it didn't.

"You said no pizza. I figured you wouldn't mind. Besides, this thing isn't really working for you, El," he said.

"I guess you're right," she said, looking away. "I'll give you boys some alone time. You don't need me hanging on every word." Her smile failed to mask her obvious disappointment.

"El, it's not like I'm going to fuck him," he said, laughing. Based on the rumor mill at work, I wasn't so sure.

"You want me to hang?" she said, her tone changing.

"Do what you want," Adam said.

"Why don't you hang out with us for a while?" I said.

"It's okay. I've got some stuff I need to finish before I hit the sack," she said, gazing at Adam. She quietly walked to her bedroom as Adam and I sat on the couch with our Zone meals and sippy cups of vodka.

As we ate, Adam explained that he and Ellie dated for a month in high school, tried sex once, then decided friendship was more important to them both. I halfheartedly believed him.

I looked at my watch and gasped, "Shit, that can't be right." I looked at the clock on the wall, and it read the same as my watch.

"What?" he said, irritated. He had string beans hanging out of the side of his mouth. *Does he eat like this in front of his clients?*

I pointed to the clock. He shrugged, then said, "Don't get so caught up on the hour! You make me nervous. Just go with it. What's the big deal?"

The clock read 2:00 A.M. "Jesus, I really gotta go," I said, prepanic attack.

"Jesus Christ, do you know how to relax?"

The fact was, I didn't. I never had. I'd been a worrier since I was a kid. After another drink, I gave my eyes a much-needed break, and dozed off until the sound of Adam's voice jolted me off the couch.

"Quick. Which rising young, naïve publicist is a two-to-one favorite in the office death pool either to quit, get fired, or worse yet, end up back in bumblefuck land?" Adam said, sitting in his chair smoking, obviously still feeling the vodka. Ellie snored on the floor beside him.

I grabbed my bag and headed for the door. "That's an easy one," I said. "You."

"Me?" he asked incredulously.

"Yeah, you."

"That's hilarious," he said.

Before he could say another word, I smiled, and replied, "I'm not naïve."

Jennie Weinstein
Public Relations JWPR

MEDIA TIP SHEET

What: Get NOTICED at the grand opening of the Meatpacking District's hottest new restaurant

When: Thursday 10 P.M.

WHO: *Expected arrivals include:* Jay-Z, Nicole Richie, Thalia, Lukas Haas, Samantha Ronson, Cynthia Rowley, Kelly Klein, Mario Lopez, Stacy Keibler, and many more.

Arrivals begin at 9 P.M.
For interview requests, please contact Mia at JWPR.
Mia_Cadelo@JWPR.com

4.

I Want to Get Noticed

SINCE I started working for Jennie, I'd felt exhausted at the very thought of walking out my front door. One thing New Yorkers quickly learn is that, while the city's energy is great at keeping you going, it's equally as great at kicking your ass. The many dreams of opportunity are matched with lonely moments. The great dichotomy of New York, a city where everyone wants to be left alone, and everyone wants to be noticed.

Jennie was apparently pleased with my organizing skills, and I was soon given more responsibilities around the office. (Or the jobs no one else wanted to do.) My new assignment was to call reporters to notify them of celebrity sightings around the city. I hadn't anticipated spending my days chasing down waiters to find out what Susan Sarandon ate for dinner. You'd think there might be more challenging and useful things that would better serve Jennie, but I was "missing the point," according to her. "At JWPR everything's about building a buzz!" Don't ask me how tofu and steamed broccoli was buzz-building. A novice might think that obtaining a celebrity sighting would be simple, but I soon learned that there was much more to it. Not only was it next to impossible to get accurate information, but trying to make idle bits of information interesting to a newspaper columnist was like trying to get Paris Hilton away from the camera.

I quickly learned that most celebrities don't hang out at trendy restaurants—ever! In fact, after working at JWPR for a few months, I learned that most stars don't return after opening night; of course that's what a restaurant's publicist *doesn't* want you to know.

Publicists and restaurant, club, and boutique owners all know that the life span of a business that caters to the jet set is about one to two months, three if you're lucky. The nanosecond the next latest and greatest opens, an ubertrendy restaurant might as well crawl under a rock and die, buried in the graveyard next to all the denizens of hip that went before, like Spy Bar, Commune, and Chaos.

These legendary places, at one time the coolest destinations on the planet, were soon forced to cater to the husbands and wives driving in from Hoboken for a night out in "the city," until finally the suburban set would realize that the food was lousy and even *their* friends had moved on to the next place, and they would quit going, too. Until, of course, the establishment closes, only to reopen under a new name and become, once again, the hottest space in Manhattan.

It's at that moment that desperate restaurant owners call Jennie and beg her to bring business back. That wasn't her specialty—she could *launch* a restaurant with ease, but when trying to *resuscitate* a dying business, she'd pay lip service to the client and eventually put the final nail in the coffin. She wouldn't even pick up the phone or send an e-mail about the restaurant, which was usually because of some vendetta she was carrying on with the owners. Perhaps they had called Natalie Bratberg to do their earlier opening instead of her, or maybe they hadn't renewed their contract, or sometimes, Jennie just didn't like them. It was all irrelevant.

Jennie informed me that Marcus Chadwick, owner of the once-trendy La Luna, was desperate to resuscitate his tapas bar. His business had been wildly successful just one year ago, until the fashionistas moved on. His bottom line was dropping fast. Marcus contacted Jennie to give his place a shot in the arm, and what injects instant chic more powerfully than a celebrity sighting? Jennie didn't mind the demand, especially for $10,000 a month.

If you connect a famous person's name to a joint, business will jump. Adam told me that Jennie had once placed an item about Lindsay Lohan partying at a particular restaurant JWPR handled; the *Post* ran the story, which claimed that the young Miss Lohan was doing shots with the bartender and making several trips to the bathroom to "powder" her nose. The real story: Lindsay was at the restaurant having a glass of wine with her mom. But once the bit ran in the papers and secured hourly coverage on E!, the "sheep," as Jennie referred to everyday people, flocked there. Who was going to deny the story? Lindsay? Her mom? With Lindsay's string of press detailing her every partying move, who would believe her denial? The gossip around the office was that Lohan was, at best, one party away from being the next Tara Reid. Worst-case scenario: She was one severe party away from being the next Natasha Lyonne. Adam said Jennie was sticking it to double-L for not walking the press line at one of her events. Jennie didn't hold grudges; she hurled them.

Jennie's interest in Marcus and his fledgling La Luna,

however, was strictly based on the cash, no vendetta needed. She knew the joint wasn't hip and frankly didn't care, as long as the fees she demanded of Marcus helped pay her credit cards down. When she handed it to me, there hadn't been any interest in his restaurant from *anyone*, and she knew it was dead in the water. Personally, I wasn't thrilled to work on it either; La Luna had turned Lauren and me away last year when I took her out for her birthday. Bastards.

But since I had no choice, I picked up the phone to ask Marcus if there was anything—*anything*—I could use to get him some ink. Gleefully, he told me, "Colin Farrell was canoodling with some mystery brunette at La Luna earlier in the week."

I hated it when words like "canoodling" were used. I wish people would just say what they mean: *They played grab ass*. Armed with all the essential questions to make it an even bigger story for the scribes, I asked him: What was Colin eating? Who was he with? What was she wearing? How much did he leave for a tip? Nothing out of the ordinary, just questions any decent publicist would ask. But his long pause indicated that he'd left something out. After further interrogation, Marcus told me that Colin wasn't actually *in* the restaurant, but was only outside hailing a cab for himself and his longtime girlfriend. What the hell was I supposed to do with that? I wasn't about to call a reporter and embarrass myself. With this piece, I'd be laughed off the phone. He had the nerve to ask if I thought I could place it with Rush & Molloy, the Daily News gossip column. I turned on my quickly evolving publicist bullshit charm. "I'll do my best," I told him, "but it will be a huge stretch." I didn't guarantee a thing.

Later that same day, I called Joanna Molloy at Rush & Molloy to let her know the simple facts: Colin Farrell was seen making out and doing body shots off some mysterious exotic beauty at La Luna earlier in the week. (In PR, the word "fact" has no meaning). She seemed quite interested: She could include it in a bigger item that she was writing on Colin's sex tape, which was on the verge of release. "Could this sex-tape woman be the same he was making out with?" she wondered aloud.

"Most likely," I said confidently. Less than a minute later she said it would be in later in the week and that I should call her if I had any more tips.

"Of course," I said. "You're always the first person I call." Though that was, of course, the first call I'd ever placed to her. I'd felt guilty, but I wasn't really lying to her. I was just leaving out some of the details like everybody else did in my profession: just using a little creative license. If it worked for Jennie and Lindsay, it could work for Colin and me. I had no vendetta against Colin—though I was a bit disappointed in *Miami Vice*—and, if anything, I was helping reconstruct his reputation as the quintessential Hollywood player.

Three days later I opened Rush & Molloy and scanned the "Sightings" section:

"Actor Colin Farrell and a buxom exotic beauty, making out voraciously in the middle of La Luna restaurant on the Lower East Side. Our spy reports that this was the same woman who shared a sexy romp with the actor that was all captured on film and is now available for download on the Internet for $19.95." God Bless Joanna Molloy! By writing less than twenty-five words in her column, the woman had inadvertently made my life at JWPR a helluva lot easier and garnered Jennie another month at ten grand.

As expected, the weekend following the item, Marcus had

called to let me know that business was booming. Yes, that one item had been enough to make schmucks like me who didn't know any better continue to go to a shitty restaurant because they thought they might see Colin Farrell enjoying another makeout session with a former porn actress.

Because in New York, everyone wanted to be left alone, but *noticeably* so.

I must have been in a zone because I didn't even hear Jennie walk in.

"Taylor," she snapped. It startled me, and I knocked over the pile of boxes also known as my desk.

"Hi!" I said, trying to sound upbeat.

"I saw the Farrell thing in Joanna Molloy's column," she said, stone-faced. "I talked to Marcus. He told me Colin wasn't even in the restaurant."

"Oh. Jennie, I only said that to Joanna—"

"You *lied*," she said.

"I—I—Yes, I lied," I conceded.

"Well, it's not an item I would've placed. It lacked a certain creativity. But nevertheless, you got the coverage. Perhaps you won't be such a waste of my time after all."

"Wow, I don't know what to say. Thank—"

"So anyway, do you have a suit at home?" she asked.

"It's probably got dust on the shoulders, but yes, I do," I joked, receiving no laughter. I bent over to pick up the invitations I had knocked over earlier.

"Don't you want to know why I asked?" Jennie quipped.

"What's up?" I asked.

"John called in sick and can't work the restaurant launch tonight. I need you to be there at seven thirty to set up."

"Sweet!" I said. She flashed me a strange look; it was obvious that she thought I didn't know what she was talking about.

"NOTICED?" I said. "The new restaurant that Steven Spielberg and Tom Hanks are backing." I took a deep breath and continued, "The chef is from Il Mulino, and Philippe Starck did the design."

Jennie was visibly stunned by the information I had just regurgitated. I'd answered the question on her face:

"I read the press kit when I was cleaning."

She gave no response. "Mia will tell you what to do when you get there. Don't make me regret this."

"I won't. Thanks again, Jennie." She walked toward the door, but there was another piece of business I had to talk to her about. It was Friday, and we still hadn't been paid. My last two checks had followed the same pattern. We'd get a check after banks closed on Friday, so the money wouldn't show in our accounts until the following Tuesday or Wednesday. On one occasion, when she gave us our checks at a record time, Friday at 10:30 A.M., I was about to race to the bank when Pena, the bookkeeper, told us we weren't allowed to make a deposit until the following Tuesday. Jennie was waiting for some client checks, we were told. Mia tried confronting Jennie about it, but she was ignored. Not surprisingly, Adam saw Jennie that Saturday doing some major damage at Barneys. Her employees were running on fumes, and she was stocking up on over a dozen Diptyque candles at sixty dollars a wick.

The thought of it made me angry and gave me courage. "Jennie, do you know if paychecks are coming today?" I asked.

The mood suddenly changed dramatically. She flashed me a cold look, and said, "That's not my department. Talk to Pena."

"I normally would, it's just that I'm 'scratching and surviving,' you know, *Good Times*?" Her face remained like stone. "In fact, I don't even have enough to take a taxi to the event tonight."

She looked at me long and hard, and said with absolutely no emotion, "Take the subway."

Then she walked out. Her total lack of concern for anyone other than herself revolted me. I was at a loss as to how I was going to survive the weekend on my almost zero bank-account balance. I felt a stabbing pain on the top of my head. *Fuck.* As much as I wanted to hold my own "ain't it awful party," I didn't have the time.

I raced home from work to find something appropriate to wear. I was a definite candidate for *Queer Eye*, but "the fab five" were nowhere to be found. The closest I had were two lesbians, who were unfortunately at Lincoln Center. Algebra's canine opinion would have to do. I tore through my clothes looking for something, anything that would pass as somewhat cool. I went through piles of shirts, pants and jackets, which I threw on my bed. I looked at my clothes and each item confirmed the obvious: I was a disaster.

"There's nothing here! I can't do this!" I shouted at Algebra. Then finally I saw it. In the farthest corner of my closet, crammed against the wall, hung the old black suit I'd worn to my first day of work at Jennie's. My dead grandfather's. It was a bit too conservative for this crowd, but it was all I had. I yanked out a multicolored striped shirt that I had worn to the Halloween parade in the West Village, hoping to add a bit of volume to the funereal ensemble, tossed on my jacket, and stood in front of the mirror.

I was horrified. *How dark will it be in NOTICED?*

It was so not me! An oversized suit that belonged with the deceased, a shirt that belonged in 1989, and a pair of shoes that belonged in Algebra's mouth. But somehow I was sure Jennie wouldn't see cargo pants and a T-shirt as trendsetting.

"Mess or Hot Mess?" I asked Algebra. He stared at me blankly and launched a special blend of carrot farts my way. I completely agreed.

Outside NOTICED, dozens of well-dressed men and women bustled next to the velvet ropes, jockeying for position near the front of the line. Through the hordes of heads, I could see Mia's tiny frame strutting like she was on a Bryant Park runway. Damn, she looked hot. She was a real woman. Not fat. But not a twig, either. She had more of that Kelly Clarkson rockin' body. Somehow I pushed my way through to the front of the line when two goons blocked my entrance.

"Yo! Back of the line, kid!" one of them shouted. Here we go again. Hadn't I already experienced enough of this bullshit?

"I'm working this party tonight," I shot back, trying to push my way in between the two men—to no avail.

Mia yelled, "Hey, Taylor, you think you could stop fucking around out there and come help me?"

She strutted over to the velvet rope and unlatched it. "Here, you're gonna need this," Mia said as she slammed a metal clipboard against my chest.

"Yes!" I said. "I've always wanted to do this." Mia rolled her eyes and turned to walk away while I scoured the crowd. I spotted a group of middle-aged women who seemed harmless. I needed to ease myself into it before taking on the obnoxious party crashers. "Good evening, name please?" I said politely.

Before I could say anything else, I heard Mia's mocking voice from a few yards away. "*Good evening, name please.* This isn't the Braxton Junior Prom, Taylor." I ignored her as best as I could.

"Barelli," the woman replied in a thick Brooklyn accent. "Tawny Barelli."

"Please hold on a second so I can check," I said. She was probably in her early forties, with big hair and white pumps—a big no-no at an event like this. But I gave her the benefit of the doubt and looked through the pages of names anyway.

"Look, I know I'm on the list. I've been standing here for over an hour," she snapped before I even got to the "Bs."

"If you just give me another minute, I prom—"

"Another minute? I've been waiting here all night," she interrupted. I had obviously miscalculated the middle-aged party crashers.

I frantically flipped through the pages desperately trying to find Tawny's name. Out of the corner of my eye, I saw Mia stop checking people in and watch my unfolding dilemma. I had to handle it so I didn't lose face.

"I'm sorry. Your name is not on the list. Could it be under a different name or company name perhaps?" I said, trying to think of anything.

"Look pissant, I'm going into that party. I've been reading about this opening for weeks. Now unhook the friggin' rope!"

"I'm sorry, I can't do that." She ignored my answer and reached for the latch. Simultaneously Mia marched over.

"Hey, you!" Mia shouted. Tawny backed up in surprise like a scolded child.

"Yeah you, Jersey Girl! Take a hike before I have to ruin my new Diors by kicking your ass." *Yikes.* Ms. Barelli winced and slunk back into the stunned crowd.

"I'm never coming back here again! No one will be at this shit hole two months from now!" she yelled from a safe distance.

"Including you!" Mia hollered back.

Mia pulled me to the center of the velvet rope box, away from the earshot of the crowd that was frothing at the collective mouth.

"Look, I'm really sorry. I'm just not used to people getting all up in my face like that," I said, before Mia could chew me out.

"Stand back. I'll show you how to work a door, Cornbread," she ordered. Mia walked to the edge of the velvet rope, where a crowd stood in front of her. She looked at them sternly, and, without looking at the list, started pointing out the people who would be allowed in. She held the clipboard to her chest and marched down the line.

"You over there," she said, pointing at a lady wearing a beautiful dress. "Yes, you. You're in. Go!"

She continued her march. "No, not you," she said, pointing at two club kids. She looked at an attractive man dressed in a black suit. "Maybe you. Show me some skin." Much to our surprise the conservative-looking man unbuttoned his shirt to reveal his well-sculpted six-pack. "Mmmm, honey, get in there and look for me later," she said with a wink.

A woman dressed in khakis and a white button shirt walked up. "Oh, no. You're all wrong," Mia said with a grimace. "It's never happening. Not tonight!" I couldn't believe what I had just witnessed. I wanted to run up to the woman to apologize, but she darted away before I could say a word.

Mia saw my stunned look, and asked, "Do you think you can handle it now?"

"Yeah, I think so." She handed me the clipboard, and I walked to ropes.

I was a bit embarrassed initially, but I quickly got over it. I saw two attractive young women and motioned them in. "You two, come in please." An elderly couple walked toward the rope, and I knew I'd be fired on the spot if I let them in. "I'm sorry, but not tonight. Please try us another time, thank you!" I felt bad, but I had to do it.

The more I let people in, the more comfortable and confident I became. A lady wearing a loud print dress sashayed in my direction, "Turn it down, sister, and try us again in the spring." *Whoa*. Did I actually just say *turn it down, sister?* I officially felt like a bitchy gay guy.

I scoured the crowd for appropriate people to complement the vibe being created inside. A large group of young women approached the rope. Contrary to instinct, I wasn't paying much attention to their faces: Mia told me to always look at the shoes. A woman with a tight black dress and black shoes with a ton of buckles walked in my direction. Without looking up, I said, "Sorry, not tonight, honey. If you hurry, you might catch the last train back to Strong Island!" I could get used to this, I thought.

"Excuse me!" the woman shouted. I knew the voice immediately. A chill ran down my spine.

"Jennie! Oh God! I didn't recognize you all dressed up!" I was motionless.

"Just open the ropes, Todd," she snapped.

"I'm so sorry . . . I—"

Jennie marched inside the box with her friends in tow.

"Mia!" Mia walked over like she was a dog who had just been punished for peeing on the carpet.

"Yes?" Mia said.

"How could you let him work the ropes dressed like that? Look at him!"

"Um, hello? I'm standing right here," I said.

"I see you, and you're lucky I don't fire you on the spot. This is the opening of NOTICED, not the Farmer's Market!" She turned her venom on Mia. "And you! This is *your* responsibility. I'm tired of your constant fuck-ups, Mia. Just give me a reason, and I'll make sure you're schlepping housewares at Sears."

Before she could respond, Jennie looked at Mia's feet, and said, "Give me your shoes."

"What? Why do you want my shoes?" Mia quizzed.

"NOW!" Jennie screamed.

Mia took off her high-heeled pumps and handed them to Jennie. She now looked like a munchkin instead of a giant. Jennie handed me the shoes. "Put these on."

Mia and I screamed in unison, "What?"

"Put them on, hurry up!" she yelled. Jennie's friends giggled and snickered behind us.

"But they're going to be too small!" I said.

"Now!" she hissed.

I took off my shoes and socks and reluctantly took the pumps from Mia. I barely crammed my two middle toes in, and balanced my heels off the back.

"Those are seven-hundred-dollar Christian Diors," Mia said.

"Something you no doubt either got on consignment or borrowed," Jennie said quickly. Mia stood paralyzed. Jennie had finally struck a nerve. "You should've thought about that before you handed him your responsibilities. Do you honestly think I'm going to allow someone from *my* staff to represent *my* client dressed in a blue-light special?" (I wanted to tell her how much higher-class Banana Republic was than the Gap, but supposed that it wasn't the time.)

"Jennie, I'm really sorry. It's all I had," I said.

"To the ladies' room," she barked.

"The ladies' room? For what?"

"You're going to be working bathroom duty."

"Bathroom duty?"

"Quit repeating everything I say!"

"But what's that?" I asked.

"You're going to sit in a stall taking notes of everything that's going on. I need some good sh—let's just say I need to know what's going on."

"But the ladies' room?" I said, horrified.

"Where else do women go to spill their guts?" she asked.

Quit. Just grow a pair of balls and quit. Mitchell may still take you back. Quit.

I could tell by the glint in Jennie's eyes that she took personal pleasure in embarrassing me in front of her friends.

"I guess I'm not clear as to what I'm supposed to accomplish in there," I said.

"God, you're daft." Her friends were smiling. "I want to know if you hear any private cell-phone conversations, any girl talk, or a person sniffing longer than ten seconds. It all goes down in the ladies' room."

I knew exactly what she meant. She wanted me to be her bitch.

"But isn't there someone else who could—"

"I'd get up there now if I were you," she interrupted. I

couldn't quit, and she knew it. I had rent to pay. And somewhere, very deep inside me, I thought if I worked for Jennie Weinstein long enough, I'd be as important as she was. She knew that too.

I looked at Mia, who was still staring at her shoes on my feet. I took my first step in her Christian Diors and nearly fell on my face. The same people I'd been snubbing thirty seconds earlier were now taking great joy in my utter humiliation. As I walked past Mia, I realized that after this moment, any chemistry she might have felt between us would be figuratively and, in about thirty seconds, very literally, in the toilet.

On the way to the ladies' room, I passed Adam, who simply shook his head. Luckily for me and my ankles, the women's restroom was close to the front of the club. Taking a deep breath, I pushed open the door just as two young women darted out. I felt like I'd just shined the light on a dark corner and sent the roaches scurrying in a frenzy. I looked inside. It was not a bathroom. It was a living room. And a nice one. Not until that moment did I understand why women always took so long when they went to the bathroom. It became clear. If I'd found a TV and a minifridge, I would have called it home.

The attendant was in her midfifties, and looked like she'd been to hell and back within the last twenty minutes. She sat by the sinks and stocked her table with lollipops, perfumes, hand lotions, mints, individual sticks of gum. It was an impressive variety.

I picked up a bottle of perfume in an attempt to make conversation. "So you like Gauthier too? You've got great taste!" I said. She wasn't going for it. She rolled her eyes and, after looking at my pumps, shook her head and pointed at the door.

"I can explain. Jennie Weinstein, the publicist for the club, wants me to sit in here to make sure everything goes smoothly. I don't mean that literally, but metaphorically, of course." Another blank stare.

"Anyway, I think I hear someone coming," I said, sliding into a stall. "I need to get to my station." I shut the door and quickly closed the toilet lid. The attendant didn't protest. Was she used to this? Another jaded New Yorker. Live here long enough and a young guy in heels is the most *normal* part of your day. I took off one shoe and rubbed my foot; a gigantic blister had already begun to form on my toe. I needed to tell Mia to stick with Star Jones at Payless.

A pair of high heels clanged rapidly into the bathroom and into the stall next to mine. I stopped rubbing my foot and stayed as silent and as still as possible.

"Great shoes!" I heard the voice from the stall next to me say. I froze. I couldn't let her discover I was an imposter.

"Thank you," I said, in the highest-pitched voice I could muster. I looked down at my feet. They looked nice, but not *girl* nice. I could see hair sprouting from one of my toes. The girl would have to be blind not to see it too.

"Where'd you get them?" she asked.

I reached down and read the label. "Dior?" I said.

"Thought so. Wow, they're so hot!" she said as the toilet paper roll spun.

"Thanks," I said, biting my mouth so hard I broke the skin.

"I gotta get back to my honey. Try some Kashi cereal, things will move faster," she instructed.

"Oh. Thanks," I said.

She flushed the toilet and walked out of the stall. I peered through a crack in the stall and watched as she took two lollipops, a stick of gum and covered herself in perfume. She took a crisp one-dollar bill out of her clutch, placed it in the tip basket, and walked out.

"A whole dollar?" the attendant said. "I'm rich."

I glanced through the cracks. My money would have said it was *the* hotel heiress herself, but I couldn't be sure.

The door shut, and I burst out of the stall. "Was that Paris?" I asked.

Before she could answer she replied, "You better get back in there, someone else is coming."

Straight journalism would be a more rewarding career path, surely. I clumsily slammed the door shut, sat back down on my throne, and sighed, resting my elbow on the toilet paper. Peering through the crack in the door, I tried to see who entered but couldn't distinguish the woman's face. I pulled off a few pieces of toilet paper and began writing a journal to give to Jennie in the morning.

I could see a pair of legs that seemed endless and another set that was short and squatty.

"There are so many men I want to fuck out there," the skinny one said, fixing herself in the mirror.

"Why am I not surprised?" the other said. As she laughed, her hair bounced.

"Oh come on, you can't honestly tell me there's no one out there you wouldn't jump into bed with!" she sneered. The other one sighed slightly.

"Don't even tell me," the skinny girl said. "Don't even utter his name!"

"What? I can't help it. He was my first. We, um, we just have something special that I can't even explain . . ." the girl with the large calves said.

"Please, Adam Hanes has something special with every girl

in this club . . . and a few guys from what I've heard." *Adam Hanes? Guys? Did she just say guys, too?* The water stopped running, and the first girl clanked her heels out of the bathroom; Chubby Legs paused for a moment, then finally left. It was Ellie.

Again I opened the stall door, but just as I poked my head out of the door, Ellie darted back inside, and walked straight to the bathroom attendant. "I'm so sorry, I forgot!" she said, placing a five-dollar bill in the basket. She looked up just as I was inching my head back into the stall. Our eyes locked. She offered me an unmistakable look of sadness. Neither of us said a word. She slowly backed up, spun, and walked out of the bathroom. The door bounced shut.

Two hours later, my writing had ceased, and I rested my head against the stall divider to get some sleep. As my eyes closed, I heard a voice from the stall next door.

"I'm outta paper in here, can you help me out?"

I popped my head down to look under the stall, hoping for other feet; surely this woman was speaking to someone else.

"Hello? Can you help me out here? I need some paper!" She was definitely talking to me, and her tone was desperately combative. Suddenly a hand emerged from under her stall. I was horrified, and nearly gasped. I had no idea that women did this; I'm not quite sure I ever wanted to know.

There was no other option: I attempted my high-pitched voice again, "Just a minute," I said as I unrolled a strand of toilet paper. I tore it off and shoved it at her.

"What in the hell?" I heard her say, just before she grabbed my hand, and gripped it firmly.

"Call me naïve, but I have never seen a woman with hands this big or with this much hair on them!" she shouted. I twisted my hand to break free, but the woman had an iron grip. I gave up, knowing that sooner or later she'd have to let go to make use of the paper. Hand and arm limp, I patiently waited. A few seconds passed, and *voilà*, she let go. I heard the toilet flush and the stall door open, but no footsteps. She had flung open her door and planted herself directly in front of mine. I was under siege.

"You better get your ass out here right now!" she shouted. She looked at the bathroom attendant, and said, "Did you know you have a man in there?" The woman shrugged and offered her some perfume.

"If you don't come out here, I'm calling security." I had no avenue of escape. Reluctantly, I opened the door and walked out in my high heels, never taking my eyes off the ground. Her eyes were burning through me as she looked me over: my oversized black suit, beads of sweat on my forehead, pants rolled up midcalf, wobbly high heels.

"I've lived in New York for nine years, and I've never seen anything quite like this," she said, chuckling.

Cautiously, I lifted my face and looked the woman in the eyes. She was beautiful. An assault of crimson-colored hair framed her porcelain face. She could pass for the devil's daughter with that hair and mischievous grin. Suddenly I recognized her.

"Wait a second, aren't you Sandy Brin?" I exclaimed, forgetting where I was.

Sandy Brin is a gorgeous and quirky-looking redhead who has been touted as "the next Liz Smith," whatever that means. Currently, Sandy was a rising star at the notorious, no-holds-barred daily gossip blog "Sandy Says." The ubiquitous Internet column wasn't just any blog: It had a daily readership of over

6 million, and she had a weekly column in *Us Weekly*. Sandy could launch a bestseller, break a pending contract, out a celebrity, win a studio an Oscar, fill a nightclub—even end a "perfect" marriage.

She was a major press magnet herself. I'd first read about her in Jennie's "Faces and Places" book at the office. As employees of JWPR, we had to know everyone in that book at all times. It was our pop-culture bible. But I was surprised how hot Sandy was in person. When I had first arrived at Jennie's, I suggested pitching our clients to her, an idea Jennie flatly refused. Mia and Adam later told me there was bad blood there, but no one seemed to know what it was or where it came from.

"Sorry, I don't mean to keep saying it, but you're Sandy Brin! You rock!" I said.

"Right. And you're a guy wearing high heels standing in a women's restroom," she said.

"It's a long story that has a very good explanation, should you want to hear it," I offered.

"I hope so, honey, because those shoes are all wrong for that suit."

It felt like someone else had taken over my body. I heard myself saying, "I never thought I'd be one of those people, but I have to tell you I'm such a huge fan."

"Great! I'm big with the drag queens. I can die now."

"Oh no, I'm definitely not a drag queen."

"Gossip writer in training?" she asked, looking down at my toilet paper steno pad.

"I'm a publicist at JWPR!" I said, excited.

"Oh God. How awful!" she said, and laughed. "I liked you much better when you were only a simple drag queen with a dream."

"Sorry to disappoint you," I said, shifting in my heels, trying to be as manly as possible. (Turns out, it's very difficult to look manly in four-inch heels.) But I definitely felt a connection between us. That, or she wanted the shoes.

"What are you working on?" she asked. "I bet you got some pretty good stuff on that roll."

"On this? No, this is just Jennie's," I explained.

"Oh come on, Jennie knows secrets before they're secret," she said, moving in closer. "We might be able to help each other out," she said, and smiled devilishly. Something told me she meant every word. "Jennie's been known to bust more than a few balls," she added.

"Yeah, it's a pretty emasculating business," I agreed. She nodded and looked down at my shoes. "There's nothing really on here that you'd be interested in," I said, putting my notes in my pants pocket.

"Listen, it's been really nice chatting with you, but I really have to get back to my friends," she said. "Call me sometime. Maybe we can meet someplace where the sound track isn't toilets flushing."

"Sounds great. I promise to wear a different pair of shoes," I said, and smiled at her.

"I think a nice canary yellow would be lovely on you," she joked. "Do you have a card?" she asked.

A card? Is she crazy? Jennie didn't give her employees cards. She wanted everyone to believe she was the one doing all the work. The only employee that she gave cards to was Adam, and I think he earned his by putting in time "after-hours" at *chez Jennie.*

"Not on me, but hold on one second." I kicked off the high heels and darted back into the stall and grabbed some toilet paper. I scrawled my name, phone number, and e-mail address on two sheets. I darted out of the stall and put the pumps back on—I do not know why.

"Here's my private cell number and e-mail address. It's the fastest way to get hold of me," I lied. "Just don't use it to blow your nose," I joked. *God, I have no game.*

"Gotcha. I'll give you a call. I haven't a clue as to why, but I like you, Mr. Green, and I'll be in touch." She looked down at my high heels again. "I hope you're still able to walk tomorrow. See you later." She walked out with the confidence only famous people have. Mere mortals do not possess it.

When the door shut, I jumped into the air and crashed into the ground, finally destroying Mia's seven-hundred-dollar Christian Diors. The bathroom attendant shook her head in shame and sucked on a lollipop. For someone who hated attracting attention, I managed to stand in front of a large crowd, walk into a nightclub, and sit in the women's bathroom in four-inch heels, and not only talk to but give my phone number to a "face."

Perhaps being *noticed* wasn't such a bad thing after all.

RICKY

5.

Brunch, Babies, Balenciaga, and Blow

WITH their hectic work schedules, New Yorkers who finally find downtime don't like to leave their apartments; especially me. However, when you haven't seen anyone outside of work for the last two months, an excursion is necessary, and imperative if your friend's girlfriend wants her to improve her "dyke apparel." On one particular Saturday, Allison and I trekked downtown to the Lower East Side to a nondescript consignment shop, a store concept that evaded me: Where I'm from we have only the Salvation Army, and it isn't the kind of place a guy goes to *improve* his wardrobe. But according to Lauren, consignment shops in New York are famous for the slogan, "I only wore it once": the claim made by models and savvy fashionistas as they drop off their old wares in exchange for cash. Of course, these same women frown upon one of their own getting caught shopping at such a store. Urban Anthropology 101.

We walked down Grand Street and felt the autumn breeze have a bit more bite. As we passed the old Italian cafes and struggling designer shops, Allison said to me, "You know, T, you can always talk to me whenever you need to talk. Seriously, we live right upstairs and Lauren is up way too fucking early and I'm up late at night, so don't be afraid to knock, okay? You can talk to us about anything, seriously."

We stopped in front of a Laundromat, and I soaked all of her in. She was quite beautiful. I knew I couldn't possibly sleep with her, but she was the kind of girl I'd marry. I liked her without the makeup, and without the high-end clothes. She was just right. Somehow if I told her that, it wouldn't come out quite the way I meant it to, so I just said "Thanks," then, curiously, "Is there something you want to know about in particular?"

"No, I just worry about you. You're new to the city, and I know how easy it is to get sucked in. It's an easy place to lose your footing," she said with a voice of experience.

I sat down on the Laundromat steps and asked, "Is everything okay?"

She sat beside me and rested her head on my shoulder. "I never thought I'd be here," she said.

"In New York?" I asked.

"No. An adult," she said faintly.

"Oh, come on, you're just as immature as I am," I joked.

"It's just so strange. I feel like a kid still, despite the fact that gravity is kicking my ass. Here I am in a grown-up relationship, and I'm not sure I don't want to be a kid again," she said.

I didn't know what to say.

"Why do I have to be so goddamn mature all the time?" she asked, suddenly standing up.

"Where is this coming from?" I asked, watching her pace in front of me.

"I'm too fucking young to have a kid, right?" she said shrieking. "Fine, we're registered domestic partners, but a kid? I'm not ready for a kid, and that's all she talks about. How do I know I'll be a good parent? What if I walk out on them both? That happened to you, didn't it?" she said on the verge of a panic attack.

"Uh," I stalled.

"Oh God, I'm sorry," she said, patting my arm.

"No, it's cool. I get what you're saying. Look, it's not easy. My dad couldn't handle it, and you don't want Lauren to raise the kid all alone if she'll be working all the time. That's what my mom did, and I barely even know her. She has a closer relationship with her customers."

"Precisely!" she shouted back at me.

"But if you're not ready for a kid, you need to tell Lauren that. I'm sure she'll understand," I offered. Until then, I'd learned all I needed to know about relationships from Ethel, and she was sour on the whole notion of children. But she was a man trapped in a woman's body. And *my* longest relationship had been with Brit Peterson: six weeks during my junior year in high school. I grew bored after the first four days, but, in typical fashion, couldn't handle confrontation; I let it drag out until she finally got bored with me and dumped me for Trevor Knudsen.

"You don't get it. Lauren has a plan for everything, and a time frame," she said, frustrated.

"Life doesn't work that way," I said. "And the beauty usually comes when you deviate from the plan."

"I guess; I just don't know how to tell her," she said, her eyes moist. I got the feeling that there was more to this. I decided to let it go and let her tell me when she was ready—or never. I preferred the latter, so I wouldn't have to lie to Lauren.

We walked farther up the street and finally stopped outside of Inca, the designer consignment shop. "So. Shall we make you a respectable lesbian?" I said, smiling.

"Clearly you don't know many lesbians," she said with a smirk. We walked inside.

As Allison grabbed several designers whose names I couldn't pronounce, I sat on the windowsill and thought of my mother and Ethel. *Do they speak to each other when I'm gone?* They barely spoke when I was around. Ethel was probably meeting the girls for a hot toddy, and my mother was probably passed out in her torn, lilac-patterned recliner, just home from church. During that moment, and others, I still couldn't believe I had landed here: in this city, with this job, surviving. They say behind every great man is an even better woman. As I looked around the shop, I considered how, in my case, I had an arsenal of them all around me; I must be fucking Jesus.

Then, suddenly, I heard a familiar voice.

"This bag has a fucking water mark on it!" she yelled. "You can do better than that. You should be paying *me* to take this crap."

"Miss, I'm sorry, but this bag is a Balenciaga," the saleswoman explained. "And it's our only one."

"A stained Balenciaga!" the voice said.

I stood up to see if, in fact, my instincts were correct. As I inched closer, I saw the long, curly hair. Before I could say anything, Mia spun around. She looked right at me, and for a split second, I saw terror in her eyes: caught at a consignment shop, with a stained Balenciaga in her hand.

I turned quickly to leave. As I walked outside, I heard Mia's heels thundering behind me; there was pure emotion in those heels.

"Hey!" she shouted, practically in my ear.

"Hi!" I said, pie-faced. "What's up?"

"What's up? Don't give me that bullshit," she said. Her upper lip began to twitch.

"Bullshit? I'm just here with a friend. Why is that so hard to believe?" I asked, annoyed.

"You think you got something on me, don't you?" she said, nearly enraged.

I backed away from her. "What in the hell are you talking about?"

She held up her black leather purse inches away from my face. "Do you know what this is?" she said angrily.

"T, is everything okay?" I heard Allison ask from inside.

"Who's that? Your girlfriend?" Mia asked.

"Not quite."

"When is she due?"

"What?" I asked, horrified.

"Never mind," she said, rolling her eyes.

"Yeah, I'll be there in a second," I said to Allison. I turned to Mia. "To answer your earlier question, I do not know what this black pouch might be, but to my untrained Midwestern eye it looks like a little purse. If you'd like to tell me more, maybe you'd like to lower your voice, have a seat on this bench, and fill me in."

After a few seconds, she sat down on the wooden bench outside the store, and I joined her. She lit a Marlboro Light and crossed her legs, swinging one violently. Her tough exterior began to fade, and I saw the human side of Mia for a brief moment.

"So, what's the deal with the purse?" I asked.

"It's not just any purse, you corn-bread moron," she snapped.

"Okay, I don't need this on my day off. I get it enough at work from Jennie," I said, standing up. I walked slowly back inside, waiting for Mia to stop me. She did not. Inside, I folded my arms across my chest and watched her, already up the block, nearing the subway station.

Then she was gone. The purse remained sitting on the bench. I quickly went back outside and grabbed it before the salesgirl thought that Mia had stolen it.

I walked back inside and leaned against the door and waited for Allison, wondering what the fuck had just happened. Mia was like the dull pain of a toothache. You keep prodding in the hopes of easing the pain, but the relief is only temporary. Eventually, you have to become numb.

Allison came out of the dressing room in a pin-striped Paul Smith shirt. It was oversized, but actually looked sexy on her in an ironic way.

"Looks good," I said, and smiled. "But isn't that a man's shirt?"

"Well, I couldn't go totally fem."

"No, you definitely don't want to do that," I said.

"Let me pay for this, and you're free to go," she said as she went back to the dressing room.

"Hey, do you know anything about purses?" I asked.

"Are you openly mocking me?" she said through the sheet divider. She quickly opened the curtain, back in full lesbian attire. "Why do you ask?"

I grabbed the black purse off the counter and walked toward the saleswoman. "How much does a purse like this cost?"

"I think we're selling that one for 470 because it has a tiny smudge on it," she said politely.

"And how much would this be if I bought it new in the store?" I asked.

"Well, that's a Balenciaga Medium Motorcycle Bag. So probably about eighteen hundred retail at Barneys or Jeffrey's."

"For a purse?" I gasped. I felt exposed. No matter how much I change my exterior, I still have a lot to learn about New York dress codes. "I'll take it," I said.

"Taylor! Are you crazy? I just use messenger bags. I'm not a purse kind of girl," Allison said, collecting her change. "And you can't afford this," she said sternly, yet quietly enough so the salesgirl couldn't hear.

"It's not for you," I said. "And I have a credit card."

"Oh, no. Not that girl you were shouting with," she said, worried. "She's a coworker, a Weinstein girl; you cannot befriend the enemy, nor should you even try. Trust me. I'm experienced."

I reached inside my wallet and winced as I handed the salesgirl my credit card and prayed that it wouldn't be declined.

"How can you afford a purse like that? That creature barely pays you, and when she does, the checks still bounce a few times." She was right, but I didn't care.

The salesgirl wrapped the bag up nicely and handed it to me, and Alison and I walked back out onto Grand Street. "So listen, Al, I have to ask you—" I was interrupted by a vibration in my pants pocket. I looked at my caller ID: Adam.

"What's up?" I said.

"Yo, I need your help, Cornbread," he said.

I knew immediately that it was Jennie that needed something. "Are you serious? But it's Saturday. Doesn't she have a calendar?"

"You know how she is. It will take thirty minutes—forty-five tops. All we have to do is pick up some art for that LIFEbeat thing next week. That's it," he said.

"We can't get it next week?" I asked.

"Come on now, since when does Jennie have any sort of logic to these sorts of things?" he said.

"Fine. I'll meet you on the corner of Houston and Broadway in ten minutes," I said. I hung up the phone and shoved it back into my pocket.

"What scandals are you off to tend to now?" Allison asked.

"Jennie wants Adam and me to go pick up some painting from some artist who donated it for her LIFEbeat event next week."

"So why can't he pick it up next week?" she said.

"Apparently she wants it now, and that's all I need to know."

"And why can't Adam go on his own?"

"I guess the artist guy lives in some housing project on Ninth Avenue in Chelsea, and Adam thinks he's less likely to get jumped if there are two of us. Look, as much as I hate it, Allison, it just is what it is; she wants it, so we go."

"I get it, I just was really looking forward to spending the day with you."

"Me too, but I promise we'll all hang out together soon. Maybe brunch at Star Diner?" I said without waiting for her response.

As I raced up Grand Street to Houston, I yelled back to her, "Take Algebra out for me!" She nodded and gave me the biggest smile she could muster. Her smile made me feel even worse about my abrupt departure. It would have been so much easier had she given me the finger.

Adam was waiting in the cab for me on the corner.

As we rode to Chelsea, I noticed the remnants of a working-class neighborhood recently made fashionable by the gay guys who had given it a total makeover. It was still peppered with working-class families, sandwiched among the rich and fabulous. And right smack-dab in the middle was a giant housing project.

"I can't believe how swank this neighborhood is," I said, making small talk as we rode thru the ubertrendy Meatpacking District.

"Uh-huh," he muttered. So maybe I sounded a little bright-eyed and bushy-tailed (my mother's phrase), but he could at least humor me. I continued to babble, in part to annoy him. I was feeling childish. I wanted to tell him, "I'm going to have a sick place on Jane Street—penthouse, just wait and see! And you won't be invited!"

Finally, he broke. "Oh God, Taylor, the innocent act is getting old. You're not in Bumblefuck anymore; you're in New York. And if you want to hang with the big guns, you better quit acting all 'ah-shucks' around people."

I should have been offended, I suppose, but at the moment I simply felt sorry for Adam. Under thirty, and already one of the most jaded people I'd ever met. The rest of the cab ride was silent. A few agitated huffs and puffs later, and the cab finally slowed down.

"Is this it?" Adam asked.

"This place looks pretty nasty," I said.

"There it is on the left," the driver said. He slowed the cab down so we could spot numbers on the decaying buildings, one on the verge of collapsing.

"That's it! Right there on the left," the driver said, pointing to the old building.

"You ready to do this?" Adam asked.

"I guess. What's the worst that could happen?" He rolled

his eyes, got out of the cab and walked quickly toward the nearly abandoned apartment building, leaving me to pay the driver.

"Wait!" I yelled, running after him.

I was already nearly out of breath when I caught up to him. As we reached the front door, two German shepherds jumped out at us from behind a wire fence.

"Jesus Christ!" I shouted. "I think I just shit myself."

"Don't be such a baby."

The dogs continued to growl, and I grew more nervous. "Do you remember which apartment number it was?" I asked.

"I think number 9."

"Nine what?"

"Huh?" he said, still shaken from the near dog mauling.

"Dumb-ass! Nine-A? B? R? V? What's the exact apartment?"

"It's hard to tell from the writing; it looks like 9-W," he said, rotating a piece of paper in his hand.

"Didn't *you* write it?"

"Yeah, but . . ." He looked again. "Yeah, it's W."

"Yes, W. W, as in 'What the fuck are we doing here risking our lives to pick up a fucking painting?'" Adam was silent. "I guess since it's for charity," I continued, "we should just suck it up."

Adam burst out laughing.

"What are you talking about?" he asked.

"We're here for the AIDS charity. LIFEbeat? Hello? Are you high already?" I said, shaking my head. "I just can't believe we're the ones out here risking our lives for it."

"You don't actually think we're here for a painting, do you? Are you that much of a fucking idiot?"

He was pissing me off, and I didn't have the patience to play the guessing game.

"Okay, fine, Adam, you're so much cooler and smarter than me, enlighten me with your knowledge as to why we're *really* here."

He ignored me and pressed the buzzer for 9-W.

"Yeah," a man's voice said.

"We're here to see Ricky," he shouted into the speaker. The door buzzed and the iron gate opened. Adam walked through and into the courtyard. I didn't move.

"Are you coming or not?"

I looked back at the two dogs still frothing at the mouth, lusting after my leg. It was either them or the Abercrombie bastard.

"Fine," I said. We walked through a regiment of dead trees and bronze planters that in its heyday was probably a rather pristine courtyard. Unfortunately for me, that was no longer the case. It smelled like piss, dead animals, and old-school Polo cologne. I ignored the shadows of rats that darted in and out of the dark corridors. The stairs creaked with every step, and the higher we climbed, the more the stench and the heat followed. We heard bits of conversations as we passed each floor, only one of them in English. Finally, we reached the ninth floor, exhausted and out of breath.

"There. That must be it. Over there," he said, pointing to an apartment down the long corridor. There was a man standing outside the door wearing dark sunglasses. He looked like some thuggish nightclub bouncer whose forearms made you think twice about mouthing off.

"How do you know?"

"All drug dealers have bodyguards, so no one steals their shit."

"DRUG DEALERS!"

"Shut the fuck up! Do you want to get us killed?" he screamed at me.

"Excuse me! I'm sorry, but I didn't realize we're starring in *The Courtney Love Story*!"

"Let's get this over with," he said. He walked a few steps ahead of me. I was moving, but I was in a daze; I was in the middle of a housing project in New York City buying drugs for my boss. *Whose life is this?*

Adam approached the huge bodyguard without fear. "I'm here to see Ricky."

He looked at Adam very carefully and in his fiercest, deepest voice asked, "And who the fuck are you?"

"I'm here to buy a 'painting'?"

He stared at Adam long, and hard, and, a few seconds later, he disappeared inside, quickly slamming the door behind him.

"Let's go!" I said. "You obviously pissed him off, and now he's not coming back!"

"Don't you ever watch any TV? He's in there getting Ricky, you idiot!"

"Oh that's just perfect. If your only knowledge of buying drugs is from watching TV, we're even more fucked than I originally thought." I shook my head, and said, "Do you realize if we get busted, we're the ones going to jail, not Jennie?"

"She wouldn't let that happen," Adam argued.

"Oh come on, you don't really believe that, do you?" I said. "Why would she say that the drugs were hers? Her career would be over!"

"Not really," Adam argued. "Do you think these celebrities and restaurant owners are going to drop her for getting arrested for drugs? Half of them are coked up every weekend anyway."

"But you're missing the point! We're the ones who'd be arrested!" I said. "If we ever get out of this disaster, rent *Midnight Express*, and you'll see why I'm so nervous!"

"Shhhh! Shut up! I really don't feel like getting fucked up the ass and murdered by Ricky the drug dealer and his bodyguard!"

Just as I was about to respond, the door opened and the bodyguard motioned for us to go inside. As a Midwestern gentlemen, I let Adam go first. Once I stepped inside, the door quickly slammed behind me, and the guy with the massive forearms locked it. The place was a palace compared to the rest of the complex. Air-conditioned rooms, marble floors, and a huge plasma TV hanging on the wall, almost as nice as the women's restroom at NOTICED. Business had obviously been very good.

"Sit down," he instructed, pointing to a leather couch.

We slowly sat down. I could see a hint of fear in Adam's eyes.

"I can't believe the shit I do for her," Adam said under his breath.

Before I could respond, in walked Ricky. He was about five-five with black hair and brown eyes. He was twenty pounds overweight and walked with a slight limp, favoring his left leg. So this was the nefarious drug dealer who caused my petrification? Then I caught a glimpse of steel protruding from his hip and suddenly found it hard to swallow. I made sure to notice everything: When the police arrested me later, I wanted to be able to give them a full description: Perhaps I would get a lighter sentence.

"You got the bills?" Ricky asked.

"Yeah, he's got them," I found myself answering. Adam's silence made me nervous, and I couldn't stop talking. "Yeah he's got the bills, lots of bills. He's the bill man. Bills, bills, bills."

Adam took the envelope full of Jennie's money out of his pocket and placed it on the coffee table. It looked odd sitting there; it was decorated with her company logo in raised gold lettering.

"Where's Connie?" Adam asked. Who the fuck is Connie? I thought. I didn't know Adam knew anyone there.

Ricky pulled five vials out of his pocket and placed them on the table.

"Hello, Connie, you old bitch," Adam chuckled.

Apparently, referring to cocaine by its name was in poor taste. Drug-Dealing Etiquette 101. Not mentioned in Jennie's indispensable "Rules of Publicity," but I suppose there are some things you have to learn in the field.

"Five eightballs," Ricky said.

"Great," Adam said. "We've got to be going."

At that moment, Ricky looked down at the bag from Inca that I was still carrying. Part of the black leather was peering through the top.

"Hold up, is that a Balenciaga in there?" Ricky asked. I ignored his question, forgetting that I was holding the bag that he was referring to. "Yo, I'm talking to you!" he said. Adam nudged me in the arm, hard.

"Oh yeah. It is," I said. I could tell by the look in Ricky's eyes that he wanted that bag.

"How much you want for it?" he asked. "My girl has been

down my throat for the last month to get her one of those." I was screwed. The bag was going to him.

Adam jumped in, "Please. For you, it's a gift. Just make sure you take care of us next time, right, Taylor?"

"No," I heard myself say.

"What?" the three men said in unison.

"I can't give you this bag," I said.

"And why the fuck not?" Ricky shouted.

I stalled, but only for a moment. "Because I can't let you give your girl a fake bag and have you and her be the laughingstock of the neighborhood."

"That shit's bunk?" he asked.

"Yeah. Canal Street," I said.

"Damn," Ricky said.

"But Adam knows people, I'm sure if you give him a call at the office, he can hook you up with a real one," I said.

"You got a card, son?" he asked. Adam reluctantly pulled a card from his wallet and handed it to Ricky.

"Well, I hate to break up this little meet-and-greet, but we have a party to get to and a boss who'll be foaming at the mouth for this," Adam said, standing up and putting the vials in his pocket.

We scurried out of Ricky's apartment. In the stairwell Adam handed me two vials. I'd never seen cocaine up close. *Who am I kidding?* I'd never seen cocaine in my life. It made me nervous, and Adam sensed it.

"This is so we both have an even stake in this; if one of us gets busted, the other won't get off scot-free with nothing on him. I'm just keeping it a level playing field."

"Fine," I said, putting the vials in my front pocket.

We flew down the stairs, passed the psychotic dogs, and

caught a cab so we could make the drop-off to Jennie's Upper East Side lair. I was told we wouldn't actually be allowed to see Jennie's apartment. We'd be leaving the vials wrapped in a sock, my sock, in a manila envelope with the concierge at her building.

I still couldn't believe what I had just done. It was the first law I'd ever broken. I was so disappointed in myself that I couldn't speak during the entire ride uptown. Adam glanced over at me a few times, and there were a couple of instances that I actually thought he was going to say something consoling, but he never did. That wasn't his style. He took out his cell phone and made reservations for dinner at Bond Street. I, on the other hand, went home to vomit.

The next morning, I got off the crowded subway and hurried up the steps. I made sure that I arrived in the office before anyone else. After I was certain I was alone, I carefully slipped the purse out of my bag. I had disposed of the Inca bag in a Dumpster two blocks away, so no one would suspect that someone was shopping in consignment. I slipped the bag under Mia's desk so that when she sat down she'd feel the package pressed against her calf. I retreated to my cloffice. Fortunately, Mia's desk in the dungeon was within my scope. Thirty minutes later, I heard a dauntingly familiar sound—her footsteps, a whirling dervish against an otherwise cold cement floor. I leered from behind the cloffice door, waiting.

She sat in her chair and inched in closer to her desk until she rubbed up against the purse. She reached under the desk, pulled out the purse, and placed it on top of her daily planner. She stared at it, stunned. She looked nervous and jittery. Then, though I'm sure she wouldn't admit it, I saw, for the first time, the hint of a smile. Then, as quickly as it came, it disappeared, as the door opened and Jennie barged in, screaming into her cell.

"The guy is a complete fuckin' asshole, Jared. I'm not working with him again," Jennie fumed. "Did you see what—

"Nice purse," Jennie said, interrupting herself. "Balenciaga?"

"Y-Yes," Mia stuttered.

"I have it in red, only mine's bigger, and you've already got a stain on it, you idiot," Jennie snipped as she marched into her office. "Jared? Yeah, I'm back. Fuck him, he came to my event last week and . . ." I heard her shut her door. Hurricane Jennie had touched down in her own office, thankfully.

I sat in silence for the first time in months. My head was swimming. At JWPR, my job was to create illusion, to dictate what people should crave for the week. Along with me, everyone in Jennie's company was spinning a new product or a new personality, but more than that, every person in the office was spinning themselves. Whether it was Mia's lack of money, Adam's dim-wittedness, or my own Midwestern naïveté, everyone had something to spin. Including Jennie.

Ten minutes later, the phones were ringing, and the week had begun. Mia did not acknowledge the purse. Neither did I.

JWPR EXPENSE REPORT

Drinks w/ Jarrett from New York Mag	$31.89
Car Service to hotel press conference	$70.00
Dinner at La Luna (Marcus hand-holding)	$120.00
AT&T Cell	$131.22
Weekly Magazines (Jennie)	$84.10
Porn (client)	$68.59

6.

Pornalicious

J ESUS Christ, what are you doing? I thought you wanted to get out of here," I shouted to Adam, while crawling on the filthy, cum-stained floor of Peepland, Times Square's own Wal-Mart of porn.

"I do, but look over there!" Adam said, pointing to a wall full of vibrators and dildos. A customer stepped over us. Apparently, two guys on all fours didn't raise an eyebrow in that store.

"Dude, I told you before, I'm not into toys."

"No! Look who's standing there!" he said.

"I assume you're talking about that gawky old man," I said, noticing a bookish man holding a giant vibrator. "So some loser is buying a vibrator. Who cares?" I began to get up off my knees.

Adam yanked me back down to the soiled ground. "That's not just some guy! That's Phil Reynolds from *The Scoop*! He's the biggest feature writer for the magazine!"

"Would you cut that shit out? You might already be a walking STD by proxy, but I don't want to catch anything from this nasty floor," I said, wiping my hands on my jeans. I took a deep breath and calmed myself. "So is this the same Phil that

Jennie's so tight with? The one who publishes every major bit of gossip to leak out of a willing publicist's mouth?" I asked.

"Ding-fucking-ding," Adam said. "If he recognizes us, or should I say *me*, I'm screwed. I can see it now: 'Porno Publicist at Peepland,'" he said, frantic.

"Calm down. He's here too! Buying sex toys, no less," I argued.

"It doesn't matter. He'll spin it to his advantage, and it'd be his word against mine. You can't win against a gossip columnist!"

"I hate to burst your bubble, but why the hell would he care if *you* are here? It's not like you're a celebrity," I snapped.

"Some consider me a male socialite, others call me a raconteur of sorts," he said, straight-faced. I couldn't help but laugh.

"A male socialite? Raconteur? Are you kidding me? You're doing exactly what we make fun of our clients for: You're believing your own hype."

We sat in silence and contemplated our next move.

Just an hour before, I'd been lying in bed asleep. For the first time in a month, I hadn't had a restaurant opening, club night, tequila launch, or an up-front party at Bungalow 8. My cell phone startled me out of a deep sleep. I looked at the caller ID: once again, Jennie. In my stupor, I stared at the phone, debating whether or not to pick up. It was two thirty in the morning.

"I need you to run an errand," she said without as much as a "hello," or "I'm so sorry for calling you this late."

"Diet Coke and smokes?" I asked groggily.

"No, it's not for me tonight," she said with a fake laugh.

"A client?" I asked, laying my head back down.

"Yes, I can't say who, but he just called me from his hotel

room. He's here for a huge presentation tomorrow, and I'm sure I don't have to mention that he's one of our biggest tech clients," she explained.

"No, of course you wouldn't have to mention that," I said snidely. My tone with Jennie had deteriorated since she had neglected to tell me that "drug mule" was part of my job description. Against Adam's, Mia's and Allison's judgment I'd confronted Jennie about it.

When I walked out of her office, Adam was foaming at the mouth, wondering if I still had a job at JWPR.

"Well, how'd that work out for you, Cornbread?" he said with characteristic pompousness.

"I flat-out told her I wanted no part of her recreational activities. That it wasn't who I was," I said.

"And you're not bleeding?" Mia asked.

"No, she was very calm and promised me she'd never do it again," I relayed. "She said, 'If nothing else, I'm a woman of my word.'"

"And you believed her?" Adam said, and smiled smugly.

"I do," I had confessed.

From that moment on, I had a new relationship with Jennie. I didn't try to kiss up to her as much; I gave her the respect she demanded, but I also garnered some of my own. It was rare that someone held their ground with Jennie, and I think it amused her. Clearly, this amusement carried into late-night "errands."

"Let me guess; he wants Tylenol PM?" I asked Jennie, snapping out of the memory.

"Not exactly," she said with a slight twinge of mischief in her voice.

"Well?" I asked.

"I need you to go to Peepland in Times Square," she said.

"That's a porno shop, I take it?" I said, a bit irritated.

"You got it!" she said. She was jovial, and I could hear someone making noise in the background. "Nicky, I'll be there in a fuckin' minute; start without me," she ordered. *It's two thirty, and there's a man over; there's no way she's sober.*

"And what am I supposed to do once I'm there?" I asked.

"He needs you to pick him up a few things," she giggled.

"Doesn't his hotel have those pay-per-view movies?" I asked.

"They do, but not the kind he likes. Besides, it can't show up on his hotel bill that he rented porn. We can't have *that* getting out," she explained.

"So what's his fancy?" I asked.

"Teenage Asian porn," she said, without a stutter.

"I'm sorry, but could you repeat that?" I asked, thinking I'd misunderstood her. I'd done stupid shit before. For my college fraternity initiation I had to walk around with a pencil tied to a stick around my . . . well, it wasn't around my neck, and collect thirty signatures before midnight. But porn? From Times Square? In the middle of the night?

"I need you. To go to Peepland. And buy teenage. Asian. Porn," she repeated slowly. Sensing my hesitancy, she continued, "You want to be a part of this firm, you do what you got to do. We've all had to do things we didn't want to for our clients. Look, if you don't want to do it, fine, I can call Adam to go with you. He's done much worse than this, I can assure you," she said.

Adam was going to be so pissed at me for not going at it alone. I also knew that he would never turn her down because she'd get rid of him. "Anyone can be replaced," she'd say at our weekly meetings. But it was too late. She was already on the line with Adam, giving him directions.

"I'll be there in five!" I said loudly.

"Just drop it off at the right hotel on your way home. I'll see you in a few hours. Don't forget I need my office spotless for the Tropical Tan Towels meeting at nine," she said, almost gleefully. "Oh, and I need you to jerk him off too."

"Funny, Jennie. Good night," I said and closed my cell phone with a snap.

"So you know who this Asian porn is for, right?" I asked Adam in a hushed voice, still crouched on the ground.

Adam peered through the racks of Vivid Videos to check on the *The Scoop* pervert. "Yup, and nope."

"Oh come on, it won't be hard for me to figure it out to-morrow."

"The less you know the better, dude," he said.

"When are you going to learn to trust me? We're crawling around in a porn store, for Christ's sake!"

"I trust you," he said. "I just feel that people's sexual tastes should be left private." I felt a shift—this was no longer about a mystery tech client or Phil Reynolds.

"I think his privacy went out the door of his hotel room when he called Jennie to get some young Asian flicks, and that's all I'm going to say about it."

"Can we get on with this please?" he snapped. I grabbed two nondescript pornos, *Asian Gangbang* and *Asian Teenage Wasteland.*

"Let's pay for this and get the hell out of here," Adam said and I rushed to the counter and set down the videos along with my credit card. Once again I was paying for Jennie's incidentals. And with a credit card that had both my name and my mother's—I couldn't get one on my own. How to explain this one? A million ridiculous excuses ran through my mind when I heard the cashier's broken English.

"Something I help you with?"

"Just what's on the counter," I said nervously. The cashier picked up *Asian Teenage Wasteland* and began reading the back of the box.

"I'm sorry, but could you ring this up now, I'm in a bit of a hurry." The clerk glanced at Adam, still on all fours and pretending to be looking at the titles on the bottom shelf, ran the credit card, bagged the videos, and handed me the credit-card slip. I signed, grabbed the bag, and darted for the exit.

Adam tiptoed his way to the exit to avoid Phil's gaze. We were nearly at the exit when—

"*Taylor Green! Stop!*" the cashier screamed.

I froze. Phil turned his head toward the commotion. Adam darted out the door. Phil and I locked eyes. He looked at me with familiarity and, for some reason, I couldn't turn away.

Keep going! a voice in my head screamed. I spun toward the exit.

"Stop! Taylor Green! Stop!" the cashier yelled. "You left your credit card," he said, handing me the bit of plastic.

"Thank you—and I mean it—*so much*," I said. "Really. That was just great of you." I grabbed the credit card out of his hand and raced outside.

"Taylor!" Adam shouted from behind a corner. "Dude, did you see your face? I thought you were going to piss yourself!" Adam burst out laughing.

"Me? You're the one who took off and left me standing there!" I shot back, but couldn't keep from smiling.

SPiN

"Could you imagine Jennie in there?" Adam asked. We both laughed like we hadn't in months. A nervous laugh, but one that strangely bonded us.

"That's funny shit, man," he said.

"Yeah, I can imagine her busting the cashier's balls," I said, laughing.

"No, that's not what I meant," he said. "It's funny how the ones who call the shots are never in the line of fire."

I could feel my face heat up; he was right. My smile began to melt.

"So to the Peninsula?" I asked.

"This was too much for me. I think I'm going to bail and leave that to you. Besides, after that, I'm pretty sure you can handle anything. You don't mind, do you? I think Ellie's waiting for me and shit," he said.

"Uh, sure I can go, why not?" I said. I went to slap Adam's outstretched hand when he moved forward and hugged me.

"It was cool tonight, man. Crazy and fucked-up, but cool nonetheless," he said and smiled.

"Have a good night. Tell Ellie I said hey," I said. He disappeared into a cab, and I walked down the street, my hand in the air, to summon the next available taxi.

I arrived at the Peninsula Hotel, still dressed in all black and with a baseball hat that covered my eyes. I looked like a cross between a robber and someone apprehended on *To Catch a Predator.* How was I to know which room he was in? Jennie hadn't even bothered telling me the client's real name, let alone a pseudonym. I knew better than to call her at this hour. She was no doubt enjoying her cannabis coma at the moment. With my black plastic bag full of goodies, I slowly approached the front desk, where a well-groomed desk clerk stood post.

"Can I help you?" he said.

"Yes, well, I hope so," I said, stumbling over my words. He looked nervous. I caught a glimpse of my outfit in the reflection on the human fish tank behind the desk. I made Christopher Walken seem nonthreatening.

"Look, I don't want any trouble," he gulped.

"Trouble? What are you talking about?" I said.

Before he could say another word I felt a tug on my shirt, then a huge force of nature shoving me into the bathroom.

"Damn it, Mia! You could've broken my arm," I yelled.

"Keep your voice down," she hushed. "You're lucky security hasn't locked you up. You look like Chester the Molester in that getup."

"What is it with you people and bathrooms?" I said, inspecting my surroundings.

"Funny," she said, without cracking a smile. "Do you have the DVDs?"

"Yeah, why?" I asked.

"Give them to me," she ordered.

"No. I had to go to Times Square at this hour to get the damn things. I want to know who the pervert is."

"Hand them over!" She squeezed my arm forcefully.

"Why doesn't it surprise me that you people would rob me even of this simple pleasure?" I shoved the bag into her hands. "Here, go have fun with him, her, or whatever the hell it is," I said.

Then I noticed her outfit.

"I know you shoved me pretty hard, but what in God's name are you wearing?" She was dressed in a full Japanese kimono, her hair pulled up into a clip. She looked beautifully awkward. "You've got to be joking? Where in the hell did you get that outfit?"

Mia was silent.

"This is never," she said through clenched teeth, "*ever*, to be mentioned in the office."

"No problem. But who has a kimono lying around the house?" I said, laughing. "I thought you were Greek or Italian or something."

She wasn't amused. "It's my mother's."

"So why the costume—wait a second! You're not going to sleep with that guy, are you? I mean, not that I care, but, well, you know what I mean," I blurted. I felt her fist make contact with my shoulder. "Damn!" I yelled.

"Hell, no!" she snapped. "Jennie told me to pick up this outfit and give the client his DVDs. She said he would much rather see an Asian-looking girl drop them off than some, to quote Jennie, 'pencil-dicked, brain-dead farm boy!'"

I couldn't help but stare. I was captivated. "I have to say, you look really hot." She slugged me again.

"Stop! This 'pencil-dicked, brain-dead farm boy' isn't about to let you go up there alone," I said earnestly.

"Taylor, please. Don't play this game with me. I've been working for Jennie a long time. Trust me, this is icing on a cupcake."

"I love cupcakes," I said, walking toward the door. "Shall we?" I asked. Mia rolled her eyes and exited the bathroom. I followed her out of the lobby and into the elevator. We got off on the fourteenth floor.

"He's number thirty-two. It's a suite, I'm sure," she said, peering at every door. "That's it, right there. I think I got it from here; just wait for me by the elevator."

"Are you crazy? No way. I'm not leaving you here by yourself." Mia began to speak, and I quickly knocked on the door, rendering her motionless.

The door opened, and there stood Jennie's client. Warner wasn't a big man; in fact, I finally understood what the word "sprite" meant when describing a person. He was elflike; an extremely hairy elf who sweated profusely—picture a hairy hobbit from *Lord of the Rings* and that would be Warner. He was disheveled and looked like he had been blowing rails of coke. His shirt was unbuttoned far more than either Mia or I wanted to see. Warner briefly glanced at Mia, then suddenly shifted his eyes to me.

"Who's this? What's he doing here?" he asked, his eyes darting from Mia to me. His speech grew more rapid. "Jennie said only the girl was coming. Who the hell are you?"

Mia was struggling for an answer, and I could see it. I blurted, "She's my mistress."

"What?" they both asked in unison.

"Not in the 'I'm married and she's my mistress' sort of way; I mean, she's my *mistress*," I said.

I exchanged a look with Mia, and, without missing a beat, she smacked my face as hard as she could, and said, "I said no talking, slave!"

"A dominatrix? Jennie said nothing about that," Warner said, crushed. Clearly, I'd ruined his late-night fantasy.

"Just hand me the bag," Warner ordered. Mia glared at him. In a monotone voice Warner corrected himself, "Please, hand me the bag . . . *mistress*." Mia handed it over, and he quickly shut and locked the door behind him. I got off my knees for the third time that night and followed Mia through the hallway, down the stairs, and out the door.

Mistress Mia and I walked down Fifth Avenue, passing several of our clients' stores and showrooms along the way. *If they only knew*, I thought. Mia was mostly silent.

I went to hail a cab when I noticed that Mia wasn't doing the same. "You want this one?" I asked.

"No, I'm good," she said quietly.

"Wait a second. You're not taking the subway, are you? Not at this hour at least!" I said.

"First, you're not my father, so I suggest you just worry about yourself," she snipped.

"And second?" I asked. She walked toward the subway. "Hey! Wait! We can share a cab!" I said. She stopped for a minute, then finally resigned herself to sharing air with me and turned around. I held the taxi door open and waited for her to get in.

I leaned into the driver, and said, "We have two stops: Upper West Side and . . ." I waited for Mia to speak up. "And?" I asked her.

"Middle Village," she said. "Yeah, I live in Queens, okay?"

"Okay," I said. I found it painfully adorable. I was gleeful about my new knowledge.

As we rode, Mia told me more about herself. She came from a big Italian family that still believed that kids should live at home until they're married. Her father had been a construction foreman, but worked for the union after he broke his back twelve years earlier. Her mother didn't work, as Mia's Italian-born father hadn't caught up with the women's movement and therefore felt no wife should ever work. Working for Jennie was Mia's way out of the Gap and T.G.I. Friday's and into Marc Jacobs and Nobu. Contrary to what I might have thought, she explained, she has a brain and she just wants the wardrobe and the recommendation to get a job at a major fashion house and work in Milan.

"From Middle Village to Milan," I said, smiling. She managed to crack a smile, but then quickly went back to her serious self.

"It's all about having an exit plan," she said. "Without it, you haven't got a thing." I thought about that for a while but found myself too tired to ask more. The rest of the cab ride to Queens we didn't speak, and Mia fell asleep on my shoulder.

Finally, we reached a modest house on a characterless street in Queens. There, a world away from Manhattan, Mia was human again. I stared at her for a moment before waking her, debating my next move. I finally tapped her shoulder. She looked at me and smiled.

She opened the cab door and stepped out into the twilight. "Good night," she called out, and walked toward her front door. Then she turned around and said lightly, "And . . . thanks for the purse."

I smiled, and the cab driver pulled away.

I headed back into the city, crossing the Fifty-ninth Street Bridge as dawn began to break. I realized that I was due at work in three hours, and I took out my cell phone purely out of instinct and checked my voice mail. I returned my only call.

"Hi, Mom."

From: Greg <greg_m@aunatural.com>
To: Taylor Green <TaylorGreen@JWPR.com>
Subject: Lunch

Taylor:

Nat and I are SO stoked you guys are coming today for
lunch. ☺ I completely forgot to ask this earlier, but does
Jennie have any special dietary needs I should know about
ahead of time?

Thanks again for all your help and championing our dream.

See you soon!

Big hug (from the both of us)-
Greg

7.

Lock & Load

IT was eleven in the morning, and Jennie and her coterie of publicists had convened at a large table in the center of Au Natural, an inconspicuous organic cafe a few blocks from JWPR headquarters. With her vast array of restaurant clients, Jennie was often invited by its proprietors to stop in—gratis, of course. In typical Jennie fashion, she brought a party of twelve.

I had brought Au Natural to Jennie after I'd met Greg, the restaurant's dreadlocked owner. I had popped in last month mainly to get out of the blowing, cold New York rain on my way home from work because I was too wet to take one more step without hydroplaning. Without noticing, I had stayed for more than two hours talking to Greg and his business partner/-wife, Natalie. Even though tempeh and spirulina weren't in my lexicon, there was something about Greg and Natalie that made me instantly love them. Perhaps it was the way they casually leaned over the bar counter when they spoke or the genuine belly laughs that reminded me of home. The twenty-something couple had moved from Oregon and sunk everything they owned into the cozy eatery. Relatively inexpensive and healthy food for organic and vegan-crazed New Yorkers: It seemed like an obvious winner to me. When I told Greg that I worked for Jennie, his eyes lit up like Times Square. He knew that she could potentially launch the joint into a new stratosphere. Au Natural wasn't typically Jennie's fare, of course—sprouts and grilled tofu on organic seven-grain bread didn't pair well with Belvedere and tonic—but I knew, with a little convincing, I could get her on board. A few weeks later, Jennie agreed to add Au Natural to her roster on a trial basis, but of course she refused to do any of the work on the account. She handed it over to me like a half-eaten bowl of cereal: a test of sorts.

Greg did his best to make sure everything—the food, the service—was impeccable, since this was the staff's first introduction to the restaurant. He had called me on my cell the night before to triple-confirm that Jennie would be there. He and Natalie were so excited that they might be working with Jennie that they had called home about it—and even their parents knew about my illustrious boss. Apparently, their parents had seen Jennie as a PR pundit on Fox News, speaking ironically from within the No Spin Zone.

Seated at the head of the blood orange table, Jennie knocked her fist on the table to get the attention of the rest of the JWPR staff, obliviously sipping their organic chai lattes and comparing notes from last night's art opening.

"Let's get this over with, people!" she said. As soon as the words left her mouth, her cell rang, and in an instant she was pitching the latest hair accessories to Cindy Baker at *Glamour. Hair accessories?* I thought. I touched my ears to make sure they hadn't started bleeding.

Adam sat near the middle of the table, typing furiously on

his BlackBerry. He looked worried, but he was one too many handmade ceramic plates covered in polenta fries away from me for me to ask what was going on. Farther down the table sat Bob, painting his nails, while Louise, stunned yet strangely delighted, looked on. Then there were the others: people sitting only a few seats away from me who might as well have been office phantoms. I'd never seen them. One perpetually tanned girl who smelled like Lysol drooled over Adam as she yapped into her cell phone. On the other side of her was a guy who chewed his gum like a twelve-year-old girl at Limited Too, popping and clicking it with every chomp and with an open mouth. The chatter around me was like white noise. I was overwhelmed. Mia sat across from me, to the left of Jennie. I tried catching her eye more than once, but she was having no part of it. Knowing that I made her slightly nervous gave me a strange feeling of satisfaction. I looked around the table and nodded in the direction of the tanorexic.

"Who's that?" I whispered to Mia.

"*Brianna.* She's worked here longer than you."

"I don't recognize her," I said.

"Oh, she definitely works here. She's in the office, but usually in small increments," she said.

"What?"

"She uses stunt props, then disappears to . . . apparently to the spray tanner," Mia explained.

"Stunt props?" I asked.

"Yeah, you know, stick a sweater on the back of the chair or leave your purse on the desk so when someone comes by looking for you it looks like you're still at the office." I continued to look confused. Mia further explained, this time adding a shrilly voice for effect: " 'Where's Brianna?' publicist A asks. 'I don't know,' publicist B responds. 'She must be around here somewhere. Her stuff is still here. Maybe at the deli? Or in the ladies' room?' " Mia returned to her normal voice. "That, my friend, is the art of the stunt props."

"Bravo," I said. Mia politely bowed. I paused and smiled. "So . . ."

"Not again," she said.

"You don't even know what I'm going to say," I said.

"I do, and it's not a good idea."

"*Eating* is not a good idea? Everybody's got to eat," I said. I looked up at her and caught a glimpse of her cappuccino-colored eyes.

"Okay, how about this: You let me know where you're planning on eating tonight, and I can go to the same place. We don't even have to sit next to each other. I'll sit on the other side of the restaurant, if that would make you happy," I said.

"You're not getting it," she said.

"That you're afraid?" I jabbed.

"I'm not afraid," she snapped back.

"So give me the name of the place you're eating."

Mia looked at me, silent.

"I'm really hoping you don't say Indian because it makes a mess of my stomach."

She cracked a smile. "That was an over share."

"Come on, gimme a name . . ." I asked again. Mia reached her hand to her head and tugged at her curls: a nervous twitch, I would later learn. She sighed and was about to speak when Jennie returned.

"C'mon, people, let's do this!" said Jennie, this time clapping her hands together like a mean substitute teacher trying to get her class to quiet down. Wincing collectively, the group quieted down, slurping only somewhat less noisily on their smoothies and lattes in a passive display of defiance. "So, who went out last night?" A few hands around the table went up, including Bob's. "I can tell you went out, Bob. Your wig has that slightly askew, druggie-Whitney look to it." Bob pulled a compact from his purse with remarkable quickness and began to adjust his wig.

"I hung out with Paul Sternley from Page Six at Bungalow 8," said Hayley, an assistant with a pixie haircut, as she fidgeted with her pita bread.

"And?" Jennie said. "What happened?"

"Nothing really. We just hung out. You know, we just, like, chilled in a banquette. We drank some Ketels," she said, brain seeping out of her ears.

"You were at Bungalow 8, and all you have to tell me is that you 'chilled and drank some Ketels'?" Hayley nodded imperviously. "Hayley, dear, you may have been hired in exchange for your mother decorating our office for free, but could you at least answer the *fucking clue phone*!" Jennie said, sliding into a scream. Before she could continue her rant, the dark-haired waiter checked on the table.

"We doing okay here?" he asked. Jennie nodded, and the cute waiter locked eyes with her. Greg carefully watched from the bar. For pomp and circumstance, Jennie leaned in and said, "This place could be huge if we got a few key players in and the right mentions." *Key players? Mentions?* I wasn't sure why Jennie switched to "PR speak" until I saw the waiter lingering. Her sex drive was higher than that of most guys I knew.

I smiled. "I agree. It's the right time, and they've got a good hook," I said, mimicking her professional tone. The waiter disappeared, and Jennie turned her head at me and smirked. It was so subtle that no one even noticed, except for Mia. Jennie leaned back in her chair and continued with the rest of the meeting.

"Anyway, what's going on with Kimora's event?" Jennie said, taking a bite of her sashimi. "Listen, Adam, there's a lot of work to be done." Adam nodded innocuously as always. "Why don't you have Taylor help you with this?"

I looked at Adam. He shrugged.

"I can handle it, if that's what you're worried about," he said.

"I *know*. Just look at Taylor like another assistant; there to help you if you need him, honey," Jennie said in her condescending tone. "Is Kimora psyched for it?" she asked.

"Yeah, excited but, you know, a huge pain in my ass," Adam groaned. Behind Jennie, Natalie and Greg hung on every bite the staff took. They nervously smiled and gave me a questioning thumbs-up. I winked while Jennie went over the details of Kimora's charity event.

"Wait," Jennie said, as if she'd had another brilliant idea. "We'll get Lexus to sponsor it. It'll be great press for them. I'm sure we can get Tyra to MC—are Kimora and Tyra speaking this week?" Before anyone could answer, Jennie continued, "I'm gonna get MAC to do the gift bags. Hmm, what other clients haven't we gotten anything from in a while?" Jennie paused and then said, "DJ AM will do the music, and Taylor, do you think this place could cater the party?"

"I'm sure they'd jump at the chance," I said.

"They'd need to do it at cost—this isn't about making money; it's about branding them as *the* place to eat good food that's good for you. They'll triple their money after this party."

"I'll go talk to them now," I said, getting up from the table. As I walked away, I heard Jennie grill the staff about press and celebrity confirmations. I walked to the bar, where Natalie and Greg had a look of terror in their eyes.

"Oh. My. God. She hated *everything*," Natalie said. She smacked Greg on the arm. "I knew we shouldn't have sent out the tofu stir-fry. Tofu is too threatening to people! They don't know what it is!" she vented.

"Relax, the tofu didn't threaten anyone," I said.

"Thank God!" Natalie shrieked.

"I came over here to find out if you think you guys could cater a party for 250 people for Kimora Simmons's charity," I said.

"Shut the front door!" Natalie said so loud that a few of Jennie's staff turned their heads. Natalie quickly covered her mouth like a six-year-old who had been scolded. Her inner dork leaked like a sieve.

"Wh-When's the party?" Greg asked.

"Next Thursday," I said sheepishly.

"I just don't—" Greg stopped as quickly as he started. "I mean, I guess we could call our—" He shot a quick look at Natalie. "Yeah, we can do it!"

"Oh, there's just one more thing. It has to be at cost. I don't want you to lose your shirt over this, but Jennie could get twenty other caterers to do this party for nothing, but she really likes your food and sees huge potential in this place," I explained. Greg's and Natalie's faces dropped. "Look, you don't have to do it. But, trust me, it will be more than worth your investment. The minute Kimora uses you, every single one of her friends will want you and, let me tell you, they throw a lot of parties. And have you seen those women? They all have amazing bodies, and *your* menu goes along with their lifestyle. Also, did I mention all of the press that will be there? Everyone from the *Times* to *InStyle*." I sounded as if I were pitching a story to a reporter.

Greg took a deep breath, and said dramatically, "We'd be honored."

"Great. I'll let Jennie know now so we can make sure you're on all the promo material. Really, this is going to be awesome. Congratulations!" I said. As I walked back toward the table, in the reflection of a nearby mirror I saw Natalie give Greg a giant hug. I could also see that her eyes were filled with tears. My feeling at that moment was one I'll never forget: as if I had a smile from my liver to my eyebrows. It felt damn good. I sat back down at the table as Jennie was in midsentence.

". . . and call Daniel at Fekkai and tell him I'll be in for a blowout at seven," Jennie said to Mia. "Well?" Jennie asked, looking in my direction.

"We're set," I said.

"Perfect. Louise, make sure they're on all the press materials we're sending out. Oh, and the invite too. Get the logo from Taylor."

Greg and Natalie approached the table holding a large plate. Jennie stopped talking and turned around in her chair.

"Sorry to interrupt," Greg said, awkwardly. "This is one of our house specialties: warm cherry flan bread pudding. We hope you enjoy it, and please accept this as a small token of our enormous gratitude to you for coming in today."

Jennie smiled as the rest of the staff clapped. It was uncomfortable, but I found myself clapping along. I wasn't sure, though, just who we were clapping for, Jennie or Greg. Judging by the grotesque smile on her face, Jennie clearly thought the applause was for her.

Greg continued, "To be working with an organization with such a great reputation and buzz as Jennie Weinstein PR humbles Natalie and me beyond belief. It's just surreal, and we're so excited about what the future holds. So with that, a giant thank-you," Greg said, and set the bread pudding on the table.

Jennie turned back around in her chair to face the staff, and just as Greg was about to step away, to everyone's surprise, Natalie stepped to the head of the table.

"Hi there! Sorry to interrupt. This will only take a second, I promise," she said. Jennie didn't bother to turn around. The rest of the staff looked at Natalie, still basking in the glow of Greg's compliments. "I also wanted to thank everyone for believing in Greg and me. Portland might not be some podunk town in the middle of nowhere, but it might as well be because it's not New York." Greg locked eyes with Natalie to encourage her to get to her point. "And the fact that we're working with you guys—and you, Jennie—my God, we've read about you in *Us Weekly* and the *Post* for years. It's insane!" The staff shifted in their seats, most likely wondering where she was going. "Anyway, I just wanted to say a huge thank-you myself, and give a very special shout-out to Taylor." Natalie looked me square in the eyes, and continued, "Taylor, you believed in us when we weren't even so sure about ourselves. You're amazing and a superstar." She giggled.

Adam snapped out of his BlackBerry coma long enough to cough "Bullshit!" into his napkin.

"One day you're going to be the PR King of Manhattan," she proclaimed, quickly adding, "With Jennie as your queen, of course." I don't quite remember my exact reaction, but Mia would later tell me that it was a combination of nervous laughter mixed with a high-pitched shrill that one makes when being bludgeoned. "That's it," Natalie said. "Enjoy the bread pudding!"

The entire staff's eyes darted nervously from Jennie to me and back. They stared at me in what I could only interpret as anticipation. The kind of anticipation where you just know somebody is about to lose an eye or a job, or in my case, quite possibly both. I sat stone-faced in my chair, as if Natalie's speech never happened. I turned and faced Jennie and waited for her next move. She cleared her throat and then smiled like I'd never seen her before. "Dig in!" she announced to the staff. "Not you, Mia. You're already a *healthy* girl," Jennie said as she slid the pudding away from Mia. The rest of the staff cautiously scooped up bites of bread pudding, and went back to their gossip. The potential tsunami had been averted. Having not breathed in at least a minute, I took in several large gulps of air.

Twenty minutes later almost everyone had returned to the office, except for Jennie, Adam, Mia, and me. Greg and Natalie cleared the remaining plates from the table. "So seven months in, and you're already bringing in clients," Jennie said, looking in my direction. "The two of you could take a page from Taylor's book," she added.

"Thanks. You know, it seemed like a good fit. Greg and Natalie are great, aren't they?" I said.

"Oh God, I need a drink," Adam chimed.

"It's not even two o'clock," Mia scolded.

"Xanax?" Adam offered. Mia rolled her eyes, and to our surprise Jennie took out four pills from her bag and handed one to each of us.

"Be my wife," Adam said, washing the pill down with the remnants of his banana-strawberry smoothie.

"Now that's funny," Jennie snickered. "Where are you residing this week? Vagina Valley or Cock City?" Jennie asked, laughing.

"What? I don't like labels, okay?" Adam countered.

"That would be a first—everything in your closet is filled with them," Jennie said. "And what about your roommate? What's her name again?"

"Ellie," Adam said. I could see his body begin to tighten with anger.

"Oh yeah, *Ellie*," Jennie started.

"Don't push me, Jennie. Job or no job, don't you say a word about her," Adam said through clenched teeth.

"Easy," Jennie said. "I wasn't going to say anything bad."

"Yeah, I'm sure you weren't. Anyway, I have to get back and work on this Kimora party," Adam said, getting up from the table. "Later."

"Should we get back?" Mia asked.

"Just a few more minutes. I want to feel the Xanax," Jennie said, leaning back in her chair. Simultaneously, Mia and I looked at each other in astonishment. A crack in Jennie's armor? For a moment, it was as if the stress of her life began to escape her body like a vapor. Watching her over the last several months, I knew it certainly wasn't easy being her, but then again, she didn't make it so. Still, the whispers and the stares had to get to her. A couple minutes passed, and Jennie's eyes fluttered a few too many times. Finally, she got up from her chair. "Let's go," she said.

Mia grabbed her purse and led us to the door, where Greg and Natalie waited to say their good-byes.

"How was dessert?" Greg asked as we reached the exit.

"It was . . . amazing," I said, lacking anything better than the publicist's catch-all phrase *du jour*.

Jennie smiled politely and reached for the door and opened it.

"So we'll give you guys a call later today to talk about the menu?" Natalie excitedly asked.

"That won't be necessary," Jennie said.

"E-mail?" Natalie followed. Jennie was silent.

"Jennie?" I said, trying to bring her out of Xanax-du.

"Oh, I apologize," she said. "You don't have to e-mail us." Natalie was as confused as me. "We won't be using you for the party," Jennie said with a smile.

"What?" Greg said.

"And I'm sorry, but we won't be able to take you on as a client," Jennie added. "My incompetent assistant Taylor failed to mention we've already been talking to a macrobiotic Chinese restaurant called Steam." I was floored. I'd never heard of Steam. "Mia's our point person on the account."

Mia cocked her head to the side. "Yeah, they're going to be huge."

"But—I don't understand," Natalie said.

"It's pretty simple really: we're not working with you. Now if you'll excuse us, we have to get back to the office. We've got a party to plan!" Jennie said, continuing to smile.

Greg exploded. "How can you do this? You come here and eat our food and fill our head with this grandiose plan of taking our food to the upper echelon, then snap it away. How can you be such a . . . I mean, you really are a goddamn . . ."

". . . Bitch," Jennie finished. She touched Greg's arm, almost sympathetically. "This shouldn't be shocking; it is, after all, my job. I have to protect my reputation and my name, and frankly, your cuisine was less than stellar." Natalie and Greg were speechless. Mia stood in the open doorway, staring at the tiled floor. "Well, I really have to get going. Thanks again." She tossed over her shoulder, "Maybe you should focus on smoothies, those weren't half-bad."

"You're unbelievable!" Greg snapped. The peaceful organic farmer had long evaporated. "Fuck you and your fucking bull-shit."

"Greg!" Natalie yelled.

"I'm sending you a bill, lady. I'm sure even you have heard there's no such thing as a free lunch," Greg continued.

"Go ahead," Jennie said as she joined Mia on the sidewalk. "But I'd hate to call the *Post* and tell them about your rodent problem."

"That's bullshit—we don't have a problem," Natalie snipped.

"I'm just saying . . . I'd rather *not* call them, but—you know," Jennie said.

"Go," Greg said calmly.

"Good-bye!" Jennie said while she mockingly blew air kisses. The Xanax had clearly reached its optimum level.

I looked at Greg and Natalie, searching my mind for the right words. "Sorry" didn't seem adequate. I'd underestimated the poison of Jennie, and apparently I was the only one unable to see my folly.

"I'll make this right," I said to Greg and Natalie. It was a lie. I knew it. And so did they. But neither of us acknowledged it. I looked at the couple one last time before making my exit. Natalie tried to fight back the tears as they fell on her cheek. Greg stood stunned. I shut the door behind me and heard Natalie wail, "I'm so sorry. It's my fault. I shouldn't have said a word. I'm so sorry." I took a few steps and grabbed on to a street pole. I was standing still, but Varick Street was spinning. After a few seconds, I put one foot in front of the other. As I walked, I heard her repeat "I'm sorry," until her voice was muffled by the sounds of the bustling New York afternoon.

It was a long and lonely walk back to the office. I remembered one morning when Allison, Lauren, and I were walking to brunch. We saw a woman who couldn't have been much older than me lying on the sidewalk on a bitter December afternoon wearing nothing except a black garbage bag. She begged for money as people strolled by. "We can't just walk past and leave her there," I said. "How can you do that?"

"You learn by example to just keep moving," Allison said somberly.

"But why?" I asked.

"You can't get involved personally; the minute you do, you become the prey," Lauren said. I never realized how right she was until now. Greg and Natalie weren't lying on the corner, but they might as well have been. Again I had kept on walking, protecting *myself*. I felt dirty.

By the time I got back to the office, everyone knew what had happened. Adam nudged my shoulder. "Shake it off," he said.

"Yeah." I sighed.

"When you get a mo', I could use your help with this event . . ." he said. I nodded and headed to my cloffice, defeated. Jennie walked out of her office and headed toward the dungeon. I glared at her with a mixture of disgust and sadness. She rolled her eyes.

"Oh God. Let's just get this out now. I do it because I *want* to, Taylor. Does that satisfy you?"

"Okay," I said as I opened my door.

"And for the *joy*, Taylor—the sheer *joy*." She snickered as she walked ahead, surprisingly effortlessly in her Louboutin heels and a Xanax-induced haze.

I went into the cloffice and sat at my makeshift desk. There was a note written in handwriting I recognized. *Angelo's. Little Italy. 8:30. Tonight.*

8.

Feels Like the First Time

I finished my second glass of Pinot Grigio and felt my cheeks getting warm. Already I'd entered the "permi-grin" phase that often accompanied my drinking. The short, balding Italian waiter approached the table and asked if we'd like another round. My mind started the great debate: *Just one more* versus *You're feeling good enough*. I waited to take her lead, as it seemed the gentlemanly thing to do. Apparently she was also caught up in the great debate, so I stepped up to the plate. "We'll take two more glasses," I said.

We deserved it. It had been a rough day. Together, we watched a couple's hopes and dreams destroyed in front of us, so it was only appropriate that we were on a date, raising a glass. To survive working for Jennie, there was little choice but to adapt and navigate through the polar opposites that our job presented.

Angelo's was crowded and noisy. It was a family restaurant, not particularly romantic or necessarily a destination for couples. It wasn't surprising, then, that we were there. Waiting for our third glass and our antipasto, I had to ask, "So why this place? Don't get me wrong, I love Angelo's. I come down here whenever I have friends visiting from out of town," I said.

"It's a New York institution!"

"But the noise. And the tourists? You don't fool me."

"What?" she said coyly. Mia recoiled back in her chair. She folded her arms and flashed a hint of a smile.

"You were afraid someone would spot us out on a date," I said.

"Oh God, please don't call it that. It just sounds so, I don't know, *official*," she said, playing with her hair. I didn't say a word, letting her dig herself out. There was a part of me, though, that was disappointed she didn't want to consider it a date. Every insecurity from junior high and high school flooded my head. *Am I not good-looking enough?* She knew how much money I made, so that couldn't be it. *What is wrong with me?* I felt beads of sweat on my forehead. At that moment, it was me who was nervous and fidgety.

"What?" she said, in response to my silence. "Okay, fine. I chose this place because the likelihood of us running into anyone from the office or one of our clients is extremely minimal."

"I knew it!" I blurted out, and nervously laughed.

"I thought it'd be nice to go someplace and not have to worry about what we said or who we talked about, because, let's face it, these people could care less."

I looked around at the mostly overweight, aging out-of-towners and agreed. There was a certain . . . exhilaration to our dinner, not only because it was our first date, but because it felt as if we were doing something clandestine. Two hip PR people slumming it. Strangely, it felt good.

"Well, they may not care, but I do. So, I know the basics

about you; so tell me one embarrassing thing about you," I said.

"Are you kidding me? That's so lame."

It was lame. I knew it, too, but I was flailing, and to put it delicately, it had been a long dry spell. My last shot at romance, over a year prior, ended with my date being rushed to St. Luke's because of an allergic reaction to nuts. Without realizing it, I must have developed an aversion to dating, emergency rooms, and pesto sauce.

"And you're avoiding the question," I shot back.

"God, you're actually serious, aren't you?"

"Oh, and by the way, I spot a lot of 'my people' also eating at this restaurant, and I've had just enough Pinot that I'd be happy to ask them to cajole you into answering my question," I said.

"'Cajole'? What other Page Six words do you plan on pulling out next? 'Canoodle,' maybe?" She laughed. The irony was that she was spot on; I had read an item earlier that morning that used the word "cajole." I'd had to look it up.

"'Cajole' as in I'm gentle but persistent when it comes to getting what I want," I flirted. Mia shifted in her seat uncomfortably.

"Fine," she said. As she took a pause, I seized the opportunity to take her in. Her eyes were piercing, smoky, and . . . those lips. Goddamn, those were some dangerous lips. "Well . . ." she started, and I shook myself out of the stare. "When I was a kid, I thought condom was short for condominium," she said, reddening.

"You *what*?" I said, aghast.

"Yeah, I walked around the house telling my brothers I was going to live in a condom in Manhattan when I grew up."

"I'm sure they had a field day with that," I said.

"Shut up! My mother made me eat soap!"

"Soap? Why? Condom is not a bad word."

"In my house it is," she said.

"Well, how was it?"

"What?" she asked, concerned.

"The soap." I smiled.

"Oh shut up!"

"So you can't say the word *condom* in your house, but you can have a mouth as bad as Jennie's when you're working the door?"

"That's different. It's work. Who I am at work is not *who I am*," she tried to explain.

"If that gets you through the day," I said, and simpered.

"No more work talk. It's your turn. Go on—spill it." The steam from my piping-hot penne à la vodka was making me sweat. Or at least that's what I hoped Mia would think.

As I was about to answer her, my cell phone rang. Mia gathered who it was from the look on my face.

"Hey, Jennie!" I answered, with false glee. As I listened to Jennie blather on, I watched Mia take tiny bites of her pasta. I'd seen her take much larger bites at the office. It was endearing: She was trying to make a good impression on me. If nothing else, at least I wasn't the only one afraid of looking like an idiot. She was utterly charming.

I don't know what got into me, but in the middle of Jennie's extolling her wisdom, I blurted, "Jennie? I'm losing you? Are you there?"

Jennie screamed into the phone, "*Hello! Hello! Jesus Christ!*" I held the phone out so Mia could hear. "*Goddamn it!*"

"Call me when you get a signal!" I said loudly into the phone. I promptly shut off my BlackBerry and placed it facedown on top of the table.

"Damn," Mia said. "I certainly didn't expect that from you."

"I'm at a very important nondate," I answered.

Mia took another sip of wine and said, "So . . ."

"Oh, I was hoping you forgot." She shook her head and arched her eyebrow to let me know I better spill it, and fast. "I played Peter Pan in our school play, sophomore year," I said. Mia burst into hysterical laughter.

"You in green tights? Genius."

"Funny." I sighed.

"Wait, are you sure you shouldn't be having this date with Adam?"

"I only did it because I wanted to get down Tinkerbell's pants," I explained.

"Okay, ew. I'm never going to be able to look at that play the same way again."

"There's more," I said. I momentarily debated if I should divulge as much on a first date, but then again I figured I wasn't known for my suaveness.

"More than you in green tights jumping around onstage?" she asked.

"Tinkerbell and I were about to have our big scene together in the third act. It was a pivotal moment where Peter tells Tink good-bye . . ." I hesitated, unable to believe I was retelling the story I'd spent years trying to forget.

"Yeah?" Mia said.

"I couldn't help it. She just looked so hot in that small pink dress with the wings and the sparkles around her boobs . . ."

"No! You didn't!" Mia gasped. The horrified look on Mia's face was almost identical to my mom's and Ethel's that night when they were in the audience to witness it.

"I got a boner. On stage. In tights."

"Oh. My. God." Mia said, shocked. "You win." I put my hand on top of hers. Surprisingly, she didn't pull it away.

"You know what I love about tonight?" I asked, as my eyes darted back and forth from her lips to her eyes.

"Yeah?" she said, with anticipation.

"No cell service," I said. "Jennie can't reach us. No one can get to us here, even if we wanted them to." Mia pulled her hand back and placed it on top of her BlackBerry.

"Why do you think we're here?" she said.

"Seriously, but how nice is it to have a conversation that doesn't involve anything to do with guest lists, gift bags, or Jennie?" I said. The minute I said Jennie's name out loud it jolted me back to the fact that I had just turned off my phone while one of New York's biggest media players was trying to call me. It scared the hell out of me. I needed the job.

"You've brought her name up twice in the last thirteen seconds," Mia said.

"Ah, do I detect a bit of jealousy?" I asked.

"Oh please, don't flatter yourself," she said. "We really should get going, though. It's a school night after all." I didn't want the night to end. I searched my brain, looking for an excuse to keep it going.

"Okay, we'll get out of here if you walk with me to the corner and get a cannoli. I saw this dessert place, and I've been thinking about it all night," I said. The truth was, I didn't even particularly like cannolis.

"Fine. I could use some fresh air." I took out my wallet to

pay for dinner and Mia tried to fight me for the bill. When I reached for my credit card a pill fell out. It was the pill that Jennie had given us at Au Natural.

"That's a strange bread-crumb trail you have to your wallet," Mia said. I picked up the pill and held it between my thumb and forefinger and studied it. "Uh, Taylor, while you may not be snorting lines on the table or shooting up heroin, nonetheless you're scaring your Midwestern compatriots around us."

"With this crowd? They're used to popping pain medication like candy." I had an idea. "Do you still have your Xanax?"

"I think so. Why?"

My nerves from not calling Jennie were beginning to get the best of me. The discovery of the Xanax was like a message from the universe. We had to do it, at least that's how I justified it to myself. "Feel like taking a little trip?" I asked deviously.

"Oh you're bad," she said. "Who knew Cornbread could be this bad?"

"My drug experience consists of eating a pot brownie, then projectile vomiting all over my mother," I said. "But I could buy you an eightball from this dealer I recently became acquainted with," I added. Based on the urgency of Jennie's voice, I gathered she wanted me to make a return appearance to said dealer.

"You too, huh?" Mia asked with a look of dread.

"Anyway . . ." I said, trying to change the subject. "Now boarding . . ." I cupped the pill in my hand, ready to pop it in.

"The booze and Xanax train?" she asked. "Of course, you would pick the more subdued of drugs, I'll give you that much. Sure, why not?" she relinquished. We grabbed the remnants of our Pinot Grigio and downed our Xanax, compliments of Jennie.

I signed the credit-card slip, and we rushed out onto Mulberry Street. The streets were packed with tourists either taking pictures of the old Italian neighborhood they'd seen in classic mob movies or buying *Sopranos* T-shirts and Italian flags from street vendors. I grabbed Mia's hand as we walked. I wondered what my mom and Ethel would think of Mia. I imagined taking Mia home with me. *Slow your roll*, I thought.

We finally reached the corner of Mulberry and Grand Streets and stood outside of Ferrara.

"Hey! You still in there?" Mia asked. Whether it was the wine, the Xanax, the Xanax mixed with the wine, or maybe even the fact I truly was falling for this girl I wasn't certain but I took a chance and pulled her closer and kissed her. Her lips tasted like vanilla, and were as soft as a pillow.

"Well, that was subtle," she said. Then wiped her mouth, "And sloppy."

"Sorry," I said. But I really wasn't sorry for the kiss.

"Are we getting those cannolis you talked about or not?" I looked at the line that overflowed out the front door; it was daunting, and there was no guest list for us to cut to the front of the line.

"Absolutely," I said, as we took our place in line behind a family of tourists. I heard music pouring out into the street from a nearby bar. The couple in front of us started to bob and sway to the melody as they picked their toddler-aged daughter up and started to dance with her. Mia nudged me and rolled her eyes.

"I forgot this is why I don't go below Houston," Mia snipped.

SPiN

"Shh, what are you talking about? Just how far does Jennie have that stick broken off in your ass?" I said with a tinge of a slur in my voice.

"Oh come on. You have to admit they're cheesy," she said.

"I think you've forgotten what it's like to let your guard down for more than an hour," I teased.

"What? I'm having fun!" she said, poking my sides as I squirmed away.

"Mmm-hmm."

"And my guard *is* down," she argued. With that I stepped off the curb and onto Mulberry Street, which was thankfully only open to pedestrian traffic at that hour of night. I offered Mia my hand.

"What are you doing?" she asked. Her body stiffened, and she looked incredibly nervous. She had no idea what was about to come.

"I'm asking my girl for a dance," I said.

"Are you high?" she said.

"Probably." I smiled. "Well?" Mia rolled those famous eyes, took yet another deep breath in, and reluctantly stepped onto the street.

"I'm just doing this so you don't make an even bigger ass of yourself in front of all these people." I took her hand in mine, and we began to dance.

"Oh you have no idea just how big of an ass I'm about to make of *us*," I said, wrapping my hands around her waist. I pulled her in so tight that I heard her nervous breathing. We continued our dance in front of Ferrara and attracted an audience.

The tourist couple turned around and smiled as Mia and I swayed back and forth.

"Now is this so bad?"

"Not if you like being stared at—not at all." Harry Connick Jr.'s version of "Save the Last Dance for Me" echoed through the streets.

"But don't forget who's taking you home, and in whose arms you're gonna be," I sang into her ear. I knew it was cheesy, but I got caught up in the moment. My singing was bad, I no doubt was buzzed, and I had told her about a boner I got in a high-school play. If this girl stuck around after all of this, we had a strong future ahead of us.

"Oh there's singing? I wasn't told there was going to be singing," Mia said. I continued my song and dance, literally.

I repeated the chorus once again, "And don't forget who's taking you home, and in whose arms you're gonna be," I sang even louder.

"Going on home with me? To Queens? At my parents' house? Not likely." Then she paused, and said, "Your place maybe." Finally, Mia joined me in my madness. I knew she had it in her. As I twirled her, I caught a glimpse of the tiny white lights strung all along the buildings that shone like Christmas as we danced down Mulberry Street. But that night, they seemed to twinkle more than any Christmas tree I'd ever seen.

Finally, Mia joined me and sang just as loudly and badly as I did. The song might have ended, but our dance continued. Until, of course, we heard applause and abruptly stopped.

"So should we get back in line?" I asked.

"Are you kidding me?" Mia said. "I'm never going to be able to set foot on this street again." Mia stared at me, shaking her head.

"What?" I moved in closer in the hopes of another kiss. I was denied.

"This," she said.

"My bad dancing? The date? The kiss? Which is it?" I said with a smile.

"All of it," she said. "What are we doing here?" Her face had a look of worry. She was vulnerable, something she never showed. I grabbed her hand and gave it a squeeze to relax her.

"I don't know, but I thought we were doing pretty good."

"It's just that . . ." She paused and again looked at me with a mix of confusion and fear. "You're a china shop and me, well I'm . . . I'm a bull." I couldn't help but laugh.

"What are you talking about? China shops? Bulls?" I said, smirking.

"Hey, I'm serious," she said.

"So am I. I'm just a guy that's out with a girl that he likes very much. Beyond that I don't know what else you want me to say," I said.

"I want you to tell me that everything's going to be all right. That we're not making a colossal mistake here," she said. I pulled her close again and whispered in her ear, "Everything's going to be all right."

"You ARE a publicist," she said, flirting. Then she kissed me. The truth was I didn't know that everything would be okay, but my intention was for it to be so. She pulled back once again to my dismay. "It's just so hard for me to believe that my prince just shows up here and not while waiting in line to go to some stupid party."

I couldn't help but laugh. "Hey, that party got me on the other side of the velvet ropes and to you."

"You just wanted to meet Leo," she said deadpan.

"I did just want to meet Leo. Speaking of which, can you still do that? I think I'd make a great wingman." Mia slugged me in the shoulder. We kissed again in the middle of the street as tourists bumped our shoulders as they passed by.

"Hey watch it, asshole!" Mia shouted.

"That's my girl," I said, and smiled.

As we got into a cab to head back to the Upper West Side, and as I powered my cell back on, the message alert chimes went off like a four-alarm fire. I panicked once again, certain that every message was from Jennie. I looked out the window and tried to remain calm. The taxi sped up the West Side Highway, and Mia cracked her window to let in the brisk night air. Then, the message alert went off once again. I stared at the phone and debated whether or not to listen. Not even the Xanax could quell my Jennie anxiety. I caught Mia watching me out of the corner of my eye as I ran my fingers over the keys on my phone. Then the cell phone rang loudly. It was Jennie. I hesitated. There were two women clamoring for my attention. The phone continued to ring, and just as I was about to choose evil over good, Mia took the decision away from me. She moved quickly, swung her leg over me, and—to the delight of our cab driver—straddled me, seductively reaching near my front pocket where my phone rested, grabbing my BlackBerry, then powering it off.

"What?" I asked.

"I'm not into three-ways," she said.

the
pearl

simple elegance.

Amenities

- "Diptyque" Luxury Candles
- 24-Hour Restaurant
- 24-Hour Room Service
- ATM/Cash Machine
- Plush Bathrobes
- Frette Linens
- Flat-Screen Televisions
- Complimentary Wi-Fi
- Francesca's Hair Salon
- Concierge Service
- Oversized Down Pillows
- Pet Friendly
- Warm Cookies and Milk Turndown Service
- White Orchids in Every Room
- Indoor Pool & Poolside Lounge
- Live Nightly DJ in the Lobby
- Art Installations
- Nonsmoking Rooms Available
- Personal Service
- Dream-Inducing Mattresses
- Complimentary Rock Spa Products
- Juicy Couture Slippers
- Minibar Essentials: Including Beluga, Moet, Belvedere Vodka, & Hot Tamale Candies

544 West 54th Street New York, NY 10019

9.

Things That Go Bump

As I rode down the elevator with Louise, I was finally able—after eight months at the agency—to get a good look at her. She was only twenty-nine, but looked much closer to forty. She stood almost as tall as me, five-foot-eleven, and rail-thin. With her strawberry blond hair and icy blue eyes, she was often compared to Nicole Kidman. In the weird elevator light, Louise's skin did have a kind of Kidman-like luminous glow, and was so like porcelain that it seemed to me if you squeezed her too hard, she really might crack into a million little pieces. Adam nicknamed her "Unbreakable" based on Samuel L. Jackson's character in the M. Night Shyamalan movie. Louise felt me staring, and we both quickly lowered our heads. She rarely, if ever, made eye contact with anyone. Her head, it seemed, was on a hinge: I rarely saw it upright, her face always buried in files and press clippings.

After a moment, Louise lifted her face and smiled at me in a way that made me feel like she once stood where I was standing. Hungry. Ambitious. But, while Louise gave up writing assignments for *Allure* and *New York Magazine*, I only gave up working for Mitchell Kern. I glanced at the conservative pearls draped around her neck—a gift from her affluent parents or maybe from her husband. Louise was from the Midwest, too, but unlike me, she hailed from the wealthy Chicago suburb of Lake Forest. I had a feeling that Louise's parents were supplementing her income; Jennie bounced too many of our checks for her to support herself. I had been forced to call Ethel on more than one occasion to cover my rent. My mother told me my empty bank account was a straight-from-Jesus sign that I should leave New York and return home. I told her it was unlikely that Jesus and Jennie were working together in any capacity.

At that moment, stuck covering a boring interview with the newbie, Louise was no doubt painfully depressed. She would have preferred, I'm sure, to have Adam or Mia alongside her. Unfortunately for Louise, Adam was primping for a benefit for the Royal Academy of the Arts, an event he looked forward to for the sole reason that he might end up on David Patrick Columbia's "New York Social Diary" Web site next to a couple of princesses, a number of lords, and a bespectacled Dominick Dunne. Adam loved to think of himself as one of *them*. Mia, on the other hand, was at the Brooklyn Aquarium covering a photo shoot with a new author. In a perfect world, Louise would go to this interview alone. Yet, sadly, here I stood, examining her pearls and her porcelain skin.

The tiny lines around Louise's eyes and mouth told me that she could've left Jennie a thousand times, but there was always a promise that made her stay. People in the dungeon often referred to Jennie as the "carrot dangler"; it was she who made the promises to employees when she needed them to do something ill-mannered. Or illegal.

"Are you loving this brisk weather as much as I am?" Louise asked, breaking the silence, which surprised me. She rarely engaged in personal conversation, mainly because she wanted to avoid divulging anything about herself.

"Yeah, it's great," I said. So it had come to this: We were talking about the weather. Of all the shit that went down in that office—the drug deals, the betrayal, the sex—she asks me about a nippy New York afternoon? *She's lost all of her social skills*, I thought. *God, don't let me end up like Louise. Despite the good skin.*

"So have you read up on the Pearl?" she asked. The Pearl was the boutique hotel in midtown to which we were en route. In the midnineties (so I'm told), the Pearl had been the place to be. The lobby was a nightclub in itself. Every staffer from *Vogue* to *Vanity Fair* hung out there. Over the last few years, however, the place had lost its luster. Enter Jennie, with promises of restored glory and hotties in stilettos with magazine spreads in hand.

"Of course," I said. "I was reading about this place while I was still in college." Louise stared at me curiously. "What? It was either celebrity magazines or cow-tipping." She let out a muffled giggle.

"Thank you," I said. "No really. Thank you for laughing at my sad, sad upbringing, Louise. That's very sweet of you."

"I'm sorry. I've just never heard anyone connect the dots from cow-tipping to *People*." She laughed.

"I'm here to educate you in the ways of Middle America. I'm at your service."

"I thought cow-tipping was an urban—or rural—legend," she said.

"Oh no, it's very real," I said. "A very, very serious sport. If you like, I'll drive you to Connecticut, and we'll tip a few ourselves."

"Get out! Really?" she asked.

"Sure! I'll revisit my childhood nightmare, and you'll watch bovines fall on their sides. It will be a hoot." I smiled. She looked at me with a wide grin. "But you'll be paying for my therapy," I added.

"Stop," she said, her white cheeks turning red. "I'm going to be a mess before we even get to the interview." She composed herself and straightened her hair, which was pulled back off her face. She was beautiful, no doubt. But she'd been *hardened*. Like so many others. Her mouth was small, her face demure; she moved her body not with determination, but with a kind of apathy, as though shrugging off what her life had become.

The elevator doors opened to the bustling lobby. As we stepped onto the sidewalk and walked up the block toward the subway, Louise asked mysteriously, "Did Jennie tell you about Todd—I mean, Mr. Martin?"

"The CEO of the Pearl? No, why?" I asked.

Louise looked quickly over her shoulder. "According to Jennie, he has a crush on me."

"Of course he does." I smiled.

"You might think it's flattering, but he doesn't care that I'm married or even about his own wife and kid. He repulses me," she said.

"Huh."

"What?" she asked.

"Such a venomous response might suggest that you're more flattered than repulsed," I said, as we approached the subway steps.

Louise was silent for a moment and paused on the top step.

"Louise, it's not a big deal. You're human! And it's not like you're really cheating. Wait—are you?"

"Of course not!" Louise shouted. "I could never. Billy is my world. And, frankly, Mr. Martin creeps me out. Jennie doesn't trust him alone with me; she thinks he might try something. That's why you're here."

"And I thought she sent me because of my business acumen."

"You've been rather good company," she teased, as we began to walk again. "But trust me; Jennie even makes me call her after I meet with him. To make sure I escaped unscathed." I looked at Louise, completely surprised. "I know it's shocking: the woman actually has, well, *emotions*."

I laughed and said, "I'll believe it when—"

"Hi!" Louise shouted, to what appeared to be nobody. "What are you doing here?"

"Hey, babe!" I heard a male voice speak out from the crowd of commuters. A short, brown-haired man stepped forward and kissed Louise on the lips: Billy, I hoped (otherwise this was going to be awkward). He was much shorter than Louise, with dirty blond, thinning hair and a bit of a flabby belly—not someone I would have pictured as Louise's husband. Though Mia had once given me the whole story on Billy—he worked in the marketing department at a big cell-phone company, and was constantly trying to extol the virtues of his company over the others, a speech no one would listen to because the caps on his teeth were so large that you were afraid he was going to take a chomp out of you while he was in the middle of a sentence. And here he was, just as described: a typical salesman/banker type, and a genuine Upper East Sider, complete with strict uniform of khakis and a button-down, no matter the destination. (Mia wondered if he wore khaki pajamas with a button-down top.)

"What are you doing here?" Louise asked, as Billy looked me up and down.

"I got off work early. Thought maybe we could grab a bite," Billy said in a thick Long Island accent.

"Damn. I wish I could, but we're off to cover an interview at the Pearl. Oh my God, I'm so rude. Billy this is Taylor Green; he's new. Taylor, this is my husband, Billy."

"Good to meet you, man," I said, shaking his hand. It felt like raw salmon. "Louise, if you guys want to go eat, I'm sure Jennie wouldn't mind."

"Ha!" Billy said. "He's definitely new."

"Thanks, Taylor, but Jennie would kill me." She turned to Billy. "I wish I could, but Jennie said Mr. Martin specifically requested that I be there. Sorry, babe," Louise said as she hugged him good-bye.

"No problem," Billy said, obviously disappointed.

"Maybe we can have dinner at the Pearl after?" Louise asked.

"Nah, you know I don't like those hoity-toity places."

"All right, I'll see you at home," Louise said, and we walked down the subway steps. I could hear the train pulling into the station, and the two of us jogged through the gates.

During the subway ride, Louise had a sullen look glued to her face. The smile she had had not less than twenty minutes ago had long disappeared. She stared quietly at the floor.

"Hey, Weezy. You still with me?"

" Weezy? God, I haven't heard that in a long time," she said, taking her eyes off the subway tiles at last.

"Ah, come on. No one calls you Weezy? *The Jeffersons*? What is *wrong* with people?" I smiled.

"My friends used to call me that in high school," she said.

"That's right. You're my Midwestern partner in crime," I nudged.

"I do miss it sometimes."

"You do? Not me. I couldn't get out of there fast enough," I said.

"Things are just much simpler there."

"And that's a good thing?" I said, horrified.

"You're young. You'll see what becomes important," she said.

"You're only a few years older than me," I countered.

"I feel twenty," she said. "I've been trying to get Billy to move out of the city for three years, but he won't do it." As Louise talked, my mind wandered to Mia. What was the protocol for this sort of thing? We both agreed that no one at the office could know. That was easier said than done—Jennie knew *everything* that happened in the office. The last few weeks I had played it cool with Mia. I called, but only every other night. I flirted, but not desperately. The truth was that I wanted to call her, *needed* to call her, nightly. Needed to tell her about the craziness of our job and that I pulled myself out of bed each morning because I knew I'd see her face. Mia had yet to spend the night at my place. Her conservative parents still expected her home each night. The night of our date when she came back to my place was a blur. It was definitely hot, but quick. Not to mention a bit awkward with Algebra watching our every move, his head slightly angled. I got lost in thoughts of Mia and me alone together, until I noticed Louise had stopped talking and had resumed her inspection of the dirty subway floor. I felt horrible.

We were supposed to be strategizing the bullet points we wanted Mr. Martin to cover in the interviews. Taking a page out of the Ian Schrager playbook, the Pearl had hired famed architect Phillipe Starck to revamp the place: Jennie's idea, of course. The terms of the deal demanded that Phillipe be mentioned in every bit of press on the Pearl, and much to the chagrin of Louise, Mr. Martin's ego didn't leave room for Phillipe, contract or no. Therefore, it was up to us to supply the interviewer with Phillipe's bio, as well as notes on the hotel's design.

"So does Mr. Martin know his script?" I asked. It wasn't uncommon for CEOs—or really any of Jennie's clients—to have a script beforehand. Our office brain trust would compile all possible questions. What do you think contributed to your company's fourth quarter earnings? What is your vision of the future of this industry? Is it true you're sleeping with your niece's college roommate(s)? Clients were coached and drilled and force-fed; eventually, their responses flowed off their golden tongues. They were, under no circumstances, to deviate from the script.

"He's a perfectionist. I'm not really worried. It's just a trade magazine," she said.

I paused. "Hey. Are you okay?" I asked. Louise looked up, and I noticed red around her eyes. The ice was melting.

"Yeah. Why do you ask?" she said. She was obviously lying.

"You seem a little, I don't know, *off*. Since we ran into Billy," I said. I was entering new territory and proceeded with great caution. "But, you know, I've been sleepwalking through this entire day."

"I've seen you worse," Louise said.

"What?"

"I've seen you worse," she repeated.

"It's that obvious?" I asked. I thought I looked pretty good, but apparently I was in the minority.

"I've been there. New kid, new privileges, new responsibilities. I get it." Apparently, Louise hadn't taken to me as much as I had originally thought.

"You don't think that I'm using the powder form of Jennie's version of 'Jesus Juice,' do you?" I said, trying to keep a sense of decorum. Even though I was on the subway where people were more concerned with the stench coming from the corner than they were with my discussion of cocaine, I felt it necessary to speak in code.

"I'm not judging. I want you to know that I know what it's like to be you."

"Me?"

"The bright, new shining star of the office," she said, and beamed. I couldn't help but smile too. Though the last thing I considered myself to be in the office was a *star*. An outsider was more how I felt. "But the thing about stars . . ." she continued.

"Yeah?" I said, fearing that she was going where I thought she was.

"They shine bright until they burn out completely. And there's nothing more tragic than a star beginning to fade." *So predictable.* I stared at Louise and searched for a reason to refute her. I couldn't come up with one. Then I was staring at the ground. I felt a tap on my shoulder. "This is our stop. We better get off before it's too late."

W e truly feel that the Pearl is a stark contrast to its old nightclub vernacular. Nightclubs can be spectacularly enchanting, but who wants to wake up in one?" said Mr. Todd Martin, current Pearl CEO, Jennie Weinstein client, and absolute dick. Mr. Martin was in the midst of an interview with

Roger Sotto, a big-deal reporter from Conde Nast *Traveler*. Louise and I had been sitting there for over an hour, listening as Mr. Martin answered each question as if it were a bother and the reporter a bore. Louise had told me, prior to Mr. Martin's arrival, of the Pearl shareholders' annoyance with his flippant attitude toward the media. The Pearl certainly wasn't what it used to be, and the board needed someone to bring back the well-heeled travelers of the days of yore. The board's idea was to launch a huge press campaign trumpeting Mr. Martin as the new face of luxury travel. Jennie suggested high-profile events at the hotel instead. The board acquiesced, but only after Mr. Martin was well covered in terms of his media wattage. Unfortunately, no matter how much Jennie or Louise coached Mr. Martin, he never once changed his demeanor with reporters.

The Pearl itself was nice enough. An understated and elegant lobby. Two giant retro-style lamps on both sides of the small reception desk. It was truly a boutique hotel. I heard him bullshit about the personal service, but come on, tell that to the guy who's been waiting in line for forty minutes for his "personal attention." No wonder sales were down. As he sat on the couch talking to the reporter, all I could think was *this guy has the hots for Louise*. He wasn't unattractive, but he wasn't Adam's level of handsome either. He was pale; borderline pasty. His body was flabby, and his wavy gray hair was meticulously parted to the left side. His suit was nice—a black tailored Zegna with a lilac-colored button-down. Mr. Martin might have been a lecherous man on paper, but in person he lacked any sort of sexuality. I continued to look for any awkward moments between him and Louise, any touch, or any dialogue that wasn't work-related. As far as I could tell there was nothing there.

"Ninety-six rooms on this property," Mr. Martin went on to tell the reporter. The amenities were "luxe," he said. They included: Frette linens, oversized terry-cloth bathrobes, Wi-Fi, a large flat-screen TV, a second resting near the bathtub, and around-the-clock concierge service. When asked about the design element, Mr. Martin shrugged, and said, "You'll have to get that information from my flacks; I'd prefer not to give Phillipe any additional lip service than he already has gotten." Louise quickly handed Phillipe's bio to Roger.

"If you'd like to speak with Mr. Starck separately, I'd be happy to set it up," Louise said. Mr. Martin stared at Louise long and hard, as if he'd just been betrayed. Louise was too busy fawning over Roger to notice Mr. Martin's disdain.

"Okay, I'm done here," Mr. Martin said abruptly as he stood up.

"If we need anything else, it's okay to e-mail you?" Roger asked.

"No, it's not. Please contact my press representative, Louise," he said flippantly. Mr. Martin shook Roger's hand, kissed Louise on both cheeks, looked in my direction without acknowledging my existence, and departed.

"Thanks so much, Roger," Louise said graciously.

"No problem. Our fact checker will most likely be calling you in the next week or so depending on how soon I get this in," Roger said. Roger grabbed his satchel and walked toward the door as Louise and I trailed behind. As he walked he said, "Are you guys sticking around? I heard the bar here makes a mean martini."

"I wish I could, but I have to meet my husband," Louise said. Roger looked at me.

"I totally would but I have a da"—I quickly stopped myself

before making an enormous mistake, the consequences of which I would feel for a very long time—"date with my laptop. We have an event in a week, and I need to go through the RSVP list and check it against Jennie's to make sure we don't have any crashers."

"So no drinks for either one of you? And you call yourselves respectable publicists. Pfft!" He smiled as he walked to the hotel bar.

"Are you headed out?" I asked Louise. She nodded. "I'll walk to the subway with you."

Louise and I walked down West Forty-eighth Street toward the Forty-second Street stop in silence until Louise could no longer contain her excitement. "I'm so glad you were there. You saw that, didn't you?"

"Saw what?"

"Todd"—she quickly corrected herself—"Mr. Martin holding his stare on me, right in front of you and Roger."

"Really?" I said, perplexed. Louise's face dropped. "I must have been focused on the décor and making sure Roger got the Phillipe Starck bullet points." I backtracked as fast as I could, but failed miserably.

"You had to have noticed, come on! Wait!" she said wildly. "The kiss! You saw that kiss!"

"Kiss?" I asked.

"You didn't see the kiss at the end?"

I had seen a polite good-bye; I didn't see a "kiss." But I decided to get on board with Louise's delusions.

"You know something, I did notice that. He didn't kiss Roger or me good-bye, so it couldn't be that Mr. Martin was just being polite. Hell, he didn't even say good-bye to me. You better be careful, Louise. He's on the prowl."

"I know!" she yelled a little too loud. I'd succeeded. "I'm just so glad you could see it with your own eyes. I've got to call Jennie to let her know how it went." As Louise pulled out her cell phone, I became more and more anxious, quietly wishing I had a Xanax. I felt sorry for her. And for me. For our life in this madness.

"Hi, Jennie, it's me. Interview is over and it went great. Roger got everything he needed. Oh, and Taylor was a complete pro. Mr. Martin loved him . . ." I turned around as I heard Louise talk into her cell phone. Mr. Martin didn't even know or for that matter care who the hell I was. Why was Louise suddenly singing my praises? I gathered because of my Mr. Martin validation. Whatever the case, I was floored. She continued ". . . Remind me to tell you all about Mr. Martin. Once again, you were right. He was all about me, and it was kind of creepy. Okay, I'm almost to the subway. I'll see you tomorrow. Bye!" She put her phone back in her purse, and we walked down the subway steps.

"Thank you," I said.

"Hey, us Midwesterners have to stick together, right?"

"Uh, right," I said. My distortion of what went on at the interview had clearly and unexpectedly bonded Louise and me. I wasn't sure what to make of it, but I could use another ally in the office. Besides, she was a refreshing contrast to the jadedness of Adam and the edge of Mia.

"So who's the mysterious date with?" Louise said stone-faced.

Shit.

"You caught that?" I said, slightly embarrassed.

"I'd be an idiot not to."

"It's really new, and I don't want to jinx it." What I really meant was that I valued my life, my job, and my balls, though not necessarily in that order. I knew better. "But I was serious when I said I have to check the RSVP list." I went to pull the CD that contained the Excel spreadsheet of RSVPs matched against Jennie's list as proof to show Louise, but it wasn't there. "Oh shit."

"What?"

"I left the CD at the office," I said.

"Can it wait until tomorrow?"

"I'm sorry, have you *met* Jennie?" I said. The N train roared into the station.

"That's me," Louise said. Out of nowhere Louise came over and gave me a bear hug. I froze in a combination of surprise and pain. She was squeezing so tightly.

"Have a good night," I said, breaking out of the hug. "Go have a nice dinner with that husband of yours." Louise looked at the N train which had just opened its doors to let straphangers off.

Before she turned to leave, she stopped. "I'm really glad we got to spend the day together. You're a good guy, Taylor; that's rare in this city." Never one to take a compliment, I laughed it off.

"You need to get out more."

"Maybe I do," she shouted as she ran toward her train. I waited for the doors to close and watched Louise head back to her "normal" life. She seemed happy. Even if it was in a Willy Wonka world of her imagination.

I'd walked the streets of New York several times at night. Whether it was walking Algebra or coming home after a long night of work, I took my problems to the pavement. It was therapeutic. The night spoke to me, providing me with an overwhelming sense of calm. The rush of the night crowd gave off a different kind of energy. Outside my door were people still awake, still alive, possibly even working. It made me feel safe.

But on that night, the SoHo streets were eerie, and something in the air was heavy. It was just after nine, but every shadow seemed an impending threat: something waiting to pounce. I walked up the steps to the brownstone with an overwhelming sense of dread and punched in the security code more quickly than usual. The building felt unfamiliar, as though it had been robbed—everything seemed out of place, disjointed. Louise's delusion and Mr. Martin's bad energy clearly had me on edge. I took a deep breath and reminded myself that I had passed through these doors a million times. *Man up!* I thought. I hurried up the creaky steps, quickly reached the front door, punched in the second security code, and walked inside.

The smell of stale smoke with an underlying hint of Thierry Mugler "Angel" washed over me, and I had to suppress the urge to vomit. It was like I had walked into a bathroom after someone had just taken a crap and lit a match, then sprayed perfume to cover the stench. I'd become immune to the odor during business hours. Then at least there was an ounce of air circulation. The odor wasn't going to be an aphrodisiac for my date with Mia, which was in approximately twenty minutes. I didn't bother with turning on the lights. The glow from a few computers guided me through the office.

As I neared my cloffice, I heard what sounded like file folders being shuffled and a desk phone hitting the floor. *Fuck.*

What the hell was that? Jennie had a cityful of enemies, and the last thing I needed was to be caught in her cross fire. I started to take a step toward the exit, but I simply froze. I suppose we all have an inherent fight-or-flight response, but not on that night. I did neither. I heard someone slamming a drawer shut somewhere in the back of the office—exactly where I was headed. Then momentary silence, followed by creaking. For a moment I debated sending text messages to Ethel, my mom, and Mia to tell them good-bye. *You're so fucking melodramatic.* Ethel would have thought I was pulling a prank, my mom would have burst into tears and begun to pray, and Mia would call me a pussy. Ah, the women in my life.

In a terribly delayed response, a rush of adrenaline kicked in and before my head could catch up, my legs walked determinedly toward my cloffice, closer to what surely was a masked killer hired by the Russian mobster that Jennie had fucked over last year at a vodka promotion. I tiptoed the last remaining steps.

I quietly opened the cloffice door and grabbed the CD from my desk. As I slid out the door, I heard a pounding sound followed by whispers . . . One thing I knew for sure, it wasn't my mind playing tricks on me. It was quite real. Someone was indeed in Jennie's office.

The door to Jennie's office was cracked maybe four inches. I took a step closer, drawn by stupid curiosity. I leaned against the wall outside of Jennie's door and reached in my pocket for my phone in case I needed to call 911 in an instant, and that's when I heard a different kind of noise. A moan. I pressed my left eye to the door for a closer look. That familiar blond hair, falling across that familiar face. My eyes adjusted. I saw a man lying on his back on top of Jennie's desk. Jennie was on top of him, riding him like she was in the Kentucky Derby. She grabbed a vial of coke, poured it on her hand between her thumb and her index finger, and snorted, all without stopping her ride. Then she leaned down and rammed her tongue into the man's mouth. It stayed there for a while, as though she were raping his mouth. *Oh God.* I felt like I was going to be sick. But once again, my feet were like cement cinder blocks. I couldn't believe what was happening.

I closed my eyes and took a deep breath, hoping to relax enough to get my legs moving again. My eyes closed, I exhaled softly, and felt all of my muscles relax and loosen . . . too much. My hand that was gripping the RSVP CD relaxed, and the CD dropped to the ground, bounced off the side of the door, and landed a few feet from Jennie's desk. *Holy Fuck.*

"Jesus Christ!" The man who was flat on the table had suddenly popped his head up. He couldn't get off the desk, as he was still inside of Jennie. Jennie was silent, staring at the door. "What the fuck?" the man shouted. Jennie dismounted, and the man quickly yanked up his pants. As he fumbled with his zipper, I caught a glimpse of his face, striped with lines of light. It was unreal, even for Jennie.

Oh God, I thought. *Louise.*

The adrenaline returned, late once again, and my legs were alive again. I closed the door and took off for the exit. *There's no way she saw me. Absolutely no friggin' way*, I kept repeating. *It was too dark. I could barely tell it was her.* And Billy stepped forward, blocking the light. *I'm cool. It's all good. Maybe she'll think she was being broken into? But what about the CD?* I told myself it could be explained. *The burglar was stealing her files?* I had seen it on plenty of TV shows. (It's amazing what you tell yourself in the midst of panic attack.) I reached the front door in record time, opened it, and breathed deeply. I was on the third step down when the office intercom squealed. The voice of the whore of Babylon.

"Don't even think about leaving this office, Taylor."

Shit.

 7 New Text Messages

10.

Like Sands Through the Hourglass

MY mom and Ethel were obsessed with soap operas for as long as I can remember. Before the birth of VCRs, recordable DVD players, DVRs or iTunes, Ethel used to tape-record *Days of Our Lives* for my mom while she was at work. She would sit the giant, clunky tape recorder near the TV and put the handheld microphone next to the speaker to capture the dramatic tones of the actors and actresses without benefit of the overwrought facial expressions and quick zooms. For my mom the show was an escape, a way for her to forget about my dad, to lose herself in the improbable dramatics, to witness the deep problems of other people. Ethel watched for completely different reasons: she loved to critique the actors' performances. Seated in her overstuffed hunter green corduroy La-Z-Boy, holding either a can of Diet Rite or a cherry-flavored Faygo, she would shout at the screen "What a hack!" or "Who taught you that? Carol Lynley?" Sometimes, she'd recognize a few of the day players from her waitressing days in New York. My poor mother—desperate for distraction, with the tape player blaring out the episode—was subjected to Ethel's rants, captured forever in the magnetic record. How if she hadn't met my grandpa, she too could've been on *Days*. Before long, I too, knew all about the trials and tribulations of the fictional and long-feuding Brady and DiMera families. Useless information, useful only for a *Days of Our Lives* trivia competition, polluted my mind. Answers to questions like "Who was the Salem Strangler?" "Who was John Black?" "How many times has Stefano been killed?" *Jake Kositchek. Stefano's pawn who was thought to be Marlena's dead husband, Roman. Ten times.* (In fact, Stefano had died so many times, he was nicknamed The Phoenix, because he always rose from the proverbial ashes and with every supposed death he'd come back stronger, slightly more twisted, and out for revenge.) I might have struggled in math throughout high school and college courses, but I could tell you that Carrie was not Marlena's daughter . . . she was *Anna's*(!). There was no possible way to know it then, but a daytime soap opera had, ironically, prepared me for that moment, standing just outside of JWPR, my feet stuck and my mind frozen, Jennie's voice echoing in the space. This was the biggest drama of my increasingly theatrical life. I heard footsteps.

I stood and looked around. Everything once familiar to me looked strangely unfamiliar and cold. I couldn't turn on the lights. Doing so would make this whole situation very real. The dark was the night, the time of dreams, allowing me the fantasy that there was a chance I could still wake up from the nightmare. When I had stumbled through JWPR's doors eight months ago, the last place I expected to be was standing in darkness waiting for Jennie to towel off before firing me. The situation was straight out of *Days*.

I was panicked. My head felt like it had been thrown in a

blender and put on puree. My thoughts were flooded with doomsday scenarios. Of all things, why had I forgotten that stupid CD? Goddamned Billy. I wished I'd never met him. And damn Louise too—why couldn't she have just skipped the meeting with Mr. Martin and gone to an early dinner? This would never have happened if she'd just gone to dinner! *How am I going to get out of this?* I thought about saying I didn't see a thing. I thought about crying. Running out the door and never returning also crossed my mind.

Smack.

I felt the sting on my cheek and just below my eye. It throbbed immediately.

"What the *fuck* are you doing?" Jennie shouted. There was still no sign of Billy. Shocked by the smack, I was speechless. "Answer me!" she yelled.

Thud.

I fell backward into the wall. I'd been sucker punched in the gut, and I felt like my kidneys were in my throat. I coughed ferociously. Over my cough I heard Jennie say, "Are you fucking *kidding* me, Billy?" The sucker-punch question had suddenly been answered.

"What?" Billy said. "It's not like he's gonna say anything. Besides, it's dark. You know, I thought he was a burglar." Jennie paced back and forth as Billy buttoned his shirt.

"I could fire you right now, you know," Jennie said. "You break into the office after hours and try to steal my database to sell to my competitors. It's grounds for dismissal—I'd be within my legal right to terminate your employment, Taylor. I could do that, you know?" I stood upright and leaned against the wall. I stared at her as she continued to pace. For me to address her obvious lies was futile.

Billy got in my face and screamed, "*You fucking pussy. You fucking breathe a word of this to anyone, and I'll fucking kill you. Don't fuck with me, you fucking pussy!*" His breath smelled like a mix of onion bagel and mayonnaise. I'm not sure what made me want to throw up more, the punch to my stomach or his breath.

"Billy, go home!" Jennie shouted. "We'll talk later." Billy's eyes remained fixated on me.

"You sure?"

"Yes, now go," Jennie said. Billy leaned in to kiss Jennie good-bye, and she stuck her hand in the air. "Go!" I stepped away from the door, and Billy lunged like he was about to hit me again. Of course, I flinched. He laughed as he walked into the hallway.

"Fuckin' pussy," I heard echo through the stairwell.

The lights stayed off, and Jennie and I were left alone.

"Jennie, I . . ."

"Shut up," she said. She walked back and forth in front of me. She continually ran her fingers through her hair while in the midst of her meltdown. "Did you have to be such a kiss-ass Taylor? You had to come back? Goddamn you. You really screwed up my night."

My cell phone chimed again. It was no doubt Mia wondering where the hell I was. I looked at the illuminated clock on Bob's desk. I was thirty-three minutes late. "Jennie, I can just go. Act like this never happened," I said. "I have someplace I need to be. In fact, I'm already late."

"I don't care about your schedule, Taylor! You're the one that ruined my night, you shit. I control you; I decide what your social life is, not you. You gave up that privilege months ago. If I tell you you're not leaving this office, you're not fucking leaving. I own you. And before you even think about calling someone to tell them about this, I'll fire you faster than you can punch in the numbers. Then you can be certain that I will make sure you're unemployable in not only this city, but in L.A. and Miami. You'll be back in shitsville quicker than you can say 'I quit.' I promise you this, I'll make it so bad for you here that you'll want to leave New York."

She was right. Jennie Weinstein did wield that kind of power in New York, Los Angeles, and Miami. Her tentacles were far-reaching, and they were fiercely sharp. I could have thrown it all away and quit. I could have probably still lived a nice mediocre life in Manhattan. Maybe I could have gotten a stable job at a bank. I could have lived without going traveling in New York's most-sought-after circles. I could have lived without going to the latest nightclub opening. I could have lived without all the free swag. I could have lived without the standing reservation at most of New York's trendiest eateries. I could have lived without the virtual all-access pass to the city. I could have lived without the insane hours. It wouldn't have been so bad . . .

But then again, I hadn't moved to New York to be a banker.

"Jennie," I said calmly.

"*What?*" she shouted.

"Fuck you." I said the words without emotion. I was calm, yet firm. I didn't say the words in passing or under my breath. I said them *to* her. Jennie stopped in the midst of pacing and cocked her head.

"What did you just say to me?"

"You heard me. Fuck you, Jennie. Quit your bitching about how this is going to affect you and your life. Who cares, Jennie? I certainly don't." One thing I neglected to mention about

Ethel and my mom's *Days* obsession: Their favorite moments were the wars of words, the good old-fashioned knock-down of verbiage. It ultimately became my favorite thing to watch too. I was on the stage now, and I was going to shine.

"Get out. You're fired."

I took a few steps and walked around her in a circle. It was as if someone else had possessed my body.

"You're not going to fire me," I said coolly.

"You certainly haven't gotten any smarter since you started working here," she said. I stopped directly in front of her and held my face just inches from her nose. If a stranger had walked in, it would have looked as though we were about to kiss.

"Let's face it. No matter how much you want to spin this, you can't. Louise's husband can't afford a nasty divorce, and you can't afford the bad press." Jennie didn't flinch.

"Really? That's it?" she said. "I honestly hope you have something better than that. If that's all you got, you're so screwed." The blue night glow washed over her face, which was clenched so tight she looked as though a thousand Botox needles had hit her at once. Her eyes, on the other hand, jutted out of her head and danced back and forth, ablaze with adrenaline. I entered brand-new territory. I was going head-to-head with Jennie Weinstein.

I reached into my pocket, pulled out my BlackBerry, and held it up. "I do," I said. "You gotta love technology. Did you know that the cameras on these things are up to ten megapixels now? Practically magazine-quality. Blog-quality, for sure."

Jennie leaned back on her heel, slightly taken aback.

"What are you going to do?" she taunted.

"Do you really want to take the chance to find out?" I

scrolled down my BlackBerry and silently punched in numbers as Jennie looked on. I took a few extra seconds to pique
her curiosity.

"Am I supposed to be scared?"

"Oh, I don't know. You're Jennie Weinstein. You don't get
scared." I glanced back down at my BlackBerry and punched
an additional number.

"Okay, I'll bite," she said. "What are you doing?"

"I just attached the video of you and supergut. And composed an e-mail to Louise, Page Six, and the rest of our staff.
All I have to do is hit SEND."

Silence. It was dark, but I think the corners of Jennie
Weinstein's filthy mouth may have quivered.

"What is it that you want?" she asked quietly. "Money?
Girls?" She leaned against Bob's desk.

"More money would be nice, but that's not what I want.
Girls? *You* are going to help *me* with a date? No offense, but
after seeing your standards, no thanks." Jennie took a cigarette
out of her purse. The fire from the match momentarily lit the
room, and I caught a glimpse of her eyes—worry? She took a
deep drag and blew the smoke in my face. The ashes from her
cigarette fell on my shoes.

"Just get to it already," she said, stoically.

"I want to do the job I was hired to do."

"What?"

"No more Diet-Coke-and-cigarette runs at two in the morning. No more drug deals. No more bullshit errands. I want to
work on accounts." Jennie took a deep breath and was about
to say something, but I continued. "*Real* accounts."

Jennie stood up and took another drag. "Can I say something?"

"Nothing's stopped you before," I said. Jennie paced the floor again as she intermittently sucked on her cig.

"I'm about to give you some very sound advice that I want you to listen to very carefully, and not interrupt me with your quips." I nodded and stood still and straight.

"Get out," she said calmly. I looked at the doorknob and back at her. "Not literally this second, you moron." I took what probably was my fortieth deep breath of the night and waited for Jennie to continue. "This is a bad business. Publicists rank about as high up on the sleaze scale as lawyers. It's often dehumanizing, mean-spirited, and downright ugly." I couldn't help but let out a smug laugh.

"I learned that my first eighteen seconds in this office."

Jennie stared at me. I could feel her anger even in the darkness. I was ready for laser beams to shoot out of her eyes and engulf me at any moment.

"It's hard to reconcile what we do, and who we are sometimes. Let's face it, Taylor, you're not cut out for this. So I suggest you think long and hard about whether or not you really want to work *here* and for *me*." I inched toward the door and grabbed the doorknob with finality. Maybe Jennie was right, maybe I wasn't cut out for this. I don't know how I had stomached even a fraction of what I'd seen.

"You know something? You're right." I walked over to Jennie and—I still do not know why—I hugged her. I squeezed her tight. She, on the other hand, didn't return the favor. "Thank you," I said as I returned to the door. "Oh, Jennie?"

"Yeah," she said softly.

"Please don't ever mistake my kindness for stupidity."

"What?"

"*Boston Legal?*"

"Have you been into my pills?"

"James Spader, I think. Delivered that same speech on *Boston Legal*, except he was talking about lawyers and delivered the lines much better than you." Jennie was speechless. I finally had the upper hand. "So, I will see you tomorrow. I look forward to working on real accounts. Don't even try to screw around and give me some of your bullshit clients, Jennie, or I will burn you." Jennie remained silent. I could almost see the PowerPoint presentation of potential solutions going through her mind. She had none. Before I could second-guess myself, I turned for the door.

"See you tomorrow." I smiled as I opened the door. Jennie stayed silent, and I quickly shut the door behind me, sprinted down the stairs, and leapt into the street. I let out a scream as if I'd just completed the New York City Marathon, a barbaric yap over the rooftops of the city, packed with emotions. Relief, anticipation, ambition, success. I pulled out my BlackBerry again: seven text messages. I was over an hour and fifteen minutes late.

Hoping she was still in the city, I texted Mia. Thankfully, she was still around; having giving up on dinner thirty minutes before, she had been walking around Chelsea. I asked her to meet me at the Starbucks on Sixteenth and Eighth Avenue. She agreed, and I began to run; my legs, like iron a few moments before, carried me like wheels across the cobblestone.

Mia sat at the table, arms crossed. She tugged on her hair and stared out the glass window. She wore tight jeans and a low, sexy V-necked black shirt with a simple pair of diamond-studded earrings. Next to her feet sat the Balenciaga bag that I'd bought for her. I watched her for a moment, watching my breath in the air, then slipped into the coffee shop.

"Hey," I said nervously.

"Hey," she replied. She was pouting, and rightfully so. I pulled out the chair and raised my eyebrows to ask permission to sit down. She nodded.

"I am so sorry. That interview with Mr. Martin ran late, then the reporter wanted to have a drink, and he just kept talking and talking—"

"Why didn't you just tell him you had to go?" she said in an irritated staccato.

"I tried . . . but I figured I needed to have another contact in my Rolodex anyway. Ninety percent of this business is who you know, so I thought it was a good idea to hang out with the guy for a while. *Please* don't be pissed."

"I texted you."

"I know you did, and I didn't get service in the hotel bar. But the minute I got to the lobby, I texted you back." She sat back in her chair and stared at me long and hard. Did she know this was all bullshit?

"Fine," she said. "Next time, call me to tell me you're going to be late. I felt like an idiot waiting at that restaurant."

"I will, and again I'm so sorry," I pleaded. "Can I buy you a cappuccino?"

"No, but you can give me a hug," she said.

I stood up from my chair and walked around to the other side of the table. She stood up and I squeezed her tight. My arm was shaking slightly—I was coming down from the adrenaline high, and I desperately wanted to be honest. I wanted to tell her about what had happened with Jennie and Billy. I wanted to tell her about Louise. I wanted to tell her how I'd blackmailed Jennie into actually giving me real work. There was just so much I wanted to say . . . but I said none of it. Something had shifted inside of me. The old me had died. But in true soap-opera fashion, I'd been reborn.

This phoenix had risen from the ashes, and was bolder, tougher, and more ruthless.

Sandy Says

daily gossip served fresh & hot.

On the Scene...

The gold will be flying tonight at Donatella's VVIP party at her Upper East Side Townhouse. I'm expecting the usual suspects like Naomi, Elton, and Christina but let's hope the Beckham's make a cameo to shake things up a bit. And of course, your very own diva of dish will be on hand. Speaking of dish have I got some for YOU.

Click HERE to read all about it.

Permalink /432 Comments (RSS)>

On the Scene...

11.

It's Good to Be (Assistant to) the King

I stood behind Jennie, watching her socialize with the global elite. Donatella Versace, or "Donna V" as I'd call her in private with Mia, was in town. She was hosting a party in her East Side town house that once belonged to her brother, Gianni. Whereas the name Versace is synonymous with bold and dramatic colors, their New York manse was decidedly pared down. It had a certain bored sophistication to it; perhaps that was the ironic intent. The room was filled with a parade of bold-face names. I knew this because Jennie had me take several laps around the party and report back to her. Diane von Fürstenberg and Barry Diller, Calvin Klein, artist Ross Bleckner, Donna Karan, Naomi Campbell, Anna Wintour, Tom Ford, Annie Leibovitz, Liz Smith, and that was just in the great room. I made it a point to pay close attention to the nuances of each and every one of them—the way they held glasses or how they turned their Baume et Mercier watches facedown or how loudly they laughed. I could barter with the gossip rags later with the information. I was floored by the tone of the party; it was decidedly light and shockingly casual. Andre Leon Talley sat in a chair and looked like a king—or queen—on his throne, as Charlize Theron and Stuart Townsend laughed at fantastically cutting comments that Andre effortlessly dispensed.

I shadowed Jennie for most of the night, watching her float in and out of conversations ranging from where to go for sushi while vacationing on the Amalfi coast to why Diana Vreeland was the premier fashion editor of the century. To my surprise and delight, Jennie brought me into conversations when an opening presented itself. However, I was still, well . . . *me*, and it didn't always go as smoothly as either Jennie or I would have liked. Jennie introduced me to Meghan Dutton, a thirty-something woman who was well dressed and terribly attractive.

"Meghan," Jennie said, air-kissing the woman in front of me. After they finished exchanging pleasantries, Jennie turned to me and said, "This is Meghan Dutton, a genius editor over at *Elle*. This is Taylor Green, he's the new Heather." I hated that.

"What happened to the old Heather?"

"Who?"

"Ouch. That bad, huh?" Meghan gasped. "Where is she now?"

"Oh, who knows—reading porn to the blind in Africa? I don't care." Meghan inspected my wardrobe, which Mia had spent hours trying to put together. I'd "borrowed" some threads from the swag closet, but unfortunately I didn't have time to get anything tailored, so my pants were loose in places they shouldn't be and my shirt was tight in places I didn't want it to be. You can take the boy out of the cornfields . . .

"Hello, Taylor, Jennie's sartorially challenged assistant," Meghan said with a bit of affectation.

"Okay, I'm not quite sure what that means, but challenged

doesn't sound so good, but at any rate—hey." Jennie rolled her eyes, a clear indication that I needed to step up my game. Jennie had said previously if I were going to work on real accounts, I needed to have real contacts . . . of my own. Sure, I'd made friends with some of the reporters at the rags, but if I wanted to pitch features, I'd have to get to know the writers. Not quite as simple.

"You guys should talk; you both love animals," Jennie said in an effort to move things along. Huh? That was her idea of a smooth transition? I don't know who was more surprised at that revelation, Meghan or me. Sure I had a great dog in Algebra, but "animal lover" implied much more.

"Well, I don't know about that." I smiled as I looked at Jennie. "I love dogs. I've pretty much had dogs all my life. Does that make me an animal lover?" I asked rhetorically. Meghan looked at Jennie, then back at me. "No, I'm not so sure you can call me that . . ." Jennie saw a passing waiter and followed him.

"Excuse me, are those crab cakes?" I heard her ask.

I continued to explain to Meghan where I drew the line as an "animal lover." "In fact, I hate cats. I think they're creepy. They're like Satan's handmaidens or something." I saw Jennie out of the corner of my eye; she chewed on her crab cake and looked around the room, strategizing who to network with next. "So what kind of animals do you like?"

"I have cats." *Shit.*

"Yeah, but I bet you're not one of those crazy cat ladies who is covered with cat hair when she leaves the house, and has *Cathy* comic strips on her fridge," I said, digging out of the hole.

"Four of them," Meghan said and smirked. *Shit. Shit.*

"Of course you do. There's a reason I typically don't talk."

"No, it's fine," Meghan said. Thankfully, Jennie was too caught up stuffing her face to notice my foul.

"I'm sorry. I didn't mean anything by it."

"Relax," she said. "I really am the crazy cat lady you always heard your friends talking about at brunch," she said. "I just dress much, much better. Have a good evening, Mr. Green." Jennie may have given me entree into this nouveau world, but, once I was in, I clearly had a lot to learn.

Over the previous month Jennie had kept to her word to bring me into the fold. She brought me to business meetings, I wrote dozens of press releases and gossip items, and I even pitched her clients to a publication other than *Big Apple Parent*. I was surprised how much she included me. I know she did it because of what happened, but there was a part of me that believed that, even though she was furious that I'd turned the tables on her, she liked that I didn't want to destroy her, that I wanted to *learn* from her. Her ego was capable of spinning even herself.

After my disastrous chat with Meghan, I found Jennie in the midst of a conversation with Tobias Walden, a writer for *Time*. Tobias explained he'd been working on an extensive book proposal on sex and politics in Bangladesh. *Personally, I'd rather stick needles in my eyes*, I thought.

"That's fascinating," I heard Jennie say. *It is?* I inched closer. *How will she spin this one?*

"There's so much corruption, so much heartache in Bangladesh. I know I can shine a spotlight on it," said Tobias. How could he say that with a straight face? The people of Bangladesh are, by most accounts, good people, and certainly, like every government, there is corruption (even a shocking sex scandal here and there), but this was coming from a writer whose previous piece for the magazine had been a story on Lindsay Lohan.

"Oh my God. I have the best idea. You should totally pitch this as a documentary while you're writing the book. They can film you in Bangladesh covering the government corruption, and you can write when you're not filming. It could be a package deal," Jennie said. Total bullshit.

"Yeah, I'm not sure I really want to *go* to Bangladesh," he said sheepishly. *So you want to write a book on Bangladesh, but don't want to go there. Priceless.*

"You'll go for a week. Ten days, tops," Jennie said. "Oh, and I'm working with Apple. I'll get you a free laptop to write the book and edit the documentary! Maybe they'll even underwrite your expenses?" Suddenly, I knew what Jennie's game was. "I just thought of something. We just started repping this high electronics boutique—like a fancier Sharper Image—I'll get you a free HD video camera! There you go; your whole trip is done!"

"You could do that?" Tobias asked excitedly.

"Yeah, Apple is my client, and they have a new series of laptops coming out, and I'm allowed to give a select number of them out to VVIPs," she explained. It was all part of the seduction in which Jennie had become a master. On the way to meet a reporter one afternoon, Jennie told me, "Most journalists are neither rich nor cool, so to be invited to a dinner party with an A-list star and a rock star they've idolized since childhood—you'll get them every time. In its basic form, it's seduction. You're *seducing* them." I was Daniel to her Mr. Miyagi. I *had* to learn more.

"But what if you can't get them invited to a dinner party or to meet their favorite aging rock star?" I asked. "Or if they could care less about either?"

"Find the rock star or actress in their own life. Meaning, through your conversation find out what really gets them charged up, and go through your mental Rolodex and figure out how you can give it to them." She so enjoyed being the teacher. "They'll be too excited and caught up in the moment to catch on, and before your new best reporter friend realizes it, they'll owe you."

I was skeptical. Editors knew the game; there was no way they couldn't see the scam. Jennie explained that of course they knew the gig, but if you waved the right thing in front of them, they'd sell their mothers on Fourteenth Street.

As I watched Jennie work Tobias, I was disappointed that I didn't pick up on this immediately. She told me that the more she bombarded her editors with freebies, the easier it became to get a mention for her client. As the gifts continued and got progressively bigger and better, the mentions turned into items and the items into features. Jennie essentially summed up what, in her eyes, was the crux of the relationship between publicist and reporter.

"I'm not sure. *Time* has strict rules about that sort of thing," Tobias said.

"Well, I'm not going to force the ultrasleek and stylish, seventeen-inch screen, titanium laptop on you. It's not *my* responsibility to protect the reputation of *Time Magazine*. It's *Time Magazine*'s job." *Damn, she is good.* Tobias stood in silence, deep in thought. "At any rate, I see Kate Spade over there, and I need to talk to her about an event we're doing together." As Jennie was about to step away, Tobias snapped out of his daze.

"Jennie, wait." Jennie stopped and turned on her heel. "I'm sure we could figure something out, right? Maybe you could come to my girlfriend Janice's birthday party and give her a gift? She's not my wife, nor is she related." Something told me Janice would never see those "presents."

"E-mail me the details," Jennie said, as she walked into a group that included Kate Spade and Chloe Sevigny. I stayed put. Way too much estrogen in that cluster.

I walked around the town house, looking at the magnificent pieces of art. On one of the bookshelves, next to the book *D.V.* by Diana Vreeland, sat a family portrait. Instantly, I was home. Since I began at JWPR, my conversations with Ethel had greatly diminished. I couldn't remember the last time I'd spoken to my mom. I barely saw Lauren and Allison, except to pass them in the elevator and make plans, which I would later inevitably cancel. Once I began working directly under Jennie, the late hours kept me from ever seeing my favorite lesbian duo. As I stared at the picture, I wondered if my sacrifice was temporary or . . . or if this would be my life. Mia was the only relationship I had outside of work, and that was, well, *tangled.*

"Well, you've moved up in the world," I heard a familiar female voice say from behind me. I turned around to see Sandy Brin looking ethereally casual in a persimmon bohemian-style shirt and loose-fitting distressed jeans. Her red hair was pulled back, allowing just a few strands of hair to frame her face. It suited her, and she blended right in among the models and the people who loved them.

"Yes, I'm not wearing my high heels. Nor am I standing watch in a bathroom stall," I said, and smiled. "It's nice to see you again," I said as I kissed her cheek.

"You as well," she said, looking around the room. Her hippie style was a welcome contrast to her acidic blog. I still found her unbelievably sexy. "Anything good yet?"

"Well . . . 'C' has made about seven trips to the bathroom in the last forty minutes, and 'J''s husband has been hitting on that cater-waiter over there. He slipped him a Benjamin, and I'm sure it wasn't because he liked the crostini. Which, by the way, is stale." Another tip I learned from Jennie was when giving bits of juice in public, never mention full names, because you just never know who's listening. It wasn't so much that she cared about spreading gossip, it was more about her wanting to get the most mileage from the information that had been so carefully garnered.

"Do you want a job?" Sandy asked.

"It probably pays a helluva lot more than mine. How's the column?"

"It practically writes itself with this industry." That was the understatement of the century.

"Wow. Somebody's gotten a bit jaded since our last encounter," I teased. I had to get some sort of credit for improving on my conversation skills from earlier, but Jennie was still huddled in the corner.

"What? And you don't get bored pitching the latest energy drink or celebrity skin-care line?"

"Ironically, I don't. I love what I do. I'm helping to shape pop culture," I said. And at that moment, I honestly believed it.

"So you're the one I should blame?" she teased. "Sorry, I'm just having one of those moments of guilt for not writing a cover story in a magazine like *New York*."

"Why guilt?" I asked.

"Two words," she said. "Jewish mother." We both laughed. "But I'll find my feature one day and make my mama proud," she said, inserting a Southern accent for effect.

"Or the feature will find you."

"Don't take this the wrong way, but how did you get invited to this?" she asked.

"Of course not. I was actually wondering the same about you." She was sweet, but oh so blunt. "Jennie brought me as her guest," I said.

"Are you sleeping with her? That's an office duty I thought only Adam performed to go to parties like this." Great, I'd just gone from being the new Heather to the new Adam. I wasn't sure which comparison was worse: someone who walked around with a stick up her ass or someone who probably *had* a stick up his ass while banging the boss.

"Ha! I'd rather stick needles in my eyes," I played. It was all I could do to keep from dry heaving. Seeing Jennie riding Billy was already burned into my brain, I couldn't handle another grotesque visual. Sandy's smile quickly faded.

"Oh my God." Her tone had drastically changed.

"What?" I said as if I didn't know what was about to come out of her mouth.

"You've got something on her, don't you?"

"Did the caterer put crack in these drinks? No, I don't have anything on Jennie." How could she know that? Of course she knew. She was one of the most feared gossips around. She made Perez Hilton look about as evil as Larry King. It was her job to read people.

"I think you're lying," she said with a slight hint of flirtation. "It only makes sense. Why else would Jennie bring her newest employee to a party like this when the rest of the staff would lie, cheat, and steal to be here? No, you're either doing her, or you're blackmailing her. I'm sure of it."

"Come on, Sandy: lie, cheat, and steal? I work at a PR firm! That's par for the course," I said with a laugh, trying to lighten the tone. Jennie was heading in our direction.

"Sandy, hi!" Jennie said.

"Hey you!" Sandy said, lips firmly planted on Jennie's butt.

"How did you get in here?" Jennie asked, cutting right to the chase. "Are you someone's plus one?"

"I am actually Brian Koppelman's date." Jennie laughed. "Why's that funny?" Sandy asked.

"Nothing. His mom was my Public Health teacher at Nightingale for, like, a minute. He used to wait outside the school." Jennie, of course, had been thrown out of the prestigious Nightingale School.

"And? Why do I get the feeling there's much more to the story?"

"And that's all I'm going to say," Jennie snipped. Jennie told me later in the car that they nicknamed Brian "the straw" because his endowment was about as thick as a McDonald's straw. After that, I took up drinking vanilla McShakes with a spoon.

"We need to jet," Jennie said as she turned her back on Sandy.

"Okay, what's up?" I asked quietly.

Jennie looked over her shoulder to make sure Sandy was unable to hear. "Tom Ford is having an after-party at Bungalow 8." Even I was surprised that a party could get even more exclusive than the one I was presently attending. Apparently, there was an upper echelon even among the superelite.

"Cool. Let's get out of here," I said.

"I'm off to say my good-byes. I'll meet you in the foyer in exactly three minutes." Jennie turned and nodded at Sandy as she continued on her way.

"It must be good," Sandy said.

"What?"

"The dirt you have on her." I laughed Sandy's accusations off.

"That's cute. It really is. I have to get out of here," I said.

"Tom Ford. Bungalow 8. I heard."

"Wow, you've got some radar ears on you," I said. "I'll speak to you soon?"

"I hope so," she said. I kissed her on the cheek and began to walk away. "Taylor," she called.

"Yeah?"

"If you ever want to talk . . ."

"Got it."

"You know, I think I finally found my *New York* cover story."

"Good luck with that," I said as I walked away, her gaze pressed into the back of my misfitted shirt.

I'd passed the neon NO VACANCY sign outside of Bungalow 8 hundreds of times. The glowing warning was always on point: every time I'd approached the doorman, I had never been granted entry—even after I started working at JWPR. This sidewalk was my walk of shame. Bungalow 8 was an habitué for the superhip or the superrich that bought their way inside. I was neither, and if ever I began to feel too good about myself, Mia would insist we walk by Bungalow 8, where I would be instantly humbled. Mia watched the doorman as though he were a master artist painting a brilliant landscape. "God, he's so good," she'd say. "Did you see the way he looked her in the eye and said 'not a chance' without blinking? It's astounding. He has no fear!" It wasn't the kind of place you went to hang out casually; it was where you took someone to impress them. Anyone who didn't know the doorman or hold a hard-fought, high-bought reservation (only granted if you were among the aforementioned superhip or superrich) was wasting their time. I'd seen girls considered to be perfect tens outside of New York plan their whole evenings around going to Bungalow, stand outside for five hours, be shown not so affectionately to the curb, and go home with nothing to show for their efforts but sore feet. There were simply some doors that would never open.

Or so I'd thought.

When Jennie and I arrived at the velvet ropes, I expected them immediately to part. But they didn't. Jennie stared at the doorman intensely.

"Jennie Weinstein," she said flatly. The doorman looked Jennie over from head to toe, inspecting each article of clothing down to her jewelry.

"I know," the doorman said. The rope didn't move.

"Amy Sacco is a friend." This was certainly a new side of Jennie I'd never seen—one that lacked self-confidence. I stood silently behind her, so as not to add any additional pressure. The two of them stared each other down for what seemed like hours. In the interim Demi Moore and Drew Barrymore were let in ahead of us. It felt like I was about to be let into a secret club, where the titans of entertainment met nightly to devise their master plan to shape the world in their likenesses. The stare-down continued, and Jennie never broke. She looked calm. Collected. But I knew she wasn't. She had a habit of rubbing her pointer finger against her thumb when she was nervous or unsure. It was a slight tell, but I noticed it, and at that moment, she was working on calluses. We waited in silence.

If I were to tell this story to my friends in the Midwest, they would laugh in my face. "It's just a club, who the hell cares?" they'd say. "Why is it so important?" The snide looks of stupidity and judgment would always follow. To them, it sounds like the pinnacle of upscale pretension. I've turned, they suppose, into one of *those* people. They fail to realize that while Bungalow 8 may be simply a small lounge, it is for all intents and purposes the new boardroom. It's where multimillion-dollar deals happen. It's where people get offered jobs, it's where new relationships develop, and, on most nights, it's a breeding ground for some of the most creative people, not only in New York, but in the world. Far more is accomplished over apple martinis at Bungalow 8 than over bagels in the boardroom. To my Midwestern counterparts I need only say: It's New York's version of the golf course.

Getting into the Bungalow was certainly not going to be a battle of intellectual showmanship or even money for that matter. I waited with curious restraint. A few tense minutes later, Amy Sacco, the club's gorgeous owner, arrived.

"Jennie, what are you doing out here?" Amy said, kissing Jennie's cheek. Jennie never took her eyes off the doorman.

"Waiting to have a drink," she said chillily. Amy snapped to attention and immediately opened the ropes and Jennie stepped inside the box and I jumped in behind her. I felt like I was watching the third act of a really great play, the part in which all was about to be revealed. The drama was deliciously intriguing. Amy walked inside, and Jennie stared at the doorman, only a few inches from his face. She reached out her left hand and in one swift motion cupped the man's nuts in her hand. I'm not sure whose gasp was more audible, mine or his. She looked down at his groin, then fixated on his eyes.

"I expected them to be much bigger with the shit you just pulled," she said dismissively. I stood stupefied. "Next time you see this face, you make damn sure you open the rope the second you see me. We good here?" The doorman nodded. Jennie revealed a hint of a smirk, betraying her sheer delight in the situation. She unwrapped her fingers and slung her purse around her shoulder and walked inside. I didn't bother to look at the doorman. He'd suffered enough.

I walked through the door and literally trembled. After so much rejection, I'd once again fought my way to the next level—I could hear the triumphant PlayStation music. I was one step closer to the Dragon.

Euro house music pumped through the speakers as I walked down the narrow path separating the banquettes. I was taking mental snapshots of the place, the people. Red velvet and beigeish embroidered armchairs. *Click.* Four- to five-foot-tall palm trees reaching up, kissing the ceiling (palm trees in New York?). *Flash.* A large display of photo murals of old pool clubs. *Click.* Black-and-white-striped banquettes. *Flash.* Tiny lounge (is this all there is?). *Click.* Lots of beautiful people. *Click, flash.* Correction, lots and lots and lots of beautiful people. *Click flash click flash click flash.*

I followed Jennie to the bar and offered to buy her a drink since she had just gotten me into New York's most exclusive lounge. "I'll take a glass of champagne," she said.

"Two," I said to the bartender. He quickly returned and

asked for forty-four dollars. That was the price of my last meal with Mia. I begrudgingly handed him my credit card and tried to think of a way to bill this back later.

"Champagne?" I asked. "I thought you only drank vodka because you don't like the taste of alcohol, and with the vodka you can shoot it."

"I do," she said as she set the glass of champagne on a waiter's tray as he passed by. "I just wanted to see you buy it for me."

I wanted to throw my champagne in her face. But the damn flute had cost $22.

"So this place is pretty intense," I said, trying to move forward.

"It's all right," she said dismissively. "The décor is a bit gauche for me. You know it's modeled after a bungalow at the Beverly Hills Hotel, don't you?"

"Oh yeah, I could tell when I walked in." I'd never been to L.A., let alone the Beverly Hills Hotel. New York was the farthest I'd been away from home.

"There's Damian McNally, the VP of AI."

"They make those really expensive cell phones, right?" Jennie didn't bother to answer me and walked toward a large banquette crammed with people. I quickly followed. Jennie hugged Damian. He was naturally photogenic, of course, and the two of them quickly sat down while I tried to squeeze my way into their table past the obvious snide stares.

An hour later Park Avenue princesses, Euro boys, and more than a few celebrities had packed the place. There were more people dancing on top of the banquette tables than on the floor. I was sandwiched between Jennie and Damian, and as they talked business, I drank. I tried to follow the conversation as best as I could, but between the music and the drinks I was having one hell of a time. The glitterazzi swayed to the music, and the glamazons around me had heard rumblings that David Beckham had arrived. They were on the prowl and paid little to no attention to me. This scene reminded me more or less of my high-school days, and my banquette felt like Homecoming Court. Jennie and Damian, of course, were king and queen.

As I sat and looked around the room I realized that, while the secrets of the universe might not have opened up once I entered Bungalow 8, something inside of me had. I'd only read about this kind of exclusivity in the pages of the entertainment weeklies, but I'd become a part of it. I felt like I had been lying dormant. I pondered this for a long moment, until I felt an elbow jut into my rib.

"Are you going to be sick? Because if you are, leave now. I can't deal with that!" Jennie shouted in my ear over the music.

"No, I'm fine. Better than fine, actually!"

Jennie dug through her purse, and said into my ear. "I need you to block me."

"What?"

"Lean forward! The last thing I need is for Amy Sacco or any of her staff to see this!" she said. I leaned forward and from my peripheral I saw Jennie do a bump of coke in the middle of the room. No one noticed. Everyone else was either too drunk or high. I saw Jennie hand her vial to Damian, who happily obliged.

"You want?" Jennie offered. "It will balance out the drinks."

Perhaps it was the alcohol, or the atmosphere. Possibly, it was even her. But I quickly nodded. I'd never touched cocaine in my life. I leaned behind Jennie and placed a tiny amount of

white powder at the base of my thumb and snorted. I immediately felt a surge and a slight burn through my nostrils, and
within seconds the back of my throat felt numb. It was the famous "drip" I'd heard Adam talk about. I felt wide-awake and
acutely alert.

"All right, I'm out of here. Hang out with Damian, lock this
account up," Jennie said as she grabbed her purse and stood up.

"You're leaving?" I was terrified. At least with Jennie there
I felt somewhat protected, but without her in that arena, I felt
incredibly vulnerable.

"I'll see you tomorrow."

"Where are you going?" I asked incredulously.

"Don't." Jennie pushed her way through the crowd as I felt
the blood drain out of my face. I sat back down and smiled at
Damian. Thankfully, he returned the favor.

"Damian, right?" I asked as I suddenly felt my teeth gnash-
ing into each other. So this is what it was like to have lockjaw.
I pulled out a piece of gum from my pocket in an effort to be
more discreet.

"Yeah, what's your name again?"

"Taylor," I said with a smile.

"Let's have some fun, Taylor," he said, pouring two shots of
Stoli.

"Sweet." I looked down at my watch and it was almost one.
Not bad.

I'm not sure where exactly the time went, but somewhere
between the drinks and the bumps I met people . . . a lot of
people. I couldn't remember all the names, but I recognized
the faces from the party pages of *Hamptons* and *Gotham*.

"This is Taylor, Jennie Weinstein's new assistant," I heard
Damian say to a sexy black woman with a Mohawk—as

downtown as you could get. I went to shake her hand, which she brushed off in favor of a kiss on the cheek.

"I'm Genevieve." She held onto my forearm. "Jennie rocks this town, she's made New York fun again. Whatever you need, you let me know." She handed me her business card, and I saw the words "Gucci" and "vice president." That was enough for me.

"Thanks! You're so sweet."

"She's not only sweet, but she's incredibly sexy," Damian shouted over the music. The pair shared a passionate kiss less than two inches from my mouth. She was so close I could smell her mint Listerine breath strips.

They stopped kissing and Genevieve turned to me, "E-mail me your home address, and I'll send you a care package." A Gucci care package? The only gift packages I'd ever received were from Ethel and my mom; they sent dish towels and homemade chocolate-chip cookies.

"Bye, boys," Genevieve said as she was pulled away by an incredibly pale woman with bright red lipstick.

"Damn! This shit is crazy!" I said to Damain. "Why is everyone being so nice to me?"

"They figure you must be somebody if you got in here. And they know you're Jennie's new right hand."

"Yeah, but . . ." I tried interrupting.

"Relax, it's not just Jennie; these people know that today's assistant is tomorrow's vice president." He was right, but it still felt too new to appreciate.

"You're hot, Taylor." That was unexpected.

"Thanks, man," I said. I felt like it was my fraternity initiation all over again and that my first eight months was Jennie's version of "hell week." Finally, *finally*, I was able to enjoy the benefits of what the job had to offer. I felt my phone vibrating in my front pocket. Mia.

"Hey, sexy!" The music was too loud. The crowd sang in unison to Pink Martini's "Sympathique." "Hello? Mia?" The revelers chanted "*Je ne veux pas travallier*" along to the French beats, which couldn't have been more appropriate for that crew. "Babe, if you can hear me, I'll call you when I get home. I can't hear a thing in here." I hung up the phone and put it back in my pocket. When I lifted my head Damian had his hand out for me to take another bump. I knew I shouldn't. But.

To say the next few hours were a blur is an understatement. I couldn't be certain, but I vaguely remember exchanging cell numbers with Matthew McConaughey and telling him that he needed a better publicist and that I was that guy. Courage in liquid and powder form. There were so many introductions, and after knowing where I worked—thanks to Damian—their sycophancy reached a new stratosphere. I was still feeling my buzz, when Damian asked if I'd go to the bathroom with him. When I shot him a strange look, he motioned like he was doing another bump of coke.

"Too many work people here now," he said. I nodded and walked through the packed lounge, and bumped into people left and right as I followed him into a private bathroom. I stood at the mirror and washed my hands. I couldn't look at myself. I was too fucked-up. If I did, I'd feel the guilt for doing the coke. Damian stood at the urinal parallel to me.

"Yo, did you see that Gillian girl? That ass! It's out of control," he said.

"She's so hot." I felt every drop of hot water touch my hands. The water was scalding but felt strangely good.

"You're pretty hot too," he said.

"Ha! Thanks, man."

"You look like you work out."

"Yeah, I try to when I'm not working," I said, trying to deflect the awkwardness.

"Yo, I'm not gay. I just fuck around sometimes when I get fucked-up." *Okay, this is definitely a new experience.* "You?"

"No; I got a girl. I'm not really into dudes, but that's cool if you are, man, I won't say a word. I'm not looking to date anyone else." I could barely hear myself.

"I'm not looking to date either, I just want to fuck," he said. I took a deep breath and waited for him to finish. He could see my uneasiness. "Fine, if you're a prude like Adam, I'm sure we can work something out," he said. *Adam? He tried this on Adam too? Did Jennie set me up for this?*

"Huh?" I said, surprised.

"Look, I'll be honest with you. I know that if you signed up AI you'd be bringing in almost two hundred grand a year to Jennie. You'd be the fuckin' hero of that office. You show me a little, and you've got our account," he said. *You've got to be kidding.*

"Now? Here?" I said in horror.

"Why not?" he pushed. He continued standing at the urinal, and my hands were turning bright pink from the burning water.

"But someone would walk in—"

"It's a private bathroom with a lock," he answered quickly.

Any person outside of the situation would be screaming, "What the fuck are you doing? Just walk away! Fuck the job!" And normally I would have agreed.

But I wasn't ready to give up on everything I had been working so hard to get just because some high horny guy wanted a few peeks at my body. Walking away wasn't an option. And I was wasted.

I began to sweat. "Yo, sorry, man, this isn't really my scene." And as I turned to say good-bye, I looked down and noticed that Damian wasn't peeing at the stall. He was masturbating, and he took a step back to show me. He took a few steps and stood in front of me.

"Go ahead," he ordered. "Take it off."

I took a big gulp and closed my eyes and began feeling the tiny buttons on my Ralph Lauren shirt. With every button I unhinged I imagined my house in the Hamptons, or my new Benz convertible, anything besides what was actually happening in front of me. I couldn't process it. I stared at the pictures on the bathroom wall, trying not to look down at Damian panting in front of me.

He reached for me. "No fucking touching!" I snapped. He quickly recoiled like a scolded child.

My face became flushed. My cheeks became hot and prickly and my eyes began to burn. I wanted to cry. Instead, I bit my bottom lip harder than I ever had. I could feel the blood drip down my throat as I stood in the cold bathroom and showed him my pale skin.

"Fuck, you have a sweet body," he said, moaning.

I couldn't stand it. I was drenched in sweat. I could hear him jerking off not more than two feet from me, and I couldn't bear to look at him. I caught a glance of his pasty skin in the reflection of the mirror, and I gagged.

The intensity increased as the moaning got louder. I could hear Dido playing outside the door. I thought to myself that I could never listen to Dido again.

I stared at the cracks in the ceiling for what seemed like hours. I wished I was one of those cracks on the ceiling, slipping from this room to the next, and out and out onto the street and through the city to the river, escaping. Finally, I heard the faucet and Damian was washing his hands. It was over. I buttoned my shirt and tucked it in.

I unlocked the door and didn't bother looking to see if he was decent. I stumbled out into the throngs of beautiful people. I was drunk, high, and disgusted.

I felt a tug on my arm. Distraught, I took a swing into the air.

"Whoa, easy, Cornbread!" I heard Adam say. I turned and stared at him.

"I need to get out of here. Please get me out of here," I said, frantic.

"Where do you want to go?" Adam said with a look of worry.

"Anywhere but here."

From behind me I heard Damian's voice. "Adam, 'sup, bro?"

Adam did the "bro" handshake and half hug. "Not much, man. We're gonna jet."

"Cool, cool. Taylor, man, cool hangin' with you." I felt a pat on my shoulder and nodded as Damian disappeared into the crowd. I felt Adam's eyes on me again. I knew that he knew. He'd been in the same situation. We fought our way out and hopped into a Town Car that I knew Adam had billed to another client for the night.

We sat in silence for the majority of the ride until finally I said, "Do you mind not . . ."

"It will never leave this car."

"Thanks, man."

"You want to come over and hang with Ellie and me for a while?" he asked. I looked at my watch; it was four in the morning.

"Yeah, that would be great." I didn't feel like going home or calling Mia to explain what had happened. In fact, I never wanted to talk about it again; and I didn't.

It was the first night I ever did cocaine. AI never hired JWPR, nor did they ever have any intention of doing so. Jennie had set me up. I couldn't prove it, but it was her way of letting me know that, despite the fact I'd seen her with Louise's husband, she still had the upper hand. It was just a simple reminder of who was queen and who was not.

Michael David Talking Points

- Nothing more than simple gossip

- Taking company in a new direction

- Striving for a commitment to excellence

- New opportunities for Michael David

- Bring the focus back to the designs of Michael David

- Excited about the MAGIC Fashion & Apparel Trade Show

- Announce Christian

12.

Intelligent Design

WHEN my brother and I created this company several years ago, our goal was to create a brand that represented the ideal man. A man of integrity, strength, and passion—a fictitious man, if you will." The gray-haired portly man smiled in an effort to give the press the okay to laugh at his remark. Approximately eight reporters and a crew from NY-1 packed the tiny conference room on the twenty-third floor of Michael David, Incorporated. Jennie and I stood a few feet behind the man and to the right of the other Michael David execs. We were just out of camera range.

"Well played," I whispered into Jennie's ear. "A joke to lighten the mood. It puts it out there before reporters have a chance to ask. Let's see what else you have planned." Jennie glared at me, as if to say, *You couldn't possibly imagine all the tricks I have up my sleeve.* As the stout man spoke, I noticed two reporters enter the conference room. They both looked agitated and rushed. They pushed themselves into the rest of the crowd of media, employees, and board members who swarmed around the podium like a thunder cloud. Eventually, they settled in and stood quietly as the gentleman continued to speak.

"We're pleased to announce that Christian Villani, formerly of the Italy-based fashion house, Etro, has joined us as the new head designer of Michael David." Under her breath, I heard Jennie say, "And cue Christian." It was as if she was directing a Broadway show. Like clockwork (Jennie's clock, that is), Christian Villani stepped by the older man's side, full of smiles as the cameras flashed.

The previous twenty-four hours had been frenzied. During the morning staff meeting, Jennie informed us that we were taking on a crisis-management client. I was unclear as to what "crisis management" entailed until Adam asked, "Who's in rehab? Who got a DUI?"

Apparently, no one. Jennie explained that the head designer for the fledgling fashion startup, Michael David, had been arrested on rape charges. While in Connecticut for a trunk show, the designer, who also went by the name of Michael David, allegedly sexually assaulted a sixteen-year-old girl that he lured back to his hotel after promising to use her as a model in his show at Bryant Park. Fortunately for the company, Michael was arrested under his birth name, Michael Lefkowitz, instead of his nom de plume. The local Connecticut newspaper where he was arrested ran a small story about the incident, and someone called it in and tipped off Page Six, who in turn called Michael David, Incorporated headquarters. Michael David, Inc.'s first phone call was, of course, to Jennie. Jennie cut a deal with Page Six that if they held off from printing the story on Michael David, she would give them an exclusive on one of her hard-partying clients. Jennie knew that it was only a matter of time until other gossip columnists heard the news, and she wouldn't be able to barter with them all; she needed to act fast.

Michael David, Inc., hired Jennie because they were set to launch globally—taking their small luxury brand into a world-wide fashion house. Michael David, the designer with a penchant for the high-school sophomore, was a liability—regardless of guilt. The company would be facing questions from their peers, potential financial backers, not to mention customers. They needed this to go away, and fast. Jennie actually liked taking on those types of clients because they were beyond the norm—a challenge for her. It meant that the staff had to do double the work for the same amount of money. For Jennie, it meant $25,000. A day.

"I'm sorry, but who's Michael David?" I asked. "I've never heard of them."

"What? They don't carry his line at Target?" Jennie snipped.

Thankfully, Bob cleared it up. "He's an up-and-coming de-signer that dresses everyone: Lindsay, Cameron, Jessica. *W* called him the next Marc Jacobs. None of this surprises me; I've seen him carry his press book out with him to the clubs to try and pick up girls. It's pretty pathetic." Bob was quite a fixture with the downtown set and provided invaluable gossip to Jennie.

"Is the girl talk over?" Jennie barked. "Compounding mat-ters, the biggest deal-making fashion trade show, MAGIC, is next week in Vegas. This kind of scandal could sink the com-pany."

"So we're defending him?" I asked. I could tell by the groans in Jennie's office that my questions were not well received.

"We're not *defending* him. Not unless you have a secret law degree I missed out on. We're doing *damage control*." Jennie tried to go on with the meeting, but I had more questions.

"Wait, so I'm lost. We're working for Michael David, the rapist?"

"Try and keep up, would you? We're working for the board of Michael David, Inc." Jennie looked at me, annoyed. "You should be writing this down." I grabbed the legal pad out of my bag and started writing. My coworkers were ready to implode with anger. This was my first "crisis management," and I wanted to make sure I knew what was going on. "At any rate, that's our challenge—and how to fix it so the company can still launch without this hanging over its head."

"Do you want me to set up a meeting with the Michael David people?" Mia asked. Jennie shook her head.

"No. Taylor will be the point person with me on this. Mia and Adam, I need you to take over whatever Taylor is working on and pick up the slack." Mia and Adam nodded in unison. Both stared ahead and never turned their heads toward me; my new assignment didn't bode well for either of them. Their jealously was only marginally comprehensible to me. What was I supposed to do, say no to Jennie? They knew better. Adam felt—obviously—that I was dulling his shine as the office golden boy. He took to spending more time with Ellie, and had stopped inviting me to hang out. If I were to ask him, he would deny that anything was wrong. So I left it alone. Mia was generally a major pouter but never said what was on her mind, telling me only that she was frustrated with work— mainly because she hadn't heard back from any of the fashion houses to which she'd sent her résumés. Stupidly, I had fanned the flames by telling her I could make some calls on her behalf. Her exact words: "Fuck you and your calls." I never brought it up again.

"We have literally twenty-four hours to figure this out, people."

"How very Kiefer Sutherland," Adam chimed in smugly.

Jennie ignored him. "The company wants a press conference tomorrow morning to put this out."

Mia asked, "But how are you going to save this? I wouldn't want to wear a label with an alleged rapist on it."

"No, but you will wear a dress made by a six-year-old in Malaysia without hesitating," Jennie snipped. Mia grimaced, and her face flushed. "We need to come up with a way to disassociate the company from the man and wrap this up quickly. The colossal mistake so many businesses make is dragging their heels. Companies that stall or deliver conflicting messages worsen a situation. Now go!"

The staff filed out of Jennie's office. As Mia walked out, I stopped her. "Hey."

"Hey," she said, obviously annoyed that Jennie had put me on as point person.

"So . . ." I said with a long pause. "I was hoping to hand you the Tropical Mystic Tan account. They have a photo shoot with *Paper* later today at four in New Jersey."

"New Jersey?"

"Yeah, New Jersey."

"Okay, fine," she said, emotionless. Clearly, Mia didn't like taking direction from me. She took a few steps and headed toward the dungeon.

"Mia, wait." She stopped walking and turned around. "It's not like I want to give you this, you heard her—she told me to hand it off to you guys. I'm giving Adam the Paragon Water interview. I figured you might want Tropical Mystic Tans."

"Oh, I *love* Tropical Mystic Tans. They're my *favorite*. They're fucking great—if you want to look like a carrot." She tugged at her hair as various staff members walked in and out of the hallway where we stood.

"Probably not a good idea to say that to *Paper*," I joked.

"I know, *Taylor*. In fact, I knew it long before you started working here. I don't know what's going on or why Jennie has taken a sudden liking to you, but you need to look me in the eye and tell me nothing's going on between the two of you. And tell me you're not working some angle."

My late nights and canceled dates clearly had taken a toll on Mia. And I'd been too tired, too busy, too distracted to notice. I'd thought she was . . . *supportive*, and for the most part she had been. Until that moment, the compounding anger had been hidden.

"Come on, we're always working an angle," I said, and smiled. My pathetic attempt at humor didn't play.

"I'm serious," she said.

"No, there's nothing going on. I think she respects my ambition and chutzpah, that's all." I couldn't tell her about Louise. Things were going too well. I was networking. I was getting restaurant reservations, getting into clubs on my own. Editors called me back within an hour. Before, I wouldn't even get so much as a "fuck you." Finally, I was a *someone*. These things didn't define who I was as a person, but they did define who I was as a *businessperson*. And they had finally brought me the respect I'd been seeking.

"Wow, I thought you'd have learned a lot more by now. Be-

cause if you knew Jennie, you'd know that she punishes anyone with aspirations that are bigger than hers. It may not be
today or even three months from now, but she waits it out—
and then she strikes."

"I'm well aware of the dangers of Jennie, thank you. So
far, I've navigated through that minefield without losing too
much," I said. "Don't be pissed at me because she likes me." I
actually believed Jennie *did* like me, as much as she could like
any of her employees. I had broken a cardinal publicity rule:
don't believe your own hype.

"You're right. You know everything."

"No, that's not what I meant." Mia stormed off, and I stood
in the hallway and wondered what the hell had just happened. I felt a tap on my shoulder. "Oh, hey, Louise."

"Hey, stranger!" Since the incident, I'd avoided Louise. She
hadn't done anything wrong; I just couldn't stand to look at
her because of my own guilt. "I wanted to say congratulations
on being point person on this—this is huge!" she said. She was
being sincere, I could tell; since that day with Mr. Martin at
the hotel, Louise had considered me her closest ally in the office. She barely talked to anyone else—except occasionally to
ask Bob about makeup tips. She was fascinated with Bob,
whose life was an open book. I think Louise secretly dreamed
of being that free with her own life. As for Louise and my
faux friendship, I went along with it as best I could.

"Thanks, Louise," I said. "It's nothing really. I'm just going
to be taking notes for Jennie mainly."

"Don't downplay it! Don't take that away from yourself.
You should be very proud. This is a big deal. I know your
grandmother would be proud." I had told Louise about Ethel

and her dreams of stardom, primarily to avoid conversation about a romantic dinner that she had planned for Billy.

I laughed. "Yeah, she probably would be." My mind wasn't with Louise; it was with Mia in the dungeon. I was worried about her, and I wanted to explain. I wanted to make things right.

"Well, I'm certainly proud of you."

"Thanks, Louise," I said as I brushed her off and headed into my cloffice. "I gotta get back to work."

I went into my cloffice and shut the door and brainstormed strategies to make the Michael David situation go away. I was, in reality, making my situation go away; I was shutting the door on Adam, Mia, and Louise. They just didn't get it, and a part of me felt guilty because they never would.

Jennie called me into the office an hour or so later to let me know that the board had fired Michael Lefkowitz. She took extra delight when she told me she got to be on the call when they let him go. She told me she could hear him sobbing. "Sobbing!" she said. "What a douche." Part of me felt bad for the guy. It was pretty much his company—the board were just the moneymen. I went back to the cloffice and outlined a proposal for Jennie, one I was certain she would rip to shreds.

Michael David, Inc.'s CEO, Ralph Breakstone, opened the floor to questions. One of the reporters who'd entered late was the first to speak. "This seems a bit coincidental when there are rumors swirling of statutory rape charges from your, I guess, now-former designer Michael David—or perhaps I should call him by his real name, Michael Lefkowitz."

I whispered to Jennie in play-by-play style, "And there it is, out in the open." Jennie quickly shushed me.

"Of course, we're very concerned about Michael Lefkowitz and the recent gossip. However, it's simply that—*gossip*." I practically mouthed along Richard's answers as I'd typed them up for Jennie earlier in the day. Talking points certainly weren't anything new for a publicist to give to a client before a speech or interview, but there was another element to that press conference. Something atypical, unprofessional, and quite possibly illegal. It was precisely why Michael David, Inc. hired Jennie.

A second reporter followed up, "So if it's just gossip, why name a new designer?" It was the question everyone in the room wanted to hear answered. Thankfully, we had prepped Ralph for every possible query.

"Uh-oh," I said to Jennie.

Ralph continued, "We were moving in different directions creatively for some time now, and we agreed that it was time for Mr. Lefkowitz to move on to new opportunities." It was a standard, safe answer. But the reporter wasn't satisfied.

"And if he's arrested on rape charges? Wouldn't it hurt *Michael David* since Michael Lefkowitz was there from the beginning?" Jennie shifted and looked as though she was about to step in. However, Ralph stood his ground, the apogee of strong leadership.

"Of course it would be a distraction. But you must understand that Michael Lefkowitz was nothing more than a garmento who was filling a role. Besides, other companies have gone through worse situations and continued to flourish. The rumors about Michael Lefkowitz are of a personal nature, and are not a company issue." Just as the reporter was about to ask another question, Jennie joined Ralph at the microphone.

"Thank you so much for your time, everyone. If you need any additional information on the company, please call my office. Thank you." The glare of the strobes was directed at Michael David's newest star, Christian Villani. I headed out to the building's lobby and watched Jennie receive praise from the executives of Michael David. She looked rather pleased with her accomplishment. Her face reminded me of Steffi Graff's after winning a long rally against Monica Seles— nodding with intent and arrogance. Michael David, Inc. had successfully distanced itself from the alleged rapist while also discrediting him. The company's CEO emerged as a strong leader, thus reaffirming the confidence of investors and company shareholders. And Christian Villani owed Jennie. Big. As I watched Jennie bask in the accolades, I took quiet solace in knowing that the seamless press conference had been my handiwork. What those executives could never know was that the two reporters were planted: an idea thought up by me, brought to Jennie after I had been staring at my wall for almost an hour. It was perfect.

Half of Manhattan was indebted to Jennie for one favor or another; it was time, I had told her, that she cash in some big chips for the press conference. Those particular reporters had committed two serious indiscretions that could have potentially ruined their careers or, at the very least, their marriages. Jennie had called them to her office and handed the meeting over to me.

"So here's the list of questions that you'll ask. I expect them to be memorized," I said as I glared at the two men sitting in front of Jennie's desk. I handed the questions to the men. "I really need you to sell it. The other reporters in the room have to believe that you're grilling Mr. Breakstone. Don't worry about him, I've—I mean, *we've* been coaching him all morning, and he's only calling on the two of you. It will be all that he has time for, then Jennie will interrupt." It was frightening how easily the lying and manipulation came to me. The older reporter was visibly annoyed and sighed every chance he got.

"And then we're done, right? No more of this?" he said, staring into Jennie's eyes, completely ignoring me. Jennie was stoically silent, as I had told her to be. We wanted these reporters on our side, and we needed them to perform.

"We'll see you later this afternoon, boys. Make sure you're on time," I said as I walked to the door and opened it.

As they reached the door, Jennie spoke, "Oh, and one more thing. I wouldn't even contemplate telling anyone about this; that is, if you ever want to work again." I felt like patting the boys on the back to say, *Hey I've heard this one before and she means it.* As we walked through the lobby, Mia had glanced up from her desk and looked at me curiously. She knew Jennie and I were scheming. I wasn't sure which upset her more, the fact that I was scheming with Jennie or that she wasn't a part of it.

Jennie finally finished with the executives and quickly fielded a few questions from other reporters. Finally, she joined me on the teak-slat platform bench. The understated bench seemed like an odd pairing in the ostentatious marble lobby. We stared out at Seventh Avenue, cars sliding by, sun covered by cloud. Without turning her head, she said, "Good work today. You've got drive, I'll give you that much. More than those other morons that work for me." The lobby had cleared out, and only Jennie and I remained.

"I don't think that's necessarily true. Everybody at the office has drive; otherwise, they wouldn't be here. They're incredibly loyal to you, almost to a fault."

Jennie turned and looked at me. "And you? Are you loyal to a fault?"

So many ways to answer. "Oh, I think you know I'm loyal." *Otherwise, you would be in the midst of a nasty scandal and the rest of Manhattan would be taking great pleasure in watching your demise.* "But not to a fault. Let's just say . . . I'm not a believer in blind faith."

As we sat, we talked. About everything from my marginal (according to Jennie) Midwest upbringing to the pathetic world of young Hollywood. Jennie thought they were "gross." They tried to be their own publicists, she lamented, by tipping off paparazzi or giving columnists dirt themselves, and it only and always backfired. "They teeter on the fine line between being famous and infamous," she said. The new generation was a threat to the PR industry, she believed, and a threat to themselves. "They have no pull, no bargaining power," she explained. "So they all come to me because they know I'm the biggest rainmaker in the city."

"Yeah, I'd heard of you before I even moved to the city," I said.

"You see," she said. "Why do you think fashion houses call me up when they have a new product to break? They know if I can get the Upper East Siders on board, they have a multimillion-selling product on their hands. It's a trickle-down effect."

I nodded in halfhearted agreement. "Sure," I said, looking back out at the street, with apparently too little enthusiasm.

"You don't believe me?" she said, irritated. "Who do you think brought Prada bags to the suburbs?"

Did she really just . . . ? I must be tired, and my brain must be fried. Did she just say she was responsible for making Prada a multibillion-dollar company?

"I had fashion executives begging me to break those little

triangle-emblazoned bags in the U.S. So I carried a couple of bags to a few high-profile parties, and gave them to a select number of celebs in the Hamptons, and the next thing you know, those same Prada bags are on the front page of the Style section. Shortly after, everyone had to have one. Thanks to me."

Her arrogance was astounding, but she was so earnest about it, it was impossible to hate her. She truly did believe she was responsible for the transition of Prada into mainstream society. Forget fashion marketing, promotion teams, or PR departments. Forget ad campaigns. Forget sociological trends and huge, uncharted fashion evolution. Forget the unnamed women who'd been carrying the bags years before Jennie's domination. No, by her account, it was all Jennie. Fuck Miuccia Prada; let's give respect to the true queen of fashion: Ladies and Gentlemen, *Jennie Weinstein.*

I could muster only a pathetic, "Wow." Which she took. She really believed I was impressed.

"I have to go to L.A. in a few weeks to meet with this new artist that Universal Records is trying to break, some girl named Jackie something. I can't remember the last name, and really, who cares?"

"Nice."

"You're coming with me. I want you to work on Jackie from the get-go. She'll be your responsibility—basically your client, under my supervision, of course."

I whipped my head to look at her. I couldn't believe it.

"It'll be you, Adam, and Kate."

Kate had begun working at JWPR a few months after me. Her father was president of an investment company and a friend of the Weinstein family. He'd called Jennie personally to ask her to hire Kate. I wouldn't say Kate had any sort of skill set, exactly, except typing on her BlackBerry and showing up to work late. But the girl loved to party and succeeded in keeping Jennie entertained. Kate in L.A. meant that Jennie had someone to get whacked out of her mind with. I suddenly understood perfectly why Kate was going along.

"That's amazing! Thank you," I said, as my eyes lit up.

"It's just L.A."

"I know, but still, this is awesome. And what about Mia? Is she going too?"

"You mean, your *girlfriend?*" *What the hell? How did she—?* I didn't say a word. If she caught me in a lie, the trip could disappear. But my silence was confirmation enough. "I've told you a hundred times, I know *everything* that goes on in and out of that office."

"I thought I was doing a pretty good job of keeping that under wraps," I said. "I guess not." I still don't know if Jennie truly knew about Mia and me or if she'd simply guessed and I confirmed it. Regardless, the proverbial cat was out of the bag. "We're dating." It was a statement of relief: no more obscure diners in out-of-the-way places to avoid coworkers.

"No shit, Sherlock." She laughed. I sat in the chair and couldn't believe my day. I'd manipulated a press conference beautifully, been asked to go to L.A. to meet a hot new music star and work with her directly, and my relationship with Mia was out in the open. I was euphoric.

"You must have a lot of self-confidence," she added.

"What do you mean?" She was setting me up. I could feel it.

"You know, with Adam?"

"What does Adam have to do with my self-confidence?"

"The fact that he used to bang your present girlfriend

doesn't bother you whatsoever?" And the euphoria was gone. I was silent.

"Oh, so you *didn't* know. Huh." That was Jennie; the sudden turn, the deep and painful twist. She knew full well I hadn't known. "So to answer your question, no, I'm not taking your girlfriend on this trip. The last thing I want is unneeded drama."

"Yeah, I hear you. It's probably for the best." What was I supposed to say? Jennie had something over me, and it made my skin crawl.

"You look like you're going to punch someone," Jennie said. I *really* needed to work on my poker face. "Relax. At my mother's funeral I walked in on my father taking his mistress from behind. He was in the same building as my mother's dead body! Is this picture becoming any clearer for you? I learned from an early age the tyrannical nature of men, and it's what has made me the success I am today. I don't thank my dad for spawning such great ambition in me. I thank his mistress."

It must have been a horrific moment for Jennie, and had it been anyone else, I probably would have felt pity for her. The pathos would have kicked in, and I would have thanked her for sharing something so personal with me, but I couldn't. She wasn't vulnerable. I was.

"And you're telling me this because?"

"I'm just saying that everyone has skeletons in their closets. Even you."

"I'm fine with it," I said. *Shit.* "Why would Mia tell me? It's in the past." *Why didn't she tell me?*

"Maybe because they still work together and see each other every single day. Next time the three of you are together, just watch the two of them. I can't believe you never picked up on it before."

"It's fine, really." *They had a familiar relationship because they had worked together for so long, right? The two of them as a couple—*

I tilted my head back and looked at her. She didn't smile when delivering the piece of news. That would have been too tactless even for her, but I knew she was incredibly pleased with herself. It showed in her eyes. They danced back and forth in wild excitement.

"Yeah, you're right. Anyway, if Adam had a choice between you or Mia, my money is on you. That boy is bi with a heavy 'twist' if you know what I mean."

"I got it. Thanks." I stood up. "I better get out of here; I need to get home to walk Algebra. See you tomorrow." I didn't wait for her.

I was more than forty blocks and three avenues away from my home, yet I didn't hail a cab. I was mentally and physically tired, but the news of Mia and Adam's dalliance weighed on my mind. It had been a long twenty-four hours. My cell phone rang as I passed my fourth Duane Reade in the last ten blocks.

"Hi, hon! It's Ethel," she said. *Ethel.* I hadn't spoken to her in what seemed like years, and her voice sounded strange and distant. I should have been riddled with guilt for my lack of communication, but I couldn't even conjure up a shred of regret.

"Hi, Ethel."

"What's wrong? You sound upset."

"You got all of that from a 'Hi, Ethel'? Who are you, Sylvia Browne?"

"No, I have better nails." Ethel never missed an episode of the psychic, Sylvia Browne, on *Montel*.

"Nothing's wrong," I said. She wouldn't let it go, of course; she didn't have it in her. When Ethel got something stuck in her craw, she pried and pried until she got it out even if some blood had to be spilled.

"It doesn't sound like nothing to me," she said. I walked past Columbus Circle and stopped to stare into Central Park as she talked. I could almost see Ethel sitting in the faded hunter green La-Z-Boy with her remote control on the right armrest as she held the phone to her ear with her left hand and kept one eye on *Wheel of Fortune*. To those outside of our small town, it probably sounded pathetic. To me at that moment, it sounded like heaven. I imagined I sat in the tattered beige La-Z-Boy next to her, the one that was usually occupied by my mother.

"It's just that people suck sometimes," I said.

"Tell me something I don't know," she said. A taxi honked at the horse and carriage that trotted behind me. It took me out of my family room and back onto the cold concrete. "Go on," she said.

"I don't want to talk about it, but I will say that people aren't what they appear to be," I said. I wasn't sure I wanted to delve into what might possibly be mere remnants of a relationship I had. I wasn't sure if Mia was still pissed at me from earlier, but, frankly, I wasn't sure that I cared. She could've told me about Adam. Adam could've told me. Anyone besides *Jennie*.

"Well you knew that, hon; you've been telling me about that ever since you started in PR," she said. Ethel's voice sounded weaker than usual. She paused a few times occasionally and coughed. She was a longtime smoker; though she had given it up eleven years earlier, the cough never quite left. I didn't want to ask her how she felt because I knew it would prompt a laundry list of ailments, and I didn't want to go there.

"Yes, but I didn't think that would be the case in my personal life, too."

"People are always going to pretend to be a certain way because it's safe. That's how you know when you're falling in love," she said. Perhaps she was right, maybe Mia was falling in love with me. I didn't know. I just wanted to get home and crawl into bed with Algebra. I could almost feel the cool sheets against my face as I drifted off to sleep.

"Huh?" I said, still reveling in my sheets. I took the phone away from my ear and looked at the time. It had been six hours since I had last spoken with Mia. I began to wonder if I would hear from her again. It's amazing how quickly insecurity plagues your mind. I refocused and heard Ethel's voice droning on about something.

"When you stop pretending to be someone you're not and open yourself up to the other person and show them the real you, that's how you know you're in love." Was she serious? Come on. Somebody had been watching too much Oprah, or dared I even think it, Dr. Phil?

"All opening myself up did was get me royally screwed, and not in a good way," I said, even though that wasn't entirely true. I hadn't fully opened up. I had been telling Mia half-truths for the last few months. I told myself that I was doing it for her own good, and that ultimately I was protecting her feelings. But the reality was that I was protecting my own. I'd grown too accustomed to half-truths, and before I knew it, I had difficulty distinguishing between a fabrication of the truth and the actual truth. I could blame Jennie as much as I wanted for making me this way, but as I once heard Ethel tell my mother when she complained about regretting ever getting involved with my deadbeat dad, "You can't rape the willing."

"Sorry for being so crass," I said.

"Molten Lava Cake," she screamed at the television. "Are you brain-dead or is your perm too tight?" she yelled.

"Hello? Ethel? Are you still with me?"

"I heard you, I heard you. It's way too late for you to apologize for being crass. You broke that boundary years ago." She laughed.

"So what's going on with you?" I asked. As I neared Ninth Avenue, I heard my name being called. I walked faster, as if running late to a meeting, unsure of where the voice was coming from. I sped up and talked louder into my cell phone saying things to Ethel like "uh-huh" and "yeah," which threw off Ethel's concentration on the other end.

"Taylor?" I heard again.

The voice was way too close to avoid it. I turned around.

Sandy.

I smiled politely and pointed at my cell phone and mouthed "Sorry." Ethel was in the middle of a sentence, and I cut her off. "Ethel, I have to go; I just ran into a friend. I'll call you tomorrow, okay?"

"Okay, sweetheart, love you," she said as I hung up, and Sandy approached.

"Are you stalking me?" I said, and smiled. Sandy looked smoking hot. She wore a black miniskirt with a tight, powder blue sweater that made her eyes even more piercing. This could be trouble.

"You wish," she said. "What are you doing in this neck of the woods?" she asked.

"*Neck of the woods?* Who are you? Al Roker?" I asked, laughing. "I live just down the street. And you? What are you doing above Fourteenth Street?"

She smiled a goofy smile. Something was off. "I was at an event at Lincoln Center."

"Oh, an *event*? You're so fancy. What was the *event* for?"

"I don't know. Oh, wait. Boob cancer," she slurred slightly. Yeah, she'd definitely been into the sauce, but she was incredibly endearing. And hot.

"Boob cancer? Is that the politically correct term for it?"

"I don't know. All I know is that they had an open bar and a great gift bag," she said, holding up a pink burlap sack filled to the brim. "It's all about the gift bag." She held her gaze on me longer than usual. I finally broke the stare-down.

"Out on a school night?" I replied. I momentarily forgot that this *was* "school" for Sandy.

"I suppose. What about you? I'm surprised you're not out on the town now that you're this new scenester." I couldn't help but laugh. A scenester? Had she met me?

"No, there's nothing more I want than to go home, take my dog out, and hit the sheets."

"You have a dog?" she asked.

"Yeah, Algebra. He's pretty freakin' adorable," I said, and smiled again.

"I have to meet him! Can I meet him? It is a him, I presume, but you never know because Algebra really isn't a gender-specific name," she rambled on. "Come on."

I interrupted, "Yes, you can meet him." She stopped talking and was staring at me again. "What?"

"Come on, let's go." *Now?* I felt a sense of excitement and impending doom. That is where my mother would have chimed in and asked me, "What would Jesus do?" If Jesus had seen Sandy at that moment, I think he would have had trouble resisting. This was the longest I'd gone without speaking to Mia since we began seeing each other. Part of me was waiting for the phone to ring, so I could be flippant and self-righteous, then have incredible make-up sex afterward. Another part of me was absolutely terrified that she wasn't going to call me, ever. And what would I do without her—I'd gotten so used to Mia in the little personal life that I had. "Well?" Sandy asked.

"I don't usually take people back to my place. It's kind of a tempest inside."

"You don't normally hang out at Donatella's town house either, but that didn't stop you that night." She had a point.

I contemplated whether or not I was actually cheating. Who knew what was happening with Mia and me? She could still be in love with Adam for all I knew. Those would be the reasons I gave myself the next morning, as my tiny studio apartment was bathed in a pink sunlight, while Sandy lay naked in my bed.

"Sure," I said. "Follow me. You'll love Algebra."

Flight Details

1. Review trip details

1 traveler, round-trip (4 days, 3 nights)   More flight details
Total airfare, taxes and fees: $ 316.99

Fri, Mar 8	Depart: **7:30** am **American Airlines 33**	**New York, NY** (JFK)
	Arrive: **10:45** am	**Los Angeles, CA** (LAX)
Mon, Mar 12	Depart: **8:00** am **American Airlines 34**	**Los Angeles, CA** (LAX)
	Arrive: **4:15** pm	**New York, NY** (JFK)

E-mail flight info

13.

JFK

THE line to go through security at JFK moved at a glacial pace. Jennie, Adam, and Kate stood in front of me as I stood in a 7:00 A.M. haze. Jennie barked into her cell phone incessantly, irritating everyone around her. The disdain she had for everyone else disgusted me. My proverbial candle had been burned at both ends. I awoke every morning exhausted. I spun stories to the press all day long, and it trickled into my personal life. Everything took on the "glass is half-full" perspective. In most circumstances, that is a positive thing. In my case, I was usually making up that the glass existed in the first place. My equilibrium was always off, and my life was in a constant spin. Publicists use the word "spin" not because they are spinning the truth, but because the world is spinning them, and the dizziness is addictive. The problem with *spinning*, though, is that, eventually, you fall down.

As we inched closer, farther up the winding line, I heard Jennie say, "Taylor, would you mind carrying my bag? My shoulder *is killing me* from hauling it around." I stared at her huge Louis Vuitton duffel bag and sighed. I was already lugging a bag of my own, weighed down both by my own luggage and by the certain gentleman's code that demanded you were always to carry a lady's bag if asked. I was the only one the code applied to, of course. Adam was literally inches away from her, yet she turned to me for assistance.

"No problem," I said, grabbing the overstuffed carry-on out of her hand. My arm was nearly torn off by its weight, and I wondered what was inside. A small child perhaps? No, she was no Angelina Jolie. A collection of porn for a client? More likely.

"It has wheels," she said, giggling. Yes, she giggled. She had already been through the prescription-pill buffet line, I gathered. It seemed that Adam and Kate had too. I had not been invited. I rolled her suitcase and carried my bag on my arm as we finally inched toward the security checkpoint.

As the three of them laughed hysterically and made their way toward Starbucks, I placed my keys and cell phone in the tray along with my bag and Jennie's onto the belt.

"Vuitton'd out," said the overweight security agent.

"Yeah," I said, and smirked. I felt like such a poser. What guy carries a huge Louis Vuitton bag through the airport who isn't either a) a rap star, b) gay, or c) both? I wasn't any of the above.

"I like that bag, playa," he said. "It's real?"

"Canal Street," I said quietly. *Saks, of course.*

"For real?"

"Yup." *Nope. It cost $23,000.00.*

"I'm gonna have to hit that this weekend. Thanks."

"No problem."

I waited on the other side, standing in my socks, my pants sagging. The security agent called over a fellow guard and pointed at the screen as the conveyor belt advanced and retreated. The huddle around the tiny screen grew. Who was the asshole who packed the squirt gun in a bag? Or the hairspray? Oh, come on already! Then I noticed that the couple that was in front of me was walking toward the gates with their bags. I was the only one with bags on the conveyor belt. *I* was the asshole.

My brow began to sweat, and I felt myself fidgeting. I was starting to convince myself that maybe I'd mistakenly packed a gun in my bag. I didn't know where I would've gotten it, but it was scary how quickly the idea became an actual possibility to me: I might have been sleepwalking the night before and packed a gun in my bag. At that moment, it seemed logical.

Forty long seconds later, my small black weekend bag came out. I quickly grabbed it, and was ready to join Jennie, Adam, and Kate for an espresso. Then I remembered the other bag, and I stopped in my tracks and turned around to find that the same security guard who complimented my Louis gear was motioning me over to a separate security area.

"What's up?" I asked. The guard asked me to come over on the other side of a large partition. I felt the stares and the whispers of the crowd behind me. I felt like I was back in Miss Barger's fifth-grade English class when I was sent to stand in the corner of the room for talking in class. I turned red as a balloon. I swallowed hard and walked to the other side.

"Sir, could you wait here, please?" the man said as he motioned to the wall.

"Uh, I guess. What's going on?" The sweat poured down my sides. I looked guilty, and yet I knew I'd done nothing wrong.

"Why are you sweating so much?"

"Because I don't know what's going on." *What the hell is in that bag? It isn't even my bag.* Two even larger burly men came from behind the partition.

"Is this your bag?" he asked, holding up the Louis Vuitton.

"No," I said. The three men looked at one another.

"You told me that this was your bag. You put it on the conveyor belt, and now you want to tell me that this isn't your bag?" He made it sound like a capital crime to lie politely. I was freaking out. I'd read about people considered to be national-security threats who had "disappeared" from airports.

"It's *not* my bag. I was carrying it for my boss, who for some reason couldn't carry it herself." The men looked at me suspiciously. "Look through the bag, and you'll see." They didn't move. I unzipped the bag and rummaged through Jennie's things and pulled out a pair of silk panties and a granny-style bra which, though it proved my point, was a little embarrassing. "You see?" I said, perhaps too proudly.

"You do realize passengers are responsible for their *own* bags, Mr. . . ." He paused to take a look at my boarding pass, and then looked back up at me. ". . . Green."

"Yes, I realize that. I was trying to be a gentleman, which is something I will never try to be again in the future."

"Well, Mr. Green, since you seem to be the one carrying the bag, and there's no one else around waiting for you, we have to assume that the bag is yours. Just give us a few moments." My nerves were shot.

"Could someone tell me why I'm back here?"

"We found an unidentified white substance in the bag, Mr. Green." *She did* not *put coke in her bag. Tell me she did* not *put coke in her bag before getting on a plane. She couldn't be that dumb. Maybe she forgot it was in there.* The older security guard snapped a pair of rubber gloves onto his hands. He rummaged through the bag and pulled out a smallish Ziploc-style clear bag filled with white powder. It was no dime bag. It was an abnormally large amount of white powder. By that point I was drenched in sweat.

"Anything you want to tell us now, Mr. Green?" the other guard said.

"I-I-It's not mine." The guard opened up the bag, wet both his index and middle fingers and tasted the powder. He grimaced almost instantly, and glared at me. It was coke. It had to be. *Damn.*

He zipped the powder-filled bag back up and threw it in the trash can. He closed the Louis Vuitton duffel bag and slid it over to me.

"You're free to go." *What? Was this some sort of a trap? What about the coke?*

"I am?"

"Unless you'd prefer to stay," the older guard said.

"No. What was with the powder?" I asked.

"It wasn't narcotics or anthrax, and anything other than those two substances doesn't involve this security organization. Have a safe flight."

I took several deep breaths before stepping away from the security area. I was beyond freaked out. This wasn't normal. I'm stopped in the airport, and my first thought is: My boss has coke in her bag. That was not a conclusion that other people would jump to. It was a complete, for lack of a better word, "mind-fuck." I grabbed the handles on my small bag in one hand and slung Jennie's bag over my shoulder and walked to the terminal where Adam, Jennie, and Kate sat and sipped their lattes.

With every step I took away from security, I became more

relaxed. After a moment, I began to laugh. The craziness that my life had become was surreal, and I felt like a lonesome cowboy as I walked that long stretch to the terminal. This didn't happen to other people. Just me. I reached gate A74 to find the three musketeers engaged in a deep conversation—as deep as one can get while under the influence of a variety of prescription drugs. It was roughly six minutes before any of them acknowledged that I was standing in front of them.

"There's my bag!" Jennie said, realizing the bag I'd lugged the entire way was magically at her feet. She reached inside and pulled out her makeup bag.

"You won't believe what just happened to me," I said, exasperated. Not one of them acknowledged my long absence. Kate and Adam stopped talking and looked up without saying a word. "I totally got stopped by security," I said finally, breaking the painfully awkward silence.

"Yeah?" Adam said.

"For what?" Kate asked.

"What the fuck?" Jennie blurted.

"I know, right? Can you believe my luck?"

"That's not what I'm talking about. Where the hell is my blotter?"

"Your what?" She dug through her bag, determined to find her blotter, whatever that was.

"My makeup blotter; it was in a Ziploc bag."

"Shut up! That's what that white powder was? Blotter? Wait, what's blotter?"

"It's what you put on your face if you start to sweat. It's like talc. How do you know about it?"

"Security threw it out." She looked at me furiously. For a

moment, I was petrified that she was going to have a full-blown shit fit in the middle of the terminal.

"What? Why? They did?" she said in rapid-fire fashion.

"Um, yeah. Actually, they did." A pang of guilt ran through me. I felt bad that I let security throw out her stuff. "I'm sorry. You don't understand. It was bad. They pulled me over to the other side of that partition thingy. I thought I was going to get a full body-cavity search—they had rubber gloves."

"Rubber gloves?" Adam asked.

"Easy, cowboy, it was to test the powder."

"For what?" Kate asked.

"I'm sorry, but did I enter crazyland and none of you are hearing me? I was almost nabbed for possession of what you're now telling me is makeup powder. They thought I was smuggling drugs or anthrax! Hello?" I sighed. I stared at the three of them, each wearing a blanker expression than the next. It was hopeless. The pills were in full effect. Jennie began to laugh.

"Finally, someone is at least getting it, but I'm still not sure I see the total humor in it as it was my ass on the line, literally," I said.

"Come sit here," she said as she patted the seat next to her. My gut told me that I wasn't going to like what Jennie was about to say, but I sat anyway. She looked at Kate and Adam and asked that they stand in front of her and have a conversation. That was certainly odd. They didn't say a word. Reflexively, they hopped to their feet and stood in front of Jennie and talked about what The Sky Bar in L.A. was like, and how they'd most likely end up partying there since we were staying at the Mondrian. Jennie pulled up the sides of her Louis to block the opportunity for any passerby to look in her bag. She placed a pink tank top over her MAC makeup bag and unzipped it. Then she pulled out a black tube of lipstick with gold trim. It looked like every other lipstick container that I'd seen at home or on my sink when Mia was over.

"You know what this is?"

"Lipstick, why?" I asked. Jennie giggled. She put the tube under the pink tank top and fidgeted with it.

"You have no idea," she said mysteriously. I heard a faint pop and a tiny compartment opened from under the gold trim. She looked around. Adam and Kate continued blabbering on. No one paid attention. With careful precision she took her middle finger and thumb and pulled. As she pulled, the tiny edge of a bag came out from the lipstick tube. As I looked closer, I knew immediately what it was.

"Aren't you so glad they didn't find this?" she said matter-of-factly. She was so pleased with herself that she'd beaten the dopes at security.

"I-I-I don't know quite what to say. This has reached an entirely new level for me. I'm stunned." Jennie thought that was the funniest thing I'd said all day and let out a cackle. Kate and Adam turned around just as Jennie secured her drugs back in her lipstick container. They turned and faced us, and joined in Jennie's laughter. I was absolutely shocked.

"You should see your face," she said, slurring slightly from the pills. She zipped up both bags and placed them back on the ground. My whole body heated up.

"You hid cocaine in your carry-on bag?" Kate said in a hush. Jennie nodded. Instead of having a reaction of horror or shock like I had, Kate high-fived her. What happened to drug-sniffing dogs? Was there no fear anymore?

"Yeah, it's in a hollowed-out lipstick container tucked in my makeup bag under my underwear." She turned to me. "Does that turn you on?"

"It turns me on," Adam interjected.

"A tailpipe turns you on," Jennie shot back.

"How could you ask me to carry that through security—" I stopped in midsentence. "You did it on purpose."

"Well in fairness, it's not like *I* could've carried it through. I've been busted once already, and I just barely kept that out of the paper—thank God for Gil Blaxon." I didn't say anything, as I was still seething with anger. "You know Gil, my attorney? Anyway, I don't see what the big deal is, everyone that's traveled with me has done it; ask Adam." I looked in Adam's direction, and he shrugged.

"I cannot believe this bullshit. Why didn't you tell me before I went through security?" Travelers began to fill in the seats around us in the terminal. Jennie leaned in closer to avoid a scene. I didn't care. I was ready to give her one.

"Because I knew you'd freak out like you're doing now. Then you wouldn't go through, and if I gave the bag to someone else, your panic would set off every alarm, and quite frankly that's the last thing I need."

"Yeah, and I get caught, and it's me who goes to jail. I would be the one who has this on my record because I can't afford an attorney on the shitty salary you pay, and after a drug conviction, I would be unemployable for the rest of my life." I was so angry that I started to shake. I felt a shooting pain from deep within my chest, and for a moment I had to take several deep breaths. I feared I could quite possibly be having a heart attack.

"But you *didn't* get caught," she said as casually as if I'd just told her that I lifted a few packets of Splenda from Starbucks for later.

"That's not the point!" I raised my voice. I think both Jennie and I were surprised by my sudden outburst. A businessman who had been typing on his computer looked up and stared.

Jennie was becoming increasingly angry as the conversation progressed. I didn't care nor did I back down. "I'm not a sacrificial lamb. I'm a publicist, for God's sake."

"I got it," Jennie said through clenched teeth as she looked around the terminal, embarrassed. I wouldn't let it go.

"I honestly don't think you do," I continued. "You can't play with people's lives like this. You can't play with *me* that way. Fire me, but don't fuck with the rest of my life like this. This is not a game, Jennie."

Adam sat down next to me and put his hand on my back. "Relax, bro, nothing happened."

"You, don't *you* say anything. You knew what was going down, and didn't even give me a heads-up. I thought we were friends, but I was way off." I quickly stood up and grabbed my bag and stared at the three of them. I looked Jennie square in the eye and, with restrained vengeance, said, "Don't EVER do that to me again." Jennie was stone-faced. I knew that nothing I could say would faze her.

I grabbed my bag and marched out of the terminal. I reached for my cell phone to call Mia. Things had been strained, but I needed her to calm me down. I got her voice mail but didn't leave a message. I didn't want to sound like a baby or a complete psycho. I walked to the bathroom and splashed cold water on my face to try to calm myself down. I had so much adrenaline pumping through my body I couldn't come down. I stared at myself in the mirror. I wasn't sure which part of the last thirty-seven minutes had been more unbelievable: the fact that Jennie had used me as her drug mule or that I'd taken Jennie Weinstein to task and rendered her speechless. This time in public, in the light of day, instead of the dark of the office. One thing was certain: I had pissed her off, and that meant she'd most certainly seek revenge. And soon.

Local Broadcast Listings   **Default**   Program Type

Station	09:30			10:30		11:30			00:30
8 WROC	The Unit	Shark			News 8 Tonight	Late Show With David Letterman			The Late Late Show With Craig Ferguson
10 WHEC	Law & Order: Criminal Intent	Law & Order: Special Victims Unit			News 10 NBC at Eleven	The Tonight Show With Jay Leno			Late Night With Conan O'Brien
13 WHAMDT2	Pussycat Dolls Present: The	That '70s Show	That '70s Show		South Park	South Park	Cops	Cops	Divorce Court
13 WHAM	Dancing With the Stars	The Great American Dream Vote			13WHAM News at 11:00	Nightline	Jimmy Kimmel Live		Paid Programmi
21 WXXI	Nature	Frontline/World			BBC World News	Charlie Rose		Tavis Smiley	To Be Announced
31 WUHF	House	Fox First at Ten	Seinfeld		The Simpsons	Friends	The Bernie Mac Show	My Wife and Kids	Russ Whitney's Building Wealth
105 USA	The Fast and the Furious				Law & Order: Special Victims Unit		Law & Order: Criminal Intent		The Dead Zone
106 TVLAND	M*A*S*H	Sanford & Son	Sanford & Son		Three's Company	Three's Company	M*A*S*H	M*A*S*H	The Andy Griffith Show
107 COMEDY	South Park	Bill Engvall: 15 Degrees Off Cool			The Daily Show With Jon	The Colbert Report	Bill Engvall: 15 Degrees Off Cool		The Daily Show With Jon
108 LIFE	The Last Trimester				Will & Grace	Will & Grace	Frasier	Frasier	The Golden Girls
110 FOOD	Throwdown With Bobby	$40-a-Day	Rachael Ray's Tasty Travels		Good Eats	$40-a-Day	Ace of Cakes	Throwdown With Bobby	$40-a-Day
112 HGTV	24 Hour Design	House Hunters	Buy Me		My House Is Worth What?	Hidden Potential	Designed to Sell	Buy Me	Decorating Cents
118 AETV	Dog the Bounty Hunter	Driving Force	Driving Force		King of Cars	King of Cars	CSI: Miami		Dog the Bounty Hunter
120 HISTORY	Ancient Discoveries	Modern Marvels			Modern Marvels		Lost Worlds		Ancient Discoveries

14.

Thank You for Being a Friend

ON the nights that Mia and I finished work at a reasonable hour, we watched *The Golden Girls* reruns on Lifetime. It was Mia's idea, and at first I resisted. "Absolutely no way," I said. "How many straight guys do you know who watch *The Golden Girls*?"

Without missing a beat, she responded, "Ones that are comfortable in their sexuality." She was damn quick. "And ones that want to make their girlfriends happy," she added. I vaguely remembered Ethel and my mom watching it when I was a kid. I never thought it was funny, mostly because I was too young to appreciate the humor. However, lying in bed with Mia late at night, watching a silly sitcom, was incredibly comforting. It was the only kind of normalcy I'd experienced in a long while.

We had a ritual when we watched. We'd start out by sitting upright, devouring a half pint of Ben & Jerry's Cherry Garcia. It got to a point where we anticipated the lines before they were spoken. We even started our sentences like sassy matriarch Sofia Petrillo, "Picture this . . . Sicily . . ." Dorothy, Blanche, Sofia, and Rose were the shit. The Miami foursome made us laugh so hard that, if someone had walked in, they would have thought we were incredibly stoned. I'd mentally file away most of the one-line zingers so that I could interject them into our work conversations at the office the next day. For example, Mia would unknowingly say something like, "I just had a thought."

To which I'd reply, "Congratulations." Fortunately—with the exception of Bob—no one else had a clue what we were doing.

After the first of the back-to-back episodes ended, Mia would lie on my chest and we'd watch these women over the age of sixty deal with love, relationships, and yes, even sex. It represented something simple and pure to both of us. It was a world away from guest lists, gift bags, and BlackBerrys, and it was our way of coming down from a long day and, most likely, night.

By the time the second episode would finish, I'd practically beg Mia to sleep over, but she always refused. She didn't want to upset her strict father, and I respected her for that. So most nights I spent curled up next to Algebra, who happily obliged.

But on that night, I was lying in bed at the Mondrian, watching *The Golden Girls* alone. The jokes weren't as funny. The characters were less interesting, and I could barely finish the first episode. I wished she were there, lying on my chest.

I sulked over what happened at the airport, and the tension between Jennie and me remained palpable. We'd spent most of our first few days in L.A. meeting with other D-list celebrities that Jennie wanted to add to her roster. We met with other publicists whom she was looking to poach, and with nightclub owners and restaurateurs to drum up business. Between meetings, Jennie vacuumed up her blow in less than two days with a little help from Kate. Once she had blown her wad, Jennie made all of us carpool to Electric Avenue, a shady section of Venice Beach, to buy more. Under the cover of darkness, Jennie sent Adam and me to meet another publicist's dealer. We sat in a rusty Kia Sportage and bought three eight-balls. I wasn't given a choice in the matter, and I had the wherewithal to know I shouldn't rock the boat any further. Besides, Adam and I were old pros at buying drugs for Jennie. We called each other Crockett and Tubbs. Of course, he relegated me to the Philip Michael Thomas part, and he got to be Don Johnson. It didn't matter that they were actually cops; what mattered was that they were partners in a cheesy town. Just like us.

Jennie wanted to expand her empire to L.A., and at one point had told me I was a strong candidate. It was safe to say that I'd probably blown that chance after freaking out on her in the airport. She avoided conversation with me. When I'd ask a question, Jennie would defer to Adam. It was beyond childish for her to feel like she was the one who got slighted.

As the TV droned on, I rolled over on my side. I asked Adam, as he brushed his teeth, "Do you ever miss Ellie?"

"What?" he said, around a mouthful of Crest.

"You know, do you ever miss her when you're not with her? I know she's not your girl, but in some ways, you know, she kind of is."

Adam stopped brushing and cocked his head. "I don't know. She's cool. I like knowing that's she around. What's with the weird questions?"

"Sorry. I'm just trying to figure out if it's possible to have any semblance of a normal relationship with this job."

"I don't know, man, you define *normal*, not someone else."

He went back to the bathroom and spit, then checked himself in the mirror. "Why don't you just call her?" Mia and I hadn't seen each other outside of work in almost three weeks. We'd had awkward hellos, and neither one of us knew what was going on, but we weren't ready to throw in the towel. At least I wasn't.

"Yeah, I will," I lied. I didn't have the right words to say. Somehow, "Hey, I'm sorry I'm getting more accounts than you, even though I've been working here for a lot less time than you have" didn't really sound like a good plan. Neither did, "I slept with Sandy Brin, but the whole time I thought of you." She was, after all, the only authentic thing I had in my life at the moment. "Anyway . . ." I said and sighed. "Where you guys headed?"

"I think dinner at Madeo's, then Jennie has a few house parties for us to hit. I'm sure her and Kate are going to be out of control."

"Cool."

"Maybe you ought to apologize to her?"

"To Mia?"

"Mia? Why would you apologize to her? I was talking about Jennie, you douche."

"*Me* apologize to *her*? I could've been arrested! Why the hell would I apologize to her?" Jennie had made me persona non grata at anything work-related. Our deal, or I should say my blackmail, apparently didn't hold outside the 212 area code. The only thing I looked forward to was meeting with Jackie Brown, the young actress/singer that everyone was saying would be the next superstar. If I had her as a client, I could run with the project and cement her into pop history. I was that confident.

"Because she's your fuckin' boss. Because she's Jennie Weinstein. Take your fuckin' pick." Adam threw on a shirt, and I pulled the sheet farther up and nested in for the night. He was dressed as if all his other clothes were in the laundry, wearing a chocolate brown polo shirt, baggy jeans, and brown-and-baby blue sneakers. The look was carefully thought out, but no one would ever suspect it. "I can't believe you're in L.A., and you won't say you're sorry so you can come out with us. Do you realize what you're missing out on?"

While L.A. might have been a far cry from where I grew up, or even New York for that matter, I was perfectly okay staying in while guarding the remaining self-esteem I had left. "Nah, I'm good. I'm going to watch some TV and chill. I want to be fresh in the morning for the Jackie Brown meeting."

"Oh God, you're so lame," he said, and smiled. "Well, good luck with that," he said, grabbing for his room key.

"Good luck yourself. Jennie and Kate let loose in L.A. You're a brave man." Adam ran over to the bed, jumped on it, and landed right next to me.

He draped his arm over my side, and said, "Save me, you big strong man." He poked on my obliques as I twitched with laughter.

"Wow, and there's a rumor that you're actually a switch-hitter. I wonder where people get this shit."

"Maybe that's because you want me," he said, poking my ass with his hand.

"All right, go," I shouted.

"Tease," he said as he got up from the bed and exited.

I looked at the TV and saw that the second episode had started. I glanced at the phone and quickly pulled the covers over my head again. I tossed and turned, until I finally picked up the phone and dialed.

"Hey. Sorry it's so late."

"You couldn't sleep either?" she said.

"I was sleeping so good I thought I'd try it in the sink," I said, quoting *The Golden Girls*. I heard faint laughter. "Can we talk?" I said softly.

"Go for it," she said.

"Picture it . . . Sicily . . ."

Tap. Tap. Tap.
   What the fuck?

This is not my problem.

15.

Meanwhile Back at the Ranch

For a moment I'm outside myself, watching a burly man holding cocaine and a half-dressed skinny boy sitting frightened in a chair. I start to tell him that the drugs aren't mine; that if he knew me, he'd know that I'm not someone that does drugs. That I've only tried drugs twice, and that was only recently, thanks to my addict of a boss. That my mother was very religious and would crucify me herself if she thought I did drugs. That if he knew me, he'd know that they couldn't possibly be mine. But I don't say any of these things because I know any explanation will be futile. I've seen the drugs before. I know where they came from, and I was there when they were purchased. It doesn't matter that the drugs aren't for me. I don't know the specifics of how the coke wound up in my safe, but I sure as hell know why. This isn't going to end well . . . for any of us.

You fucking bitch, you ain't that good.

"The drugs aren't mine." Is this really the second time in less than a week I'd uttered that phrase?

"Stop talking," the man bathed in a sea of beige demands. *This is not my problem.* I say this in my head over and over. I close my eyes with the hope that when I open them, the security guard will be gone and all of this will have been a dream. Part of me (the delusional part) thinks if I concentrate hard enough, I can rewind, stop myself from calling security to open the safe, and all will be well. The other part tells me to run. I'm quick. Kind of. (Maybe I'm *all* delusional.) I open my eyes. He's still there pacing.

"I'm telling you, the drugs aren't mine. The room is registered under Jennie Weinstein. Check with reservations—they'll tell you. Trust me, coke is not my thing. You don't even want to know what happened to me the only time I ever did it," I say with a nervous laugh.

"Shut up!" the security guy shouts. I know I have to think fast as it's only a matter of time before the cavalry arrives. I look at the TV as Ann Couri reads the news on *The Today Show*. I love Ann Couri; she's kind of a dork, but a hot one. *Think, Taylor!*

"Look, I'm sure we can work something out." I'm not quite sure where I'm going with this, but I'm all about flowing downstream. Beige's interest is piqued.

"Come on, you gotta want something," I say. "No one is here yet, and no one has to know what you saw in this room. It could be an honest mistake. Maybe you called for assistance because the safe is jammed, and you needed someone to slice it open. There's still time to, you know, cancel . . . the police."

"Keep talking," he says in an even tone.

"Call and retract the request. If you think I'm full of shit or can't offer you anything, then call them back later. You outweigh me by a good hundred pounds. I'm not going anywhere." *Keep it going, Taylor. Make the pitch. Make the goddamn pitch.* The only problem is I don't know what I'm offering. The

SPiN

guard finishes with his internal debate and walks over to the
phone on the desk.

"Don't move."

"I'm not going anywhere."

"Becky, it's Larry; cancel the police. Yeah. It was a misun-
derstanding. My mistake." He pauses for a moment, then says,
"Yeah, I'm sure." While Larry is on the phone, I desperately try
to think of something to offer him. He hangs up the phone
and sits on the edge of the bed, across from me. "You have five
minutes."

"Can you throw me a shirt? I think better when I'm fully
clothed." He doesn't answer me. For a moment, I think I'm
about to have a repeat performance of my bathroom encounter
at Bungalow 8. "Or not." Finally, he walks to the closet and
opens it. He rummages around and grabs one of Adam's ultra-
formfitting T-shirts. I slide it over my head and it's as tight as
gauze. I don't dare ask for another.

"Three minutes," he says. He looks at the ill-fitting shirt and
shakes his head in disapproval.

Okay, here goes. "Can I get up?" Larry nods. I walk to the
closet and grab two hundred dollars from my suit jacket. It
was petty cash meant to last for meals for the entire trip.
Luckily, I'd spent most of my time in the room getting delivery from Pink Dot. "Here's two hundred dollars. I can get
more, I just have to wait for my boss and my roommate to get
back, and I swear I can get you more." Always lowball even in
cases of desperation, I once heard Jennie say. Larry walks to
the phone and picks up the receiver. "Wait!" I yell. "What do
you want? Gift certificates? BlackBerry? Free dinner? Your
name on every club VIP list in L.A.?"

He puts the phone back down. "It's a start. Don't jerk me around, son. You could be on your way to jail right now."

"Okay. Why don't we do this, Larry? Can I call you Larry?" Larry nods. "Why don't you be as direct as possible and tell me what it is that you want?"

"I don't know."

"Well, I'm happy to give you all the things I promised a few minutes ago if you're willing to forget all about this. That's totally cool with me and totally doable." Larry stares at my carry-on bag, then at the luggage tags.

"I want to go to New York," he says. *Here we go.*

"Done," I say. I knew Jennie had a ton of travel vouchers that she was supposed to use as a giveaway for a charity event we did. She tucked them aside for herself in case of "emergency" (and by "emergency" I mean "if she felt like going to Miami for the weekend"). "I can get the vouchers FedEx'd to you by tomorrow morning. Would that be okay?"

"Yeah." Larry pauses and walks to the window and looks outside onto Sunset Boulevard. "I want a new job." My eyes are wide now. I'm not quite sure what I mumble next, but I know for the most part it's unintelligible.

"I can make some calls and get you some bouncer work at some of the clubs."

"A bouncer? Are you fucking kidding me, dude? You think I'm going to leave working security at a hotel to be a *bouncer* at some loser nightclub? No way. The business cards on the table say Jennie Weinstein Public Relations. I'm sure you can hook me up with some of her celebrity clients for personal security." *This is not my fucking problem.* I say again to myself.

"I don't really have that kind of power." I feel my face becoming flushed.

"Call some people. Make this happen. I know your boss is some big shot, she's stayed here before, and I've seen the people she rolls with. How many times do I have to say this? *Get it done.*"

"Okay, I'm sure we can come up with something. My boss knows a lot of people in L.A., and I'm sure they need security. If not, we'll make sure they do, right?" I say, trying to lighten the mood. My stomach lets out a large growl. I need to eat something, anything. Pancakes. I need something comforting at this moment because I'm not sure how the hell I'm going to get this man a job doing personal security for a celebrity that I don't even know. *Yes, pancakes would be ideal right about now.*

"Not in L.A. I want to work security in New York."

I'm not hungry anymore.

"In New York?" I ask. I feel heart palpitations as I nod continuously like a real-life bobblehead.

"In New York."

"Okay. Let me see what I can do."

A few hours later, I sit on the floor of my hotel room with my back pressed against the wall. The room is completely silent. All I can hear is the sound of my breath. I'm somewhere between consciousness and meditating. I pose several questions in this dreamlike state and wait for the answer to come to me. *If I quit today, could I get hired somewhere else?* Maybe. Maybe not. I haven't been with Jennie for even a year; though it feels more like ten years than ten months. Most employers frown on anyone's leaving a job before a year—that coupled with an almost certain bad review from Jennie would take me back to square one. *Do the perks outweigh the bad?* Yes. Or no. I was awarded luxuries that were meant only for celebrities or the careless elite. And I was neither. On the other hand, I had purchased cocaine for my boss; had done cocaine; had smuggled cocaine through an airport security line, albeit unknowingly; had let a person jerk off in front of me while on cocaine and staring at my abs; and I was keeping my boss's adulterous affair with her employee's husband a secret. In only ten months. *But what about all the stories you have for Ethel?* As much as I wanted to tell myself that I stayed because I wanted to make Ethel proud, I know that's bullshit. I stayed because I'm addicted to *this* life. I turned away from the red flags so I could convince them—and myself—that I had Manhattan at my fingertips. That was then, but now . . . the life had seeped into my bloodstream. Now it's my own hunger that makes me stay.

I can hear the morning-rush-hour traffic on Sunset through the window above me. It's nothing like New York traffic, nothing like Manhattan's continuous stream of sirens and horns. I open my eyes and look around at the tiny white room. I read and reread the television screen that gives me the option of cable, movies in theaters, movies recently in theaters, video games, and porn. The accompanying *Super Mario Brothers* kind of music plays on a loop, but, strangely, I do not want to bash the TV.

Time passes. Who knows how long. Finally, I hear the keycard being slipped into the door. Voices. Adam is the first to walk in.

"Hey," he says. He looks at me, confused. I'm sitting on the floor, still wearing his tight T-shirt. "Shirt's a little small for you, don't you think?" he says.

"Yeah."

"Where you going in that?"

"Nowhere," I say somberly. I look to my left and Adam follows my line and sees the reason for my discomfort.

"Okay. I'm not sure what that's about." Adam sets his key on the bureau, and Jennie stands in the foyer on her cell phone.

"I'm going to be back tomorrow," she says into the phone. "Can't you get her out of the house? I have painters coming tomorrow." She pauses. "I want to see you, too." Jennie notices me sitting on the floor. She turns her back to me and whispers something into the phone. It couldn't have been more obvious that she's talking to Billy. I'm too numb to care about Jennie and her philandering at this very moment. Jennie hangs up the phone, and asks, "What the hell are you doing here?"

"How did I know you would be surprised to see me?"

"I'm surprised you're not at breakfast or at the very least on the phone with New York to see what the hell is happening with your clients." Jennie walks in the bathroom and turns on the light. She fixes herself in the mirror. Surprisingly, the blow out I gave her earlier in the day is still intact. Perhaps that *could* be a fallback career.

"Bullshit."

"Oh, are we going down this road again? You temporarily grow a set of balls, then back down after you realize you're no match for me." She leans in closer to the mirror and takes her pinky to clean the corners of her eyes. I can see half of her from where I'm sitting.

"The coke in the bag at the airport wasn't enough for you?" I say.

"Are you still on that? Jesus, get over it. Nothing happened." I stay seated on the floor.

"I know you view me as expandable, so to speak, but I have one question . . ." I lock eyes with her in the mirror.

"Well?"

"When is enough enough for you? Because apparently I pissed you off enough at the airport for you to leave cocaine in my safe and ask me to call security to get your 'watch' out because you'd forgotten the code." Her mouth remains closed.

Adam interrupts, "What?" He looks genuinely surprised, but I don't believe anyone anymore.

"Don't, Adam," I say quickly. "Just shut up. How could you have *not* known? You were with her all night and this morning."

"Dude, I had no idea. I was chilling with Kate in her room for a bit." *That's rich.*

"Is it a prerequisite that you sleep with everyone at the office?" I ask. "Jennie, Mia, Kate? It's pathetic how you're willing to fuck your way to the middle." I hear Jennie snicker.

"I'm glad you think that's funny; seeing as you're probably still high. But I'm seriously at a loss. I don't know what to do anymore: Is all of this worth it?"

"It must be. You're still sitting in here, in the hotel room I paid for." Jennie shuts off the bathroom light and moves back to the foyer.

"*You tried to get me arrested!*" I shout. I want to pierce her with my stare, but I cannot look at her. I want to take off my shoe and throw it at her. And then throw the chair, and the table. I want to crush her under furniture and shoes. Instead, I absently pick at the bright blue carpet. "You're an unattractive behemoth with short, stumpy, sausage fingers. No matter how many Prada dresses you buy, how many blow outs you get, or how much money you have, you'll always be an ugly person. Inside and out."

In one remarkably swift motion, Jennie reaches for her BlackBerry and hurls it at me, hitting me on my left cheek.

"*Jesus Christ!*" I shout. Damn my slow reflexes, which were not honed while I played dodgeball in gym class. Adam stands up to see if I'm okay; I wave him off.

Jennie walks toward me, our eyes locked. There is nothing in the room except for the two of us.

"You're a fucking child. A stupid Midwestern child," she says in a venomous half-whisper. I stare back at her and shrug. *Is that all?* For a moment she stands in front of me, completely transfixed by the sight of me. She's stunned. I haven't run, broken, or begged for forgiveness. And she doesn't know quite what to do next.

"I may have sausage fingers and be a behemoth, but I'm rich, and everyone in that fucking city wants to be my friend. I make magic, and if it wasn't for me, that city wouldn't be nearly what it is today. I bring it to the people!" In her mind, she was floating above the metropolis, tossing gifts and glitter to the awed, uplifted faces.

"Bring it? What exactly is *it*? You think you're responsible for all of the city's nocturnal activities? Right. And, let's not forget, you invented Prada!" I laugh loudly in her face.

"I don't know how you did it," she says, almost to herself.

"Did *what*?" I say. Pushing her, leading her to the trough. *Drink, Jennie. Drink.* "Come on, Jennie? Whatever are you talking about?"

Adam leans in closer. "For real, Jennie. Did you set him up?" Adam says.

"You should be in jail right now on the phone to me begging for bail money and an attorney." She's as angry as I've ever seen her. Angry at the surprise.

"So you put the coke there?" Adam says.

"Yes, you *dumb-ass*. Taylor needed to be taught a lesson. What the hell do you think?" As Jennie turns her head to mock Adam, she notices what Adam noticed several minutes ago: Larry the Beige is sitting on the other twin bed, dressed in earth tones, blending in with the bed and the wall, and out of Jennie's peripheral version. He is not smiling. "Who the fuck are you?" she demands.

"Oh, Jennie, this is Larry. Larry, Jennie," I say. I finally get up from the floor. "Larry is the head of security at the hotel. He thought the coke was mine too, and was ready to let the LAPD take care of me, until I convinced him otherwise."

Jennie is stunned.

"So . . . you're going to arrest me?" she asks.

"No, no," I interrupt. "Larry is your new personal security guard, that is until you find him a job with a celebrity or with one of your socialite friends." I walk to the bed near the window and pull out my bag, which is already packed.

"What? My security guard?"

"You figure it out," I say, grabbing my carry-on.

"Where the hell are you going?" Jennie asks in awe.

"Home," I say. "I'll see you on Monday." I walk to the door and turn back. "Bye, Adam. See you soon, Larry." I open the door, push it open wide, and walk out. I'm four steps down the hall when it shuts behind me. I'm in the lobby in seconds, as though I teleported there, and am standing at LAX before I remember to breathe. Six hours later, I arrive in New York, where Mia meets me at my apartment. She turns on *The Golden Girls,* and I fall in and out of a deep sleep. The swirl in my head is dizzying. I feel drunk, and I wrap my arm around Mia's waist. She's the only thing that can make me stop spinning.

Jennie Weinstein Public Relations
welcomes you to the launch of

manifesto

512 West Gansevoort Street
New York City
9 P.M.–Midnight

only the sexy need apply

16.

Dangerous on the Dance Floor

OUTSIDE a gray, nondescript building in the meatpacking district, I suck on a Marlboro Light. Yes, I now smoke. I certainly didn't aspire to be a nicotine addict; it just sort of happened. Between the cloud at the office and Mia's lighting up in my apartment, I put away so much secondhand smoke that I figured I might as well join in. Ironically, Mia quit two weeks ago, cold turkey, joking that I'd joined the dark side. She had no idea how frighteningly accurate that statement was. I hadn't said anything and wasn't planning to, now that things were back on track. To Mia, Jennie and I simply had a cantankerous relationship—she was completely unaware of its volatility. And I intended to keep it that way.

It's a bitter November night, and the rest of the JWPR staff is inside escorting the press around a party: the launching of a new clothing store by a hip-hop star turned fashionista. The scene is purposely made to look like a fashion tent's backstage—glam yet slightly edgy. The place is just too tragically hip for me. The entire staff is cloaked in gear provided by the store, and to me they all look ridiculous: twenty- and thirtysomething white kids wearing double XL shirts and ultrabaggy pants. Adam's wearing a white velour sweat suit and has been strutting around the party like he's on a catwalk: perfectly K-Fed. Mia's in a dark denim skirt with a baby pink T-shirt and heels so high she's easily an inch taller than me. She's sexy when she's standing still, but when she walks she looks like a clumsy twelve-year-old. The models look even more awkward. The only people who appear comfortable are the designers and the waiters, who know how to work the threads and look painfully cool without trying. Except for the fanny pack. The designer is trying to bring them back. Unfortunately, it's just not possible to rock a fanny pack.

I, on the other hand, am terrified to don anything from the store for fear of bringing the party to a grinding halt. Cornbread and hip-hop don't mix. My sartorially challenged intuition could certainly set the rap movement back a decade: me in Kangol hat and baggy jeans would be uncomfortable for us all. Instead, I chose a black sweater and black pants sent to me by a publicist at Prada in exchange for putting her and her three girlfriends on the guest list. Jennie isn't the only one who knows how to barter.

I puff on my cigarette and watch Larry trail Jennie. When I left L.A., I wasn't sure what would become of Larry, but it's no longer my problem. To my surprise (and delight), the following Monday Jennie showed up with Larry in tow. No one mentioned what had happened, not even Kate, who typically spills everything. Adam later told me that Larry was staying with Jennie, in her third bedroom/home office, but the arrangement was only temporary until the room above one of the nightclubs she represented became available.

Jennie walks around the party in her usual black dress. She

was not about to change her style for one night, no matter how much she is getting paid. As she and Larry walk, I can see a certain delight on her face: Jennie Weinstein has her own personal security guard, and everyone in the room is buzzing about it. Jennie is now even more of a powerhouse among Manhattanites. *What have I done?*

When I showed up at the office after L.A., I had no idea what to expect. But it was business as usual. For Jennie, I was her very own reality show, unfolding in her very own office. Why would she fire her biggest entertainment? Until now, I was the only one who had put up with her insults and abuse—my predecessors had either quit or been fired (one even went to rehab, and Jennie fired her when she returned because "she just wasn't any fun anymore")—and a part of her liked the challenge. Personally, I was growing weary of being played, of dancing for the queen: The stakes—my life, my freedom—were just too high.

I finish my cigarette and pace behind Brody, the new intern, who is working the guest list. Brody is young, hot, and, most likely, Jennie's next conquest. Brody is also only nineteen. Jennie thought this would be a good way to get his feet wet, and surprisingly he doesn't falter when turning people away like I did. I look at the time: 11:30. *Where are Lauren and Allison?* I'd invited them to the party since I hadn't seen them in months, and as an incentive I told Allison that the oversized shirts would come in very handy as maternity wear. Allison and Lauren were full steam ahead on "operation gay-by." I look across the street and watch several men dressed in soiled aprons from one of the last remaining meat shops in the district load boxes onto a large generic white truck. It's cold, and I cram my hands into my pockets.

Just shy of a year ago, Allison, Lauren, and I stood in a line much like the one in front of me, clamoring to get inside. Maybe I was the only one "clamoring," but the three of us nonetheless braved the cold and waited with the rest of Manhattan to get into a Jennie Weinstein party. How much things change in such a short time. In a New York minute, my New York year.

One day soon, I tell myself, I'll have a company of my own, and I can invite whomever I like to whatever I like. I will fly Ethel and my mom to New York and let them see the craziness of a red carpet like this one. The looks on their faces. I'm thinking about Ethel harassing the paparazzi when I feel a tap on my shoulder. Thinking it's Allison and Lauren, I turn around excitedly.

"Oh, hey Brody, what's up?" I say, disappointed.

"These girls over here swear that Jennie personally invited them when she was at the restaurant they work at."

"Which girls?" Brody points at a group of girls, and all of them are quite attractive. They're all Indiana tens, but New York sixes. They look at me as Brody points. They smile. I know that smile. I've owned that smile while waiting in line: *You could make my entire night*, it says, *make my entire month if you let me into this party right now.* I've *been* them. They seem cool enough. I scratch behind my left ear, and on cue Brody walks in front of the velvet rope.

"Sorry, girls, not tonight."

"What? She *invited* us. Come on, look at us! Do we look like party crashers?" I heard one say. One of the other girls shouts, "Don't be a dick!" The security guard beside Brody steps in.

"Let's go, ladies; keep it moving. You don't have to go home, but you can't stay here."

I turn my back on them, mainly out of embarrassment. Jennie probably did invite them, but she didn't care enough to put them on the guest list, so that meant her invite was bullshit. Had I let them in, Jennie would have reamed Brody in front of everyone at the party. I've actually saved him from a lot of grief, I tell myself, maybe even from a potential firing. Or maybe I've changed. How could I not? What's the famous line? "Leave New York before it hardens you." Too late.

Brody returns with his hand outstretched, ready to shake mine.

"Thanks, bro, I owe you one," he says as he slides a tiny vial into my palm. I take it and put it in my front pocket.

"No problem," I say.

It's my other habit since returning from L.A. Can you blame me? I can't spin around in my office without landing on someone doing a bump here and there. With all the bad experiences connected to the white horse, you'd think I would have continued to resist. Not only does it numb the back of my throat, it numbs my mind, especially my memory of the last few months. I'm extremely discreet by insisting to anyone that I do a bump with not to tell Jennie—or Mia. I can't afford to let Jennie have anything on me. And I can't stand the thought of Mia knowing. The old me would politely turn Brody down, but here I am, taking coke from a kid still in school.

I duck around the corner and find a vestibule in one of the many abandoned factories in the middle of transforming into a Pottery Barn or Starbucks. The entryway is a respite from the heavy wind. I step up, huddle in a corner, pop off the cap, and pour a little from the vial. I place my finger on my right nostril and inhale deep. It burns. I pour the same amount into the cap again and repeat, switching nostrils. The burn. I can't get used to that burn. It feels like someone blew out a match and then stuck it up my nose, singeing the inner walls. I close my eyes and inhale. I stand still, listening to the wind shake the posters on the side of the building. They flap and rattle.

I hear a set of heels clapping on the cobblestone. I quickly screw the cap back on and throw the powder into my pocket. I step out of the doorway and recognize the dishwater blond hair five steps in front of me.

"Al!" I shout. Allison is dressed in a long, black-wool winter coat, with black pants and bright red patent-leather boots on underneath. She turns around and flashes me a smile so genuine it could warm your toes.

"Hi there."

"Wow, look at you. The hair, the makeup, you clean up real nice," I tease.

"I try to keep the lipstick in lesbian."

"And the boots? Damn."

"I had to do something to distract people from my fat belly," she says, and laughs, grabbing my hands. "It's really good to see you again, stranger."

"You too! No Lauren?"

"No, she sends her regrets, but she has an eight o'clock tomorrow." I'm actually relieved that it's only Allison. When Allison is solo, she's truly herself. Around Lauren, she tries to be the person she thinks she ought to be. I look at Allison, and she emits such a happy energy that I tell myself from now on I will schedule a weekly dinner with her and Lauren so we never lose touch again. Every Sunday we'll have Italian food. I'll even

SPiN

babysit—with Mia's help. We'll be friends again. It's a euphoric delusion: More likely, I'll be out working on Sunday night, and the thought of being stuck with a screaming baby for more than an hour makes me jittery. Maybe just coffee instead. "Hello?" she says, for apparently the second time. The coke clearly had kicked in: I was on a tangential thought, interminable.

"Sorry. I was just thinking we should get together more."

Allison locks her arm around mine, and we walk down the street. "That would be wonderful. I'd really like that." I smile and pick up the pace. "What were you doing out in the cold and around the corner?" she asks.

"You know, I was trying to call Ethel to tell her about the party, but for some reason I wasn't getting cell reception, so I kept walking until I did." I'm perfect at it by now.

"You called her this late?"

"You don't know Ethel."

"How's she doing?" she said, as we approached the velvet ropes.

"I think she's okay, I didn't reach her. I left a voice mail," I say, stopping in front of the rope, catching Brody's eye. Allison and I stand on the exit side of the rope, away from the fifty or so people waiting in the frigid November air to eat crab cakes with Heidi Klum and Usher. Brody immediately races over to us, opens the rope, and we walk inside the magic box. Still arm in arm, we step up the tiny stairs leading to the store.

"You look really great yourself, by the way," Allison says. As she looks up at me, the lights above the doors hit my face and the glare takes her by surprise. She breaks from our armlock.

"What?" I say. Allison inspects me like a new shirt she's

267

brought home from the store. "What's wrong?" She wipes her nose. "What?" I ask again. She wipes her nose again. I'm not getting it.

"You have blow on your nose," she says flatly.

My hand flies to my face. "Okay, this is awkward."

"You weren't calling Ethel."

"It's so not like that, Al. I rarely do it; I was just really wiped and, you know, needed a little something to make me, er, shine."

"Things that shine don't usually leave a residue." I feel dizzy and hot, like I've just been busted by my mom. The door opens and drunken, random strangers pour down the steps past us.

"Can we please talk about this later? You can ask me anything you want." I say this knowing full well we won't. Hoping we won't. Because I have no logical explanation for my behavior. Stockholm Syndrome, maybe? It worked for Patty Hearst. *Focus.*

I open the door, hoping Allison won't back out. She pauses, then says, "I did put on boots and makeup." I put my arm around her.

"Attagirl." I smile.

"And you did mention a gift bag."

"I did."

Just as we are about to walk inside, she says, "It's just—I do worry about you. That you'll get too deep into this world, that you have already."

"Don't worry; I'm toying with an idea for an exit strategy," I say cryptically. "Actually, it's more like an 'in case of emergency' strategy."

"You're going back to work for Mitchell?" she says optimistically.

"Nah, I've got bigger dreams now."

"That's what scares me," she says, as we walk inside.

The interior of the place is cavernous and set up almost like a nightclub. In each little side room is a different type of clothing; one holds made-to-order suits that are mainly navy with pinstripes in primary colors; another displays clothing with logos slapped on everything (my personal favorite is the denim jacket with the designer's name in Swarovski crystals for fourteen hundred bucks); still another offers only women's shoes. With so many separate rooms, I can't tell how many people are inside, but it doesn't matter: The main room is jammed, and that's where we're headed. A giant disco ball descends to the center of the room and hovers above floors covered in faux-fur carpeting. I'm sure the faux fur *sounded* like a good idea, but on a cold and wet November night, it looks more like a wet dog with matted hair than the glam plush vibe they were going for.

"This is so over-the-top," Allison says over the loud hip-hop beats pulsing through the speakers.

"What do you mean?"

"The carpet, the discoball, the ghetto fabulousness! They went all out for this!"

"Oh no, that's the standard décor. It wasn't for the party." Allison's eyes practically fall out of her head. I laugh and see Mia escorting Gina Hoggett from E! Online around the room. "Come on, I want you to meet someone," I say.

This is the first time my two worlds have met on a level playing field; my old life and my new one, merging into one.

The first time Allison and Lauren met Mia was when I stood in line with the dynamic duo, and Mia refused to let all three of us into the party. The second time Allison saw Mia was when she bitched out the salesgirl at Inca. I remember this as we almost reach Mia. This might not have been such a good idea, I think, as we step up to her.

"There you are." I smile. Mia smiles back, and Gina Hoggett sips on a pomegranate martini.

"Gina, you remember Taylor Green."

"Hi, Gina," I say, kissing her on the cheek. "Did you get that item I sent you on the J-Lo perfume thing?" Gina nods. "Are you going to be around tomorrow? I want to pick your brain about one of my new clients and see what you think I should do." A trick of the trade: play dumb to the reporter and give them the power. Make them think they're teaching you and that by covering your client in their lousy video blog, they've saved your ass and instructed you how to do your job in the process. They fall for it all the time.

"You must be Allison," Mia says politely.

"That's me," Al says, with a skepticism only I register.

"Mia. Nice to meet you," she says, reaching out her hand.

"Oh, put your hand away and give me a hug! Taylor is like family to me, and from what I hear, you've entered our fold." I wince. Mia and I haven't been able to keep our relationship a secret around the office, but we have been successfully secretive with our press pals. Luckily, Gina is too busy looking around the room for potential gossip. Mia and Allison hug briefly. Is this what normal people do? Gina excuses herself to the ladies' room and leaves the three of us standing in the middle of the room.

"So when is the big day?" Mia asks. Allison stares at her

blankly. After an uncomfortable pause Mia says, "The baby?"

Allison looks at me. "What baby? Who's having a baby?" The color drains out of Mia's face, and she twirls her hair. Allison's generous that way: She doesn't make just one person feel uncomfortable, she lets *everyone* feel that way.

"Oh, I-I—," Mia struggles.

"I'm totally kidding!" Allison says before Mia has a stroke.

"Oh, Jesus, that was so messed up!" Mia laughs. Her laugh is infectious, and I love that Allison took the piss out of her.

"I'm sorry, I just couldn't resist. Plus, I had to get you back for being a royal bitch the first time I met you." Ever since I've known Allison, she's always had a penchant for saying what's on her mind. She didn't have the opportunity to jab Mia that night or at the consignment shop, but Allison waited like an expert marksman for the right opportunity to go in for the kill.

"Oh my God. I'm so sorry. I was probably so awful."

"Oh please, don't worry about it. I just have thin skin. Besides, I've heard stories from Taylor about how awful people can be when waiting in line. It's all water under the bridge."

"Thank you for saying that." Mia looks at me and smiles. She likes Allison—I can tell. "We should get together one of these days, preferably when I'm not working a rope line."

"I would love that," Allison says.

"It's a date," I concur.

"If you'll excuse me, I need to go check on Gina and make sure she's not seeing anything that she shouldn't be."

"Go!" Allison says.

"We're definitely getting together," Mia says, hugging Allison good-bye. Mia gives me a subtle wink, and I watch her walk toward the bar. I turn back to Allison, who is beaming.

"What?"

"You've got a girlfriend," she sings. I feel like I'm back in middle school. "As much as it kills me to say it, because Lord knows I wanted to hate her, I think I kind of like her?" she says, ending her sentence as a question.

"Yes, you like her, and its okay to come out of the closet with it." I laugh.

"I'm being serious."

"And I really appreciate it, your being serious, that is."

"You're such a shit."

The party is in full swing. Girls in Stella McCartney and Trina Turk. Men in clothes that look like they were bought at the Salvation Army on Eighth Street instead of where they were actually purchased: Barneys. The banquettes set up for the VVIPS are filled to capacity, and six stripper poles are being used by some of the best girls from Scores. Giant framed black-and-white photos of scantily clad male and female models adorn the robin's-egg-colored walls. Allison and I awkwardly attempt to bust a move on the dance floor. She sways like a sixties flower child back and forth to the music, while I look like I'm having a seizure. As I flail about, I see Louise walking toward me. The coke has made me gregarious, and I wave my hands at Louise, grabbing her arm and dancing around her while Jay-Z pounds into my ears.

"Where have you been all night? Are you just getting here? Jennie's gonna kill you!" I say. She's silent as I try to convince her to dance with me. She doesn't move. Something's wrong. Allison is oblivious, her eyes closed, swaying. I look closely at Louise and see that her mascara has bled to her chin, and her eyes look like a raccoon. Her hair is askew and her outfit looks like she just got—or fell—out of bed.

"Are you all right?" I ask. She stands and stares blankly into the crowd. "Louise? Louise?" I snap in front of her face and her eyes lock with mine.

"He left me."

"What?"

"He's gone."

"What are you talking about? What do you mean *gone*?"

"I must have really screwed things up. I'm just not sure how." Louise's eyes are swollen. It reminds me of when Ethel brought home a cat, and my eyes turned into tiny slits—I could barely open them and had to sit in a hot shower for an hour, the steam helping to open them. I wish Louise had a cat allergy instead of a shitty husband. That would be a much easier thing to fix.

"Let's go over here. It's more private." I nod at one of the many cubbyholes. I grab Louise's arm and nudge Allison out of her transcendental dance and motion her to follow us. I quickly guide the women past one of the cubbies that includes bedazzled dildos, harnesses, and lingerie. Instead, we walk into the "COATure" section, a clever moniker for a room that's filled with winter coats that are blinged out to resemble couture collections. Louise and I walk ahead as Allison trails. We each grab a corner and sit down on one of two white-leather footstools. We let Allison have one to herself.

"Thirteen years, and that's it." I grab Louise's hand. She continues, "I just don't get it. I'm not that girl." There's really no authentic way for me to respond. Every word would be a lie.

I offer a measly, "Yeah."

"When you met him . . . we seemed good, right?"

"For the thirty seconds that I met him, yes."

"Taylor!" Allison rebukes.

"Sorry, I didn't mean it that way. You did seem good to me. Maybe he's just stressed at work, or he's having some sort of midlife crisis." I try to divert her away from the topic of another woman. I'm not sure I'll be able to keep *that* from her. My face will give it away.

"Do you think he was seeing another woman?" Allison asks. I look at Allison, returning the rebuke. So much for my strategy. I know it as fact: No woman wants to hear that their man is cheating when he asks for a divorce. Somewhere deep inside they know he probably is, but they don't want to hear it. Once the phrase "there's someone else" is uttered, their worst fears are realized. I know this because of my mom; I learned while listening to her heart break when my dad left.

"And you thought *I* was being insensitive! Come on, Al! Of course he wasn't cheating on her. I mean, look at her!" *Shut the hell up, Allison!* She returns my look with one of total confusion. I stare at the room, a gaudy explosion of color mixed with white leather. It's all kinds of wrong, and once again I lose myself in thought, analyzing the décor—it's the coke, I know: it makes me feel like I suffer from constant A.D.D. Louise is in crisis, and I'm distracted by the eighties-inspired neon colors, wondering about a Fiorucci motif.

"Taylor?" Louise says loudly.

"What?" I say, snapping out of my temporary distraction.

"Do you think he's seeing someone else? You're a guy. Be honest." Louise wipes her nose.

"I don't know." I fidget. "Maybe?" Louise starts to cry. I've

never done well around women and waterworks. And never before have I seen Louise or anyone at work weep. It's unbearably
uncomfortable. Her head is in her hands. I look at Allison, unsure of what to do.

Allison whispers into my ear, "High or not, you need to
pull yourself together. Look at this woman. She's about to
implode." I look at Louise. Her hands are covering her face.

Allison looks at me and shakes her head in disgust. I stand
up and pace around the room. Allison sits next to Louise and
places her hand on Louise's back. The room feels like a tiny
refuge from the frenetic and blurring energy. It's silent except
for the echoes of a few drunk girls who linger on the edge of
our room, talking loudly over the music that's being pumped
through the main room.

"I just don't know what to do. Am I supposed to date again?
I'd rather shoot myself." Louise looks up at me, her eyes literally dripping tears. "No, we made plans together. It wasn't just
me, he did too. We did . . ." Her voice crumples. She pounds
her fist against the footstool.

"You'll get through this," Allison says, rubbing her back. Out
of the corner of my eye I see Jennie with her minientourage,
including Larry, passing our room. She sees me and walks in.

"Why aren't you out working the party?" Jennie says in a
huff. I shrug. "Why aren't you saying anything?" Jennie notices Louise slumped over. "What happened to her?"

"Billy wants a divorce. Can you believe it? What a scum-
bag!" I say this last bit for effect as I stare deep into Jennie's
eyes. Jennie marches over to Louise.

"Who are you?" Jennie asks Allison coldly.

"Allison."

Jennie sighs. "Great, now could you get your ass up so I can sit down and have a conversation with my employee, please?" Allison stands up, shakes her head, and stares at me.

"Get me the hell out of this crazy town and its reigning queen," Allison says. Had this been ten months ago, I would've apologized on Allison's behalf, grabbed her by the arm, and escorted far away from Jennie. At this moment, I revel in her disdain for Jennie. I stay silent as Allison stands next to me. Jennie ignores the both of us.

"Men are stupid," Jennie says quickly, flatly, offering some pathetic semblance of comfort. Louise shakes her head, still staring at the ground. "What happened?"

"I was getting ready to come here, and he walks in and tells me he can't do this anymore. I wasn't sure what he meant. I thought he meant me working late. Then he tells me it's us, and he's not in love with me anymore, and that he hasn't been in love with me for a while."

"How awful!" Jennie says. I wonder where Jennie was when Billy practiced this very speech with her. Were they having dinner in some secluded restaurant? Were they doing lines? Was he taking her from behind? He must've gone off script— Jennie was much more creative than this.

"He had already packed a bag and said he was going to stay with his friend Dennis from work." Yeah, I bet. A hundred bucks says he is at Jennie's this very moment, sitting on her Ligne Roset sofa, drinking a Stella and scratching his nuts. I feel a nudge from Allison.

"Can we get out of here? I think I've had all I can handle for one night."

"Just five more minutes," I say. "I want to see how this plays out." Allison looks at me curiously and instantly reads my face: I know more than I'm letting on.

"I think I'm going to go. I've seen all I need to see." I don't acknowledge her implication.

"Okay, I'll call you tomorrow and fill you in." I lean in to kiss her good-bye. She pulls away.

"You're not going to walk me out to get a taxi?" she says. "Never mind. Good-bye, Taylor." I'm about to respond when Jennie turns to make an announcement.

"I want everyone out of here. I need to speak with Louise alone." I hang around, thinking she means everyone but me. "You too, Taylor." I look at Louise, and she turns away from me, buries her face in Jennie's dress, and sobs uncontrollably. Has Billy also packed Louise's brain in his bag? Why the hell would she seek solace from Jennie? Affair aside, Jennie has never been known as a solace for the tearful. She's more often the sharp edge that causes the tears. Larry, Allison, and I obey, and walk out of the COATure room.

"I need to wait here to make sure she's okay," I say to Allison. "Larry, can you help my friend get a taxi? Take good care of her, and don't hit on her. She's a lesbian, and she's pregnant."

"What? I don't see what—I'm just at a loss with you, Taylor. I don't get it. What's up with you?" Allison says, sneering.

"Can we talk tomorrow? I want to clear up some things about tonight with you." It's a conversation that I am sure won't happen until much later, but I need to give her something, however small. A promise at least, so that I have one friend left when the dust settles.

"Tomorrow. Sure. Thanks for . . . I don't know . . ." she says, searching.

"I'll talk to you later." She turns, and I watch as L.A. Larry and Allison merge into the crowd like a Town Car on the

Long Island Expressway, dodging crazies, swerving to avoid a collision, and finally breaking free to the open road.

Twenty minutes later, Jennie and Louise emerge from the coat atelier arm in arm. For a moment, I think I've overdosed and am delusional. Louise looks stronger and stands upright. Her makeup is fixed, and it appears as though she's even run a comb through her hair. Just what the hell was in that room?

"Where's Larry?" Jennie snips.

"He just stepped out for a minute."

"Typical."

"Can I help you with something?" I ask, looking at Louise.

"I need you to walk Louise out and flag down Gene, my driver, and have him take Louise to my place."

"Your place?" I ask, exasperated. This wasn't the resolution I was hoping to hear.

"Yes, why? Is there a reason Louise shouldn't go back to my place?" Jennie asks, knowing that if I implicate her, I will drag myself down too. *Rock, meet fucking hard place.*

"No, I'm just surprised. I thought Billy was the one who moved out." Theoretically, Billy could be at Jennie's apartment this very minute waiting for her.

"It doesn't matter. I don't want Louise to be alone. She's part of the JWPR family, and I will not let one of my family members go through this alone." She says it so strangely, almost stoically. The content of the statement doesn't fit with her voice and her heart: bad acting.

"Okay," I say sheepishly. "You ready, Louise?" Jennie's secret has gained power and morphed me into a coconspirator.

Louise turns to Jennie and grabs both of her hands. "Thank you. For . . . this. I don't know what I would've done without you. No . . ."

Still have a marriage, I think. Louise breaks one hand from Jennie and grabs mine in the other. ". . . the both of you." I feel a stabbing pain in my chest, like someone has taken a ballpoint pen, pierced my body, and made contact with my heart.

"All right, I have to get back in there to see if everyone's happy. Louise, you're good?" Louise nods. "I'll see you back inside," Jennie says to me. "You're still working, so don't putz around outside." I ignore her last comment and grab Louise's hand. We push our way through the crowd to the solace of the street. I see Gene leaning up against the wall smoking a cigarette a few feet away. I motion him over. Gene's in his midsixties, but looks and acts like he's eighty-five. Jennie keeps him around because he says whatever he wants, and she finds it amusing. I've ridden with him on a few occasions, worrying every time that he's going to run over a small child or a careless bicyclist, and so I've opted to take cabs or subways on these kinds of nights.

"Hey, Gene. Jennie needs you to take Louise uptown to Jennie's apartment, then come back down here." Gene heads off to fetch the car without saying a word.

"How you doing?" The sounds of the West Side Highway fill the night air, mixing with the movement and chatter of people still waiting in line, though the party is over in ninety minutes. Their voices, and their laughter, are like static that strangely calms and soothes me.

"I think I'm in shock. I just can't believe this is what my life is now," she says, shaking her head. "Hey, who knows? Maybe there's a book somewhere in all of this. I always wanted to write." She momentarily smirks, but the half smile fades quickly.

"One day at a time. And remember: Don't feel like you

can't go home. That's *your* place, and he left. You keep that apartment." Louise has more money than Billy, and her parents bought her that apartment years ago. Plus, I wanted her out of Jennie's apartment, like, yesterday. The black Town Car pulls up, and Gene slowly gets out of the car and opens the back passenger-side door. "Your carriage awaits." Louise hugs me tightly and stares into my eyes.

"Thank you for being such a good friend. You're an amazing person, Taylor, and I'll never forget how good you've been to me. Not just now, but at the office, too."

"Stop!" I say. "I'm supposed to be making *you* feel good." I follow Louise as she steps into the car. She sits down, and I say, "Now try and get some sleep if you can."

"Oh, I will," she says, holding up a prescription bottle with Jennie's name on it. I roll my eyes and, before shutting the door, say, "Just be careful." The car pulls away and I watch it blend in among the taxis and Town Cars and I eventually lose sight of it. I walk back past the lingering line of hopefuls, and back through the velvet ropes. I stop Brody and whisper in his ear. He discreetly hands me the vial—our ritual—and I pocket it before entering the fray.

I need to forget.

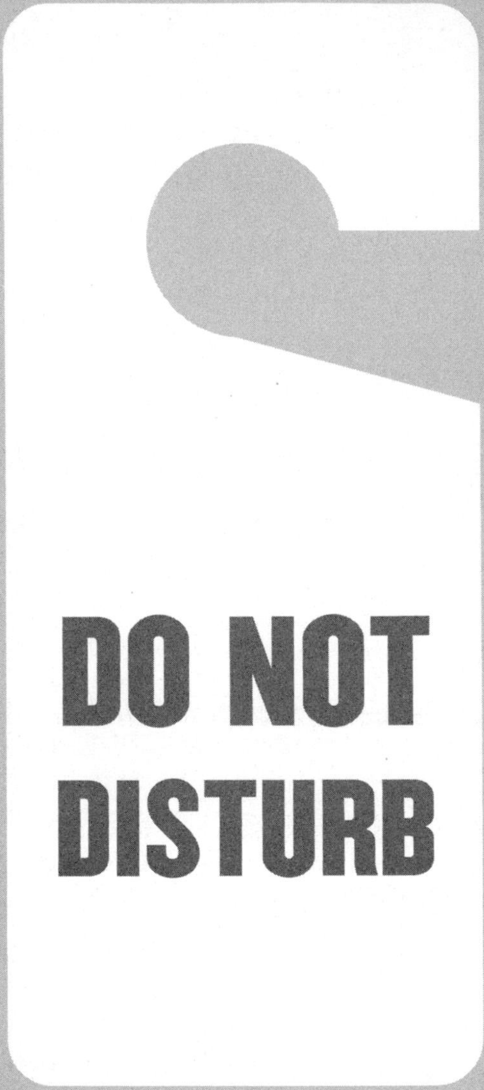
DO NOT
DISTURB

17.

He Comes Unspun

THE water is cooling off. I stretch out my big toe and pull the silver knob toward me, causing a steady stream of hot water to pour out of the faucet. I wrap my leg back around Mia's, and she leans back on my chest as we sit in the giant bathtub. I close my eyes and wish we could never leave. I wish I could wash off all the bullshit, all the lies, the drinks, and the drugs. I'm naked in the moment—literally and figuratively—hiding behind nothing. And I'm emotionally spent.

I feel like I could cry, *should* cry, but I'm not someone who often does: not because of some macho bullshit; I'm just not that guy. It's a physiological thing, I guess. Or maybe a psychological one. I'm numb, all emotion drained from my body. Power and privilege in New York demands that you do a dangerous dance, a seduction akin to the vampire Lestat's. He pulls his victims in with his beauty, and with the promise of a life beyond the formerly possible. By the time he goes in for the bite, you're too far gone to turn around, too far in to do what you must do to survive: run like hell. You've been enchanted, and you offer yourself without a shudder. "Close your eyes and give in to your darkest dreams," he whispers to his victims. You've become possessed, and you've been smiling the whole way. The sweet intoxication is much too powerful, and one's soul seems a reasonable price. *Close your eyes. Give in to your darker side.* And you do. I did. Do. This is my relationship with Jennie Weinstein, the reigning vampire queen of the night.

"Where are you?" Mia asks, twirling the little bit of hair that I have on my chest.

"I'm right here," I say blankly.

"Don't think about Louise, Jennie, or anything that has to do with work."

It's hard not to, as the very bathtub we sit in is a product of that world. A new boutique hotel on Spring Street had signed with us—with me—and my new client offered a complimentary weekend stay. If I experienced the impeccable hotel for myself, they had insisted, I'd better be able to sell it to the press. This kind of thing didn't help sell anything, of course, but why would I tell him that? I thought of using the freebie by surprising Ethel and my mom with a luxury weekend in New York. I was going to hook them up with house seats to whatever Broadway show Ethel was dying to see that week from a publicist friend I knew, and score them a comp meal at Platter, my newest restaurant client on the Lower East Side. They would have loved it. But one night after a few too many Jack and Cokes, I called Mia and asked if she wanted to spend the weekend at the hotel with me. Ethel and my mom got thrown under the love bus.

"Let's quit," I say. Mia reaches for her Pinot Grigio and takes a sip.

"Trust me: The minute I get hired at one of the fashion houses, I'm going to tell Jennie to fuck right off." Mia is biding her time until she gets hired in the PR department at a place like Christian Dior, Gucci, or Ralph Lauren. The connections at JWPR provide her with a real shot at getting hired—a better shot than she'd have if she worked at a small fashion label. She has the contacts and the experience with heavy hitters. I would never tell her, but I think her rough edges kept her from some of the jobs she'd been interviewing for lately. Most of those places hire girls from Brown or Cornell, not tough girls from Queens.

"Just play along and tell me where we'd go if we both quit AND we couldn't work in PR or live in New York. Play with me," I say, taking a sip of vodka now watered down from the melting ice.

"How about Rome?"

"Roma!" I say in an awful Italian accent. "Nowa youa speaka my language," I say.

"And close," she says, pushing my lips together. I laugh and sink farther into the tub, hitting a pocket of warm water.

"What would we do in Rome?" I ask.

"We'd drink wine. Eat a lot of carbs. And drink more wine."

"And?"

"Espresso?" she asks.

"Espresso is great. Now you're playing along. Are we working in Rome or are we gypsies?"

"Oh God no, I could never be a gypsy. We'll own a small trattoria. You can work in the back and cook the food, and I'll greet our Italian friends as they come in and seat them at their regular tables." I can tell by the tone of her voice that the notion of living in Rome and having a restaurant greatly excites her.

"So you basically would be a waitress?" I laugh and grab a

bottle of the sandalwood-and-lime soap from the hotel gift basket. Thank God the soaps aren't perfumey. Mia hates anything overly sweet-smelling because it gives her terrible headaches. When Jennie bathes in her "Angel" the day after a long night out, Mia's head feels like it's going to explode. I pour the shampoo into my hands and massage Mia's scalp. This is how it's been for us for the last month, steamy yet sweet. The passion replaced the guilt I felt about Sandy. I still hadn't told Mia about Sandy. What would be the point? Unless to clear my own conscience. The only one who would get hurt was the person I wanted to hurt the least. Luckily, Sandy understood; she seemed more embarrassed than hurt.

"No! A hostess slash owner!" she says, relaxing into my hands.

"Owner?" I tease.

"Yes, you'll be working for me. Do you have a problem with that?"

"I'm happy to be a kept man." I wrap my arms around her bare stomach and fold my hands on top of her belly button. I kiss her neck gently.

"Lean back," I instruct. Mia leans her head back as I pour the water onto her head and let the soap drip from her soft hair onto my chest. I love every inch of her, yet neither of us has been brave enough to speak that word to the other. I shut my eyes and enjoy the smell of sandalwood and Mia's skin. I'm dozing off. This is heaven.

My cell phone rings loudly in the other room. I lift my head from the inflatable bathroom pillow and look at the clock in the bathroom: almost 1:30 A.M.

"Does she ever leave you alone?" Mia's body stiffens.

"I don't think it's Jennie. She's got Brody to do her errands now, among other things," I say. I relax my head into the pillow and close my eyes. *I don't need to know who's calling. It can wait until tomorrow.* Mia lays her cheek on my chest and kisses my nipple and I twitch in delight. After a few seconds I hear a long chime.

"She left you a message," she says into my chest. The sound vibrates on my skin. Something doesn't feel right. I tap Mia on the shoulder and she leans forward and I step out of the bathtub, dripping water onto the marble floor. I kiss her softly.

"This will take one minute, I promise." Mia nods. I walk into the bedroom and grab the phone and return to the bathroom. Mia leans back in the tub and sips her wine and shuts her eyes. I stand naked in front of her, holding my phone, watching her fully enjoy the moment. I'm envious. I look down at my phone. Missed call: "MOM."

I pause to stare at every inch of Mia's beautiful body, then listen to the voice mail: "Hi T, it's Mom. You're probably fast asleep or, knowing you, still working, but . . . call me back as soon as you get this." Her voice sounds as though she couldn't catch her breath. I press one and listen to the message again: I realize that she's crying.

My eyes are on Mia's face. She senses the staring and the silence, and she opens her eyes.

"What?" she says, annoyed by my stares. She looks at my stunned face closer. "What's wrong?"

"It's Ethel," I say, barely able to say her name.

"Yes?"

"Something's wrong."

"Oh my God." Mia stands, wraps herself in a towel and steps out of the bathtub. "Are you sure?" she asks, putting her hand on my arm.

"No, but my mother . . . She was crying. This can't be good." My mother is not the type to ring the alarm. If anything, she downplays every situation.

"You have to call. Call her back."

"I'm not sure I can." I'm stunned. Mia grabs the phone out of my hand and searches the last number called, presses send, then holds it to my ear.

She sounds shaky when she answers. "Taylor?"

"Hi Mom, what's up?" There's a long pause. "Mom . . . what's going on?"

"Your grandmother—I mean, Ethel," she says.

"Is she?" I didn't want to hear her say the word.

"No . . . it doesn't look good . . . she's . . . she had a . . ."

"What, Mother? Just tell me, goddamn it!" I never swear in front of my mother, never "take the Lord's name," as she would say. With Ethel I cussed all the time, but never with my mom.

"She's had a stroke," she says.

"But that's not as bad as a heart attack, right?" Oh my God, I'm even trying to spin my own grandmother's condition.

"She's not awake. It's touch-and-go."

"I'll take the first flight out in the morning," I say.

"I'm sorry. I know you're busy at work, and I know Ethel would hate for you to miss anything good, but . . ." Her voice begins to crack. She struggles to stop herself from sobbing uncontrollably.

"Mom, it's okay. Don't worry about me. I'm glad you called. Are you okay?"

"I'll be fine," she says. I know she's crying on the other end and is trying to be brave for me. Mia sits on the toilet and runs her fingers through her hair and watches my every move, listening for any inflection in my voice.

"She's at St. Joseph's. Room 1218."

"I'll be there as soon as I can." As I'm about to hang up, I catch myself. "Mom?"

"Yes?"

"They say people that are unconscious can still hear you. Tell her I'm coming and to hold on. I'm on my way."

"Okay," she says. I close the cell phone. Mia wraps her arms around me and squeezes me. The ultrasoft plush towel feels good against my skin. She holds me tightly.

"It's going to be okay," she says softly in my ear.

My eyes burn, and I want the tears. But still nothing.

I cannot even fucking *cry*.

18.

O Holy Night

MY mother sits across from me, sipping her coffee. She takes no cream or sugar—just black. She's always been no frills; she's straight up and honest, often to a fault. Maintaining truthfulness and integrity was a constant theme in her parenting: She was adamant that I be an honest person. I once took two sour balls from a candy shop at the Eagle River Mall when I was seven, and my mother made me go back to the store, and, while sobbing, tell the owner my crime. Her guilelessness could be overwhelming.

My mother, Elizabeth, was named after Elizabeth Taylor, as was I. As one might guess, Ethel was obsessed with the actress and offered my mom a new car if she'd name me Taylor. It was an easy decision. I thought back to the days after my dad left: Mom played the disciplinarian while Ethel was my partner in crime. Being the heavy was a role my mother didn't particularly care for, but one she took on with great vigor. She worked twelve-hour days to make sure I never had to ask for a thing . . . within reason. However, I would've traded a few pairs of basketball sneakers for some extra time with her. She fascinated me. Even more since my father left us, and she had retreated far inside, becoming more a mystery than ever. My mom is the type of woman who makes her child her sole purpose, making sure he is taken care of, not spoiled. She was devoted, and I was her world: But she had a hard time expressing that. Sitting in the plastic hospital chair next to her, I realize this is the first time we've sat alone together in many years—the last time was 1996, when Ethel went on a bus tour with "a bunch of blue-haired ladies" to a casino in Iowa, a six-hour bus ride. While the other ladies went for the nickel slots, Ethel went for Tony Orlando. Ethel would travel far to see some "real entertainment" as she'd say, so the long trip didn't bother her. Unfortunately, Tony's performance did. For weeks, his name dominated conversation, and very nearly became a curse word on its own.

When I met my mom in the lobby of the hospital, her hug was long and tight, and it immediately brought me security: Things would be okay. But then she pulled back, and I saw her swollen eyes. My mother cries as often as I do. And her eyes—things are bad.

As she sips her coffee, I wonder aloud why the cafeteria can't get an espresso machine. Midwestern people certainly like cappuccinos and espresso, much like the rest of the world.

"I can't really see a need for that here," she says plainly. She's always practical, never extravagant, which makes my chosen career path seem frivolous to her. I'm too exhausted to explain that an espresso machine is not actually about need, but about pleasure. The distinction eludes her.

"Yeah, you're probably right," I concede.

"You must be tired; you didn't even try arguing that one," she says, perusing the remaining bits of coffee cake resting in the middle of the table. I smile. She knows me better than I think. "Eat this. You're getting way too skinny."

"I could actually stand to lose a few pounds. Have you looked at the people around here? They're a good twenty pounds overweight . . ." I say. After it comes out of my mouth, I regret saying it. It sounds snotty, like something a city kid says to a country bumpkin. "Sorry, I didn't mean it like that." I often step all over my sentences around her. I take my fork and stab at the last piece of cake and shove it into my mouth.

"Emotional eating?" she says, finally cracking a smile. I smile and scoop up the remaining crumbs. They're dry and tasteless.

I still haven't been able to face Ethel. My mom understood and suggested we go to the cafeteria until I was ready to go upstairs. That was two and half hours ago. My phone chimes. I glance at my BlackBerry.

"That thing's gone off every ten minutes. How do you stand it?"

"It's part of my job, Mom. Sorry—do you want me to put it on vibrate?" I say, scrolling through the menu.

"No, I just was wondering what's so important that some-one could be bothering you when your grandma is in critical condition."

"You've never met Jennie."

"Oh, I've seen her on Fox News talking about this and that. She doesn't strike me as a nice person."

"She's all right," I lie. "Besides, that wasn't Jennie on the phone, it was Mia."

"This is the young lady you mentioned earlier? Maybe you

can bring her here one weekend to meet Ethel and me," she says with a glint in her eye.

"Sure." Pause. "Yeah, we'll see." She senses my level of discomfort. My eyes dart around the cafeteria and land on a man with an oxygen tank ordering a cheeseburger.

"If you're not too embarrassed for her to meet us."

"Mother, come on. I'm not. It's just that . . . I don't know. Let's see what happens with Ethel; then we can worry about you meeting the woman I'm sleeping with."

"I'm sure she loves to be called that." Her tone changes. "I didn't raise you to talk like that."

She's right, she didn't. I've changed. But she would've too if she had been in my shoes. Then again, she might have been: My mother once had the opportunity to live in New York. Ethel practically shoved her out the door. But Mom returned home after only two weeks of staying with one of Ethel's friends, convinced that the city had nothing to offer her and that the people she met didn't either. They weren't the types that were interested in starting a family, and that was all she ever wanted. She never mentioned her time in New York except to say that "it wasn't for me." I wondered how we could possibly be related: this woman who had seen the city and found it repulsive and me, whose heart beat in sync with it. Soon after her return to Indiana, she met my father. He duped her into falling in love with him, with talk of a family he never really wanted. But we've already been there, haven't we?

"She's a good girl. She comes from a good family," I say, wiping my mouth with a napkin. "She kinda reminds me of you." I flash her a shit-eating grin.

"I'm afraid to ask."

"She doesn't take any sh—um, stuff from anyone. She keeps me on my toes."

"Well, I'd love to ask her how the heck she's able to do that. I tried for I don't know how many years," she says, leaning back in her chair.

"She keeps me honest, and I'm a better man when I'm around her." This is true. She does these things—though I resist in ways she does not know.

"I like this girl already," she says. My cell phone chimes again. Another text message. "Wow, she really needs to speak with you. Why doesn't she just call you instead of spending all this time punching letters into the phone?" I shake my head. My mother and I are part of different generations, the gap between us the size of a microchip.

"You're right. It'd be a lot easier." I grab the phone again, but this time the message is from Jennie. It reads in all caps, "CALL ME!!!!!!!!!!!" Jennie had been fairly sympathetic when I told her I was taking a few days—at least until we knew what Ethel's prognosis was. As long as I had my BlackBerry, access to a computer, and could maintain all my client work, she was surprisingly fine with my absence. Most likely, she didn't want me around Louise, who had been showing up to the office looking more and more despondent. Louise continued as Jennie's tenant, and Jennie served as Louise's personal pharmacist. The two of them bopped around the dungeon as if they were best girlfriends. The rest of the staff found it incredibly strange. Adam tried to ask Jennie what her motivation was, but her evasiveness was palpable. Mia asked if I knew what was going on, and I shrugged my shoulders. Everyone knew something was up, but no one quite knew what, and Louise had become a shell of her former self.

ROBERT RAVE

"You can call her if need be. We can go check on Ethel after," my mother offers.

"It's my boss," I say irritated.

"Oh. Go take care of it, and get it over with so she won't
bug you while you're upstairs."

"You'll be okay here?" I ask.

"I'm going to run to the ladies' room. How about I meet
you near the elevators in a few minutes?"

"Perfect," I say, getting up from the table while dialing my
cell phone. I walk straight to the lobby and stop just short of
the automatic doors and stare outside at the cold Indiana day.
"Jennie Weinstein PR; please hold." *Shit.* I had mistakenly
called the office instead of Jennie's cell. Before I can hang up
I hear Bob on the line. "How may I help you?"

"Hey, Bob, it's Taylor. Jennie texted and asked me to call
her ASAP."

"Oh, you have no idea," he says.

"What?" I watch the snow fall on the deserted parking lot.
A man in his midfifties is mopping a small section of tiles previously covered with some kind of bodily fluid.

"Are you serious? You really don't know?" Bob had a shrill
in his voice. I could hear his delight that he had the privilege
of spilling a huge piece of gossip.

"No, what?" I'm getting increasingly agitated. I don't have
time to play a guessing game when Ethel is lying upstairs near
death.

"D. R. A. M. A.," he spells out.

"Jesus, Bob, just tell me the goddamn news!" Bob sighs deeply,
letting me know he's not happy with the way I snapped.

"It's Louise."

"What about her?" I say, stepping toward the automatic

door. Bone-chilling air rushes into the lobby, and I quickly take a step back.

"Billy asked for a divorce."

"I know, and . . ." I say trying to hurry Bob along.

"He was definitely having an affair," Bob continues.

"Are you sure about this?"

"Yes."

"Okay. That was the big emergency Jennie's been texting me about?" Maybe Jennie was worried that I'd told Louise. Maybe she wanted me to do damage control. I hear Bob laughing quietly so Jennie doesn't hear him.

He whispers into the phone, "He was sleeping with Jennie." Here we go. It had to come out sooner or later, and I'm relieved it didn't come from me.

"Jennie? No!" I say.

"Oh yeah," Bob continues. "When Jennie was out one night, Louise stayed behind and wanted to take a hot bath. She started the bathwater, poured herself a glass of wine and was ready to dip her toes into the tub when she realized she'd forgotten her towel. She went to the linen closet and grabbed a towel from a large stack, absentmindedly knocking the stack onto the floor. When she bent down to pick the towels up, she found a pair of loafers that looked similar to Billy's. Then she noticed a red polo that was strangely familiar. Next to the polo was a silver dop kit that resembled the one that came with the Issey Miyake cologne she'd bought Billy for Christmas a few years back. Severely suspicious, she opened the kit, and there were his initials."

I can't believe what I'm hearing. The pace of it tells me Bob has told this one before. How could Jennie be so stupid? How could she leave Billy's things—and with Louise in the house?

Had she forgotten they were there? Did she purposely want Louise to find out? I am dumbfounded.

"I'm speechless," I say. "What did Louise do?"

"She took a bath."

"She what?"

"She took a bath, drank her glass of wine, and waited for Jennie to return from her night out with Kate." I could only imagine the amount of chemicals that were pumping through Jennie's system at that hour.

"And?"

"Jennie came in and saw Louise sitting on the couch. On the cushion next to her were Billy's polo shirt, his shoes, and the dop kit. Jennie looked at Louise and the small pile, and said, 'I'm sleeping with Billy' just as matter-of-fact as if I said to you, "I'm running out to get a manicure.'"

"She didn't!" I say loud enough for the janitor to shush me.

Bob pauses, then asks, "Are you finished?" Always the diva.

"I am," I say modestly.

"Anyway . . . Louise got up from the couch and started screaming at Jennie. Saying things like how could you; you fucking bitch; whore; you know, the basics."

"Wow. That is just unbelievable."

"Wait, there's more!" Bob says, sounding like an infomercial on QVC. "In true crazy-town fashion, Louise grabbed Jennie's arm to get her attention and out of fear Jennie blurts out, 'Don't hurt me I'm pregnant, with Billy's baby!'" I step forward and again split the automatic doors. This time I stand still, feeling the cold air shoot through my clothes.

"You're not serious. You can't be serious."

"It's true. Jennie's pregnant and Billy's the baby daddy," Bob says, ghetto fabulous.

"Bob, tell me you're lying." Part of me still isn't able to comprehend this, and I can only imagine how Louise must have felt.

"Nope, it's all true. And Jennie followed up that bombshell with the news that she and Billy are getting married."

"*Shut up!*" I shout. I shake my head in disbelief.

"Hey, you, get out of the doorway! You're letting all the cold air in!" I hear the old janitor shout. I step to the side, hold back the urge to tell the old man that I couldn't possibly be letting *all* the cold air in, then move away from the door sensors and put my forehead on the cold glass. I shut my eyes and turn my head from left to right, feeling the frigid glass against my warm skin.

"Are you there, or did you go into cardiac arrest?" I hear Bob say.

"I'm here." The cynic in me kicks in, and I fire off a list of questions, hoping this is nothing more than gossip. "How do you know this is true? Who told you this? Is this drag-queen gossip? Are you high? Have you spoken to Louise?"

"Oh, it's true all right, and I haven't even told you how I know." I raise my head from the glass and place my hand against the large window to steady myself. I'm not sure I want to know. I finally manage to speak. "Go on."

"After Jennie made her announcement, she told Louise she was going to bed. She didn't care if Louise stayed the night, Jennie just couldn't bother to look at her any longer. Jennie went to bed and locked her door, just in case Louise cracked completely and tried to kill her in her sleep." Apparently despite the drugs, Jennie had had her survival instincts intact. "Jennie woke up a few hours later to get some water, and when she turned on the kitchen light she found Louise lying on the floor, unconscious, next to an empty bottle of Jennie's Xanax. It's so old Hollywood, couldn't you just *die*?"

My legs wobble, and I try my best to stay standing. I can't. I collapse onto a radiator, grabbing the edge to keep from toppling like a stack of blocks. The room feels as though it's spinning. I can't breathe. Oh God, I can't breathe. I look down the hall at the old man whose back is to me. I try to call out for help, but nothing comes. I gasp for air, and still he can't hear me. I hear Bob asking, "Are you there? Hello? These damn cell phones." I cannot answer. I close my eyes and try to calm myself. I want to die. I feel like I could die right here in the lobby, with my mother and Ethel mere yards away.

"S-S-She's dead?" I finally exhale.

"No, she's alive. Jennie had to call 9-1-1. In a fabulous twist of fate, it was Jennie that saved her life." I could see Jennie seizing this opportunity. She would be lauded as a hero for saving Louise instead of skewered for being the cause of Louise's attempted suicide.

"Hero?" I gasp.

"Before you go getting all crazy, know this is a nightmare for Jennie; don't forget Louise was found in Jennie's apartment and with her boss's prescription pills." Right. I feel better.

"And Louise?"

"She's still in the hospital . . . recovering. My guess is she's going to be in the psych ward any day now." I look at the elevator bank and see my mom waiting. She stares at her watch and points for me to hurry up.

"I'm glad she's okay," I say. "I really need to get going and see my grandmother."

"Wait," Bob says, excited. "I haven't even told you the best part."

"Yeah?" I ask, unaware that there could be something good to come of this.

"Before Louise downed the pills, she sent an e-mail to Jean over at Page Six telling her everything. It was the lead friggin' item in today's *Post*. The phone has been ringing nonstop from the press wanting a comment from Jennie. She's in the middle of a media firestorm." I'm gobsmacked, unsure of what to say. I see my mom looking at me strangely. She's worried. I look into her eyes and give her half of a smile. She motions me to come to the elevator bank. I've kept her waiting for over ten minutes and I'm sure visiting hours are nearly over. I've stalled as long as I can, and I need to see Ethel to face the reality of Ethel's mortality. One foot in front of the other, I begin to walk toward the reassurance of my mother's face. With each step I gather more strength from her.

"Is that it?" I ask, praying that there isn't anything else.

"That's it, lamb chop," he says. "Jennie's walking out now, let me hand the phone to her."

"Wait, I'm going up to see my grandma now. I'll call her back," I say, trying to catch Bob before he places me on hold. It's too late.

Within a second Jennie's on the line. "Get back to New York and handle this. I'm disappearing for a while. You're just as responsible for Louise as I am, and you know why."

"What? Jennie, you know that's not—" I don't hear anything. "Hello? Jennie?" She's hung up. I reach my mother who locks her arm in mine and we step onto the elevator. My head is spinning.

"Are you okay?"

"Yeah, Mom, I'm fine."

"You don't look so good. I know this is a lot for you to deal with, but I'm right here, and your grandmother, I mean Ethel, will be so elated to know you're here."

"She's not even going to know that I'm here."

She turns to me and looks me in the eye, her eyes red and tear-ready. "It means a lot to *me* that you're here. You're a good boy." My mother has an unfaltering faith in me, and she hasn't a clue how guilty her belief makes me feel. Mainly because I'm still thinking of Louise, Jennie, and the office. My head is not where it should be. It's certainly not on Ethel. Here I stand, next to my mother, probably the most selfless, giving person on the face of the earth, and I've got Jennie, the most unscrupulous figure I've ever known, in my mind. Between the two, I feel a moral dilemma where there should be ab-solute clarity. I literally have a choice between the physical embodiments of good and evil.

"You ready for this?" she asks, squeezing my arm.

"I think so," I say. I'm dazed. Ethel's illness has brought my mom and me together for our first real conversation in years. If the trip ends in tragedy, I can at least be grateful for that.

I take a deep breath and follow my mom off the elevator. The walk to Ethel's room is spent in silence. The stale smell of the hospital is making me nauseous. If death has a scent, this is certainly it. Sweat gathers on my upper lip and the back of my neck—the strange cold-and-hot amalgam I get when I have the flu. Outside of Ethel's room, I feel I may pass out. My mother goes in first, and I hear her say hello to the nurse.

"She's very weak," the nurse says to me, as my mother nods soberly in agreement.

SPiN

"What's her prognosis?" my mom asks.

"She's not out of the woods yet," the nurse replies. I look at Ethel, slipping in and out of consciousness. At the moment, she's out. Her bed is upright as if she's in her La-Z-Boy ready to watch *Wheel*. I notice a hint of blush on her cheeks, and a subtle bit of pink lipstick on her lips. I catch my mom's eye and nod at the makeup.

"I did it when she was out," she says. "I really wanted to go with the purple lip gloss." I can't hold it in. Finally, a reason to laugh. *Pop*. It was akin to the pressure that you feel when you're sitting on a plane and your ears just won't seem to pop no matter how much gum you chew or how many yawns you attempt. When they finally do, it's the greatest sense of relief you've ever felt.

I turn to the nurse. "You don't know Ethel—this isn't a dramatic enough way for her to go. It lacks a proper sense of theater." I manage half a smile. My mom allows herself to laugh. I'd forgotten what an incredible sound that is.

"She's a fighter, all right," my mom says.

"What are her chances of recovery?" I ask.

"It's too early to tell. I've seen it go both ways," the nurse says. My smile turns into a frown. Damn honesty. Before I can say anything, I hear a groan coming from the bed. I can feel her fighting for lucidity. We stand by her bedside.

"Mom, it's me. We're here," my mother says, leaning in close to Ethel's face. I stare at Ethel, hoping she'll wake up again. She's only had a minute here and there of alertness since I've been in the room. Then the groans subside. I feel like I've swallowed my heart. My mom continues. "Mom, its Elizabeth, Lizzy." Nothing. "Taylor's here, too. He flew in from New York to be with you. He put all of his famous folks on hold just for you, Mom. Mom, can you open your eyes?" I shake my head. This is futile.

My mom nudges me to say something. I look at her blankly, "What am I supposed to say?"

"Whatever you're feeling." I shrug and sit on the side of the bed and grab Ethel's limp hand.

"Ethel? It's Taylor." I wait for some sign of life or cognizance, but still nothing. I notice the nurse walking toward the door. This is hopeless. I look at my mother again.

"Go on," she says.

It takes me a moment, then I look back down at Ethel. "Ethel, can you please say something? Just say anything. Tell me about when you lived in New York. Tell me about your days as a cabaret girl. Just tell me anything, Grandma." I feel a twitch against my hand, and I hear Ethel faintly murmur something, but I can't quite make out what she's saying.

"Ethel?" I say excitedly.

"Talk to us, Mom," my mom says, leaning in closer. Ethel repeats the same thing and mom leans in closer, trying to decipher what she might be saying.

"What, Mom? One more time."

"What's she saying?" I ask.

"Shhh."

Ethel speaks again, this time louder. My mom looks at me and cracks a giant smile.

"What?" I ask, confused.

"She said, 'Don't call me Grandma.' "

"She did, did she?" I laugh. Ethel's eyes flutter, and she's once again awake; and this time there's an alertness that wasn't there earlier. She stares at Mom and me and examines us from head to toe.

"My babies," she slurs. The stroke has affected her speech. She's startled by the sound of her own voice.

"We're here," I say. She mumbles something that I'm unable to hear. I look to Mom again.

"Well?"

"I think she said 'Kirk Douglas.' "

"Kirk Douglas?" I say, aghast. Maybe he was one of Ethel's paramours in New York and my mom is his illegitimate love child. It would be just like Ethel to tell us this because she thinks she's about to die. I look at my mother, and Ethel says some words and again ends the sentence with "Kirk Douglas."

"I think . . ." I say to my mom.

"What?"

"I think she's saying she sounds like 'Kirk Douglas.' "

Ethel nods and tries to smile.

"I think you sound wonderful," I say as I squeeze her hand. Ethel calls me closer with her finger. I switch places with my mom and sit inches away from Ethel's face. "Don't speak. Save your energy," I say. "That's what they always say in the movies anyway." She will like that last bit; in her mind, she is reveling in the histrionics of the moment. Ethel smiles at me and starts to mutter something, and I place my ear to her mouth.

"I-I-I'm proud of you," she finally blurts out. Damn. She does sound like Kirk Douglas.

"It's the medication," I say, deflecting. Ethel shakes her head and squeezes my hand hard.

"I'm proud of you," she repeats louder. I shudder. *Proud of me?* If she only knew. My mom starts to cry. I lay my head down on the bed in front of Ethel, and she pats my hair gently with her hand. "I'm proud of you." *Stop. Stop saying that.* The words, she does not know, ache in my brain, burn.

I begin to cry, weakly, then fully. I cannot stop. I cry for Louise. I cry for my mom. I cry for Ethel. I cry for Mia.

I cry for me.

Several hours later, I'm standing in the hospital lobby again, waiting for a taxi to take me to the airport. I've told Mom about Louise, but just the bare minimum. She looked at me, unsure, unknowing. She didn't ask me why I'm leaving when Ethel is the way she is. But she didn't argue either. "You have to go and take care of it, I suppose. It must be important, or otherwise I know you wouldn't go," she'd said. She was right: It is important that I go back. But I wasn't exactly clear as to what my reasons were—Louise or handling damage control for Jennie. I'm going back to New York for one reason, but I couldn't speak it. Not with her eyes on me. There is an opportunity back in New York that I cannot walk away from. Ethel, of course, told me to go. She didn't like my seeing her debilitated anyway. *I'm proud of you.* I said my good-byes upstairs, and here I stand. *I'm proud of you.* I think about the part I played in Louise's attempted suicide. *I'm proud of you.*

It comes to me.

I reach inside my pocket, pull out my cell phone, and dial the number. It rings twice, and I expect voice mail. We haven't spoken in quite some time. The silence had been for the best.

On the third ring I hear, "Hello." The woman's voice is cool.

"Hey, it's me."

"Hey, you. This is a surprise."

"Yeah, for me, too."

"So what's up?"

"Are you still looking for your cover story?" Silence. "Are you there?"

"Yeah," she says.

"We need to talk." I see the taxi pulling into the parking lot. As I reach for my carry-on bag behind me, I see my mother standing in the lobby. Her arms are folded, not in judgment but as mothers do. She smiles, raises her right hand, and waves. I mouth to her, "I love you."

Her eyes fill with tears. She nods, and says quietly, "I love you too." I grab my bag and walk outside.

"Hello?" I hear the woman say.

"I need a little time to figure out how I want this to play out, but I'll be in touch very soon," I say. I hang up the phone and get in the taxi. For the first time in a long time, I am, for better or worse, in control of my destiny.

19.

For No Mere Mortal Can Resist the Evil of the Thriller

THE office feels more like a subway stop than my place of employment. My visits are quick; collecting phone messages, bringing a soy chai latte to Mia, managing a quick game of gin rummy with Adam. I've been covering most of Jennie's meetings, client interviews, and photo shoots. Over the past several months she had taken me with her to all of her appointments, so I was the only person in the office that the majority of her top-tier clients felt comfortable with. I wasn't Jennie's first choice; she would have rather had anyone *but* me handling them—Mia, Adam, even suicidal Louise, but the clients weren't familiar with any of them. As much as I felt guilty for saying it, Louise's attempted suicide had been remarkable for my career.

Jennie's been gone for nearly five weeks from the day that Louise swallowed a bottle of pills. Immediately following the Louise debacle, Jennie released a statement to the press to the effect that she and Billy are nothing more than "friends" and that any insinuation to the contrary would be met with legal action. For his part, Billy confirmed the divorce and denied all the other accusations. In response to Louise's suicide note to

Page Six, Jennie was swift in turning the tables. Louise's behavior had been erratic and paranoid over the last few months, Jennie had told the press, but she remained "hopeful" that Louise would get the help she so desperately needed. It was Jennie's word over that of a girl who tried to kill herself, a girl painted in the press to look highly unstable in some items strategically placed by Jennie herself.

Jennie had prior experience in this area. I had watched her feed fake item after fake item about a pop diva, making her look so completely insane that by the time the singer had heard everything written about her, she had actually started losing it. This had all been because the chanteuse had refused to do press at one of Jennie's events; Jennie had gotten it stuck in her craw and had grown bound and determined to destroy the girl. The rest is history. When the songbird came back stronger than ever, Jennie had taken credit for that too.

The army of attorneys around Jennie tried to quash any negative story regarding her involvement with Louise, and for the most part the story was restricted to the New York press. Although word of Jennie's participation in Louise's near demise spread from people in the "scene" all the way to peripheral bloggers, the story was nothing more than speculation and hearsay. There was only one person who could corroborate Louise's story, and I wasn't about to say a word.

Tired of all the questions and the constant swirl of rumors, Jennie's been holed up at the Hotel Costes K in Paris, waiting for the next headline to replace her own. She checks in with the office almost hourly, either by e-mail or phone, and manages to bark just as many orders as she does when she's actually in the country. In fact, thanks to her forced sobriety due to her pregnancy, she accomplishes something I think isn't possible: her rude behavior is even worse. I can smell her perfume from here.

Jennie may have told the staff that she was going away to avoid being spun around in the rumor mill, but I know better. Jennie is much tougher than that; she is a New Yorker. She would be showing soon, and how would she explain a mysterious pregnancy? I'm sure she's considered immaculate conception, but was persuaded otherwise.

If I have to guess, Jennie will be announcing a whirlwind romance between her and Billy resulting in a Paris wedding in the next week or so. Jennie has been spotted out at various Parisian restaurants like Taillevent and Astrance with Billy on her arm. The two of them being seen together was no accident; it was a well-crafted and well-executed plan. My prediction is that when the announcement of a wedding finally comes, the trail of budding romance could be tracked backward in image and text. Billy, it has been said, has been traveling a great deal to Paris for "work," the result of Jennie's pulling some major string-age. I could even imagine Jennie's quote in the *Times*: "It was fate that brought us together on the Champs Elysees." The wedding would be an event like no other, especially since this was Jennie's first trip down the aisle. It is pretty ingenius, I must admit. Sick? Absolutely. Diabolical? Definitely. But still . . . pretty ingenius.

When I shared my theories with Mia, she was frightened that I was able to get into Jennie's mind with such ease. And baffled as to how I knew so much. I couldn't tell her the truth. She'd never forgive me. Instead, I told her I'd heard the majority of it from a gossip reporter friend.

With Jennie "on vacation" I've done more than take care of her clients. I've befriended them. They love me. And why wouldn't they? I work my ass off for them and check in with them constantly. I do everything Jennie doesn't. I make them trust me. I show them that I'm a trustworthy boy from the Midwest, and not some slick and slimy New York publicist who flits off to Paris for five weeks on a whim. I barrage them all with swag from one another without them knowing, and my generosity makes me linger in their subconscious; as they listen to their new red iPod nanos, they think of how they received them via messenger from me, or when they sip on Ketel One martinis, they think of the vodka that I personally delivered. I call in every favor that I've stockpiled with reporters and columnists over the last year and place items and feature stories for my clients, completely unprompted. I simply send courteous e-mails alerting them of the placements, then follow up with copies of the actual clippings. Like clockwork, I receive phone calls within ten minutes, praising my hard work and dedication—usually a dig at Jennie's general lack of respect and at her extended absence—and telling me I'm the greatest publicist in the city.

Then they suggest I should be running my own company.

My usual response to this is dumbfounded surprise. "Aw shucks," I give them, pretending that the idea has never crossed my mind. "Do you really think so?" I reply. "I mean, I don't know anyone that would leave Jennie. Everyone loves her." I vary this slightly with each account, but have found the responses identical: "You'd be surprised. Please call us if you ever leave."

Feelings of guilt have entirely disappeared. Jennie would do the same to me had the roles been reversed. In fact, she had stolen all of her former boss's clients before opening JWPR. Adam told me that her old employer, Donna, now works at

Ann Taylor at the Short Hills Mall. Donna had hoped, I'm sure, to slip into anonymity after Jennie sank her successful firm. But Adam ran into her while accompanying Ellie on a shopping trip, and told Jennie in passing. One call to Page Six and the item landed in the "Scene" section. *Former PR Player Donna Hewitt seen working at Ann Taylor at the Short Hills Mall.* Jennie must have called in a few favors to get them to print the tiny piece—no one knew or cared about some disgraced ex-flack—but Jennie couldn't leave the woman with even an ounce of dignity. Yep, feelings of guilt are gone. Besides this, the world of entertainment has not lived up to its end of the bargain. I was supposed to have been awestruck, amazed at the fast and glamorous life I'd read about in magazines and seen on countless entertainment news shows for years. I was supposed to have marveled at the incarnation of the dreams of my childhood among cornfields. It was supposed to offer the promise of everything I didn't have. In return for offering this mesmerizing magic, they would continue to have both my adoration and my money. I would continue buying the movie tickets, would gladly attend the overpriced concerts, read the book-club selection, scour the rags to read about their private lives. They would provide me with wonder, and I would provide them with loyalty. This is the deal the average American strikes with celebrity. But the longer I work in this business, the more parties I attend, the more stars I cater to, the more disappointed I become. I have pulled back the curtain and seen the industry for what it is: a pathetic addiction to affirmation and relativity, with Jennie Weinstein controlling the machine.

I walk into Ale House on Ninth Avenue around two in the afternoon. It's a new neighborhood bar just north of Chelsea. It still has the new-bar smell. There's no vagrant smell, no pee and vomit permeating the air. In fact, I smell warm pretzels and popcorn. I look to my left and near three dartboards sit a popcorn machine and soft pretzels. Several plasma TVs surround the bar, and various basketball games are playing. Bruce Springsteen is on the jukebox, transitioning to Dave Matthews. It's the kind of bar that I would've hung out at in college—only because there was no other place to go, and this was the closest thing to a social scene my school had. Perhaps for such nostalgic reasons, this had become my head-quarters for the last several weeks. I nod at Josh, the bar-tender, a robust guy in his early forties, and take my seat in a booth near the dartboards in the back. I had offered to help Ale House with press in exchange for use of the back booth exclusively from one o'clock to four thirty, just before their after-work crowd pours in. The owners treat me well and the down-home vibe makes me feel safe. I couldn't trust any-one sitting in a place like Cafeteria or Cipriani.

I take out my legal pad and the black ballpoint pen my mom gave me for Christmas three years ago and set them on the wooden table. ("You need a good pen," she'd said. "No-body likes to do business with somebody who looks like he picked up a Bic at the drugstore." Business philosophy from my mother was a questionable arena, but something stuck: I tore up my apartment all morning looking for the damn thing.) Josh brings two mugs of water to the table without saying a word, as he's done for the last two weeks. I check my Black-Berry and respond to a few e-mails. Jennie wants my daily sta-tus report e-mailed to her in the next hour since she has a dinner reservation at Buddha Bar. While she's been gone, Jen-nie has required me to keep her abreast of everything that's been going on with her clients. I happily oblige; I just don't tell her the complete version of everything.

Mia sends me an e-mail asking if we're still on for dinner later. I reply that I need to push it back thirty minutes as I will be running late. As I type, I hear a set of men's dress shoes hitting the tiled floor.

I look up and see Dan Aston, senior vice president of marketing and public relations for Xi Energy Drink.

"Hey, Dan," I say, standing to shake his hand.

"Interesting place," he says with a smile.

"Yeah, I figured this was a good place to meet for obvious reasons," I say, as we sit down in the booth. "Do you want anything? Vodka and soda? They have kick-ass barbecue wings here if you're hungry."

"No, no. I'm good. I can only stay for five minutes. Do you have the papers?"

I reach into my Jack Spade file case, a Christmas gift from Mia. And most likely from Inca, the same consignment store where I'd bought her purse. But it didn't matter. Her thoughtfulness was as abundant as her growing love for me. When she gave it to me, I looked at her and smiled. "You're getting soft," I told her. She rolled her eyes and sighed. And then she followed with a nostalgic, "Fuck you." I looked at Mia and thought we'd switched roles. She was once the cold, cutthroat businessperson, me the doofy naïve kid following her around with gifts and hope. Now . . . I know better than to tell her this.

"Everything's here," I say, handing him the papers. He glances at the papers for maybe a millisecond and looks me in the eye.

"You're going to make us bigger than Red Bull, right?"

"Who?"

"That's what I'm talking about," he says excitedly. He doesn't bother reading the paperwork. He signs and pushes the stack back to me.

"Welcome to Taylor Green PR," I say with a smile.

"Congratulations on your new venture. Oh, I almost forgot." He grabs a check from inside his jacket and sets it face-down on the table.

"Thanks so much," I say, laying the innocence and trustworthiness on thick. *Payment? You're going to pay me? Gosh, thanks.* "Are you sure I can't get you anything?"

"No, I've got an appointment downtown. Then I want to try and make it to the gym." He starts to leave.

"Thanks again, Dan, for the opportunity. Your trust in me means a lot."

"Don't thank me. You've done more for us the last four weeks than Jennie has in nine months. All the cases of samples she asked for," he says, shaking his head.

"I know," I say, frowning in pretend disgust. I purposely invited Dan to JWPR to meet right after Jennie left. We met in the cloffice, where there were stacks upon stacks of Xi Energy Drinks stored. Jennie had been hoarding them while telling Dan she was using the samples for high-profile parties, and for sending a case here and there to different celebrities. I knew Dan would be livid when he saw all the product stashed in the corner. I played dumb, like I didn't know what was going on.

"So when you gonna tell Jennie?" he says, heading for the door.

"Soon," I say cryptically.

"Do you own a bulletproof vest?" he says. I laugh as if it's the funniest thing I've heard all day.

"No, seriously," he says deadpan.

"I can take care of myself," I say.

"All right, man. If you're not going to sweat it, neither will I."

"Thanks." Dan exits and I sit back down in the booth. I take a deep breath and turn the check over. Ten thousand dollars. One month's work. I feel flush. I just guaranteed myself one hundred twenty thousand dollars by the yearlong contract he signed. He's the third client I've met with. My goal is to hit half a million by Friday. I've gone from scratching and surviving to something else entirely.

As I count my potential income in my head, I look up and see Sandy coming toward the table. The Ale House is definitely not Sandy's style. She likes her bars sleek and shiny, not frat-house grubby.

"The doorman told me this is a private party," she says, holding a Starbucks cup. She's decidedly understated in loose-fitting jeans and a tight black turtleneck sweater. There's barely a hint of makeup on her face. I've seen her like this only one other time: the morning she left my apartment. This is only the third time I've spoken to her since that night, and the meeting with her feels awkward. I called her a week later—obligatorily—so I wouldn't be labeled as "that guy," but it didn't matter. I already knew I was him. That wasn't even my real reason for calling that day—I needed to get a mention for our new celebrity chef's cookbook that was being released the following week. She was happy to do so and thanked me for the call, but it still felt weird. Other than an e-mail telling her to meet me here today, we hadn't spoke since I was heading for a taxi outside an Indiana hospital. I needed time to set things up; moreover to ensure that I had some source of income after it all went down. Sandy had been in London promoting "Sandy Says," trying to take her brand global.

"It is a private party," I say. "For you and me."

"I'm sorry. I thought I was meeting with Taylor, not Adam," she gibes. I give her a hug and smell her perfume. She smells incredible, and I'm slightly turned on.

"How are you? What have you been up to?" I suddenly find myself wild with energy. Maybe it's the ten-thousand-dollar check. Maybe Sandy's perfume. I stare into her eyes and study the few freckles on her face.

"Little of this, little of that." She tries to play it extremely cool, but her body language betrays her, and her forearm twitches slightly. Apparently, I make Sandy Brin nervous. This is good.

"I'm sure probably more of *that* than this."

She looks at me and shrugs her shoulders as if to say, *What do you want me to say?*

"London was good?" I ask.

"Very English." She reaches in her purse for a Marlboro Light. "You want?"

"I really shouldn't." I hesitate, then say, "Yeah, give me one." She hands me a cigarette, and I light her up, then me. Even though New York City has a strict antismoking law, it's the middle of the afternoon. And the law's not really that strict.

"So?" she says.

"Yeah," I say, nervously staring back at her. I shift in my seat. Now it's Sandy who is making me nervous.

"Look, let me just say this now and put it out there to end the weirdness." *Phew.* "What happened happened."

"Yeah, I've been meaning to—"

"Let's not," she says, interrupting. I'm a bit taken aback. "Don't worry about it. I'm *so* not that girl," she says, proving to me she *is* so that girl.

"Um, okay. I do want you to know that if I wasn't with someone right now—"

"But you are." I leave it alone. "What's my cover story?" she asks.

I reach into my bag and pull out four file folders of print-outs, photos, and receipts. I push the stack toward her.

"Your trash is my cover story?"

"My trash is your cover story," I say. She looks at me, confused. I open the top folder. "This is my personal and private diary detailing everything that's gone on inside Jennie Weinstein's offices over the last year. Everything's documented. There are so many drugs being bought and ingested it makes Studio 54 look like kindergarten."

"Drugs? That's it?" she says, slightly annoyed. "That's maybe enough for a couple of paragraphs."

"No. I have receipts."

"Drug dealers give receipts nowadays?"

"No, I have false expense account reports detailing the scam Jennie's pulling on her clients. She's charging them for services she doesn't provide: messenger services, FedEx shipping, color copies, airfare when she has free vouchers from other clients, car services when she takes her own. It may not seem like a lot, but take all that and multiply it by twenty-five or so clients, and it adds up. Moreover, it tells you a great deal about her business practices. Plus, I have all of the lies. All of the scams. And all of the incestuous relationships publicists and reporters have—none of that has *ever* been talked about."

"All right, I'm slightly intrigued. Go on."

"Check your phone."

"What do you mean?"

"I sent you a text message a few minutes ago before you got here."

"I didn't get anything."

"It's a video file, it takes a while." Sandy pulls out her phone from her purse, looks at it, and then back at me in surprise. "Open it." She clicks on the video file, and I sit back in the booth and wait. Sandy gasps.

"Oh my God! Is that Jennie?" she asks horrified. "She did not just do blow off that guy!" she shouts. This is precisely why I request the booth at the back of the bar.

"She did."

"Wait, who's the guy?" Sandy asks.

"Billy Phillips." It doesn't register. "Louise Phillips's soon-to-be-ex. The same JWPR employee who tried to off herself a short time ago and swore up and down that Jennie was sleeping with her husband. The same Louise Phillips Jennie has vilified in the press, making her sound bat-shit crazy."

"This is incredible!" she gasps. She sits in the booth, stunned, unsure of what to say. I smile like the Cheshire cat.

"I told you."

"But, Taylor, I can't *use* any of this. *New York* would be sued. *I* would be sued. *You* would be sued!"

"I'm two steps ahead of you. I already spoke with an editor at *New York* about it. I didn't give her all of the details but just enough to whet her appetite. She said the piece could be written roman à clef with just enough information to get tongues wagging."

"Someone's not playing here," she says, leaning forward.

I swallow hard. "Oh, this isn't a game anymore." I pause for a second, then continue, "I said the only way I would hand over this story was if you wrote it and if I was never mentioned in the piece. "

"But why are you giving this to me? You could go anywhere with it. Hell, you could even get paid a lot of money to sell this story."

"I'd get fifty thousand tops. And after I sold 'my story,' I could never work again. Who's going to hire the guy that gave away his boss's best-kept secret? No, this way people might guess, but they won't ever know for sure who your informant was. With some crafty writing, a reader might even think the source is Louise Phillips herself."

"I suppose they might," Sandy says, taking another puff on her cigarette.

"Secondly, I trust you, and of all the people in this insane industry, you deserve to get your cover story and everything that comes along with it."

"Oh God, don't PR me, Taylor. You know that we both need this. I want a cover story to get paid legitimate money to work at a real publication instead of out of my studio apartment writing a blog. And you want to see your shrew of a boss eviscerated." She's nailed it. Mostly.

"No, I want to see you get this. This has huge potential for you—maybe even a book or movie. I like you, Sandy," I say, putting my hand on top of hers. "You're such a cool girl." Sandy leans back in her booth and looks at me quizzically. I'm nervous. I don't know if she's going to throw her coffee at me or kiss me.

"Okay," she says, after a long pause.

"Okay?" I say excitedly. I can't believe it. I've sold it. She grabs my file folders and places them in her bag.

"I'll need to get your contact at *New York* and we'll go from there." She reaches for her bag, slings it over her shoulder, and stands up.

"You're leaving?" I ask.

"Yeah, why?"

"I don't know. I just thought you'd want to know more, or . . . want to hang for a little bit," I say, stumbling. This is my first takedown, after all. I was hoping for some hugs or a little cheer perhaps. *Hats off to the whistle-blowers!*

"I've got a lot to pore over here. But seriously, thank you for the opportunity." She says it so formally you'd think I just hired her to be my assistant. "I am a bit surprised, I have to admit."

"You are? Didn't think I had it in me?" I say cockily.

She looks at me long and hard, then answers. "No, actually I didn't." I nod like I'm hot shit. "I would have expected something so damaging, disturbing, and dark from Jennie, but never from you, Taylor." What? I feel like she's punched me in the gut. I even put my hand on the table to steady myself.

"I'm not like Jennie at all."

"I don't know. Maybe you are; maybe you're not. But from an outsider's point of view, you look a lot alike. You've got a lot of things about to take off, I'm sure; I'd even guess you'll open your own firm when the dust settles. My only suggestion would be to make sure you don't take such a running leap into the dark side as she did."

I'm speechless yet again.

"Thanks again for the story," she says, and she walks out of the Ale House. I fall back into the booth.

They say every man, at least once in his life, has a crisis of conscience where he looks in the mirror and sees a stranger staring back. I wish I could have been so lucky. When I looked in the mirror, I saw Jennie staring back. She had seeped so far into my soul, even my reflections had gone histrionic.

I don't know who I am anymore, and I'm not sure I want to.

Taylor Green
Public Relations

Taylor Green
President

20.

And So It Begins

EVERY publicist has a story to tell about a tyrannical boss or a maniacal client. Somewhere in that story lies a semblance of truth. Unfortunately, he or she has spun it so many different ways, they've pitched it to listeners so many times, that even they're not sure what's truth and what's not.

My story is not that different from most. I just know how to sell it better.

I believe a publicist coined the phrase "blind ambition." Who else could spin a person's selfish desires into such a neat and tidy couplet? If "blind ambition" is when one's ego drive prevents people from seeing the truth of what's happening around them, then what's the phrase for when you're completely aware of what's happening and choose to plow through it anyway?

Close your eyes. Give in to your darker side.

I'm proud of you.

Standing on the corner of East Eighty-third waiting for Mia, I'm in a reflective mood. I'm purposely fifteen minutes early, and I am looking at the brownstones, imagining the lives of people living there. I pull out my cell phone and call the office; as usual, Bob picks up after the second ring.

"Jennie Weinstein PR, please hold." As I'm placed on hold, I smile, thinking about big, beautiful, Winona Judd–looking, drag queen, Bob. I'm going to miss his quirks, his advice.

Over the past two weeks, I've saved all my contacts and client documents on an external hard drive. I've made color copies of all the stories I've ever secured. I slowly but surely have been preparing for my departure since the afternoon Sandy called with the date the *New York Magazine* piece would be coming out. Next Monday to be exact. But I know the publicists at *New York*, and I'm sure they'll be placing items with the gossips today. Therefore, for all intents and purposes, today will be my last day at JWPR, whether I am ready or not.

"Jennie Weinstein PR, can I help you?"

"Hey, Bob!"

"Who's this?"

"Very funny, Bob."

"What's up, sugar? When you headed back in?"

"I should be in a little later. Mia and I have an appointment. Everything good there? No drama?"

"Every day is drama in this office. Haven't you learned anything?" I laugh and ask to speak to Adam. I know this is the last time Bob and I will speak.

I rush a word in before he can place me on hold. "Thanks, Bob . . . for everything. You rock." There's a long silence, then I hear the double beep indicating I'm on hold again. I'll never be certain if Bob placed me on hold before or after I said thank you. I like to think he heard me, and that his matchless perception told him that I was jumping ship, and he didn't want to have to send out the battle cry against me.

"T-Money?" Adam says. He had stopped calling me Cornbread and replaced it with an equally bad moniker.

" 'Sup?"

"I'm putting together the guest list for BUMP and trying to get some of my peeps to make a cameo." BUMP was a new mod-looking lounge on the Lower East Side that was formerly a fish market. It was the most-anticipated bar opening since . . . the last most-anticipated bar opening. "So you know why I'm calling . . ."

"I do."

"And."

"I thought long and hard about it, man, and it's a great offer. I don't know. As much as I would love to work with you— and I think we could really tear it up—I just don't think I can jump ship like that. Jennie might be a major bitch, but she gave me this really great gift, and she has been incredibly good to me. I can't turn my back on that."

This stings. When I asked Adam if he was interested in working with me at my own shop, I wasn't sure how he'd respond. But I was highly optimistic. He'd bitched about Jennie to me since the day I started. I thought he would be a part of my new team.

"No, I get it," I say, shakily.

"Did you tell her yet?"

"I'm going to call her after I hang up with you." Adam doesn't know about *New York*. No one does. Louise is the source of the article, it will seem, not me.

"Good luck to you," he says, with a laugh.

"I'll be all right."

"Yeah, I know you will be," he says poignantly. Adam and I have an unspoken brotherhood: By all accounts he was the closest thing to a brother I'd ever had. We fought, we teased and taunted, we did the things normal brothers do (if buying coke and Asian teenage porn was included in the bonds of brotherhood). "So come by this weekend if you're around. Ellie's been asking about you. Bring Mia if you want." I still wasn't a hundred percent comfortable with the two of them hanging out together, considering their history. But it wasn't the right time to say so.

"Sounds good," I say, knowing it won't happen. "Give me a call and let me know when."

"All right, will do."

"I better jet and make that call," I say nervously, momentarily feeling like my old, scared, Midwestern self.

"You'll be fine. You're always going to be fine, Taylor."

"Talk to you," I say.

"Talk to you."

I hang up the phone. I have only a few minutes before Mia will be here. The wind is kicking up, and I'm beginning to freeze my ass off. Winters in New York. It's now or never, and I'm sure Page Six will be calling Jennie in the next hour for a comment on the pending *New York Magazine* story. I stare at my phone, on the verge of getting lost in the contemplative nature of the call. Before I drift in thought, the bitter cold pushes me to dial the number. Jennie Weinstein picks up on the first ring.

"Hi, honey," she says. Honey? Her hormones are clearly out of wack.

"Hi," I say, slightly caught off guard by the salutation. I hear a man's voice in the background. I assume it must be Billy.

"Do you have a second?" I ask.

"That's about all I have. Why, what's up?" she says, tone

changing. My heart is beating so fast and so hard I wonder if she can hear it through the phone. It echoes in my head. My body has become incredibly warm, and the agonizing cold has become a nonissue. *What am I doing? Can I really handle my own firm? Do I think I can go toe-to-toe with Jennie Weinstein? Do I want to make an enemy of her? I can still call this whole thing off. I can send back the monthly retainers I've received. It's not too late.*

"I wanted to say thank you so much for the last year and the great opportunity you've given me." I hear the words coming out of my mouth, but I'm not sure where they're coming from. Someone else is talking for me. "I think—"

"You're quitting?" She cuts straight through my line of bull-shit.

"I am."

"Uh-huh," she says. Her emotional range expresses its variations with remarkable speed.

"I learned so much and I so appreciate—"

"Don't return to the office. We'll have your things sent to you by messenger," she says.

"Okay, that's fine." Silence. I look down at my phone:
JENNIE DISCONNECTED.

Almost instinctually, I call home. My mom answers, and I check to see how Ethel is doing with her physical therapy. "She got a good report from the doctor," she says. Ethel's asleep; otherwise, she'd have answered the phone. I tell my mom that I've quit. When I announce to her that I'm opening my own agency, her tone brightens, and our conversation is punctuated with questions like: "What does that mean exactly?" "But is she mad?" and "Are you eating?" Her ruminations are at the very least entertaining. Then finally she says, "I knew you'd be famous one day." I explain that I'm not the one who's famous, I only help make other people famous. She still doesn't get it, though I've explained PR to her hundreds of times. I tell her I will check in on Ethel later tonight. We say our good-byes, and I exhale.

A few minutes later, Mia arrives, bundled up, and we cross the street against the wind to a large high-rise. We stand in the lobby and wait for the concierge to deal with the UPS man.

"And that was it?" Mia asks.

"That was it."

"I can't believe she didn't threaten to boil your balls—at the very least," Mia says, just loudly enough for the UPS guy to turn around and stare at me.

"No, my balls are safe." I nod at her, ignoring him.

"Well, that's a relief. I hope she takes it that well when I call."

When I told Mia that I was leaving JWPR, she was my biggest supporter. She said that after I quit, she would do the same. She felt like she needed to make the jump, or otherwise she'd be stuck working in agencies for the rest of her life, and her dream of working in fashion would evaporate. I offered her a job, which she declined. For the best. There was only one boss . . . and that was her.

She did offer to help me get things going, and to help with the hiring until I was up and running. For the time being, my office would be run out of my apartment—alongside Algebra, of course. Lauren offered to be my assistant while she stayed home with the baby, to which I happily agreed. It wasn't JWPR, but it was a start . . . my start.

The concierge finishes with the UPS man, looks at Mia, and asks, "Who are you here to see?"

"Louise Phillips," I say.

"Name?"

"Taylor Green."

This is the first time I've seen Louise since everything went down. I couldn't face her before, but now I'm ready. The doorman calls up.

"Go on up. Thirteen-B."

As Mia and I walk to the elevator, her cell phone rings. She picks up. "This is Mia." She pauses for a minute. "Oh hey, Chris." As she talks on the phone, I stand in the elevator bank staring at the grains in the marble floor, thinking about what's transpired in the last year, in the last twenty-three minutes. I hear Mia say things like, "Okay," "I'm not sure," "I haven't a clue," and "Can you tell me more?" She hangs up the phone and looks pale.

"What?" I ask.

"That was Chris at Page Six asking me about some *New York Magazine* story about Jennie."

"About Jennie?" I say, feigning surprise.

"Well, it's about her without actually *being* about her. It's a thinly veiled story on a New York power player. He's dying to know who the source in the article is because it mentions some major insider stuff. He wouldn't tell me what."

"Really? That's insane. Who wrote it?"

"Your bathroom-stall buddy Sandy Says," Mia says as we step into the elevator. "Did you pour out your soul to her while you were on the toilet?" she says with a smile.

"Sandy Brin? I think we spoke maybe three words to one

another, and I gave her an item one time after that night. I'm dying to read the story." I look at Mia curiously, without saying anything.

"What? I'm sorry, I didn't mean to imply that you—that wasn't my intention."

"Well, good, because that's not the kind of person I am."

"Maybe it was Louise!" Mia gasps, as if she's just unraveled a great mystery.

"Yeah, maybe," I say.

The elevator doors open and we walk down the long hallway to Louise's apartment, where we will no doubt offer a sympathetic ear and wish her nothing but the best, never mentioning the article or Jennie.

Mia rings the doorbell, and I exhale.

Ding dong, the witch is dead.

Epilogue

Five Months Later

ABOUT an hour and a half outside of Manhattan, depending on traffic, lies the quaint upstate town of Millbrook, New York. It's the destination for New Yorkers who want to unwind and get a slice of small-town life. People spend their days there antiquing or perusing the shelves at the Merritt Bookstore on Front Street. The evenings are low-key with early dinners by the wood-burning fireplace at Charlotte's restaurant on Route 44. The pace is slow and the people warm. It's ironic that so many of us who moved from small towns to experience the big city can't wait to escape on the weekends, spending top dollar to return to the small-town atmosphere we once were desperate to escape. Unfortunately—or fortunately, depending on whom you ask— Millbrook is also a town fast becoming a mini-Hamptons, with its palatial homes and lavish house parties thrown by some of New York's elite.

My energy-drink client, Xi, was one of the first to spot this growing trend and quickly snatched up a six-bedroom house on six acres just north of town. It's a rental with a price tag larger than my retainer for the entire year. The Xi reps have asked me to hold celebrity-filled parties at the house to build the brand and help with imaging during the social lull before the Hamptons' summer season kicks into full gear.

Over the last few spring weekends, the Xi Corporation has paid young starlets and Hollywood heartthrobs anywhere from ten to twenty thousand to show up at Xi events and basically party their asses off. In return, I was allowed to witness everything, then place items in all of the celebrity rags and blogs about what happened at the "Xi house." The goal was obvious: Kids and adults alike would be more apt to choose Xi over its competitor if they read something about the brand in *Us Weekly*. Hence, we associate the caffeine-laden drink with the likes of Lindsay and Pharrell. Sadly—or happily, again depending on whom you ask—the strategy worked.

This weekend, the second of May, there are no events on the books. I invite Mia, Louise, Lauren, Allison, and baby Beatrice to spend the weekend at the Xi house—my very own *Charlie's Angels*. It doesn't bother me to be in a houseful of women; I grew up in one, after all. Besides, who could resist staying gratis at a stocked mansion for the weekend? Adam, apparently, who sent his regrets.

Mia and I are the first to arrive at the house, and my mind is full of five months of euphoria, agony, chaos, and guilt. The *New York Magazine* piece was as controversial as it was empowering. The article never mentioned Jennie or me by name, but for those among the gawker.com and entertainment set, it couldn't have been more obvious. It was the exact boost my little company needed, and within hours of the story hitting the newsstand, my BlackBerry lit up. I was atop the New York social heap. For two weeks.

Fifteen days later, *Gotham* magazine featured a very pregnant Jennie on its cover, looking matronly and almost saintlike. It basically spun her sordid lies, adultery, drug use, and ruthlessness into a story of redemption and newfound devotion to motherhood. She had found her conscience and purpose, it said. A bitter and brutal New York rivalry between the two of us had been sparked, and the battle had every social circle buzzing—which was exactly the point.

Jennie went into labor prematurely (I think she planned it as a publicity stunt) and spawned a son named Jeremy. Though we've run into each other at various restaurants and the occasional lounge, and even once at the gym, we haven't spoken since I called to give my notice. I've been too inundated with my own clients to worry about Jennie, though everyone has told me to keep one eye permanently over my shoulder, and to never sit with my back toward the door. I ran into her at Bungalow 8 one night very late after she gave birth, and she asked that I be removed from the club. I was ceremoniously kicked out and asked not to return. Other than that expulsion, we've never actually spoken, even when at the same venue. Only the occasional stare-down, like we're in the fifth grade. I've never turned away first.

I still run things out of my apartment—with Mia's help. I've signed a lease for an office in Hell's Kitchen that begins June first. I didn't want to be anywhere near Jennie's old offices, even though a much cheaper office became available in the same building. The modeling agency I stumbled into that first day had gone under. What a shame.

Louise arrives in Millbrook an hour after Mia and me. She freelances for me and works at her own pace, often from home. She mainly writes the press materials: bios, cover letters, press releases, and media alerts. Louise loves to write, and I need a strong writer on my team. And I wanted to do penance for not telling her about Jennie and Billy. It would be a long purgatory.

Mia and I open a bottle of Pinot Grigio from the wine cellar and take a moment to come down after a traffic-laden drive.

"Do you want a glass of Pinot, Weezy?"

"Zoloft and Pinot Grigio are probably not the best combo. I'll stick with my Orangina. There's no FDA warnings against mixing those, at least not yet."

"To a fun and relaxing weekend," I say, raising my glass.

"To a *work-free* weekend," Mia says, clinking our glasses.

I glance at Mia while she sips her wine. She's relaxed and at ease with herself—a welcome development. When working for Jennie, she was forever on edge. I sensed a shift in her soon after the break, and now she's coming into her own. God, it makes her even sexier.

I raise my glass yet again. "To Mia, for being my strength and for her invaluable advice and guidance, especially with my choice in clothing." Instead of clinking glasses, I lean in and kiss her deeply.

"Hello? I'm still standing here," Louise says. My eyes are shut, and I'm tasting the Santa Margherita on Mia's lips. "Hi, I had a nervous breakdown because the man I loved was screwing the boss, remember that?" Louise interrupts.

"God, Louise, you're so selfish," Mia jokes as she pulls away from me. Mia and I have settled into something of a normal existence—as much as one can have when you work twenty-four/seven. Our only arguments come when I go out, but she ultimately understands it's the only way I'm going to get new business.

Lauren and Allison and baby Beatrice are the last to arrive, late as usual. Luckily, they have a babysitter so the adults can have some fun. They quickly pour themselves glasses of wine and kick off their shoes as the sitter settles Beatrice into one of the upstairs bedrooms.

"The babysitter's kinda hot," I tease. Allison had already told me that she wasn't sure that she liked having a buxom twenty-two-year-old brunette around the house when she was feeling not so hot and, well, not so twenty-two. Mia slaps my arm.

"It's okay, T, I get the same knee-jerk reaction from Al," Lauren says as she sits on the corner of Allison's chair. The baby had bolstered a relationship that at times had waned. Overall, they're better than ever. To my great disappointment, they'd found a larger apartment in Park Slope. The move is set for late June.

"She's going to hear you," Allison shushes.

Over the next few hours, we move our conversation out to the large front porch that overlooks the enormous grounds. We talk about everything—politics, music, religion, travel, even debating whether or not baby poop had a discernible smell during a child's first few weeks of life. (Lauren and Allison are convinced it doesn't. I remain completely convinced it does.) Work never comes up. All BlackBerrys are left in the kitchen. We lazily watch the day disappear into night.

"What time is our reservation?" Allison asks.

"Nine," Mia answers. The ladies have a camaraderie that

I'm not a part of, and I don't mind. I'm happy everyone is getting along. I have no time for additional headaches.

"It's supposed to be quite a scene, I hear," I say. This probably isn't the best audience for that kind of thing.

"You'll never change," Allison says and smiles.

"I thought we left Manhattan to avoid *the scene*," Lauren interjects.

"We did . . . sort of." I smile. As the cool wind blows, Mia moves over to sit on my lap. She kisses my forehead softly.

"Would you look at that?" Louise says.

"Sorry," Mia says.

"No, not you two. The sky."

It is the perfect mix of purples, baby blues, and pinks swirled together. It's the most beautiful thing I've ever seen, and the colors are more vibrant than any neon club marquee in Manhattan. The traveling circus that is my life has calmed. Even the circus takes a day off every once in a while.

We arrive at Autumn, Millbrook's new restaurant, at five minutes to nine. We would've arrived earlier except that Allison didn't want to leave Beatrice. "I get a pain in my boobs when I'm away from her," she says.

"Okay, eew," Mia says.

"What?" Allison says, smiling. "We have that strong of a connection."

"Your boobs are sore because B's been sucking on them six times a day," Lauren chimes in. Adamant that something bad is going to happen, she resists until the final moments. Finally, we assure her it's normal mommy anxiety, that she'll see Baby B in a few short hours, and that if she doesn't walk out the door immediately we will label her "Twitchy Tits."

Autumn is packed, and the parking lot is at capacity. New York has definitely descended upon this small town and livened up its local dining and nightlife scene. I feel partly responsible, since we'd been importing so many celebs for the Xi parties. I shake off the thought.

I go inside to check in with the hostess and find the place as bustling as I'd expected. The tiny dining room is painted a pale green that sets off the details of the old Craftsmen house, while the floors are dark wood and the thick crown molding a soft white. A large fireplace sits in the corner of the room, and I manage to catch a glimpse of the open kitchen on the other side. I can smell the homemade quality the place has; burning wood and baked bread. Recognizable faces are here and there, but it is too crowded to discern who exactly.

"We're running fifteen to twenty minutes late," the hostess tells me. It's too loud to wait inside, and, frankly the noise would send the girls over the edge—it was hard enough to convince them to leave the quiet and serenity of the house. I walk back outside and let them know of the small delay.

"Twenty minutes?" Allison says, annoyed. "Let's just make something at home." Lauren rubs the small of Allison's back to calm her down.

"Come on, we agreed we'd relax and have some fun this weekend," I say.

"Do you want me to go get you a drink at the bar?" Mia offers. Allison smiles and declines.

Autumn's small porch is packed with diners who need to smoke, seeking sanctuary from those who frown upon the habit that I have personally come to enjoy. We stand near the valet lot to escape the crowd, and I wrap my arms around Mia's waist from behind and kiss the back of her neck. She has eased into my public displays of affection over the last few months.

"I can't wait to get you home," I whisper into her ear.

"Oh really?" she says playfully. "Tell me why."

As I hold Mia, I hear Louise say, "What's he doing here?" I turn around and see Adam leaving the restaurant. He's dressed in jeans, a T-shirt, and a leather jacket. The outfit is very pared down by Adam's standards. I let go of Mia for a minute.

"Hey! What are you doing out here?" I say, walking toward him.

"You know," he says, and smiles. "I go where the party circuit is. I gotta keep my finger on the pulse." He gives me a hug hello and nods at the ladies behind me.

"Wow. Did you really just say that?" I joke. "You already eat?"

"Sort of," he says mysteriously.

"Sort of?" Before I can ask what he means, I hear a familiar voice screaming at the hostess I'd just seen.

"Who the fuck are you?" I hear her slur. It's Jennie, and she's on a tear. Her sobriety ended within twenty-four hours of giving birth. "You're actually throwing me out? I don't think you have a clue as to who the fuck you're dealing with, restaurant bitch!"

"So you sort of ate," I say to Adam.

"She was talking a bit too loud into her cell phone, and management asked her to leave," he explains.

"What is she doing here?" I hear Louise say from behind me. "I want to go. I want to fucking go now!" She digs through her purse and opens her bottle of pills. She pops one into her mouth and looks at the other girls. "Can we just go? I can't be here right now with her here."

"We can just make something at home," Mia agrees.

"Guys, she's leaving. Why should we leave because of her? I'm staying right here. She'll be gone in less than five minutes," I say. Louise huddles with Lauren and Allison and turns her back so she no longer has to see Jennie. Mia moves forward and stands with Adam and me as the three of us stand and watch Jennie scream at the hostess. She finally punctuates the argument by calling the woman a cunt. It still rolls off her tongue.

Jennie marches toward the valet lot and stumbles, nearly falling in the mud. She yells something into her cell phone, and a few minutes later, the valet arrives with her car. Adam turns to me. "Well, I guess that's my cue to go."

I smile and say, "Some things will never change." I look at Adam and punch his shoulder. "It was great to see you, man." As he goes in to hug me, I hear the car door slam shut. We both turn around and see Jennie already in the car about to take off.

"Or it looks like you might be giving me a ride home," he says, and smiles.

"No problem," Mia says. "You're family." Louise, Lauren, and Allison are in their own little world only a few feet away, trying to keep Louise distracted.

I can't help myself. I lift my head and stare at Jennie's car. Perhaps I'm hoping for another stare-down like we've had for the last several months, but I can't really be certain. I catch her eye in the driver's side mirror for only a moment, but this time something is very different. And within a matter of seconds, everything changes.

Flash.

The lights come toward us at breakneck speed. The engine roars. The car accelerates . . . at us . . . at *me*.

Screaming.

I hear screaming, but I'm not sure from where or from whom. Was someone hit? Oh my God. Mia? Lauren? Allison? Louise? Where's Adam? The screams echo through my ears. Then the car is suddenly here, nearly on me.

Bang.

Thud.

Oh shit. The press is going to eat this up.